D1433106

MAGNUS
AND THE CROSSROADS
BROTHERHOOD

ROBERT
FABBRI

MAGNUS
AND THE CROSSROADS
BROTHERHOOD

CORVUS

First published in eBooks in Great Britain in 2011, 2013, 2014, 2015,
2017, 2018 by Corvus, an imprint of Atlantic Books Ltd.

This collection published in hardback in Great Britain in 2019
by Corvus, an imprint of Atlantic Books Ltd.

10 9 8 7 6 5 4 3 2 1

A CIP catalogue record for this book is available from the British Library.

Hardback ISBN: 978 1 83895 043 9
eBook ISBN: 978 1 83895 044 6

Printed and bound by CPI Group (UK) Ltd, Croydon, CR0 4YY

Corvus
An imprint of Atlantic Books Ltd
Ormond House
26–27 Boswell Street
London
WC1N 3JZ

www.corvus-books.co.uk

This one is for Anja again, with all my love.

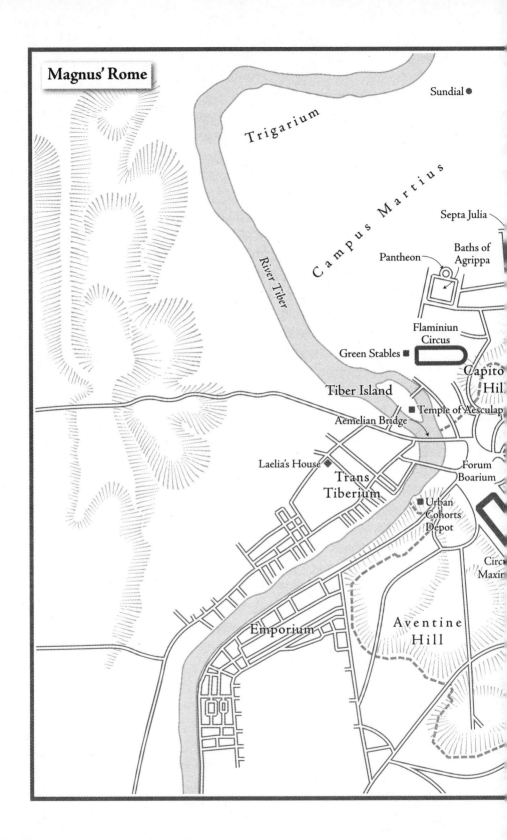

Magnus' Rome

Sundial •

Trigarium

Campus Martius

River Tiber

Septa Julia

Pantheon

Baths of
Agrippa

Flaminiun
Circus

Green Stables ■

Capito
Hil

Tiber Island

Temple of Aesculap

Aemelian Bridge

Laelia's House ◆

Trans
Tiberium

Forum
Boarium

Urban
Cohorts
Depot

Circ
Maxir

Emporium

Aventine
Hill

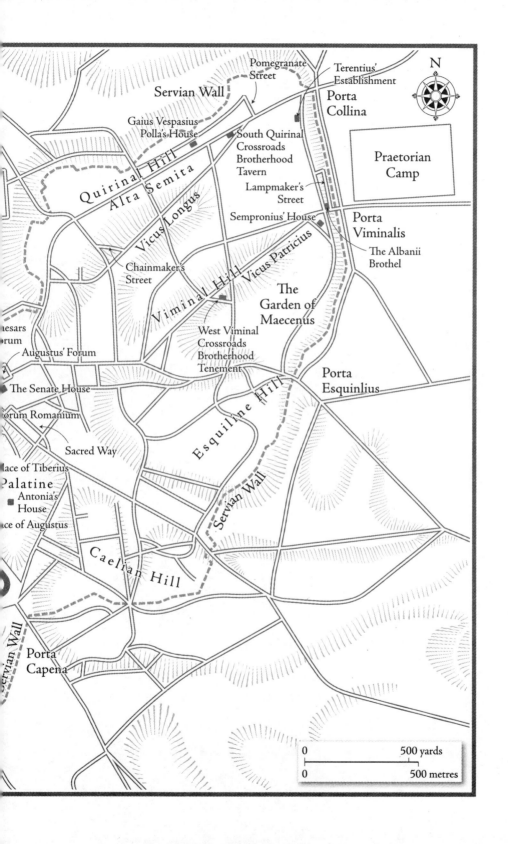

THE CROSSROADS
BROTHERHOOD

I had not planned Magnus, he just stepped out into the road on the day that Vespasian and his family entered Rome in the opening book. I had originally intended Vespasian to rescue a brother and sister from the clutches of the Thracians later on in *Tribune of Rome*; their indebtedness to Vespasian for saving their lives would provide the basis for lifelong loyalty. But, instead, Magnus got up from his table outside the South Quirinal Crossroads Brotherhood's tavern and waylaid the Flavian party. And I'm so glad that he did.

I immediately saw that with Magnus being a part of Vespasian's story I could explore that part of Rome – the underbelly – which, because of his rank, I could not with my main character.

And so the South Quirinal Crossroads Brotherhood was conceived and Magnus, Sextus, Marius, Servius, Cassandros and Tigran, as well as other lesser characters, were born, along with Magnus' arch-rival Sempronius and his West Viminal Brethren.

But Magnus needed to be attached to the higher echelons of society, otherwise who would have the influence to get him off the hook after another rampage through Rome behaving very badly indeed – badly at least to our modern way of thinking? So to make him a client of Vespasian's uncle, Gaius Vespasius Pollo, and indebted to him for saving his life over a silly misunderstanding that left someone or other dead was an ideal way to have Magnus cross the divide between the two sides of Rome. Thus Magnus' present difficulties in Rome's underbelly could be solved at the same time as looking after the interests of his benefactor operating in far higher circles.

The final ingredient that I needed were subjects for the six stories that I planned; however, that was easy as the human condition does not change much – it was ever thus. And so each story deals with something that is still relevant today, and in the case of *The Crossroads Brotherhood* it is child prostitution. The Albanians that I mention are not the same as what we know of today but, rather, from the ancient Kingdom of Albania on the west coast of the Caspian Sea, next to, rather confusingly, Iberia!

This first story concerns what Magnus was doing in the lead-up to his first appearance in *Tribune of Rome* and finishes with his first line in said book; I have to admit that was my wife Anja's idea and I can make no claim to it!

ROME, DECEMBER AD 25

'MARCUS SALVIUS MAGNUS, I've come to you as my patron in the hope that you will right the wrong that is being done to me. In the three years that you have been the patronus of the Crossroads Brotherhood, here in the South Quirinal district, you have seen that I've always paid the not inconsiderable dues owed for your continuing protection in full and on time. I have always provided you with information on my clients, when you have asked for it. I have always offered you free use of my establishment, although you have never availed yourself of that, as my goods are not, I believe, to your taste.'

Magnus sat – leaning back in his chair with his elbows resting on the arms, his hands steepled, his forefingers pressed to his lips – and looked intently at the slight, auburn-haired man standing on the other side of the table as he continued to list examples of his loyalty to the Crossroads Brotherhood, under whose protection lived every trader and resident on the southern slope of the Quirinal Hill. Wearing a tunic of fine linen, outrageously unbelted, and with long, abundant hair tied back in a ponytail, he was of outlandish appearance, but not unattractive – if you liked that sort of thing. Although in his late thirties, his skin was as smooth as a young woman's, clinging tightly to his fine-boned cheeks and jaw. His sea-grey eyes, lined with traces of kohl, sparkled in the soft lamplight and watered slightly in reaction to the smoky fug produced by the charcoal brazier in the small, low-ceilinged room that Magnus used to transact business with the more important of his many clients. Through the closed door behind him came the muffled shouts and laughter of the well-fuelled drinkers in the tavern beyond.

Magnus had no need to hear of the man's commitment to him and his brothers, he already knew him to be trustworthy. What interested him was the fact that he felt compelled to affirm it at such length. He was evidently, Magnus surmised, building up to ask a very large favour.

Next to Magnus, his counsellor and second-in-command, Servius, shifted impatiently in his chair and scratched his balding grey hair. Magnus shot him a displeased glance and he settled, stroking the wrinkled skin sagging at his throat with a gnarled hand. Servius knew full well that a supplicant had the right to fully state his claim – however long-winded – to the protection of the only organisation in Rome that would look after the interests of his class.

'And finally, I am always at your disposal to help repel incursions from the neighbouring brotherhoods,' the man eventually concluded, causing Magnus to smile inwardly at the thought of such an effeminate in a street fight, 'should they try to take what is rightfully ours – as they did, not one hour ago.'

Magnus raised his eyebrows, concern seeping on to his battered, ex-boxer's face – this was unwelcome news. 'You've been robbed, Terentius? By whom?'

Terentius pursed his lips and almost spat on the floor before remembering where he was. 'Rivals from the Vicus Patricius on the Viminal.'

'What did they take?'

'Two boys, and they cut up two others; one very, very badly.' Terentius looked down and indicated to his groin. 'You understand?'

Magnus winced and then nodded thoughtfully. 'Yeah, I take your meaning. You did right to come to me. Who are these rivals?'

'They aren't citizens – they came from the east a few years back.'

Magnus looked at Servius in the hope that his counsellor's long lifetime's supply of knowledge of the Roman underworld would extend to these easterners.

'They're Albanii,' Servius informed them, 'from the kingdom of Albania in the south-east Caucasus between Armenia and

Parthia on the shores of the Caspian Sea. Like a lot of eastern barbarians they're inordinately fond of boys.'

Magnus grinned. 'Well, there's a big market for them here as well. I can understand why they've set themselves up in competition to you, Terentius. Have you lost much business to them?'

Terentius looked at the chair in front of him and then back at Magnus, who nodded. With a grateful sigh he sat down – not used to being upright for so long, Magnus mused with a hint of a smile.

'It was fine for the first couple of years,' Terentius said, taking the cup of wine that Servius offered. 'They were no threat to me: cheap with substandard, dirty boys who took no pride in their appearance. And besides, the house was more than half a mile away. But what it lacked in class and service it made up for with turnover.'

'A quick in and out, as it were?'

'What? Oh yes, I see. Well, they worked their boys hard, day and night, and soon were making good money but still they didn't trouble me as their clients were from the lowest part of society. I kept my elite clientele: senators, equestrians and officers of the Praetorian Guard, some of whom still occasionally ask for me.' Terentius smiled modestly and smoothed his hair with the palm of his hand.

'I'm sure that a professional with your experience is a sound investment for an evening,' Servius commented diplomatically, his hooded eyes betraying no irony.

Terentius inclined his head slightly, acknowledging the compliment. 'I do not disappoint and neither do my boys.' He took a delicate sip of wine. 'However, at the beginning of this year these Albanians decided to move upmarket, competing directly with me; and by this time they could afford to. They bought a more lavish place, close to the Vinimal Gate, and began to stock it with the best boys that they could find.

'As a result of Tacfarinas' revolt being crushed last year, the slave markets had started to fill up with the most delicious boys from Africa and, naturally, I wanted my pick of these brown-skinned beauties.'

'Naturally,' Magnus agreed.

'Unfortunately so did my rivals and, regrettably, they too have good taste. I suggested an agreement with them whereby we wouldn't always bid against each other, but they refused. Even on the very young ones that we train up so they are able to do most things with finesse by the time they're starting puberty; you can charge a premium for them. I couldn't let all the best ones go: my stock would have deteriorated over the next few years whilst theirs went up – I would lose my standing. So, I bid over the odds for the best.'

'Which must have pissed off our Albanian friends no end,' Magnus observed.

'Yes, but they still ended up with a goodly amount of beautiful, if over-priced, young flesh, and because the Praetorian Guard's camp is just outside the Viminal Gate, I started to lose some trade. I had little choice but to lower my prices and do deals: two for the price of one, eat and drink for free on your second consecutive evening, and that sort of thing. But they responded with similar policies and now, because of the huge outlay that we've both made this year, we're slowly driving each other out of business and, what's more, our clients all know it so they bargain even harder when they walk through the door.'

Magnus shook his head; he could see the problem: if Terentius' business went under then the South Quirinal Brotherhood would lose quite a chunk of its income. 'And so this evening the Albanians decided to up the stakes and try and force you out.'

'My men beat them off but the damage to my reputation is done; there were quite a few clients in the house when we were attacked.'

'So you want me to negotiate a financial settlement with Sempronius, Patronus of the West Viminal?'

Terentius' pale eyes hardened. 'No, Magnus, this is beyond that now. I want you to get my two boys back and then I want you to destroy these Albanians. Kill them all and their boys. The money that I've paid over the years to this Brotherhood entitles me to that.'

Magnus looked at Servius and shrugged. 'He's got a point,

Brother; and besides, we can't let an attack like that in our area go unpunished – but how do we do it without starting a war?'

The counsellor thought for a few moments, looking at Terentius. 'How well protected are these Albanians?'

'They have the best protection: the Vigiles. One of their tribunes has been using the Albanians as a way to ingratiate himself with the Praetorian Guard. So the Vigiles ensure there's never any trouble near the house and provide an escort for the boys to and from the Praetorian camp should an officer wish to enjoy them in the comfort of his own bed and suchlike services.'

Magnus stared hard at Terentius and sucked in his breath through his teeth. 'This is a big favour. If we do it we'll have the Vigiles and the Praetorians as well as the West Viminal Crossroads after us.'

Servius smirked coldly. 'You've got it, Brother: If *we* do it. We'll just have to make sure that it looks like *we* didn't.'

Magnus turned slowly to his counsellor; a trace of a smile cracked his lips. 'You're right. So first we need to get Terentius' two boys back and bring the matter to an honourable conclusion so everyone can see that we have no more interest in it. Then we set someone else up.'

Terentius bowed his head in gratitude. 'Thank you, patronus.'

Servius looked thoughtfully at his fingernails. 'And who will seem to be responsible for the Albanians' demise, Brother?'

'It has to be a group that's untouchable but one that could logically have done it. People who hate both the Vigiles and the Guard as much as they're hated by them in return.'

Servius raised his eyebrows. 'Your old mates?'

'Exactly; the Urban Cohorts. I think that we should call a meeting of all the neighbouring brotherhood chiefs for tomorrow.'

'I think so too. And I think that we should take a gift to show our good intentions.'

'I'll leave you in charge of the arrangements, Brother.'

'I'll send the invitations out immediately. Usual time and place?'

'Usual time and place.'

*

Magnus was woken by a knock on the door of the small room that he called home, above the tavern that was the headquarters of his Brotherhood.

'Magnus?' a voice called from beyond the door.

'Yeah, what is it? It's still dark,' Magnus replied sleepily, feeling the warmth of a woman in the bed beside him and trying to recollect her name.

'It's Marius, Brother. Servius says that you should come down and take a look at what Sextus, me and some lads brought in just now.'

Magnus grunted and eased out a fart. 'All right, bring me a lamp.'

The door swung open and the silhouetted bulk of Marius filled its frame with a lamp in his right hand – his left hand was missing.

'Leave it on the table, Marius,' Magnus said, sitting up.

As Marius walked across the room Magnus pointed to the sleeping form beside him and mouthed: What's her name?

'Dunno, she's new, just turned up last night.'

'Thanks, Brother, very helpful. I'll be down in a moment.'

Magnus slapped the woman's arse and got out of bed as Marius left the room. 'Up and at 'em, my girl. I've got to go. What do I owe you?'

The woman rolled over sleepily and peered at him through a tangle of well-ravaged black hair. 'It was a free one, Magnus. Aquilina, remember? I said I'd do you for free if you'd let me work the tavern.'

'Ah, that's right, you're new,' Magnus replied, trying to remember the conversation through the haze of last night's wine. 'Well, you've passed the test. See old Jovita later and tell her that I said it was fine for you to work here. She watches the girls; you report to her if you leave with a customer or if you're just giving your favours in a dark corner. We take twenty per cent of everything you earn from the tavern, payable in cash the following morning. If you try and cheat us, you're out on your ear and you won't find a cock willing to service you in this district ever again, not even for nothing, because you'd be too ugly, if you take my meaning?'

Aquilina smiled, getting to her feet – a pretty smile Magnus thought, she should do well. 'I won't cheat you, Magnus, I just want to earn my keep,' she said, slipping on her tunic and picking up her discarded loincloth and sandals. She gave him a kiss on the cheek. 'Any time you want me, I won't charge.' Giving him a playful squeeze, she left the room.

Magnus watched her go, frowning.

'What've we got here then that's so important?' Magnus asked, walking into the tavern's main parlour that still stank of stale wine, vomit and sweat from the previous evening.

Servius looked up from a scroll of accounts that he was going through on a table in the centre of the room and nodded towards two small figures, bound with sacks over their heads, slumped under the amphorae-lined bar. Marius and Sextus watched over them.

'Servius sent us fishing,' Sextus said slowly, as if reciting, 'and we caught a couple of slippery fish. They're nice and greasy, especially in certain places.' He broke into deep, shuddering laughs.

Marius smiled at Magnus, shaking his head in exasperation. 'He's been practising that line for the last hour, Magnus; it ain't even funny 'cos fish are slimy not greasy, but he can't see the difference.'

'Well, he'd soon find out if he came across a slimy arse. Let's have a look at them.'

With Sextus incapacitated by mirth, Marius pulled the sacks off, to reveal two very attractive, but slightly bruised, brown-skinned youths in their early teens. They looked at Magnus with dark, fearful eyes and huddled closer together.

'The lads did well, Magnus,' Servius observed.

Magnus was impressed. 'A couple of the Albanians' boys? How did you get them, Marius?'

'They was on their way back from a visit to the Praetorian Camp.'

'But they have an escort of Vigiles.'

'Yeah, but what do Vigiles do when they see a fire?'

Magnus grinned. 'First they negotiate a fee with the owner for putting it out; then they put it out.'

'So I had some of the lads start a fire when we knew they was on their way, and these poor little fish got forgotten about whilst their minders tried to make a profit out of some poor bastard's misfortune. So Sextus and me decided to escort them home. We just took a few wrong turns, that's all, and happened to end up here.'

'Well done, lads; such a pretty gift for the meeting later. Lock 'em up safely until this afternoon and then get the altar ready for the morning sacrifice.'

Marius visibly swelled with pride at the praise and he and Sextus, who was still chuckling fiercely, hauled the terrified boys to their feet and dragged them away.

Magnus turned to Servius. 'Have the invitations gone out?'

'Yes, Brother, and all the replies are back in. All five of the surrounding *Patroniae* will be there an hour before sunset.'

The sun was slipping behind the Aventine Hill throwing the raked-sand track of the Circus Maximus into shadow and bathing the stepped-stone seating and the colonnades that soared above in a warm evening glow.

Magnus stood, in a freshly chalk-dusted white toga, at the end of the spina, the central barrier that ran down the middle of the track, facing the massive wooden gates that opened out on to the Forum Boarium. Servius, flanked by Marius and Sextus, waited behind him – they too sported gleaming togas, worn with pride by the free and freed citizens of Rome, however lowly, and worn today, as custom decreed, at a meeting of Crossroads *Patroniae*. Four other similar groups of a patronus, his counsellor and two bodyguards, stood around the edge of the track, two to Magnus' left and two to the right, all keeping a good distance between each other as they awaited the final arrival. A light breeze, blowing along the length of the track of the eerily silent stadium, played with the folds of their togas.

'Fucking typical of Sempronius to keep us waiting so that he can make a grand entrance,' Magnus muttered over his shoulder to Servius.

'A futile gesture, Brother; you will all be equal in the middle, no matter who arrived last.'

Magnus grunted. A moment later a small door to the left of the main gates swung open to reveal the missing party led by a tall, blond-haired, young man. As he started to walk forward, Magnus and the other four *Patroniae*, followed by their entourages, did the same, coming to a halt in a circle exactly halfway between the spina and the gates, one of the few public places in the crowded city of Rome where a private conversation could be held without fear of eavesdroppers.

'Greetings, Brothers,' Magnus said, looking each of his counterparts in the eye. 'I, Marcus Salvius Magnus, of the South Quirinal, called this meeting to deal with an issue that has arisen between us and the West Viminal Brotherhood.'

Sempronius pursed his lips, pulled his broad shoulders back and glared at Magnus with cold, piercing, sapphire-blue eyes; the jaw muscles beneath the tight flesh of his cheeks twitched rapidly. His counsellor, equally young and equally handsome but dark-haired, leaned forward and whispered in his ear. Sempronius nodded, never once taking his eyes off Magnus.

'I wish to settle this issue now,' Magnus continued, 'in front of witnesses, in order to avoid it escalating into a war. None of us here would wish to see that, as we all know from past experience just how damaging for business that can be.'

Sempronius looked down at his left arm, held rigid across his stomach, supporting the folds of his toga, and stared at it for a few moments as if examining in fine detail the blond hairs on the back of his hand. His eyes suddenly flicked back up to Magnus. 'We had nothing to do with the raid on the whore-boy house.'

'I am not saying that you did; yet you know about it.'

'I know of it,' Sempronius corrected, 'but not much about it. As I said: it was not done by us.'

'No, but it was done by people from your area; Albanian

clients of yours, who you would be honour-bound to avenge if we exacted the correct price for their actions.'

'And what would you consider that price to be?' Sempronius asked slowly, one side of his face curled up in a sneer.

'Death. And not a quick one.'

Sempronius smiled mirthlessly. 'That would be grievous mistake.'

'No, Brother, that would be justice, but I'm not naive enough to think that we both have the same sense of justice so, in order to maintain the peace between us, I offer this compromise.' Magnus put two fingers in his mouth and whistled shrilly. A couple of his lads led two small figures out of one of the entrance tunnels in the rows of seating; knives were held across their throats.

Sempronius regarded them for a few moments and then shrugged. 'More whore-boys; what are they to me?'

'They're nothing to you, but they're worth quite a bit to their Albanian owners – in the condition that they're in at the moment, that is. Unfortunately their condition is worsening.' Magnus raised a hand and brought it down quickly. A knife flashed golden in the evening sun; there was a screech and blood started to flow down the face of one of the boys. 'That was just a small cut across the top of his forehead; nothing too disfiguring so it won't reduce his value that much.'

'What do you want?'

'The two boys that your Albanian friends took from my client. If they are returned tonight, unharmed, then I will return those two with their fingers, tongues and cocks still in place and without sharp knives rammed up their arses. In other words, in perfect working order to carry on their trade. My client will also forgo his revenge for the two other boys that were cut up in the attack and that will be an end to the matter.'

'And if they're not returned tonight?'

'It will be their tongues first, then we'll have our vengeance on the Albanians and all our businesses will suffer as we fight out a blood-feud.'

'That can't be allowed to happen, Sempronius,' the patronus to Magnus' left stated. 'My area, the North Viminal, is right between you two, we would suffer badly. Magnus' deal is fair and you should accept it; if not and you take us to war, then we will be against you.'

There were murmurs of agreement from the other three Crossroads leaders.

Magnus kept his expression neutral but smiled inwardly as anger briefly flashed across Sempronius' face; he would have to back down and lose face or find himself ranged against all of the brotherhoods on the Viminal and Quirinal.

'Give him something to take away from the meeting as a sop,' Servius whispered into Magnus' ear. 'Otherwise his pride may prevent him from accepting.'

Magnus nodded. 'To show our goodwill, Sempronius, I'll give you one of the boys to take with you now, on account as it were.'

Sempronius turned to his counsellor who inclined his head indicating his agreement. 'Very well, Magnus, I'll take the boy. The Albanians will return the two that they've got this evening and pick up the second one then. After that we're square, yes?'

'Square, Sempronius, and these brothers are our witnesses. Tell your Albanians to have the boys at my tavern by midnight, I'll guarantee their safe conduct. After that they're to keep out of my area if they value their lives.'

It was dark by the time Magnus and his comrades got back to the Crossroads; the tavern was filling up and business was brisk.

'Take him into the back, clean him up and keep watch over him, Cassandros,' Magnus ordered one of the two brothers accompanying the visibly terrified remaining whore-boy. Dried blood matted his hair and covered his face.

'A pleasure, Magnus,' Cassandros replied with a grin.

'And keep your filthy Greek hands off him, and any other part of your body for that matter: he's not to be interfered with.'

Looking disappointed, Cassandros led his charge off as Magnus and Servius took a corner table. A jug of wine and two cups were quickly set before them by a plump, grey-haired woman.

'Business looks good this evening, Jovita,' Magnus commented as she filled his cup.

Jovita indicated with her head to the far corner where Aquilina was perched on the lap of a busy-handed freedman. 'That new one who started today seems to be very popular; seems to be pulling a crowd. That's number six so far.'

'Busy girl,' Servius commented to the old woman's back.

Magnus looked away from the girl, taking a slug of wine. 'So, Brother, they seemed to believe us.'

'Yes. So now we wait.'

'Just a few days, let things settle.'

'Have you worked out how we're going to do it?'

'Almost, there're a couple of things that I ain't sure of yet but I'll go and see an old comrade from the Cohort discretely tomorrow; he'll be able to help me.'

Servius looked over Magnus' shoulder. 'Not another whore-boy?'

Magnus turned to see a beautiful youth in his early teens swathed in a hooded cloak and sighed. 'Does he want to see me, Arminius?'

'Yes, master, can you come at once?' the youth replied with a guttural Germanic accent, pulling back his hood to reveal luxuriant, flaxen hair.

Magnus nodded and downed his wine. 'Deal with the exchange if I'm not back when the Albanians arrive, Brother.' He got to his feet and, indicating to Marius and Sextus that they should follow him, stepped out into the night after the young German.

'Magnus, my friend, thank you for coming so quickly,' Gaius Vespasius Pollo boomed, turning his huge bulk in his chair as Magnus and his companions were shown into the atrium by a very decrepit and ancient doorkeeper. 'Arminius, take Magnus' friends to the kitchen and find them some refreshment.'

'Good evening, Senator,' Magnus replied as his erstwhile guide led Marius and Sextus from the room.

'Come and sit down, it's a chill night.' Gaius indicated with a full wine-cup to a chair across the table from him, in front of a blazing log fire, set in the hearth.

'How can I be of assistance at this time of night?' Magnus asked, sitting and adjusting his toga.

Gaius handed him the cup. 'Yes indeed, not really the business time of day, is it?'

'It is for my sort of business.' Magnus took a long draught of wine, ignoring Gaius' disapproving frown at the rough treatment of such a fine vintage. 'That's a nice drop of wine that is, sir.'

'I'm glad that you appreciate it.' Gaius reluctantly topped up Magnus' proffered cup. 'What do you know about the Lady Antonia?'

Magnus shifted uneasily in his chair and took another slug of wine. 'She's the Emperor's sister-in-law, grandmother to the children of the late Germanicus and a very formidable woman. I believe that you are in her favour.'

'I am.'

'When I was a boxer I attended a few of her dinners as a part of the entertainment.'

'Yes, I'm aware of that, although I've never understood why a citizen would choose to become a boxer.'

'The money mainly but also the notoriety – look at all them young gentlemen who choose to fight a bout or two in the arena for wagers or just to get their names heard.'

'Rather excessive, to my mind.'

'Yeah, well, it helped me become the patronus of my Crossroads – you don't do that by just asking nicely, if you take my meaning?'

Gaius' eyes twinkled with amusement in the glow of the fire. 'No, you did that by murder for which you would have paid with your life – had it not been for me, if you take mine?'

'I do, Senator, and I will always be in your debt.'

'Enough to commit another murder?'

Magnus shrugged and held out his cup for another refill. 'If you require it.'

'*I don't*,' Gaius emphasised, pouring more wine, 'but Antonia does. This evening she asked – or rather ordered – me to organise one for her. She's not a woman that one can say no to.'

Magnus looked away and tried to keep his face neutral. 'I can imagine.'

Gaius chuckled, causing his tonged ringlets to sway gently over his ears; he took another sip of wine.

'Who does she want done and why doesn't she organise it herself?' Magnus asked.

'There's absolutely no reason why she couldn't organise it herself, so I've a hunch that the answer to the second question is that it's a test to see how far she can trust me. If I succeed then I will have a place in her inner circle of friends.'

'And be one step closer to the consulship.'

'Quite. So you can see how important it is for me. As to the first question, that's simple: a Praetorian Guardsman.'

Magnus banged his cup down on to the table in alarm. 'A Praetorian? Is she serious?'

'Oh yes, quite literally deadly serious. And it's not just any Praetorian either, it's Nonus Celsus Blandinus.'

'Blandinus? One of the tribunes?'

'I'm afraid so.'

'What's she got against him?'

'Nothing that I know of; it's rather unfortunate for him really.'

'Then why?'

'Earlier this year, Antonia managed to persuade the Emperor to forbid the Praetorian Prefect Sejanus to marry her widowed daughter, Livilla. Now she wants to send a message to Sejanus that in making that request he went too far; and what better way to do that than to have one of his deputies killed?'

'I can think of a lot of better ways. When does she want it done?'

'Within the next couple of days. But she wants it done in a way that Sejanus will know that she's behind it but be unable to accuse her of organising the murder.'

'So we can't just slit his throat in a dark alley.'

'Absolutely not, this demands subtlety.' Gaius leaned forward and put his hand on Magnus' forearm. 'I'm relying on you, my friend. If you do this well for me then Antonia will owe me a favour. My sister and brother-in-law are bringing their two boys to Rome. I may be able to use this to have her further their careers as well as my own.'

Magnus raised an eyebrow at his patron. 'And the higher you and your family rise the more you can do for me, eh, Senator?'

'Naturally.' Gaius smiled and patted Magnus' arm. 'We could all come out of this very well.'

'You might, but I could come out of this very dead.'

'If I thought that for one instant then I wouldn't have entrusted you with one of the most important favours of my career,' Gaius asserted, raising his cup to Magnus who smiled mirthlessly, raised his in reply and then downed it in one.

The night was cold and clear; Magnus' breath steamed as he walked, deep in thought, down the quiet streets of the Quirinal followed by Marius and Sextus. Turning left on to the wider and busier Alta Semita, jammed with the delivery wagons and carts that were only allowed into the city at night, the pavement became more crowded but people stepped aside in deference as they recognised the leader of the area's Brotherhood. Those who were not local and failed to move were roughly shoved out of the way by Marius and Sextus.

Magnus accepted a charcoal-grilled chicken leg from the owner of one of the many open-fronted shops, occupying the ground floor of the three- or four-storey insulae that lined both sides of the street. The walls to either side of the shop were covered in graffiti, both sexual and political.

'Thank you, Gnaeus; one for each of the lads as well.'

'My pleasure, Magnus,' the sweaty store-holder replied, retrieving, with a pair of tongs, two more legs off the red-glowing grill.

'Business been good?' Magnus asked, biting into the dripping flesh.

'We had a very good Saturnalia, however it's trailed off a bit in the last few days but I'm sure that it will pick up for the New Year. The trouble is that the price of fresh chicken has gone up considerably in the last couple of months and it's eating into my profit.'

'And you've raised your prices as much as you can?' Magnus asked, realising why Gnaeus had offered him some of his wares.

'As much as I dare without pricing myself out of the market.'

'Where do you buy your chicken?'

'Ah, that's the big problem: the small market at the Campus Sceleratus, just inside the Porta Collina; the prices are usually better there than in the main Forum markets, and it's in our area. However, I'm sure that the traders have started fixing their prices and the market aedile is colluding with them.'

'I see.' Magnus gnawed thoughtfully on his chicken leg. 'That sounds less than legal to me. I'll send a couple of the lads up there tomorrow. They can offer anyone I suspect of price-fixing the opportunity of joining the Vestals who were buried alive beneath that Campus for breaking their vows.'

Gnaeus inclined his head in gratitude. 'I'm sure that's an offer they would be happy to refuse, thank you, patronus.'

Magnus threw his cleaned bone into the gutter. 'How's that daughter of yours? Have you found her a husband yet?'

Gnaeus raised his eyes to the heavens. 'The gods preserve me from wilful women. I—'

A series of loud shouts from a nearby shop interrupted the store-holder's catalogue of domestic woes. A bearded young man came pelting along the pavement towards them, clutching two loaves of bread to his chest.

'Marius? Sextus?' Magnus said, stepping aside and nodding at the fast approaching thief.

Seeing his path blocked by two burly men in togas, he tried to sidestep to his left, into the road. Sextus thrust out his massive, right fist and caught him a stunning blow to the side of his head, sending him crashing into a mule-cart and startling the beast pulling it. With a speed that belied his size and quickness of thought, Sextus was down on the stunned man, hauling him up by his ragged tunic, semi-conscious, to his feet; the loaves of bread were left in the road to be trampled by the spooked animal.

A tubby little baker in a grease-specked tunic puffed, pushing his way through the gathering crowd of onlookers. 'That man stole from my shop, Magnus. I want payment for that bread.'

Magnus walked over to the still-dazed thief held upright in Sextus' powerful grip. He lifted his chin roughly in his hand, squinting at his face. 'I don't recognise him, he ain't from round here.' Letting his chin go he gave him an abrupt slap across the cheek. 'Where're you from, petty thief?' The man's head lolled on his chest, a trickle of blood worked its way through his beard; he said nothing.

Magnus grasped the captive's right hand, folding his fingers in a firm grip, crushing them, causing a groan of pain as he recovered his senses. 'What are you doing stealing from this area?'

The man opened his eyes and tried to focus on Magnus, his face grimacing with agony as the pressure increased on his crushed fingers. 'He cheated me couple of days ago,' he managed to whisper, in thickly accented Latin. 'He gave me a counterfeit *as* in change.'

Magnus eased his grip. 'Can you prove that?'

The man reached for his belt and pulled a small copper coin from a leather pocket sown into the reverse side. Magnus looked at it; the surface had been scratched revealing the dull-metallic hue of iron. He took the coin and brandished it at the baker. 'Did you give him this, Vitus?'

The baker reddened and held up his hands. 'Of course not, Magnus, I wouldn't be so stupid; I'm well aware of the punishment for passing dud coinage.'

'I think that I had better have a look in your shop. Marius, ask this gentleman nicely to escort us to it.'

'My pleasure, Magnus,' Marius said, stepping forward and placing a firm hand on the reluctant Vitus' shoulder, slowly turning him around; he pushed his stump into the small of the baker's back and propelled him forward the few paces to his open-front shop.

Sextus followed, hauling the thief after him.

'Where do you keep your money, Vitus?' Magnus asked, looking around the shelf-lined premises and enjoying the smell of freshly baked bread.

Vitus glanced sidelong at his accuser, still secure in Sextus' grip. 'There, under the oven.' He pointed to a recess below a sturdy iron door. Next to it two elderly female slaves were kneading dough on a wooden table. They continued with their work, ignoring the intrusion.

'Show me.'

Vitus retrieved a wooden box from behind a couple of full, small sacks and opened it; it was a quarter filled with low-denomination coins.

'That's not where he got my change from,' the thief exclaimed. 'One of the slaves got it from a bag in a draw in the table.'

The two women stopped the work and looked at their master, who paled.

Magnus smiled grimly at the baker and held out his hand. Vitus nodded at one of the women who opened a draw, pulled out a small leather bag and threw it to Magnus.

'Well, well, Vitus,' Magnus said as he tipped a dozen or so coins into his hand, 'evidently you are stupid; lucky that it was me that caught you and not an aedile.'

Vitus fell to his knees and clutched at the hem of Magnus' toga. 'Please, Magnus, don't report me to the aedile; I'll lose a hand. I'm sorry, I won't do it again.'

'Too fucking right you won't do it again; I won't have it in my area; it will give us all a bad name.' He turned to the thief. 'What's your name?'

'Tigran, master.'

'Where're you from?'

'Armenia, master.'

'No, I meant: where are you from in Rome?'

'Oh, I live in the shanty town amongst the tombs on the Via Salaria.'

'You're not a citizen, are you?'

'No, master. I arrived here a few months ago.'

'Then I'll give you a warning: you don't steal here. Next time you're cheated in my area come and see me, I won't have people taking the law into their own hands. Explain that to him, Sextus.'

With a sharp jab, Sextus rammed his right fist into Tigran's stomach, doubling him over with a loud exhalation of breath.

Magnus put the counterfeit coins back into their bag and

tucked it into the fold of his toga. 'Get me two loaves of bread, Vitus.' As the baker rose to his feet and scuttled to a shelf Magnus removed four *asses*, the equivalent of one sesterce, from the money box and gave them to Tigran, who still struggled for breath. 'Give him the bread as well, Vitus.'

Vitus quickly handed over the loaves.

'Now get out of here and don't come back unless you plan to behave honestly,' Magnus said, cuffing Tigran around the ear.

'Thank you, master.' Tigran turned quickly to go, clutching the loaves to his chest with one hand and clasping his money in the other. He pushed through the crowd of onlookers and disappeared.

'As for you,' Magnus growled, pulling Vitus by the collar so that their faces were nose to nose, 'I want a list of everyone that you can remember passing that shit on to, plus the name of the person who supplied it, with me by morning, or it will be your last, if you take my meaning?' He brought his knee sharply up into Vitus' testicles and then walked away leaving the baker to crumple to the floor, eyes bulging, unable to breathe and with both hands grasping his damaged genitals. The crowd parted for him, voicing their approval having witnessed justice well done.

Magnus and Servius sat at a table in the shadowy, smoky confines of the small room behind the tavern that they used to conduct business. A jug of steaming hot, spiced and honeyed wine stood between them next to a single oil lamp. 'So we need to kill a Praetorian Tribune in a way that doesn't look like an accident and doesn't look like an obvious murder but is suspicious enough for Sejanus to recognise it as a warning from Antonia,' Servius summarised.

Magnus looked gloomy. 'That's about it, Brother. How the fuck can we do that?' He took a swig from the cup that he held in both hands and scalded his tongue.

Servius looked on with amusement as his superior called on various gods to curse or strike down the obviously half-witted slave who had prepared the wine. 'I think that was a good lesson,' he observed once the tirade had subsided. 'Drink the wine before it's ready and it will hurt you; drink when it's just right and it will please you. So let's not rush into this—'

'But we have to rush into this,' Magnus interrupted – the burn had not helped his temper. 'Antonia wants this done in the next couple of days.'

Servius raised a calming hand. 'Yes, and it shall be. All I'm saying is that at the moment we don't know how to approach it. The difference between an accident, death in suspicious circumstances and murder is the situation in which the body is found. A man may die falling from a horse that he rides every day; he may genuinely have fallen off, in which case it is an accident; or the horse may have been spooked on purpose by someone in order to get it to throw the man off, in which case it's murder. However, if a man is found dead having fallen from a horse but it's known that he never goes riding, then that's death in suspicious circumstances; it would be highly unlikely to be an accident because what is he doing on the horse in the first place? And yet you can't prove that it's not; nor can you prove that it was murder because people die all the time from falling off horses.'

Magnus' face brightened; the pain from his burnt tongue forgotten. 'Ah! So you're saying that if we stage an "accident" whilst Blandinus is apparently doing something that he never normally does then Sejanus will suspect it was murder but be unable to prove it.'

'Exactly.'

'So we need to use the rest of tonight and tomorrow to find out all that we can about the unfortunate tribune.'

'Precisely, and then we will have to somehow lure or force the poor man into that unusual circumstance in which he will be found dead.'

'Tricky but not impossible. Get the lads on to it immediately.'

'I will, Brother,' Servius confirmed as a knock sounded on the door.

'Yes?' Magnus called.

Marius stuck his head into the room. 'Magnus, they're here waiting outside, them Albanians, and a strange fucking sight they are too.'

'I don't care what they look like, so long as they've got the boys.'

'Yeah, they got them all right.'

'Good. Go and tell Cassandros to bring the boy into the tavern; I'll send for him when I need him.' Magnus rose to his feet. 'Shall we go and do business, Brother?'

'I think we should,' his counsellor agreed, following him out.

Magnus surveyed the four bizarrely attired easterners waiting in the moonlight by the tables outside the tavern. Two pretty youths in their early teens, one with blond hair and one dark, stood next to them, staring at Magnus with frightened eyes, knives held to their throats.

'Who speaks for you?'

'I do,' a middle-aged man said, stepping forward. He wore a long-sleeved, saffron tunic, belted at the waist, that came to just below his knees, half covering a pair of dark-blue baggy trousers bunched in at the ankle to expose delicate, red-leather slippers. His oiled hair was jet black and fell to his shoulders framing a lean, high-cheekboned face dominated by a sharp, straight nose. Two dark, mirthless eyes stared back at Magnus; his thin mouth was just visible beneath a hennaed red beard that came to an upwards-curling point.

'And you are?' Magnus asked, trying to keep the contempt that he felt for this outrageous-looking whore-boy master out of his voice. Behind him Sextus and Marius led half a dozen brothers, armed with knives and cudgels, out of the tavern.

'Kurush,' the Albanian replied, resting his right hand on the hilt of a curved dagger hanging at his waist. 'And you must be Magnus?' His Latin was precise and with little trace of an accent.

'I am. Let's get this over with; show me the two boys.'

'They have not been harmed or even interfered with; I can assure you of that with my word.'

'I'm sure you can but, nevertheless, I wish to see them closer.'

'A man who won't take another man's word is not worthy of trust himself. Let me see my boy. His condition will determine the state of the other two.'

'Sextus, tell Cassandros to bring him out,' Magnus ordered, keeping his eyes locked on Kurush.

They waited in silence, staring at each other, for the few moments that it took Cassandros to appear with his charge.

'Bring him here,' Magnus said as the Greek dragged the struggling youth through the tavern door.

'This man raped me,' the whore-boy shrieked at Kurush, pointing an accusatory finger at Cassandros, 'and paid nothing.'

Magnus spun round. One look at Cassandros' face confirmed that the boy was telling the truth: he could not meet his eye.

'It would seem that we have a problem,' Kurush observed. 'I don't take kindly to people making free with my property.'

Magnus grabbed the youth from Cassandros' grasp with his left hand and cracked his right fist into the Greek's face, felling him. 'I'll take care of it once we've done the exchange; he'll be punished, I give you my word.'

'Why should I take your word when you wouldn't take mine just now? But I'm not interested in him being punished, you can do what you like to him; I'm interested in a fair exchange.'

'This is a fair exchange, more than fair. I've already given you one of your boys; let's complete the transaction and then we need have nothing more to do with each other.'

Kurush smiled icily and turned to his three companions speaking to them in their own language. The blond-haired boy was brought forward. Kurush took him by the neck and propelled him towards Magnus. 'There, an untouched boy in payment for the one you sent me earlier.'

The boy stumbled and fell at Magnus' feet. Marius stepped forward, hauled him up and pulled him away.

Kurush looked back at Magnus. 'Now that leaves us with another untouched boy to exchange for a soiled boy; I don't consider that fair.' He barked a command in his own language.

The dark-haired boy was forced down over a table. He started to shriek as two of the Albanians grabbed his arms, holding them firm, at the same time pressing their weight down on his back, pinning him. The third Albanian, a young, effeminate-looking man with a wispy beard, barely out of his teens, pulled up the boy's tunic and ripped off his loincloth, raised his own tunic and opened the flap in the groin of his trousers, his gaze never leaving the boy's exposed buttocks. The boy screamed as the Albanian forced himself into him. The screaming stopped and the boy stared down at his white-knuckled hands gripping the table's edge as the Albanian took to his task with all the savagery of the abused that has become the abuser.

Magnus stood and watched in silence, indicating to his men that they should do so too, knowing that to interfere would jeopardise the deal; Kurush was not a man to lose face and besides, it was nothing to him whether the boy was raped or not, the important issue was to get him back to Terentius unmarked, his value intact if not his dignity.

'Is this absolutely necessary, Kurush?' Magnus asked as the Albanian quickened his pace and grunted to a climax.

'Yes, Magnus, for two reasons: firstly to show you that whatever is done to me or mine will be repaid in full, and secondly, to demonstrate that *my* men do as they're told.' He pointed down to Cassandros still lying prone on the ground. 'Unlike yours.'

After a few moments collecting his breath, the Albanian withdrew and wiped himself clean on the boy's tunic, grinning at Magnus as he did so.

'Very educational I'm sure, you've made your point. Now take your boy and give me mine.'

Kurush barked another order and the boy was immediately released, grimacing with pain and clutching his loincloth. Magnus pushed Kurush's boy towards him and as the two passed each other they paused for a moment, sharing a look of mutual sympathy, before carrying on back to their enslaved lives over which they had no control or say and in which the best that they could both hope for was to get through each day with as little misery as possible.

'Now get out of my area by the quickest route,' Magnus growled at Kurush as the boy passed him. 'The offer of safe conduct doesn't extend to any sightseeing. If you ever go near Terentius' house again you'll be a dead man, no matter who protects you.'

'I think Terentius understands, well enough to make a second visit unnecessary, that there is only room at the top end of the market for one of our establishments.'

'I know he does,' Magnus muttered under his breath as the Albanians turned and left. 'And so do I.'

'Do we have anything interesting on our tribune yet?' Magnus asked Servius. They were making their way in the crisp and clear dawn air up the Via Patricius, one of the main thoroughfares of the Viminal. Cloaked and deeply hooded to avoid being recognised, they had especially chosen this chill time of day so that their attire would not stand out as suspicious.

'Nothing yet,' Servius replied from within the depths of his hood, 'but it's only been one night; give the lads time. I've got quite a few of them going round and asking questions, one of them should come up with something soon enough.'

'It needs to be today.'

'Then I suggest that you help matters by going to see Senator Pollo after you've met with your mate from the Cohort. He may know something about him.'

Magnus muttered his agreement as the Viminal Gate came into sight.

'It's just up here on the left before the junction with the Lamp-makers' Street,' Servius informed him. 'We should get on to the right-hand side of the road.'

They crossed at the next set of raised stepping-stones, designed to keep pedestrians' feet free from ordure but also to allow the passage of wheeled vehicles, and disappeared into the throng of people opening shops, buying bread, firing up braziers, visiting patrons, clearing drowsy beggars from doorways. Pushing through the crowd, Servius led Magnus to a tavern with an outside bar.

'Two cups of hot wine,' he ordered, placing a small-denomination coin on the wooden counter.

Once they had been served, Servius turned and nodded to a large two-storey, brick-built house. 'That's the Albanians' place. As you can see it has no windows opening on to the street, no shops in its facade, it's just a blank wall and a door.'

Magnus looked at the two huge, bearded doormen in eastern garb, armed with cudgels and knives, guarding the entrance. 'Is that door the only way in and out?'

'Fortunately not.' Servius pointed to a small street that led off from the Via Patricius two houses up from the Albanians' establishment. 'That's the Lamp-makers' Street. There's an alley that runs from it along the rear of all the buildings opposite; I sent Cassandros to have a look at it last night after the swap; he says that the wall is only ten feet high and we could easily scale it and get up onto the roof.'

'He's making up for his mistake.'

'I gave him a dangerous assignment and he understood why.'

Magnus grunted approvingly. 'We need to teach the randy sod a lesson; but that can wait. Do they keep a guard in the alley?'

'Cassandros said that there was no one there last night, we'll walk past in a moment and see if there's one during the day.'

'So, we get in and out over the roof, but we've still got those two brutes on the door to deal with. When they hear noise inside at least one of them will come in – that'll make it easier.' Magnus took a sip of his wine. 'So if we have a group of our lads close by they could deal with the remaining one and then take the door; that sounds like a job for me and Marius, he's not much good at shinning up walls in a hurry with just one hand.'

'Yes, but you'd have to be quick to get the door before it's bolted again on the inside.'

'Unless we can make them think that some of their own are in danger out here in the street and are running for safety.'

'How?'

'I met an easterner last night and he owes me a favour. His name's Tigran, he lives in the shanty town on the Via Salaria; find him and see if he speaks Albanian or knows anyone who does.' A well-dressed figure striding up the street with two bodyguards and a woman in a hooded, dark-brown cloak caught Magnus' attention. 'Well, well, our friend Sempronius is paying the whore-boys a visit; I wouldn't have thought that that was his sort of thing.'

'He's probably just come to check that the exchange went all right last night. But what's really interesting is who he's got with him; I think I recognise that cloak.'

Sempronius' party approached the two doormen, one of whom immediately knocked rhythmically on the door; it opened and the doormen stepped aside to allow Sempronius in. As the woman followed him in she pulled down her hood.

Magnus' eyes widened. 'Minerva's wrinkled arse, that's the new girl, Aquilina! I thought that there was something wrong about her when she offered to let me have her for nothing; nobody does something for nothing.'

Servius downed the last of his wine. 'Evidently someone else paid her. It seems that Sempronius has put a little spy in our midst.'

Magnus slapped his counsellor on the shoulder. 'I'd say that was a piece of good fortune. I think that's just solved my last problem.'

'You're late!'

Magnus chuckled looking down at the shadow cast by the seventy-feet-high Egyptian obelisk on the Campus Martius; it was a couple of inches short of the third-hour line. 'I didn't think that anyone had the brains to read the sundial since I left the Urban Cohort, Aelianus.'

'True enough, mate, I'm probably the only one who can, which is why they made me quartermaster,' Aelianus replied, grasping Magnus' proffered forearm.

'A moment of madness on their part but one that's proved extremely lucrative for us, eh, my friend?'

Aelianus' florid, round face creased into a gap-toothed grin and he passed his hand through his thinning copper-coloured hair. 'And how are we going to exploit their moment of madness this time?'

Magnus put an arm around the Aelianus' shoulders and led him away from the tourists admiring the hundred-feet-long, curved hour-lines emanating from the base of the obelisk sundial – set up by Augustus a generation before – and on towards the first emperor's mausoleum on the bank of the Tiber, as it curved back northwards after a brief foray east. 'Get me twenty Urban Cohort uniforms, minus the armour and shields.'

'What for?'

'To pay a visit to an establishment that has caused me some grief. Oh, and I'll also need you to set fire to your depot.'

Aelianus raised his eyebrows. 'Just like that?'

'Yes, my friend, just like that.'

'And what's in it for me?'

'Half of what we find in the place, but with a guarantee of at least two hundred and twenty-five denarii.'

Aelianus whistled softly. 'A year's pay for a common legionary. Well, the tunics, belts, boots and cloaks will be no problem – I can have those for you by this evening. The helmets, swords and scabbards are slightly harder because I'll have to wait until all my staff have left for the day – but I could bring them round to you personally by the third hour of the night. When do you plan to do this thing?'

'The day after tomorrow, an hour before dawn when there shouldn't be any clients in the house; so tonight will be fine, you can bring it all then.'

'Good. But as to the fire, that's a different matter: I need to think that through very carefully.'

'Well, don't take too long about it, my friend. I need that warehouse doing its best imitation of a beacon an hour before dawn in two days' time.'

'Oh it will be, Magnus, don't you worry.'

'That's why I'm paying you so well, Aelianus, to take away my worries.'

The ginger quartermaster grinned again. 'If only you had more worries, I'd be a very wealthy man. I'll see you later with the gear; can you send a few of your lads to escort me?'

'Sure, they'll be at your depot by the second hour of the night.'

'Thanks, mate,' Aelianus said, turning to leave.

'Before you go, Aelianus,' Magnus said, stopping him, 'there's one more thing that I'll need you to do when you come over tonight.'

'It's included in the price, I suppose?'

'Yes and it's not negotiable.'

'Go on.'

'I need you to fuck one of my girls.'

Aelianus sighed melodramatically and shook his head slowly. 'Magnus, you're a hard taskmaster.'

The forum romanum was packed – three treason trials were being conducted simultaneously, part of a recent upsurge in the legal hounding of enemies of the emperor or the rivals of his praetorian prefect. To Magnus, how the equestrian or senatorial classes treated each other meant nothing, provided it did not affect the daily running of the city's institutions that were close to his heart: the games and the grain dole.

Pushing his way through the mass of spectators, food vendors, beggars and jurists, Magnus eventually came to the steps of the Curia, the Senate House. The doors were open and the Senate was in session. Magnus peered into the gloomy interior and, once his eyes had adjusted to the light, soon made out the corpulent figure of Gaius Vespasius Pollo. Knowing that he had no right to enter the building he descended the steps, bought a grilled sausage and a hunk of bread from a street vendor and settled down to wait.

Prodded by a red-shoed foot, Magnus awoke to the booming voice of Gaius. 'Sleeping on the Senate House steps like some vagrant? Have your brethren finally kicked you out as you did your predecessor?'

'Yeah, but less violently it would seem, seeing as I'm still alive.' Magnus grinned and got to his feet, rubbing his numb behind. 'Actually, I was waiting for you, Senator.'

'Is there a problem with our business? It's meant to be done by tomorrow at the latest.'

'Not as such. I have a question for you.'

'Walk with me,' Gaius requested, turning right along the front of the Curia, heading for the Quirinal.

Magnus fell in step and explained Servius' plan.

'I see,' Gaius mused as they started to climb the hill. 'That counsellor of yours is shrewd. Suspicious circumstances, very good.'

'So what do you know about this Blandinus? What doesn't he do?'

'I'm afraid he does most things: goes to the games and the theatre, he drinks, he gambles, he goes whoring; in fact, he frequents an establishment in your area, owned by Terentius.'

'But that's just boys; does he like women?'

'I think so; he's married and has children.'

Magnus looked disappointed. 'There must be something that he wouldn't be seen dead doing.'

Gaius' flabby face, glistening with sweat from the exertion of the uphill walk, suddenly brightened. 'Of course there is: men!'

'Men?'

'Yes, men. I can almost guarantee you that he has never even contemplated being buggered, let alone countenanced it.'

Magnus smiled. 'Of course; so simple that it was too obvious. Thank you, Senator, I'd best be going.'

'Won't you have some honeyed cakes and wine, we're almost at my house?'

'No time, Senator, I've got a lot to organise; it seems that I can wash two tunics in one tub.' He ran off leaving Gaius wondering just what he had been talking about.

'Bring it forward to dawn tomorrow?' Servius asked, throwing a handful of kindling on to the small fire on the altar of the Crossroads' lares next to the front door of the tavern.

Magnus sprinkled incense over the flame; it flared, giving off a pungent aroma. 'Yes, provided Terentius, with the good help of our lares, can entice Blandinus to his place this evening. Send one of the lads to fetch him here immediately.'

The counsellor nodded and went over to Marius and a group of the brothers sitting playing dice on one of the tables outside the tavern. After a brief word from Servius one of them got up and left.

'What about the gear?' Servius asked, returning to Magnus by the altar.

'That'll be here tonight but I want you to write a note to Aelianus telling him that I need his fire to happen one hour before dawn tomorrow, not the next day; ask him to acknow-ledge that in writing.'

'I'll do that now.'

'What about Tigran, any luck?'

'Yes, he's waiting inside to see you; he's very keen to repay the favour. He speaks a little Albanian but he's brought his cousin, Vahram, who's fluent.'

'Thank you, Brother,' Magnus said, looking up the Alta Semita towards the Porta Collina. A party of travellers caught his eye. 'Marius, take one of the lads and do the honours with that lot,' he said, pointing at the group. 'They look wealthy enough to be in need of our services.'

Marius grinned and got up from his game. 'Right you are, Magnus. Normal rate?'

'Yeah, normal rate.'

Marius slapped his neighbour on the back. 'Come on, Lucio, let's get busy.'

Magnus sat down at an empty table, watching the two brothers waylay the travellers and offer their protection whilst mulling over the plan for the night in his head; he knew that it was risky bringing the raid on the Albanians forward but it was too good an opportunity to miss and he smiled to himself as he thought of how Blandinus was to be found. Poor bastard.

Eventually a cough brought him out of his reverie; he looked up. 'Ah, Terentius; sit down, my friend. How's that boy?'

'Still passing blood, so I've had to put him on lighter duties,' the whore-boy master replied, elegantly placing himself on the bench opposite Magnus. Out in the street money was changing hands.

'I'm sorry to hear it. Do you know the Praetorian Tribune Blandinus?'

'Of course, he's one of my regulars.'

'Does he ever, how shall I put it, take his turn around?'

'No, never; some of our clients ask for that but never Blandinus. He only gives and he gives very well; I can personally vouch for that.' A misty-look came into Terentius' eyes that Magnus found disconcerting.

'I'm pleased to hear it. Will he be coming this evening?'

'I don't know, he comes most evenings. Why?'

'I need you to ensure that he comes this evening.'

'I suppose I could send him a note saying that I've got a new boy that may be to his taste.'

'And do you?'

'Yes, I've had to replace the ones that were cut up.'

'Then do that and when he comes I need you to drug him; can you do that too?'

Terentius looked uneasy and hesitated. 'Of course,' he answered after a few moments.

'You seem reluctant?'

'No, Magnus, I'll do it.'

'Good. Send me a message when it's done and keep him sedated until I pick him up.'

'What's this for?'

'Terentius my friend, it's part of something that will make you very happy.'

Out in the street Marius and a group of brothers led the now very well protected travellers off.

Night had fallen and the tavern was packed. Magnus sat in a corner watching Aquilina and her fellow whores plying their trade. Tigran and his cousin looked to be enjoying their wait for the night's mission.

Servius slipped on to the bench next to Magnus. 'The lads have left for the Cohort's depot.'

'They should be back in an hour then. Any news from Terentius?'

'Nothing yet, but Aelianus sent a message saying that he can do the fire tonight.'

Magnus nodded. 'Well, that's something. I suppose if Terentius fucks up then we could postpone it until tomorrow night, although the senator won't be happy about it.'

'What are you going to do about her?' Servius asked as Aquilina led another customer outside. The ever watchful Jovita made a mark in her ledger.

'Use her to deliver a message and then ... well, we'll see.'

'I assume this message is for Sempronius.'

'Exactly, Brother. When my mate Aelianus comes with the gear tonight I'm going to make a big fuss about him and offer him a girl and the use of my room. He's going to let a piece of pillow-talk drop.'

Servius smiled coldly. 'And she'll run straight to Sempronius with this titbit.'

Magnus grinned and watched a young slave come through the door. The boy would have been pretty, had it not been for an ugly, badly stitched wound running from left corner of his mouth to his ear. He walked over to Jovita and after a brief conversation was directed over to Magnus' corner.

'Magnus?' the youth asked, speaking with some difficulty. He held out a wax tablet.

Magnus inclined his head.

'My master, Terentius, sent this.'

Magnus took the tablet and gave it to Servius to read.

The counsellor glanced at it briefly. 'Our tribune is sleeping peacefully.'

A look of relief spread over Magnus' face. 'Excellent. Tell your master we'll be along in three hours.'

The slave bowed and slipped out of the room.

'Make sure all the lads are here within the hour, Brother,' Magnus said, getting to his feet.

'They will be.'

'And the first delivery?'

'Already here.'

'Pile them up over there in the corner, next to the ladders,' Magnus ordered as Aelianus and four brothers pushed a couple of laden handcarts off the street and through the double doors of the storeroom at the very rear of the tavern.

Within moments the doors were shut and a pile of twenty Urban Cohort uniforms, minus the armour and shields, lay in a heap on the floor.

'Right, lads, sort it all out into twenty sets,' Magnus said, putting his arm around Aelianus' shoulders. 'You, my friend, are coming with me to fuck the best-looking girl we have working here, and all for free.'

'What's the catch, mate?'

'No catch, I just want you to tell her what the Cohort are planning to do in three nights' time.'

'I don't know what we're planning in three nights' time.'

'Of course you don't; quite rightly you take no interest in the doings of your unit, but I shall enlighten you as we walk.'

'Aquilina, come and meet my very good friend and one-time comrade, Aelianus,' Magnus shouted as he led the quartermaster through the door into the fug of the tavern.

Aquilina disengaged herself from a disgruntled old man and walked through the crowded room. A plumper colleague took her place.

'Aelianus has just done me a huge favour,' Magnus informed her as she came up to them, smiling sweetly, 'and I want you to be very, very nice to him. I'm paying so anything he wants, if you take my meaning?'

'Oh I do, Magnus.' Aquilina ran her hand up the inside of Aelianus' thigh. 'Anything he likes, for as long as he likes.' Aelinaus' mouth fell open as he gawped at her with undisguised lust. 'But there's no need to pay me, Magnus – any friend of yours is a friend of mine.'

'If you insist.'

'It'll be a pleasure.'

'In that case you can use my room.'

'Thank you, Magnus,' Aquilina purred, leading Aelianus off and flashing Magnus a sweet smile over her shoulder.

As they disappeared through the door, his eyes hardened. It was a shame that she was going to have to lose that pretty smile.

Almost an hour later, Magnus was sitting in the back room when he heard footsteps on the bare wooden stairs coming down from the first floor. He put down the knife that he had been sharpening and looked at Servius. 'Seems like Aelianus has had his fill of Aquilina.'

'I would say that it is probably the other way around, Brother.'

'Yeah, too true,' Magnus laughed, getting up. 'Let's hope that he's still got the energy for a bit of fire-starting.' He opened the door and, stepping out into the dingy corridor, saw Aquilina appear at the bottom of the stairs.

'Your friend has quite worn me out, Magnus,' she said with a touch of exaggeration, 'I'm going to call it a night, if that's all right with you?'

'Nothing to do with me, my girl – you work as and when you want to, so long as you pay your percentage.'

Aquilina smiled brightly. 'Of course. Well, I'll see you tomorrow then.' She disappeared into the tavern with a little wave.

Servius joined Magnus. 'Do you want me to have her followed?'

'No, she might notice, and it wouldn't do for her to become suspicious. Anyway, we know where she's going.'

Aelianus lumbered down the stairs looking conspicuously florid. What was left of his ginger hair stuck out at odd angles.

'How did it go?' Magnus asked.

'Very well,' Aelianus replied with a grin. 'I surprised myself and, I like to think, the lovely Aquilina too. You heard her – she said that she wouldn't be able to have another customer for the rest of the night after my performance.'

'Yeah? Well, don't take it too hard but that was just her excuse to get out of here and go and tell a few tales to her real master. I meant how was the pillow-talk?'

Aelianus looked slightly downcast. 'It was fine. I told her that I'd come to warn you, as an old mate from the Cohort, that the Urban Prefect was planning a raid on one of your clients' establishments in a few days' time, someone called Terentius. That's why you wanted me to have her as a reward.'

'What then?'

'Well, after that she started saying that I must be very important to have that sort of information and how much important men like me excited her ... What she can do with her—'

'I know, mate,' Magnus cut in, 'I've had her too. Just tell me the part I need to know.'

'Sorry. Well, she carried on asking me about the Cohort and the raid ... you know ... now and again ... until I told her that it wasn't to be the first raid, there was going to be one in three days' time on an establishment on the Viminal owned by easterners.'

'And she swallowed it?'

Aelianus raised his eyebrows and nodded, grinning. 'Yeah, all of it.'

Magnus slapped him on the shoulder. 'You did well, my friend, I hope you'll be as successful with the fire.'

'It won't be a problem, Magnus, but I'd appreciate a couple of your lads to help me spread some oil.'

'Fine. Come over tomorrow and collect your money.'

'I'm looking forward to it.'

'Oh, and leave those handcarts here, mate.'

'They're no good to you – they've got Cohort insignia branded all over them.'

'I know.' Magnus turned to his counsellor. 'Brother, we've got work to do. Get a couple of the lads for our good friend here and see him out, and then slowly get the rest moving up to the Lamp-makers' Street in twos and threes. I'll meet you there in a couple of hours.'

The two doormen outside Terentius' establishment were equally as large as those guarding the Albanians' place. Magnus, however, had nothing to fear from them as he and his party approached the house awhile later.

'Evening, lads, your master's expecting me,' he said, striding up the worn steps to the door of the elegant marble-fronted house. Torches attached to each of the two columns of the portico illuminated the well-crafted drawing of an erect phallus, above the door, succinctly advertising the business transacted within.

The doormen immediately stepped aside, one giving a coded knock on the door as he did so. The viewing slot slid back and a pair of eyes perused Magnus for a few moments before the door opened.

'One of you show my boys around the back,' Magnus ordered, pointing down the steps where Marius and his mates stood with the handcart. Behind them the inevitable night-time parade of carts and wagons rumbled past in both directions. The shouts of the drivers and the clatter of hooves and iron-rimmed wheels filled the cold air, and the moonlit darkness was given substance by wisps of smoke and the breath of both man and beast.

Once satisfied that his brothers were being taken care of, Magnus walked through the open door into a small vestibule lined with cloaks. He recognised one as that of a Praetorian. He stepped out into an atrium furnished with couches, some empty and some holding youths in various states of undress. Oil lamps and the orange flicker of flaming sconces gave the room a feeling of intimacy and homeliness. The sweet chords of a lyre blended with the gentle patter of a couple of fountains at either end of the impluvium and any conversation between the boys was conducted in a soft murmur.

A slave in his late twenties, evidently too old to be of interest to most of the clientele but strikingly good-looking nonetheless, proffered Magnus a tray holding cups of wines. He took one at random as Terentius appeared at the far end of the room.

'You honour me with your presence,' the whore-boy master said formally, walking elegantly through the room, one foot placed exactly before the other, dressed in a woman's stola. His long auburn hair fell loose to below his shoulders, half-concealing two drop-pearl earrings. Kohl lined his sea-grey eyes, rouge delicately enhanced his cheeks and his lips were painted a soft pinkish-red.

Really not bad at all, Magnus found himself thinking as he downed his wine, if you like that sort of thing. 'Thank you, Terentius,' he replied, placing his empty cup back on the tray and helping himself to another. 'We have business to discuss.'

'Come.' Terentius beckoned with his left arm and inclining his head so that a few strands of hair fell across his face; with an unhurried brush of his right palm he eased them back into place as he turned and walked back the way he had come. His body swayed sensuously beneath the fine fabric of his stola.

Magnus followed, glancing left and right at the whore-boys languishing on their couches and realised that Terentius had not been exaggerating about his taste. They were all exquisite but each in a different way, whether it be skin, hair or physical build; however, they all had one thing in common: they were undeniably beautiful. Each was immaculately turned out, clean and well-groomed and although the perfumes with which they adorned themselves were thicker and headier than those of women, they were still intoxicating.

Magnus raised his eyebrows and found himself wondering whether he might not take advantage of Terentius' offer to sample the goods on display. He followed the whore-boy master into a corridor with a slanted ceiling. On one side lay moonlit windows looking out onto a courtyard garden; on the other, six evenly-spaced doors on with oil lamps set into a niche in the wall. Four of the lamps were burning.

'He's down at the end,' Terentius whispered.

As they progressed down the corridor Magnus realised that the lit oil lamps were a sign of occupancy.

Terentius reached the last door and knocked three times. After a brief pause it was opened by the same scarred boy who had delivered the message earlier.

'Is he still sleeping deeply, Bricius?' Terentius asked, stepping into the room. Magnus followed him in.

'Yes, master, I've poured a few more drops down his throat and he hasn't stirred,' Bricius replied, wincing in evident pain from his wound.

Magnus walked in; the room was of a good size and decorated with homo-erotic frescoes depicting acts between men and youths. It was furnished sparsely but with taste and was dominated by a large, richly covered bed upon which lay the recumbent form of Tribune Blandinus, breathing deeply.

'You've done well, Terentius,' Magnus said approvingly, patting him on the back.

Terentius looked down sadly at Blandinus and stroked

his short-cropped black hair before running his hand over his tanned, high cheekbones and then tracing the line of his straight jaw. 'I won't ask what's going to happen to him but I imagine that I won't see him again. A pity – he was always very good to me, never too gentle but never too bestial, I shall miss him.'

'Yeah, well, that's one of them things,' Magnus mumbled. 'Fortuna wasn't kind to him and he drew the long straw. Nothing you can do.'

'No, I understand.'

'Now, my lads are around the back with a cart, I need a couple of them in here to help move him.'

'Yes, of course,' Terentius replied in a small voice, running his finger along the drugged man's lips. 'Bricius, go and fetch them.'

The boy ran off, leaving Magnus watching uncomfortably as the whore-boy master continued caressing Blandinus' face, kohl-stained tears trickled from his eyes.

Fortunately after a few moments the sound of footsteps came from the corridor. Marius and Sextus came through the door.

'Right, lads,' Magnus said with relief, 'an arm over each shoulder and drag him out to the cart.'

'Drag *him* to the cart,' Sextus repeated slowly, pointing at Blandinus, anxious not to get anything wrong.

'Yes, Sextus, that's right, the man on the bed.'

'Right you are, Magnus.'

As his brothers lifted the sleeping tribune, Magnus found himself putting an arm around Terentius. 'I'm afraid that this comes from people far above us and there ain't nothing that I can do unless I risk my standing with them, which I wouldn't do for no one.'

Terentius sobbed gently. 'Nor would I, Magnus; I understand how favours work, I'd be a fool not to. It's just that he was a decent man, who knows what sort of bastard will take his place.'

Magnus nodded and slapped Terentius jovially on the shoulder. 'You'll have good news in the morning, my friend.'

'I hope so. Bricius will see you out.'

As Magnus turned to follow the slave boy out he paused and

looked back. 'Get rid of that Praetorian cloak in the vestibule, just in case someone comes asking any questions.'

Terentius raised his eyes and smiled. 'I shall have it made into a blanket for my bed.'

Magnus shook his head disbelievingly and left the room.

Magnus walked briskly and with confidence up a narrow street ascending the northern slope of the Viminal. Moonlight and the occasional spill of dim lamplight from an open window provided just enough illumination for him to keep up a quick pace without fear of losing his footing on the uneven, wet paving stones. Behind him Lucio, Cassandros and the two Armenians struggled with the handcart containing their swords, helmets and the sleeping tribune, who was covered with a leather sheet. Marius and Sextus brought up the rear, hands on the hilts of their daggers at their waists. Now and again a snatch of conversation or the harsh tones of an argument floated out from the dwellings on either side but otherwise their route was comparatively peaceful. The few figures that came into view melted into the shadows before they passed, unwilling to confront or be confronted by a relatively large group led by a man with such an air of authority and purpose.

Upon reaching the top of the Viminal, Magnus turned east towards the looming bulk of the Servian Walls before turning back south and entering the Lamp-makers' Street at the end furthest from the Viminal Gate.

Signalling to his brothers to stop he looked down its length. He could make out nothing to concern him unduly – a couple of stationary delivery carts off-loading their consignments of blocks of clay wrapped in damp cloth to various workshops on either side of the street.

Servius appeared out of the shadows of a nearby doorway. 'I've had a couple of the lads take a look at the place, there's no one down the back alley but there was a group of four Vigiles chatting with the doormen at the front.'

'With luck they should be called away very soon,' Magnus

replied, looking west in the direction of the Tiber. 'Where're the rest of the lads?'

'They all arrived here without mishap; they're scattered around within earshot of a whistle.'

'Good. Get a man up on the wall and tell him to keep a look-out for a nice big orange glow from the banks of the Tiber. I'll take eight men to get rid of those carts.'

Servius nodded and gave a brief, shrill whistle and within a few moments the full complement of eighteen other brothers had assembled; all were wearing Urban Cohort tunics. Urban Cohort cloaks were quickly exchanged for their own, and helmets and swords were distributed from the carts. Cassandros scaled the wall by one of the many sets of steps constructed to allow defenders access.

'Right, lads,' Magnus said quietly, addressing the eight men gathered that were to accompany him. 'Remember, we're Cohort, so we're smart, just like we used to be in the legions or the auxiliaries. You march in step and stop as one when I command. If I give any of you an order, you reply, "Yes, sir" or "Yes, optio", is that clear? Now form up.'

A few of the lads grinned, trying out Magnus' new title quietly as they arranged themselves into two files of four. At Magnus' signal they marched forward and turned right into the Lamp-makers' Street.

Approaching the carts Magnus counted a dozen or so men unloading them. He brought his men to a smart halt ten paces away and walked forward with the strut of a man used to command. The work ceased at the sight of a unit of the Urban Cohort.

'Whose carts are these?' Magnus demanded, looking around the faces in the gloom.

A couple of men stepped forward, indistinct in the patchy light.

'We're the drivers,' one of them replied nervously.

'Then you had better drive them out of here now unless you want them to be impounded and find yourselves up before the aedile.'

'But we've got every right to be unloading at this time of night,' the other man protested.

'Not tonight you haven't.'

'Why not?'

Magnus pulled back his cloak to reveal his sword. 'Look, son, I don't make the rules, I've just been told to keep this and a couple of other streets clear until dawn. You can come back tomorrow. Why? I don't know, nor do I give a fuck. I just do what I'm ordered because it's easier that way. Now, I'm doing you a favour, I could just impound your carts and take you in but instead I'm giving you the opportunity to bugger off in good order. Which is it to be?'

The two carters looked at each other and came to a mutual agreement. 'We'll come back tomorrow.'

'Good choice, lads.' Magnus looked at the assembled lamp-makers and their slaves. 'Inside, all of you, and if you know what's good for you keep your windows shuttered until after dawn.'

With a deal of muttering, but no outright dissent, the tradesmen dispersed with their slaves and whatever clay they had managed to grab.

The carters mounted their vehicles.

'I'd turn them around if I were you, lads,' Magnus suggested helpfully. 'If you go towards the Viminal Gate you might find a brother optio of mine who's not nearly as good-natured as myself.'

Muttering their thanks and looking nervously over their shoulders the carters turned their mules, brought the carts round and disappeared back down the street. With a barked order, Magnus turned his men about and they followed.

A whistled double note came from the wall as Magnus reached the end of the street; he looked up to his right to make out the silhouetted figure of Cassandros waving at him. Leaving his men with Servius he jogged over to the steps and mounted them, two at a time, to arrive puffing on to the wide walkway at the top.

'Over there.' Cassandros pointed west.

Magnus followed his gaze over the shadowy rooftops of the Subura below, past the white marble edifices of the Palatine and on to the warehouse district in the lee of the tree-lined Aventine. There, sure enough, was a faint orange glow outlining the group of Cypress trees surrounding a temple on the side of the hill. 'Good man, Aelianus,' he muttered to himself. 'Cassandros, go and tell Sextus to have the lads stand by, I'm just going to watch the fire for a few moments to make sure that it's growing.'

Cassandros nodded and then clattered down the steps, the hobnails of his Cohort sandals causing a few dull sparks on the damp stone. Magnus took in the view. Almost a million people resided in this city – most of them crammed into half of it whilst the lucky, elite minority enjoyed the rest. From where he stood it seemed almost peaceful, hardly a sound reached his ears and the only sure sign of habitation were the many trails of smoke climbing high into the air to form a hazy, moon-drenched ceiling over the Seven Hills. He glanced over his left shoulder towards the brooding presence of the Praetorian camp, just two hundred paces outside the Viminal Gate. Constructed like any other legionary camp its torch-strewn layout was very familiar to Magnus, even though he had never visited it. He offered a silent prayer to Jupiter and Fortuna that it would remain that way after the events of the next half-hour, then checked the progress of the fire. Satisfied that it was escalating, he made his way back down to his brothers who stood ready in a column three abreast. The Armenians stood to the rear with the hand-carts that held the ladders and the still recumbent tribune.

Taking his position at the head, Magnus raised his right arm, brought it down swiftly and the column set off in step down the Lamp-makers' Street. As they progressed, Magnus saw a few shutters on either side of the street open and close quickly, the occupants wanting nothing to do with a unit of the Urban Cohort marching down their road. Magnus smiled to himself, knowing that when questions were asked there would be more than a few witnesses able to swear that they saw the men of the Cohort.

Bringing the column to a halt just before the alley, he turned to Servius. 'All right, Brother, get your boys into position. And remind the lads we need two people left alive: one of their whore-boys and that bearded bastard who raped the boy the other night.'

Immediately the five ladders were unloaded, and the four-teen men who were to accompany Servius over the rear wall made their way up the alley.

Once the ladders were set against the wall with three men waiting behind each one Magnus patted Servius on the shoulder. 'Keep the boys quiet, Brother, whilst I go and take a look at the front. I'll come back and tell you once it's clear.'

Taking his four lads and the Armenians with the second cart, he made his way to the end of the street and cautiously peered around the corner. The Vigiles were still there with the doormen but their attention was on the orange glow in the sky to the west.

Magnus waited for what seemed an age, praying that what he had counted upon would come to pass. After many a muttered entreaty to the whole pantheon of gods, a Vigiles optio eventu-ally came pounding up the Via Patricius.

'You men! Follow me at the double,' he shouted to his subor-dinates.

'But we're meant to stay here for the night, optio,' one of the Vigiles protested.

'Fuck the whore-boys, that's the Cohort's depot on fire. The Urban Prefect will have our guts out if he hasn't got anything to dress his toy-soldiers up in tomorrow. Macro's ordered every available man down there.'

With a shrug the four Vigiles jogged off towards the confla-gration leaving the two doormen alone.

Magnus ran back to the alley. 'Now, Servius,' he hissed.

Instantly five men scaled the ladders, then crouched and leant back down to help their comrades. Once all fifteen were on the roof, the ladders were pulled up after them and they split into three groups.

As they disappeared from his vision Magnus went back to join his party. 'Tigran and Vahram, get our guest ready.'

The Armenian cousins pulled back the leather sheet and, with a degree of difficulty, hefted Blandinus out of the cart and supported him between them, an arm around each shoulder.

Faint shouts and screams suddenly emanated from within the Albanians' establishment. 'Right, they're in,' Magnus whispered, looking at the two Armenians. 'When I give you the signal you run around the corner hollering in Albanian for all you're worth that the place is under attack and you've brought a wounded man from round the back. We'll be twenty paces behind you so you won't have long to hold the door once you've killed the doormen. Don't worry if you drop matey-boy here, he won't feel a thing and we'll pick him up.'

Tigran and Vahram grinned and nodded.

Good boys, Magnus thought as he peered around the corner, could be useful in the future. The doormen had now heard the fighting and were knocking violently on the door. Magnus heard the bolt slam back. 'Now!'

The Armenians leapt around the corner, dragging Blandinus between them, shouting in an incomprehensible language. The two doormen glanced up at them in alarm and then at each other. They pulled the cudgels from their belts and one stepped through the now open door whilst the other held his position, with a puzzled look on his face, keeping the door clear for his comrades approaching from the shadows shouting for help in his own language. By the time they were close enough for him to make out their features, it was too late. He died looking into a stranger's eyes with an unforeseen blade in his heart.

Magnus hurtled around the corner with his brothers in his wake as the doorman slumped to the ground. Within moments he made the door. Tigran held it open, the second doorman and the doorkeeper lay dead in a pool of blood at Vahram's feet. Just inside the vestibule, Blandinus lay cast to the ground.

Lucio and Cassandros dragged the dead doorman in from outside and Marius shut and bolted the door.

Magnus looked through the curtains into the dimly lit atrium. Kurush and four or five of his men were struggling to hold back the Crossroads Brothers as they tried to force their way through from the courtyard garden. A gaggle of three frightened boys huddled in one corner. To his left the stairs leading up to the first floor were deserted. 'Right, Sextus, you stay here guarding the door and keep an eye out for anyone coming down them stairs. Kill anyone who isn't wearing a Cohort tunic.'

'Kill anyone not dressed like me,' Sextus said thoughtfully, digesting his orders.

'And look after Blandinus. If he starts to come round knock him on the head, but gentle like.'

'Knock him on the head gently; right you are, Magnus.'

'Marius, get those boys, one unconscious but alive. All right, lads, let's do this.'

Magnus sprang through the curtain with a savage roar and his sword held steady at his side. Marius, Lucio, Cassandros and the Armenians followed, each yelling at the tops of their voices.

The sudden distraction from behind caused the Albanians to falter for an instant. Two went down immediately to the swords of their attackers in front whilst the rest gave ground.

Magnus leapt over a couple of the sumptuously upholstered divans that littered the room and pounced on Kurush, locking his forearm around the whore-boy master's throat. 'I don't take kindly to greasy foreigners fucking with my clients,' he growled in his ear.

'Magnus!' Kurush managed to gurgle through his constricted windpipe. 'I thought we were square.'

'Now we're square.' With a brutal thrust he forced the finely honed blade of his sword into Kurush's side, up under the ribcage, slicing through his liver and into a lung. Blood spurted from the Albanian's mouth onto Magnus' forearm as Kurush went rigid with pain. Around him his brothers despatched the remaining defenders in a welter of dismemberment and savagery. With a final upwards thrust that lifted Kurush off his feet, Magnus felt the man go limp. He let him fall to the floor with the sword still embedded, his eyes open in sightless shock and his beard redder than it had ever been in life.

Magnus looked around, breathing heavily, wiping the blood from his forearm on the side of his tunic. The only men left standing were his brethren and the Armenians, all also trying to catch their breath as they looked down at the Albanians sprawled at their feet. Magnus looked closely at the dead. None of them was the young rapist.

Servius came in from the garden flanked by four brothers. 'It's all clear back in the rooms. As you predicted there were no customers at this time of night so no tricky questions will be asked. We've suffered two flesh wounds and Festus got a nasty gut wound. I've had him sent back with a couple of lads already.'

'Good. Where's the rapist?' Magnus asked.

'Not back there, Brother.'

Magnus looked around the atrium. Marius stood over the bodies of two of the boys, a third lay unbloodied to one side. 'He must be upstairs.' He turned to walk back to the staircase but stopped in his tracks.

Sextus was standing over the body of a young man looking pleased with himself. 'One tried to sneak out, Magnus,' he said, wiping his sword on the dead man's trousers.

Magnus closed his eyes and bit back his anger. Sextus had only done as he had been told and killed a man not in Cohort uniform. 'Shit!'

'What is it, Brother?' Servius asked.

'How can we get the rapist to fuck Blandinus if he's dead?'

'Ah yes, I see. We'll have to improvise. Cassandros, this is your area of expertise, I believe?'

Cassandros pursed the thumb and fingers of his right hand together and grinned. 'I just need a bit of oil.'

Magnus raised his eyebrows. 'Unbelievable. Well, if that's our only option we better get to it, it'll be dawn soon. Have some lads search upstairs to make sure it's clear and get the rest of them looking for cash and jewellery. Sextus, bring the dead Albanian. Lucio and Marius, you get Blandinus. Cassandros get the oil.'

As Magnus led his brothers carrying the dead rapist down a corridor overlooking the garden, very similar in set-up to Terentius' place, he stepped over the occasional body of a whore-boy or one of their masters.

'In here, lads,' he said, pushing the door to the last room open. It caught on the dead weight behind it but with a little additional effort he managed to slide it back far enough to slip inside. He pulled the body of its former occupant, lying face down on the floor in a bloody tunic, out of the way. 'Strip Blandinus and put him kneeling on the bed, then get the Albanian behind him and this dead boy in front of him.'

As Marius and Lucio removed Blandinus' tunic and loincloth Cassandros came in with a small jug.

Before long all the three bodies were lined up on the bed with the boy placed with his back to the wall. Blandinus knelt before him, a trail of saliva trickled from his mouth and he breathed shallowly.

'All right, Cassandros,' Magnus said, pointing to the Albanian lying behind the tribune, 'get it over with. Lucio, Sextus, hold Blandinus firm.'

Cassandros smiled and, evidently relishing the prospect, began pouring the oil.

Magnus turned his attention to other matters. 'Marius, run and tell Servius to get everyone out of here with whatever they've got and make sure that boy is still unconscious; give him a wound to the shoulder so it don't look like he was left on purpose.'

Marius nodded and left as Blandinus groaned and abruptly tensed, his eyes flicked open as his arms twitched but remained useless. He turned his head groggily to stare unfocused at Magnus.

'Sorry, Tribune.' Magnus crashed his right fist into Blandinus' face.

He went limp and a few moments later Cassandros grunted deeply in satisfaction.

Magnus winced. 'Good, now stab him then slit his throat and then we can get out of here.'

Cassandros expression of sexual gratification turned to one of uncertainty.

Magnus put his hand on his dagger's hilt. 'Just do it,' he hissed as he heard the brothers run down the corridor to the ladders. 'If you could keep yourself under control you wouldn't get the shitty jobs.'

Cassandros took his knife from its sheath and, looking extremely unhappy at the prospect of such coldblooded murder, plunged it, after a slight hesitation, brutally into Blandinus' naked back. Pulling the knife back out, releasing a flow of dark blood, he moved along the bed and as Lucio and Sextus held the shoulders firm placed the blade to the tribune's throat and ripped it across. The wound began to gurgle and hiss as the innocent and hapless man started to drown in his own blood.

'Well done, Brother,' Magnus said approvingly. 'That's your debt paid.'

Cassandros looked at Magnus wide-eyed and nodded vacantly.

'Let's go.'

The brothers did not need to be told twice and immediately ran out of the room. Magnus paused for a final look at the tableau they had left and smiled grimly to himself, hoping that some good would come from this highly unpleasant deed. With a muttered prayer to Fortuna to keep him safe on the way home, he left the room without looking back and ran to the last of the ladders up against the roof in the garden as the first light of dawn stated to warm the eastern sky.

'There you go, my friend, that's almost four hundred,' Magnus said, slapping three heavy bags of coin down on the table in his back room.

Aelianus looked greedily at his share. 'That's almost double what you guaranteed.'

'We were lucky, they must have had a busy few days. How did the fire go?'

Aelianus shrugged. 'The Vigiles managed to save some of the stores because the depot was right next to the Tiber. They ran around for a couple of hours pouring water on it until they finally got it under control. One of their tribunes was there putting the fear of death into them, marching up and down, shouting and kicking arses – nasty piece of work. I'm glad he's not in the Cohort, we wouldn't get a moment's peace.'

'But you're in the clear, aren't you?'

'Yeah, mate. I was doing my best impression of a quartermaster who considers all the stores as his personal property

– which of course they are – and even made a couple of heroic forays into the building to save a few things.' He showed Magnus a burn on his right forearm to prove the point. 'I was almost in tears over my loss.'

Magnus grinned. 'I bet it was the loss of your ledgers that upset you the most.'

'Too right,' Aelianus replied solemnly, 'if only I could have saved them. Now I've got no record of what was in there.'

'Or not, eh?'

'Yeah, well, you bringing it forward a day meant that there was slightly more in the building than I intended there to be, but this will make up for it.' Aelinaus patted the bags on the table in front of him as the door opened and Servius stuck his head into the room.

'Senator Pollo has sent a slave to escort you to his house, Brother. Marius and Sextus are waiting for you in the tavern.'

'I'll be right there,' Magnus replied, standing to show Aelianus out.

'Give me a shout when you think that we can exploit their moment of madness again, mate,' Aelianus said, hefting his coin bags into a leather satchel.

'Of course,' Magnus confirmed, gripping his forearm, 'it's always good to have someone honest to do business with.'

Aelianus returned the grip and then, slinging his satchel over his shoulder, walked past Servius with a brief nod and out of the room.

'A useful mate,' Magnus commented.

'Very,' Servius agreed. 'Trustworthy?'

'As much as you or me. On that subject I've been thinking about what to do with Aquilina.'

'Don't trouble yourself, Brother, it's done.'

'What is?'

'I realised that we couldn't risk her working here when Aelianus told us how persistent she was at asking questions. If Sempronius had any suspicions about what occurred she'd have got it out of one of the lads in no time. Just imagine what Sextus would say if she had him by the cock?'

'That's the conclusion I came to. Where is she?'

'All over the place.'

'Shame,' Magnus said, walking through to the tavern, 'she had a pretty smile.'

The ancient doorkeeper showed Magnus into Gaius' study. 'Magnus, my friend, come and sit down. A cup of wine would slip down a treat, I'm sure.'

Magnus took a seat across the desk from Gaius as his host poured him a full cup of wine and passed it over, unwatered.

'Thank you, Senator,' Magnus said after taking a gulp. He smiled inwardly as he noticed that it was not the finest of vintages.

'My friend, it's me that should be thanking you. I had a visit this morning from the Lady Antonia's steward, a Greek by the name of Pallas. A man of discretion and considerable influence with his mistress, despite his slave status.'

'Yeah, I've come across him.'

Gaius' moist lips pulled back into an appraising smile. 'Yes, of course you have. He came to tell me how pleased his mistress is today. Very early this morning, apparently, one of Sejanus' tribunes, by the name of Blandinus, was found dead after a raid on an establishment close to the Viminal Gate. You might know of it?'

Magnus shrugged noncommittally.

'Well, the only survivor of the raid, one of the boys, swore that it was men in Urban Cohort uniform that had attacked them. A handcart with Cohort insignia branded on it left outside and a Cohort sword embedded in the owner of the establishment confirmed to Sejanus that it was indeed the Cohort who were responsible. As you can imagine that caused rather a stir. Sejanus accused the Urban Prefect of heavy-handed tactics against premises frequented by his officers and the Urban Prefect accused the Praetorians of burning down his Cohort's depot in mistaken revenge for an act that they didn't commit.'

Magnus shook his head slowly. 'Nasty business.'

'Indeed, but what makes it nastier is that Sejanus did eventually believe the Urban Prefect's word that they were not involved. He went immediately to the Lady Antonia and accused her of murder; something, Pallas informed me, that she vehemently denied.'

'I can imagine.'

'Yes, so can I. She asked him what grounds he had for such an accusation and the good prefect replied that it was the manner in which Blandinus was found. He said that the raid must have been set up as a screen to disguise the murder.'

'That seems overly fanciful, Senator,' Magnus observed, proffering his cup for a refill.

Gaius obliged him. 'According to Pallas, the Lady herself said something along those lines. She then asked Sejanus what was it about the way in which Blandinus was found that had led him to such a bizarre conclusion, at which point the prefect exploded in anger. He almost screamed at her that his tribune had been found with his head languishing in a dead, naked boy's lap, his throat cut, a stab wound in his back and an easterner's arm, with its bearded but deceased, trouser-wearing owner still attached to it, hanging out of his backside.'

'What some people get up to, eh?'

'I know. Shocking, isn't it? As you might well expect from a lady of Antonia's breeding she was appalled by the image and suggested to Sejanus that in future he should spend more time looking to the moral standards of his officers and less time involving himself in the politics of her family.'

'Good advice. Did he take it?'

'Pallas didn't know because Sejanus stormed out at that point, but he rather doubts it. Still, as the Lady Antonia said after he had taken his leave: "He can't say that he hasn't been warned."'

'Well, the machinations of the powerful are nothing to do with us, eh, Senator?'

'Indeed not, Magnus, but I thought that I'd tell you because now that establishment on the Viminal has been closed down I would assume that Terentius' place will be making a lot more money, a goodly percentage of which will come your way, I believe. That should please you tremendously.'

'Yes but Sempronius, my counterpart on the Viminal, won't be so thrilled.'

'Oh, I wouldn't worry about him. I guessed that might be his reaction so I shared my worry, as your patron, with Pallas, without reference to your name, of course.'

'That's very good of you, Senator.'

Gaius waved his hand airily. 'Don't mention it. Pallas has promised that should Sempronius come to the mistaken conclusion that it was *not* the Cohort who was responsible for his loss of income, then the Lady Antonia will see to it that he is fully compensated. Until, of course, he has set up a new business – she doesn't approve of whore-boys. The offer will naturally come with a warning to him not to look too deeply into her affairs.'

Magnus inclined his head, acknowledging the favour. 'That should do it. So no more whore-boys on the Viminal and Sempronius will think that it was either the Cohort or the Lady Antonia. That's a very satisfactory conclusion, Senator.'

Gaius beamed. 'Yes, but what makes it even sweeter, from my point of view, is the real reason for Pallas' visit this morning. It wasn't just to share idle gossip.'

'Of course not.'

'Apparently the Lady Antonia has been put into such a good mood by all this that she will be inviting me to an intimate dinner in the very near future. Not one of those lavish affairs with scores of guests where one can never get a chance to speak privately to the hostess, just myself and a couple of close friends.'

'A step closer to the consulship.'

'Yes, and a chance to promote my nephews' careers. They should be arriving any day now.' Gaius took a self-congratulatory swig of wine and stood up to show that the interview was at an end. 'Where would we be without patronage, eh, Magnus?'

'It makes you wonder, don't it, Senator?' Magnus said, getting up and heading towards the door.

'Before you go, my friend,' Gaius said, stopping Magnus as he opened it, 'as I'm sure you're aware, being a keen supporter of the Greens, there are races tomorrow. I'll need you and some of your lads to be here soon after dawn to escort me and my clients down to the Circus Maximus.'

'I'll see you tomorrow then, Senator,' Magnus said, stepping out into the atrium and closing the door behind him.

'Having our very own tame senator so close to Antonia has to be a good thing, surely?' Servius said, shaking the dice cup vigorously.

'I wouldn't call him tame,' Magnus replied, taking his eye off the street to watch the dice roll across the table. 'Ah, two threes and a two. Eight. Double it, Brother.' He slammed four sesterces down and scooped up the dice in his cup. 'Like all rich men he just wants more power and more wealth.'

'And poor men don't?'

Magnus grunted, acknowledging the point, as he made his cast. 'Pluto's balls, four, three, one. Eight again. And anyway, being in Antonia's favour may be lucrative but along with that comes some high expectations. He'll have to work hard to maintain his position with her and that will mean some rough jobs for us.'

A raucous shout of satisfaction from the crowded table next to them indicated a large pot had been won. Lucio snapped his fingers under a glum-looking Cassandros' nose and Sextus chortled, slapping his palm on the bench, as Jovita stepped out of the tavern carrying two plates of roasted pork and bread.

'We can afford to take on a few new faces with what we got last night plus the extra income that's sure to come from Terentius, that should help,' Servius pointed out, taking his turn. 'Twelve! Double it again.'

Jovita placed the food on the table as Magnus matched the bet. 'Festus has slipped back into unconsciousness again,' she said, wiping the grease off her hands on to her tunic, 'and the wound's started to ooze. There's nothing more I can do.'

'Call for a proper doctor, then,' Magnus said, shaking the dice cup. 'We owe it to him and it ain't as if we can't afford it.'

Jovita nodded and walked off.

Magnus slammed the cup upside down on the table, keeping

the dice hidden. 'What about Tigran and his cousin? They did well last night and they've got nothing, so they'd be loyal if we give them a chance.'

'They ain't citizens.'

'We'll give them less of a percentage then, like auxiliaries, if you take my meaning?' Magnus lifted the cup slightly towards him, peered under and cracked it back down. 'Shit! Fortuna spent the last of my luck last night.'

Servius scraped his winnings towards him. 'Then I can't see a problem. I'll send one of the lads to find them later.'

'Marcus Salvius Magnus.'

Magnus looked up to see Terentius standing at the end of the table, holding a purse.

'I've come to thank you for looking after my interests,' he said, placing the purse in front of Magnus, 'and to assure you that I won't tell anyone what I know about the events of last night.'

'That would be wise, for both our sakes, Terentius.' Magnus pushed the purse back. 'There's no need to pay me, it was covered by your percentage.'

'This isn't a payment, Magnus. This was Blandinus' purse that he brought to spend with me yesterday. It would be wrong for me to keep it. I've heard how he was found and I'm sorry that I was, in a way, responsible.'

'Yeah well, that's the thing about patronage, it goes both ways and you never get something for nothing not even if you're the emperor.'

Terentius nodded, smiling sadly. 'Still, one good thing came out of Blandinus' death: that bastard Macro has got his wish, he's taken Blandinus' position. I shan't be missing that particular tribune patrolling our streets. Keep the purse.'

Magnus picked it up and felt its weight. 'Perhaps I'll use it for what it was intended for and spend it in your house.'

'You've no need to bring any money if you visit me. As I've always told you: you can have the run of my establishment for free.'

'I know, Terentius my friend; but as we all know, no one gives something for nothing.'

Terentius inclined his head, turned gracefully and walked away.

'Are you really thinking of giving that a try?' Servius asked, taking a mouthful of pork.

'Why not? Don't judge it until you've tried it and besides, change pleases. And it would be on Blandinus.' Magnus grinned and tipped out the coins onto the table. His eyes widened in surprise. 'That's forty Denarii or so.'

'Blandinus must have been planning quite a night.'

'Yeah. And Terentius must be feeling very bad about him to give up that amount of money.'

'Strange morals for a whore-boy master.'

Magnus looked up and watched Terentius walking away along the Alta Semita. 'Very strange,' he agreed as a party of travellers on horseback followed by a litter, coming towards him, caught his eye. He picked up the dice and threw them. 'Three sixes, Venus. Fortuna's back with me.' He looked over to his brothers still playing dice on the table next to him. 'I'll do this one, lads, they've got guards and a litter; I'd say that they could well afford our services. Stay alert.'

He studied the party as they approached. Behind three mounted guards rode an equestrian in his mid-fifties flanked by what looked to be his two sons. He was talking animatedly with the youth riding on his right who had a look of awe on his round, sun-tanned face as he looked about.

Getting up off the bench, Magnus timed his walk so that he got between the party and their guards and stood, four-square, in front of the leading traveller's horse, forcing it to stop. Magnus looked up at the man, his face set hard and menacing. 'You'll be needing protection, sir, if you're thinking of going down that road.'

THE RACING FACTIONS

This story takes place after the end of *Rome's Executioner*; Magnus, who has all his life been a passionate supporter of the Green Racing Faction, gets cheated out of his winnings by a dodgy bookmaker – a guaranteed way to annoy him considerably – and vengeance is required. What better way to have it than by fixing a race, a thing that people still try to do all over the world to this day?

Meanwhile, Gaius Vespasius Pollo is attempting to get his nephew, Sabinus, elected as a quaestor, the position in which we find Vespasian's elder brother serving in Judaea in the prologue of *The False God of Rome*.

Ruthlessly pursuing self-interest was a natural goal for Romans of all classes; however, there were other things that united the citizens of Rome and one of the most important was the succession of religious festivals that punctuated the year with public holidays; I decided to start having festivities – in this case the Lupercalia and the Equirria – act as the backdrop for each story giving extra flavour to my imagining of life in the greatest city in the empire.

I also was able to expand Magnus' world by bringing other characters from the *Vespasian* books and seeing one of them, in particular, in a situation that only Magnus could witness, not Vespasian ...

ROME, FEBRUARY AD 32

THE STALLIONS' EYES rolled; specks of foam flew from their mouths as they answered their charioteer's call and accelerated down the track. Barrel chests sucked dusty air into their straining lungs whilst pounding hearts pumped blood to the muscles in their legs working to the very limit of their power as they pulled a light chariot seven times around the track. They felt the reins tug back; they slowed, their current sprint over and another corner to be rounded. The inside horse wheeled left in response to a sharp pull on the reins and led his three stable mates, at a speed at which they could just keep their footing, around the turning post at the far end of the spina, the central barrier of the Circus Maximus. Feeling another bite of the four-lash whip, they looked up the 350 paces of the dust-clouded straight and they were away again, inciting each other to greater effort in the fury of the race in which they were leading.

Their driver, in the colours of the Green Racing Faction, risked a quick glance over his shoulder to one of the three White chariots, just four paces behind, but gaining; beyond it his Green team-mate drew out into the track in an attempt to pull level with the chasing White. The leading Green driver snatched a small skin of water thrown at him by a boy from his team stationed on the spina; he squirted its contents over his dirt-encrusted face and into his parched mouth, discarded it and pulled his team to the right to avoid the mangled wreckage of two chariots, a Blue and a Red. A couple of well-aimed curses, written on folded lead sheets and studded with nails, flew past him as he neared the spectators; pulling back to the right, closer to the spina and out of range of the hurled missiles, he sped on, showering grit all over the crash. Within it, public slaves struggled to cut loose writhing horses entangled in the debris, whose screeches were lost in the tumult of a quarter of a million voices roaring on the ten remaining chariots. Waving the flags of their favoured faction, the citizens of Rome screamed themselves hoarse, stamping their feet on the stepped-stone seating, urging on the teams upon whom over a million sesterces was riding in bets.

The Green driver pulled on the reins wrapped about his waist and slid his team, in a spray of sand, around the turning post closest to the twelve starting boxes positioned next to the towering wood and iron arched gates of the circus; the next lap began. High on a column above the spina the fifth of seven bronze dolphins, marking the progress of the race, tilted down and the noise of the crowd escalated even more, echoing around the Palatine and Aventine Hills, overlooking the Circus Maximus on either side, and on to the rest of the Seven Hills of Rome.

'Come on, you Greens! This one has to be ours, lads!' Marcus Salvius Magnus bawled in excitement to his two companions as the second-placed White chariot misjudged the corner, losing crucial ground and allowing the second Green team to come alongside. Magnus' breath steamed as the temperature fell with the sun. The baying, sweat-reeking crowd around him, on the Aventine side of the main gates, sported Green colours and had worked themselves up into a frenzied celebration at the prospect of their team's first win of the day.

'Twenty-five denarii at eight to one! That's two hundred, or eight hundred sesterces; Ignatius ain't going to like that, Magnus,' the huge bald man next to him shouted, punching the stump of his left wrist in the air.

'Too right, Marius, we've finally got that bastard bookmaker this time, and with our biggest bet of the day.' Magnus' scarred, ex-boxer's face creased into a grin; he looked down at the wooden receipt for the bet, signed by the bookmaker Ignatius, grasped in a massive fist of his other companion. 'Two hundred denarii – that's almost as much as a legionary earns in a year! It'll make Ignatius' eyes water and swell the Brotherhood's coffers nicely. Fancy a couple of whores tonight, Sextus?'

'A couple of whores?' Sextus ruminated, slowly digesting the thought whilst keeping his eyes fixed on the action down on the track far below, where the second Green driver was drawing a small knife from the protective leather strapping around his chest. 'Right you are, Magnus, if you're sure we can afford it after what we've lost today.'

'We've lost five denarii in nine races, my slow friend, that's forty-five; we're one hundred and fifty-five denarii up. We could afford five hundred whores.'

Sextus' ox-like face creased with strained concentration as he tried – but failed – to get to grips with such advanced arithmetic. 'With learning like that, Brother, I can understand how you got to be the patronus of our Crossroads Brotherhood.'

'If the leader of the Brotherhood can't count, Sextus, then how is he going to be able to check that everyone in the South Quirinal has paid their rightful dues to us in order to enjoy our continued protection?'

'Then that rules me out of ever becoming leader.'

'Yes, that and the fact that you'd have to kill me first.'

The crowd's thrilled roar drew Magnus' attention back to the race as the White and Green chariots touched wheels, shattering the eight spokes in both of them in a hail of splintering wood. The Green immediately slashed at the reins tied around his waist with his knife and, severing them, bailed out as the wheels of both vehicles fragmented. At a speed of more than thirty miles per hour, the chariots' unsupported sides juddered down on to the sand, their naked axles gouging deep furrows, abruptly slowing them and jerking the traces of the two teams of horses, causing them to slew into each other and rebound. With the weight of its driver gone, the Green chariot twisted up into the air, its remaining wheel spinning freely, and arced, with delicious inevitability, over on to the White charioteer. The fast-rotating iron tyre scraped through the skin of his neck with a spray of blood as it knocked him sideways off the chariot to crunch down, unconscious, on to the track with the reins still wrapped about his waist; his team ran on, dragging him along the scouring sand as his vehicle disintegrated around him.

The leading Green was clear.

'A selfless act, and the best way to deal with the favourite,' Magnus pronounced at the top of his voice, watching with approval the downed Green charioteer scrabble to his feet and leap on to the spina, narrowly avoiding a trampled death beneath the hooves of three chasing teams. 'One and a half laps to go and nobody near our man; we'll collect the money, brothers, and then go and wait outside the senators' enclosure to escort Senator Pollo home.'

With the result of the race now a foregone conclusion most of the crowd sat back down and amused themselves by watching the attempts of the crashed White's *hortator* – the single horsemen attached to each of the twelve racers for exactly this purpose – to pull up the bolting team before their charioteer had all the skin scraped from his limbs. Only the Green faction stayed standing to cheer on the progress of their hero of the moment.

Sure of victory and uninterested in the White charioteer's fate, Magnus looked around for one of the bookmakers' slaves who patrolled the crowd with leather bags around their waists, taking bets on behalf of their owners. 'You, boy!' he shouted, spotting one of Ignatius' many slaves circulating amongst the spectators. 'Over here.'

The elderly slave gave a deferential nod and made his way through the celebrating Green supporters, who had begun pointing and droning crude chants at the White faction on the Palatine side of the gates; they replied with obscene gestures and jeering.

The seventh dolphin fell as the Green chariot, its driver punching the air, crossed the winning line in front of the White faction's seats; the Greens' joy was completed by the sight of the White charioteer being carried away, quite evidently dead.

'Where's your master, boy?' Magnus asked as the slave approached.

The old man pointed to the colonnaded walkway above the seating. 'Up there, sir, next to the statue of Neptune.'

Magnus tugged at the sleeves of Marius' and Sextus' tunics.

'Come on, lads; let's cash our bet with the man himself so that we can have the pleasure of seeing his face.'

His Crossroads Brethren grinned in anticipation of Ignatius' expression as he counted out what would, in all likelihood, be his biggest payout of the day. The thought of supplementing the considerable income paid to the South Quirinal Crossroads Brotherhood by local traders and residents in return for protection from rival brotherhoods was a cheering one. They barged past the old slave, who was immediately set upon by other Green supporters who had laid wagers with Ignatius and were now keen to claim their winnings.

The noise of the crowd died down as teams of public slaves poured on to the track to remove mangled chariots and the carcasses of horses and to clear it of thrown objects in preparation for the next race. Magnus and his brothers forced their way to the steps leading up to the walkway and negotiated a path through the tangle of individuals using them as overflow seating. Eventually, after pushing through the crush of people, who, unable to get a seat, were obliged to stand along the colonnade, they managed to get to the walkway that ran along the entire Aventine side of the circus.

'Now where's the statue of Neptune?' Magnus muttered, looking along the carved images of gods and great men that punctuated the colonnade; between them, at regular intervals, were wooden desks at which bookmakers sat counting coinage and clacking abacuses, surrounded by piles of wax tablets, and guarded by thuggish-looking men with cudgels. 'There it is; I'd know Neptune's trident anywhere.'

Ignatius' four guards shifted warily, nervous at being approached by three men just as brutish as themselves; they slapped their cudgels into the palms of their hands, feeling their weight with threatening intent.

Magnus raised his hand in a conciliatory gesture. 'No need for that sort of behaviour, lads; we're here to collect our rightful winnings from my old friend Ignatius.'

The man seated behind the desk looked up, midway through tallying a pile of bronze sesterces; his face was as fearsome as

those of the men guarding him: lantern jaw, broken nose, dark
eyes sunken beneath an overhanging forehead. His attire,
however, was not that of a street thug: those days were long
behind him, their memory preserved in the livid scars on his left
cheek and well-muscled forearms; beneath his white, citizen's
toga he wore a saffron-coloured tunic of finest wool and around
his neck, falling to the pectoral muscles on his expansive chest,
hung the heaviest and longest gold-linked chain that Magnus
had ever seen. 'Magnus, to what do I owe this dubious pleasure?'
His voice was deep and gruff and his accent betrayed his lowly
roots in Rome's poorest district, the Subura, although he did his
best to cover it. 'I trust that I've been having a good afternoon at
your expense?'

'A very good afternoon for the first nine races, Ignatius, you
took forty-five in silver off us; a pity about the last race, though.
Give him the receipt, Sextus.'

Ignatius leant forward and took the proffered piece of wood
bearing his signature along with the number of the bet. 'Two
hundred and eleven.' Taking up a wax tablet from the top of a
pile, he scanned it quickly, raising his pronounced eyebrows and
tutted. 'It seems I owe you money.'

'It does look that way.'

Ignatius pulled out a heavy-looking strong-box from under the
desk. 'I'd better pay it then, although I don't understand why you
came all the way up here for such a trifling amount when you could
have saved yourself the trouble and had one of my slaves pay it out.'

'Yeah, very funny, Ignatius; that's going to be your biggest
payout today. Now get on with it.'

Ignatius shrugged and unlocked the box; he scooped out a
large double handful of silver denarii and began to count them
out into stacks of ten. When he had completed four and a half
such piles he stopped and pushed them across the desk, toppling
them with a metallic clatter.

'That's our business completed, I believe.'

'I may not be able to read, Ignatius, but I can certainly count,
and that is nowhere near two hundred denarii plus our original
twenty-five stake.'

'You're absolutely right, my friend; that's forty denarii and your original five stake.'

'We put down twenty-five. Sextus, tell him, you laid the bet.'

Sextus nodded slowly at the memory. 'Yeah, Magnus, the slave was a young lad with curly black hair; I gave him twenty-five in silver on the Greens' first chariot at eight to one.'

'Well, my friends, I've written down on my ledger: bet two hundred and eleven, Sextus, five denarii, Green first to win, eight to one.' He picked another tablet up from a different pile and proffered it to Magnus. 'And this is the slave's record of all the bets he took on the last race; it says exactly the same thing, but I suppose it's a waste of time showing it to you gentleman as it probably just looks like a collection of squiggles to you.'

Magnus knocked the tablet away and jabbed his forefinger towards the bookmaker's face. 'Listen, Ignatius, I don't give a fuck about what you wrote down; we made a bet and expect it to be honoured.'

Ignatius remained unruffled; he added another five denarii to the fifth pile. 'Take the money I owe you plus, as gesture of good-will, an extra five so that we're completely even on the day's transactions as I've recorded them; in fact, I'll even make it easy for you.' He scooped back the fifty denarii. 'You can have it in gold.' He smiled, coldly and without mirth, in a take-it-or-leave-it manner and placed two golden *aurei* on the desk with a couple of hollow clacks. 'And now piss off before I'm forced to have my lads break open your skulls.'

Magnus tensed, as if he was about to leap over the desk, and felt a heavy hand clamp on to each shoulder.

'I wouldn't, mate,' a voice growled in his ear as the other two guards squared up to Sextus and Marius.

Magnus' eyes locked with those of Ignatius; he breathed deeply, suppressing the urge to explode into foolhardy action. After a few moments, feeling an icy calm settle on him, he shook himself free from the restraining hands, looked with menace at their owners and then scooped up the two aurei. 'We're not even, Ignatius, not by a long way. I now owe you and I pay my debts. Always.' With a final glare at Ignatius, he pushed past the heavies and walked calmly away.

'What are you going to do, Brother?' Marius asked, catching Magnus up.

'Go back down and find that slave.'

'I swear to you, master,' the young slave pleaded through gritted teeth, 'I wrote down twenty-five denarii.'

'And you gave Ignatius all the money?' Magnus pulled back the lad's thumb even further as Sextus, looking puzzled, sat with a massive arm around him as if they were having a friendly chat. Marius stood right in front of the group to block the view of the slave's pained face, but no one in the crowd was taking any notice; their attention was held by the twelve chariots in the second-to-last race parading around the track.

'Yes, master. Ignatius blinded the last slave he caught cheating him.'

Magnus increased the pressure. 'So why do you think that he wrote down five instead of twenty-five?'

'I don't know, master, but it's happened before when he's stood to lose a lot of money with a big bet.'

'Has it now? And what about your records?'

The slave's face screwed up even further. 'They're written on wax, master, the two Xs can be scraped clean leaving just the V.'

'What's your name, boy?'

'Menes, master.'

Magnus released his grip. 'If you know what's good for you, Menes, you won't mention our little chat to Ignatius. Now piss off.'

Menes scuttled away and disappeared into the crowd.

Sextus frowned. 'So did we get the right money or not, Magnus? I mean, can I still have a couple of whores tonight?'

'No, Brother, we did not, but we will; and until we do you'll just have to make do with one.'

'Do you think the slave's lying?' Marius asked, sitting in Menes' place.

'No, Brother; I think that Ignatius' dishonesty means that he has just unwittingly declared war on the South Quirinal Crossroads Brotherhood.'

'That's very foolish of him.'

'Very.' Magnus stood. 'Come on, lads, we don't want to be late for our senator.'

'Magnus, my friend, I trust you've had luck?' Senator Gaius Vespasius Pollo boomed, waddling down the steps from the senators' enclosure in a flurry of wobbling belly, jowls and chins.

'Quite the opposite, Senator.' Magnus took up his position in front of his patron, the man to whom he owed his life, with his brothers at either shoulder, ready to beat a path for him through the departing race-goers disgorging into the urine-scented, cavernous belly of the Circus Maximus.

'That's what comes of just betting on your beloved Greens without paying any attention to form.'

'Once a Green, always a Green, sir.'

Gaius' full, moist lips broke into a grin as he pushed away a carefully tonged curl of hair from his eye. 'I find it much better to have no such affiliations; it gives me far more room for manoeuvre and a better chance of backing the winning team. That, of course, goes for politics as well as racing.'

'I admire your lack of loyalty, sir.' Magnus shoved a slow-moving, old man out of the way as they emerged through an arch into the Forum Boarium where the four Racing Factions had their race-day camps; horses and wagonloads of chariots trailed out, heading back to their permanent bases on the Campus Martius, north of the city. The fading, late-afternoon light washed the grand marble buildings on the Palatine above them with a warm glow, despite the dropping temperature.

'I reserve my loyalty for family, patrons and my clients, such as yourself; it's generally wasted elsewhere.'

'Except on the Greens.'

Gaius laughed. 'Have it your own way, Magnus. If it makes you happy to lose your money needlessly, who am I to dissuade you? In the meantime, I have a favour to ask.'

Magnus stopped for a few moments, giving way to a party of higher status. 'Of course, patronus.'

Gaius nodded at the passing senator, one of this year's praetors, preceded by his fasces-bearing lictors. 'As you know, my eldest nephew, Sabinus, has failed for the last two years to get elected as a quaestor; obviously I can't allow that state of affairs to continue.'

'Indeed not.'

'I have to make sure that he gets in this time because next year his younger brother, your friend Vespasian, will be old enough to stand and I certainly won't be able to afford two sets of bribes; not to mention the friction it'll cause in their already strained relationship.'

'Surely your patron, the Lady Antonia, could help; the support of the Emperor Tiberius' sister-in-law for Sabinus would be invaluable.'

'I'm nervous about asking her to involve herself in matters, like quaestor elections, so far beneath her.'

'She involves herself with some matters way beneath her.'

Gaius chuckled. 'She's always loved a boxer; is she still demanding your services?'

Magnus grunted. 'Yeah, well, now and again I get a summons.'

'I've made an appointment to see her tomorrow morning concerning another issue and I wouldn't want to make two requests of her at the same time; you know how demanding her reciprocal favours can be.'

'I do – at first hand, as it were.'

'So I have to look elsewhere for support for Sabinus and that's where I'll need your particular skills.'

'I assume, therefore, that pressure needs to be applied or an incentive offered, if you take my meaning?'

'I do indeed; but in this case pressure would be risky.'

'So you have someone in mind?'

'I think it would help if the Senior Consul publically supported Sabinus.'

'Gnaeus Domitius Ahenobarbus?' Magnus turned in horror to Gaius. 'You must be mad, begging your pardon, to think about influencing him, sir, he's a monster.'

'He is.'

'He pulled an *eques'* eye out in the Forum just because he criticised him.'

'And only last month he purposely ran over, with his quadriga, a small boy playing on the Via Appia. What better person to support Sabinus? If Ahenobarbus backs him a lot of other people will vote for him too, to keep on the right side of the monster.'

Magnus looked dubious as Marius and Sextus, either side of him, used their strong arms to ease their way through the crush. 'Why don't you just bribe him?'

'I will, and handsomely so; but everyone else is too. He's taking money from all the candidates and will end up supporting the one who pays him most. The trouble is I don't know whether my bribe will be enough and I can't afford to increase it; somehow it needs to be supplemented.'

'So you want me to ease him in the right direction.'

'Exactly, but without him realising that I'm behind it as I fully intend to have both my eyes still in place once Sabinus is elected quaestor.'

'And how do you think I can manage that?'

'I've no wish to know, Magnus my loyal friend; but you've served me well before and I've complete trust in your ability to solve even the most delicate of problems.'

The ceaseless night-time clatter and rumble of delivery carts – banished from Rome's packed streets during the day – had begun in earnest by the time Magnus and his companions reached the tavern that served as the headquarters of the South Quirinal Crossroads Brotherhood, at the junction of the Vicus Longus and the Alta Semita. Magnus checked the flame on the altar of the Crossroads' lares – the deities of the neighbourhood – the upkeep of which was the original purpose of the formation of the many such brotherhoods in Rome; satisfied with it, he patted the brother guarding it on the shoulder and stepped through the door into the fug of the crowded tavern.

'A legionary back on leave called in to see you,' an old man with gnarled hands informed him, looking up from a scroll on the wine-stained table before him.

'Did he leave a name, Servius?'

'Just the one: Lucius. He said that you'd remember him from Thracia and Moesia a couple of years ago; he's serving with the Fourth Scythica.'

Magnus looked at his aged counsellor and second-in-command, recalling the name for a couple of moments, and then smiled. 'Lucius? Yeah, I remember him; Vespasian saved him from execution in Thracia; he owes him big. He used to work as a stable lad for the Greens before he joined up; he's still got contacts there, promised me a few tips.'

'He's going to be at the Greens' stables on the Campus Martius from noon tomorrow; he said you should drop by, he'd give you the tour that he promised when he last saw you.'

'Did he now? I may well take him up on that, it'd take my mind off a couple of problems we've got; come through to the back room, we need to talk.'

'Gnaeus Domitius Ahenobarbus!' Servius exclaimed as Magnus finished talking; his gaunt, lined face appeared waxen in the light of a single oil lamp. 'He's a monster; no one in their right mind would meddle in his affairs.'

Magnus poured them both a cup of wine from the jug on the table between them. 'That's what I said, but the senator needs him to back Sabinus.'

'I suppose Sabinus getting elected and taking a seat in the Senate could be useful for us.'

'Possibly; and then his younger brother, Vespasian, will follow him and we'll have three tame senators to call upon should we run into difficulties with the authorities; but Sabinus first.'

'If we can get Ahenobarbus to support him.'

'Which is a big "if", Brother. So what do you know about him?'

'Apart from the fact that, just like all his ancestors, he's violent, cruel and arrogant?'

Magnus waved a dismissive hand. 'I know all that.'

'He's very greedy; he hoards money and hates giving it away. When he was a praetor he used to refuse to hand over the prize money to charioteers in the games he sponsored; he found it bad enough being forced to put on the games without having the extra expense of rewarding the winners. It's ironic really because he loves chariot-racing; he attends every race and is a fanatical supporter of the Reds. All his family are because their beards grow that colour.'

'I fucking loathe the Reds almost as much as I do the Blues.'

'I know, don't we all? But the Whites loathe them even more than we do.'

'I ain't that keen on the Whites either. What else?'

'He's married but doesn't have children.'

'Likes it rough the other way?'

'Likes it rough any way. He married his wife four years ago when she was just thirteen; apparently every time she's been seen in public since she's had bruises all over her face and arms.'

'He sounds lovely.'

'Oh, he is, believe me.'

'So how do we get to him?'

'We've got time to think; the elections aren't for another few months. What was the other problem? You said there were two.'

'Ah, yes; Ignatius.' Magnus downed his wine and related the events of the afternoon.

'What are you thinking of doing?' Servius asked, having heard the story without a flicker of emotion.

'We could kill him but he's well protected and anyway that's too clean and quick for what he did. I can't allow people to humiliate me in front of a couple of the brothers; that sort of thing gets around and before you know it there're mutterings about a change of leadership. I want to see him suffer and I want the brothers to be reminded about what happens to men who cross me.'

'Ruin him, then; but the problem is how to place a bet with him big enough to do that and certain enough to win.'

Magnus thought for a few moments and then smiled; his dark eyes twinkled in the lamplight. 'We need to fix a race.'

Servius pulled at the loose, wrinkled skin of his throat. 'Of course we do.'

'You can get odds of forty or fifty to one for all three chariots of one team to come in first, second and third.'

'Yes, but he's got to be worth at least a million denarii; you'd still have to bet at least twenty-five thousand denarii to have a chance of ruining him. That's a thousand aurei. We don't have that sort of money; and, even if we did, how would we make him pay up?'

'No, we don't have that sort of money, nor would Ignatius be terrified enough of us to honour the bet even if we did, but ...' Magnus paused and winked at Servius.

The old man broke into a brown-toothed grin. 'I take your meaning: there is someone who would frighten Ignatius into parting with his last sestertius, and he certainly does have that sort of cash. But how could you make Ahenobarbus place such a bet with him?'

'That's where Ignatius' greed will be his downfall. I think, Brother, that, despite how much the idea repulses me, we're going to organise a Red one-two-three.'

Magnus pushed his way through the drinkers in the tavern, past the amphorae-lined bar and on to his table in the far corner, giving him a good view of the door; the regulars knew better than to occupy it and passing customers, who lacked the benefit of such knowledge, were soon made aware of their transgression.

A Greek with a nasty scar along his jaw, which reduced his beard to clumps, brought a jug of wine and a cup and set it on the table.

'Thanks, Cassandros,' Magnus grunted. 'Sit down a moment.'

Cassandros complied whilst pouring Magnus' wine.

'I need you to do what for you should be a pleasant job.'

Cassandros grinned lopsidedly. 'So I'll be mixing business with pleasure.'

'Very much so. Tomorrow I want you to go down to the Campus Martius and hang around the Red stables.'

Cassandros' face fell. 'But tomorrow is the Lupercalia.'

'And you're going to miss it. I know you enjoy watching patrician youths running naked through the streets whipping women with thongs of goatskin but, let's face it, the ceremony is to help women conceive and therefore completely irrelevant to a man of

your tastes. Instead you're going to find yourself a nice attractive
Red stable lad or whatever and show him a good time; Servius
will give you some cash to cover your expenses. Take him home,
give him a serious going-over and leave him panting for more, if
you take my meaning?'

'I do indeed, Brother. How long do you want me to keep him
desirous of my services?'

'Shouldn't be more than a month I'd guess; and then I'll be
wanting some information from him.'

Cassandros frowned. 'You're not thinking of betting on the
Reds, are you?'

'Why would a lifelong Green do a thing like that? Don't you
worry about what I'm thinking of doing; you just concern yourself with making a nice young lad very friendly.'

'Only the aedile in charge of the games can do that,' Gaius
informed Magnus as they made their way up the Palatine, rife
with crowds, the following morning. 'Only four bookmakers are
licensed to operate in the senators' enclosure: Albus, Fabricius,
Blasius and Glaucio; and all of them have paid very hefty bribes
for the privilege, as I'm sure you can imagine. It's a very lucrative
position.'

'Do you know the aedile?' Magnus asked as a group of women
came running, laughing and screeching in excitement, towards
them.

'I do.'

The women dashed past, their laughter and footsteps echoing
off the grand buildings of the Palatine, pursued by a group of
naked youths, in varying states of arousal, lashing at them with
freshly cut, bloody strips of goatskin. The crowds on the pave-
ments cheered them on; young girls held out their hands to be
whipped, giggling as the youths obliged them.

'And?' Magnus asked as Gaius eyed the youths in appreciation, turning his head as they passed.

'And it makes no difference. There're already four bookmakers with the senatorial-enclosure licence.'

'What would happen if there were suddenly three?'

'Ah! That would be a different matter altogether; then there would be a vacancy which the aedile would be duty-bound to fill.'

'Do you know him well enough to make a recommendation?'

Gaius tore his eyes from the retreating youths' buttocks and gave Magnus a sly look. 'And whom should I be recommending?'

'Ignatius.'

'A friend of yours?'

'Quite the opposite.'

'Then why help him?'

'It's partly to do with Sabinus.'

'In which case I'll be only too pleased to help – but it'll be expensive.'

'Don't worry, Senator, you'll be able to recoup that money and a lot more besides.'

They stopped outside a single-storey house that, although tall and grand in structure, was not ostentatious compared to other buildings on the Palatine. Its windowless walls were painted a plain white, and it lacked any extraneous decoration.

Gaius slapped Magnus on the shoulder. 'Thank you, Magnus. If you wouldn't mind waiting for me whilst I have my interview with Antonia, I shouldn't be long.'

'Of course, Senator. One thing before you go in: does Antonia have anything to do with Ahenobarbus?'

'He's her nephew, the son of her late elder sister, another Antonia. And he's married to her granddaughter, Agrippina.'

'Is he now? Does Antonia have any influence over him?'

Gaius rapped on the bronze-studded oaken door. 'A little, but not enough to make him forgo all the bribes from the other candidates.' A viewing slat slipped back and after a brief pause the doors were opened. Gaius walked in leaving Magnus deep in thought.

'I thought the offer of a tour would be of interest to you.' A broad-shouldered young man with military-style cropped hair and a tanned face greeted Magnus at the entrance of the Greens' stables in the shadow of the Flaminian Circus.

'More than you would know, Lucius, my friend.' Magnus

grasped the proffered forearm. 'It's good of you to remember your promise. When did you get back from Moesia?'

'A couple of days ago; I've got a month's leave in the city. Let's go in.'

Lucius led Magnus through the arched gate, acknowledging two guards who made Ignatius' protectors look like boy-players in the theatre.

'How come they let you in?' Magnus asked, eying the two colossi.

'All my family work for the Greens; my uncle's the stable-master now, I can come and go as I please.'

They walked into a busy, rectangular yard, two hundred paces long and half that across. The two long sides consisted solely of stables, hundreds of them; whilst the shorter sides housed a mixture of workshops, forges, warehouses and offices. The air was scented with the sweet, animal smell of horses and filled with the sound of their hooves clattering on the paved ground as they were exercised in groups of four or in pairs. At one end, teams of carpenters were repairing those chariots only mildly damaged in yesterday's racing, replacing broken struts in the light frames and restretching green linen over them. Next to them blacksmiths fitted glowing-red iron tyres on the eight-spoked wheels and dipped them, steaming and hissing, into tubs of water, contracting the metal so it fitted tightly around the rim. Everywhere there was activity: hunched leather-workers stitching harnesses and traces, dusty grooms currying horses, sweating slaves unloading bags of feed from a covered wagon, boys running errands, axles being greased; hammering, joking, neighing, sawing, shouting and whickering – all the business of a faction's stables on the day after a race.

'Were you there yesterday?' Magnus asked as they wove their way through the plethora of pursuits.

'Of course, I was helping my uncle in the Forum Boarium; we had a hundred and forty-four horses in the teams yesterday, plus all the hortatores' mounts and the spares. Busy day.'

'And only one winner.'

'Yeah, shit, weren't it? We haven't had a day like it for years even through it was only a half-day's racing. The faction-master was livid; although judging by the size of his purse at the end of the day he wasn't just betting on his own team.'

'Bastard.'

'Yeah. Especially as it's not allowed for anyone who works in the faction's stables; one rule for them and one rule for us – you know how it is, my friend. If we get caught betting on another team we get expelled from the stables.'

'Why's that?'

'It's assumed that the only reason you would want to bet on an inferior team is because you've been fraternising with them and got some tips in exchange for information about your own team's plans or, even worse, you've bribed the drivers to throw a race.'

Magnus stroked the muzzle of one of the finest pieces of horseflesh he had ever been close to: a beautiful bay Gaetulian mare from the province of Africa.

'Spendusa,' Lucius informed him. 'She's a rarity.'

'I know; most racehorses are stallions.'

Spendusa whickered gently, her breath and soft, flaccid lips warming the palm of Magnus' hand.

'We have one team of mares. It's a new idea: we don't expect them to win but we're going to use them when they come on heat. The hope is that they'll distract the stallions in the other teams and allow our other two chariots to come in first and second.'

'But they'll be just as distracted as the rest.'

'Not if they're two teams of geldings.'

'Nice.' Magnus grinned and stroked Spendusa's well-muscled flank. 'Will it work?'

'My uncle says that it already has in experiments in the Flaminian Circus. The stallions under-perform – they're too busy trying to get a sniff; whereas the geldings just press on thinking about nothing more than their feed-bag at the end of the race.'

Magnus whistled appreciatively. 'That'll piss off the other factions.'

'It'll cause a riot.'

'It will. When are you going to try it?'

'They're next on heat at the calends of March, Mars' birthday. We're going to put them in one of the races on that day, after the armed priesthood of the Salii have finished their round of the city.'

'Which race?'

'I don't know yet but I'll tell you when I find out.'

'Now that's the sort of information that's worth a lot of money.'

'I know. And I'm telling you because I want you to pass it on to Tribune Vespasian as a thank-you for his saving me from execution back in Thracia. Hopefully he'll be able to profit from it.'

Magnus laughed and slapped an arm around Lucius' shoulders. 'And Vestals will stop taking a close interest in their middle fingers. I'm afraid you've got the wrong thank-you gift there, my friend; Vespasian's about as likely to put money down on a wager as I am to take it up the arse from a Nubian. And, besides, he's away from Rome for a few months at his estate in Cosa. I, on the other hand, will be only too pleased to profit in his stead.'

Lucius shrugged. 'Fair enough, I owe you as well. I should know which race we're entering them for by Equirria festival, two days before the calends. Come and see me then.'

'What do you know about the bookmakers Albus, Fabricius, Blasius and Glaucio?' Magnus asked Servius. They were sitting on one of the rough wooden tables outside the crossroads tavern, idly throwing dice; no money was involved. Around them, the Brotherhood was similarly occupied whilst at the same time keeping their eyes on the constant stream of passers-by making their way to and from the Porta Collina, just a couple of hundred paces away along the Alta Semita, or frequenting the open-fronted shops on the ground floor of tenements that lined the street.

'Aside from the fact that they are all licensed to operate in the senators' enclosure in the Circus Maximus?'

Magnus smiled, impressed by the speed with which his counsellor made the connection. 'Yes, I know that.'

'Albus and Glaucio both come from the Aventine: born and bred in the tenements on the far side by the granaries; but they now live in far grander houses on the summit. They've known each other and been rivals since boyhood; their mutual loathing is surpassed only by a hatred of any other bookmakers. Despite their antipathy they work together to fix odds to protect their businesses.' Servius threw the dice and grimaced his disgust.

Magnus retrieved the offending articles. 'So they need each other?'

'Yes, it's a perverse sort of loyalty but a strong one.'

'What about the other two?'

'Fabricius is a freedman; he lives on the Caelian, close to the Servian Wall. He's completely ruthless and deals harshly with everyone who crosses him; he even had a neighbour's house torched because the man built up another storey and took the sun from his garden. Four people died, including the owner, but nothing could be proved, of course. Apart from his bodyguards and bet-takers, Fabricius' whole household is made up of female slaves who are – how shall I put it? – extremely well fed.'

'Big and bouncy, eh?' Magnus chuckled, shaking the dice cup and throwing.

'Which is ironic as he has no spare flesh on him whatsoever; although I'm told he eats like a slave at the Saturnalia.'

Magnus examined his score. 'So he wallows in copious amounts of female flesh to make up for it; I suppose it keeps him warm in winter.'

Servius wrinkled his nose. 'But what about in a hot summer?'

Magnus pushed the dice across the table. 'Don't bear thinking about.'

'Quite. Blasius, however, lives on the west slope of the Esquiline, not far from the Querquetulian Gate. I don't know anything about him other than he is, like the other three, fabulously wealthy. They're all as well guarded as people who regularly take huge chunks of senatorial money can expect to be and they all pay for the protection of their local brotherhoods; so they're very hard to get at – if that is your intention, which I assume it is.'

'I just need one vacancy so that I can get Ignatius into the senators' enclosure.' Magnus glanced past Servius' shoulder to a party of half a dozen well-dressed, eastern travellers, clearly newly arrived in the city. 'Tigran! Looks like one for you and your cousin; squeeze them hard.'

A young, almond-skinned man with a pointed, hennaed beard got up from the table next to Magnus. 'Our pleasure, Magnus. Come, Vahram, let's show our Roman brothers how to extract the correct toll for travelling through our area.' His cousin's eyes glinted and white teeth showed under his beard; the two easterners walked off towards the travellers.

'Keep an eye on them, Marius, back 'em up if negotiations don't go smooth.'

'Right you are, Magnus.' Marius got to his feet, indicating to a couple of the brothers to follow him.

Magnus turned his attention back to Servius. 'So what do you suggest?'

Servius rubbed the palm of his hand over the rough grey stubble on his chin and thought for a few moments. 'If you're determined to get at one, then Fabricius is your man.'

'Why?'

'Because of where his house is situated; go and have a look tonight.'

An abrupt scream followed by shouts and the clatter of hardened leather soles on stone cut through the background calls of shopkeepers, street-traders and haggling customers. Magnus swung round and immediately leapt to his feet, drawing a short, street-fighter's knife from his belt. One of the two cousins lay writhing in the road whilst the other, Tigran, was fending off the swords of two of the travellers with only a knife as Marius and his two brothers weighed into the rest.

'With me, lads!' Magnus shouted at the rest of his brethren, who were jumping to their feet in a scraping of wooden tables pushed forward and benches falling back. Magnus powered into one of Tigran's opponents, body-checking him to the ground and slashing his blade across the man's forearm as the young easterner fell to his knees clutching at a bloody wound in his shoulder. Stamping on the downed man's kneecap with a brittle crunch, Magnus twisted and grabbed the flowing hair of Tigran's second assailant; as the man raised his weapon for the killing blow to the wounded brother, Magnus jerked back his head and pressed a blood-slick blade to his exposed throat. 'I'd drop that if I were you, bum-boy, it's illegal to carry swords in our city.' Ramming his knee up between the man's buttocks to emphasise the point, Magnus slowly applied pressure to his knife; the easterner's sword fell ringing to the ground and he went limp.

Magnus threw the man down on to the ground, spitting at him in disgust, and looked around; the fight had drawn a crowd. 'Get rid of them, Marius.'

'Right you are, Magnus.' Marius headed off without sheathing his knife; the crowd began to disperse without needing to be told to mind their own business and not that of their local Crossroads Brotherhood.

The six travellers were all down and in various states of consciousness and pain; their slaves, carrying the baggage, hung back, looking with fearful eyes at their masters, unsure what to do. Tigran still clutched his wound, trying to stem the bleeding, his face contorted in agony and sorrow as he stared down at the glazed eyes of his cousin, Vahram.

'What the fuck happened there?' Magnus exploded. 'It's meant to be a generous offer to provide protection, for a small fee, through our territory; not a fucking declaration of war!'

Tigran tore his eyes from his cousin's immobile face and stared up at Magnus. 'It was all agreed: a denarius for each traveller and two for the slaves.' He pointed to an easterner lying next to Vahram, moaning softly in a pool of blood that oozed from his abdomen. 'He said he would pay the eight denarii and put his hand under his cloak; we thought he was getting out his purse, but instead out comes a sword and he plunges it into Vahram.'

From along the street came the staccato clatter of hobnailed sandals.

'Fucking great!' Magnus spat. 'Now the Urban Cohorts are getting involved.'

'The Urban Prefect will have to hear of this,' the Urban Cohort centurion informed Magnus, staring down at the dead and wounded. 'He's issued orders for us to crack down on street violence, especially involving the brotherhoods.'

Magnus nodded, feigning a look of sympathetic understanding. 'Rightly so, Centurion, some of them are vicious; it's getting to the stage that decent folk can't walk about the city in safety. We, however, try and enforce the law in our area.' With his foot he flicked back the cloak of one of the wounded easterners to reveal a scabbard. 'See? Carrying swords in the city; only you lads and the Praetorians are allowed to do that. We were just trying to explain that to them, as they were obviously new to Rome and must have been unacquainted with that particular law. It cost one of my men his life.'

The centurion looked down at the evidence whilst his men continued to surround the area with their weapons drawn. 'I'll still need to make a report.'

'Of course. I would have done the same when I was in the Cohorts.'

'You were in one of the Urban Cohorts?'

'I finished my time ten years ago. I believe my mate, Aelianus, is still the quartermaster down at the depot?'

The centurion grinned. 'That old crook, yeah; he should have been discharged years ago but he seems to cling on.'

'It's a very lucrative business being in charge of all that gear.'

'I'm sure it is; I've been trying to get new boots for my century for the last two months.'

'What's your name, Centurion?'

'Nonus Manilus Rufinus.'

'Well, Rufinus, today is your lucky day; I'll have a word with Aelianus and the next time you put in a request for boots mention my name, Marcus Salvius Magnus. I think you'll find Aelianus very accommodating and I'd be surprised if your lads get their pay deducted for the new gear.'

'That's very good of you, Magnus.'

'Not a problem, my friend. Now what are we going to do about these fucking easterners that killed one of my men with their illegal swords?'

Rufinus scratched the back of his head. 'I'll take them down to the cohort depot and lock them up until the Urban Prefect decides what to do with them.' He looked closely at the belly-wound of Vahram's killer. 'If they survive, that is. Obviously I'll have to make a report; we can't allow people to flout the law like that. Naturally I'll emphasise that it was self-defence on your part.'

'Naturally. And there won't be any mention of the South Quirinal Crossroads Brotherhood?'

'Of course not; that will just get the Urban Prefect upset and we wouldn't want to do that; he's getting on.'

'A wise precaution, Rufinus; I believe he's going to be eighty this year.' Magnus indicated the easterners' slaves, who had been rounded up into a tight group. 'Shall we just take the blood-money now, out of whatever they've got in their baggage?'

Rufinus shrugged. 'I suppose that would make matters easier; if you're happy with the blood-money then the murder could be forgotten about. Take what you like.'

'It'll be simpler if we just take everything; you will come round and pick up your share once you're off duty this evening, won't you?'

'Of course. I'd better take the slaves, though, just in case … you know.' Rufinus waved his hand in a vague manner.

'I do indeed,' Magnus assured him. 'You never know.'

'Quite.'

'Would you like some of my lads to help your boys carry the bastards to the depot?'

'We'll manage, Magnus. I'll see you later when I come for my … er …'

'It'll be waiting for you, my friend.'

'A third goes to Tigran, a third to Rufinus and a third to the Brotherhood,' Servius said, clacking at an abacus. 'Which means that, in coin, one share is one hundred and twenty-one aurei.'

Magnus whistled softly and stopped pacing around the small

back room. 'No wonder they were armed, walking around with over three thousand denarii on them. What were they going to do with all that money?'

'I don't know; but what is for sure is that they won't like losing it. They'll come looking for it if they're freed.'

'They'll be dead in a few days; they're not citizens. Rufinus will make his report very damning once he's seen how much he stands to gain by their execution. I wouldn't worry about it, Brother, and it's no more than they deserve after killing Vahram. We need to concentrate on more important business: it's time I took a gander at Fabricius' house.'

'You can see right into it!' Magnus muttered in surprise as he looked down from the Servian Wall into the torch-lit courtyard garden of Fabricius' house, just fifty paces away.

Servius smiled and patted Magnus on the shoulder as they strolled along the walkway. 'Only because Fabricius burned down the house between here and the wall a couple of months ago; they haven't started rebuilding it yet.'

Magnus glanced down at the burnt-out ruin below, just visible in the weak moonlight. 'Silly man, he doesn't realise just how much that bit of extra sun is going to cost him.' He stopped and scrutinised the house. The courtyard garden, surrounded by a portico with a sloping, tiled roof, was a decent size for the tightly packed Caelian Hill, stretching forty paces by twenty; although the wall surrounding it was a good twelve feet high, from where he stood, thirty feet up, Magnus could see the door that led into the tablinum and on into the atrium of the house. 'From here to the door must be almost a hundred paces; if Fabricius walked out of it, it wouldn't be an impossible shot for a good archer. Tigran's our man, he's an easterner; they're born to the bow.'

'My thoughts entirely; but he's not going to come out at night at this time of year and it would be too dangerous to try during the day; Tigran needs the dark to be able to escape cleanly.'

'Then we'll have to come up with something that'll bring him out from under his fat slaves and into the garden. Have Marius and a couple of the lads watch the place for the next few days; we need to get an idea of the household's routine. In the meantime we've got to work out how to prevent three Blue teams and three White teams finishing ahead of the Reds.'

'What about our Greens?'

'That's the easy part, Brother; I saw how to do that this afternoon.'

Magnus' face fell as he walked through the tavern door. A Greek in his late twenties, with a thick black beard and dark, expressionless eyes, sat at his table in the corner. 'Does she want to see me, Pallas?'

'She does, master,' Pallas replied, getting up and bowing his head.

'There's no need to do that.'

'I am a slave and you are freeborn.'

'Maybe, but you're also steward to the Lady Antonia.'

'But still a slave.'

'Which is what I'm going to be for the rest of the night.'

'That's a matter of perception, master. If she demanded it of me I could not refuse to go to her bed; you, on the other hand, could.'

'And if I did that, then I wouldn't benefit from her favour.'

The Greek steward raised an eyebrow a fraction. 'But that would be your free choice, whereas if I refused she'd be within her rights to have me crucified.'

Magnus turned and headed for the door with Pallas following. 'Yeah, well, however you argue it there's no getting around the fact that she's a powerful woman and we all have reason to do her bidding.'

'And some of her requests are a little more demanding than others, which is why she sends me to fetch you so that she can preserve her dignity and as few people as possible know that she ... er ...'

'Likes to get a hard fucking from ex-boxers?'

Pallas cleared his throat. 'Precisely.'

*

'You may go now, Magnus,' Antonia murmured, lying back on the pillow and staring up into the gloom of the ceiling high above, beyond the reach of the few oil lamps placed around the bed. 'And take your things.'

'Yes, domina.' Magnus looked down at the most powerful woman in Rome and wondered how it had come to this. During his two years as a boxer, after leaving the Urban Cohorts, she had often hired him to fight as an after-dinner entertainment for her friends; like many other respectable Roman matrons, she would sometimes retain him for services of a different nature after the party broke up. He had always performed his duty with diligence, acceding to all her demands – which were numerous and some-times not for the faint-hearted. However, once he had retired from fighting, the massive difference in their social status precluded any liaison until he had met his patron Senator Pollo's nephews, Vespasian and Sabinus. They had been favoured by Antonia and because Magnus' loyalty was to Senator Pollo and his family, his and Antonia's paths had crossed a few years previ-ously; since then she had made regular demands on his services. It was not so bad, he reflected as he retied his loincloth; for a woman in her mid-sixties she was still attractive. Her skin remained smooth with only a few wrinkles around her sparkling green eyes: eyes that never missed a single detail. She wore very little make-up; her high cheekbones, strong chin and full lips needed no embellishment. Even with her auburn hair loose and dishevelled she still managed to look like the high-born patrician that she was; an image helped by the fact that she had not run to fat and her body had not yet creased and sagged.

Magnus slipped on his tunic, gently rubbing the bite-marks on his shoulder. '*Domina?*'

'Are you still here?'

'I have a favour to ask, domina.'

'What is it?'

'I would like you to give someone a racing tip.'

'To whom and why?' Antonia turned over languidly to lie on her belly, her eyes closed and her face nestled into the pillow; the sheet fell away from her buttocks.

Magnus admired his handiwork. 'To your nephew, Ahenobarbus.'

'You don't want to get involved with him; he's probably the most unpleasant member of my family. I'm just pleased that he and Agrippina haven't managed to breed yet; a child of that union would be atrocious.'

Magnus knew enough about the imperial family to understand that was condemnation indeed.

'I don't want to get involved with him; I was hoping to do this without him ever knowing where you got your information from – until it's been proven reliable, if you take my meaning?'

'Why do you want him to win at the races?'

'I don't want him to win as much as I want him to place a bet with a bookmaker called Ignatius, big enough to ruin Ignatius when he does win.'

'If he wins.'

'Oh, he'll win all right; it'll be a sure thing.'

'How much do you want him to put down?'

'A thousand aurei on a Red one-two-three at odds of around fifty to one.'

'And if he wins then the bookmaker will owe him over a million denarii; it would probably break him.'

'Yes, domina.'

'This bookmaker has upset you, I take it.'

'Very much, domina.'

'Ahenobarbus might not believe me.'

'I know, so before he places the big bet we'll have a practice run on the races on the calends of March; then he can judge just how good the information he's getting is. If you're willing to grant me this favour, have Pallas meet me at the Temple of Mars in Augustus' Forum that morning at the third hour.'

'I'll think about it, Magnus; now leave me.'

'Yes, domina.' Magnus scooped up his sandals, took the short black-leather whip from off the bed and left the room.

'The Whites bring their teams out of their stables' gates and turn right, past the Pantheon and the Baths of Agrippa; they then pass between Pompey's theatre and the Flaminian Circus and on to the Fabrician Bridge and over the Tiber Island,' Servius informed Magnus as they stood in the rain outside the Villa Publica on the Campus Martius, three days later. 'They cross the river, turn left along the Via Aurelia and go across the Aemilian Bridge and then through the Porta Flumentana and into the Forum Boarium, the race-day camp for all four teams. The Reds also take that route; however, the Urban Prefect never lets the Reds go at the same time as the Whites – that way he avoids any faction trouble.'

Magnus digested the information for a few moments; drops of rain trickled off his wide-brimmed leather hat. He shivered and pulled his cloak tighter around his shoulders. 'What about the Sublician Bridge?'

'To stop any rabble getting into the teams' camp, that's always closed on a race day as it too leads directly into the Forum Boarium.'

'So the only ways to cross the river near the Circus Maximus on a race day are across the Tiber Island and the Aemilian Bridge.'

'Precisely.'

'What about the Greens and Blues?'

'They take a different route. They don't cross and recross the river; they enter the city through the Porta Carmentalis and then cross Velabrum and enter the Forum Boarium from the east.'

'Why are there two different routes?'

'To avoid congestion.'

'And they always stick to the same route?'

'Always. You wouldn't know this because our connections mean we can always get into the circus whenever we want; however, hundreds of thousands of people can't and they line the routes so that they can see their favoured teams pass.'

'How the masses live, eh?'

Servius spat; his saliva was immediately lost in a rain-battered puddle. 'Fucking rabble. Come on, Brother, let's get back before my old bones seize up.'

'How far in advance do they bring the teams in?' Magnus asked as they turned to go.

'Normally, on a twenty-four-race day, they start by bringing in the twelve chariots for the first four races plus the spares for the day and all the hortatores; then they do relays of twelve throughout the day so that the Forum Boarium doesn't get too crowded.'

Magnus grinned despite the rain. 'So if we were to stop the Whites bringing their last relay of twelve in then they wouldn't have any teams in the final four races, would they, brother?'

'Don't forget the spares.'

'How many do they have?'

'It depends on the fitness of the horses, but normally between three and six teams, never more because of shortage of space.'

'So we could guarantee the last two races being free from Whites?'

'It's possible; but how would you do it? They're very well guarded and if you were to block the way they would just go back and take another route to the circus.'

'Not if we block the bridges and trap them on the wrong side of the river.'

'But the Reds would be trapped as well.'

'Not if we time it right. Let's invite Nonus Manilus Rufinus over for a little chat when he gets off duty this evening.'

'So what have you learnt, brother?' Magnus asked, rubbing his hands over a portable brazier as Marius walked into the tavern's back room.

'Fabricius doesn't go out much and when he does he's very well guarded.'

'As we expected,' Servius commented, taking a sip from a steaming cup of hot wine; his eyes watered from the brazier's smoke.

Magnus indicated the jug on the table. 'Help yourself, Brother. What about his household?'

Marius poured himself a cup, chuckling. 'Well, every morning two of his fat slaves – and they really are fat, you should see 'em, Magnus, you'd have to roll 'em in flour and look for the damp patch. Anyway, every morning the same two head off for the market to buy whatever they need that day. They come back a couple of hours later laden with stuff; it's unbelievable how much they all eat.'

'Fabricius likes to keep them fat and he can well afford it.'

'Well, I ain't ever seen the like of it, Magnus.'

'Are they guarded when they go?'

'No, who would want to touch 'em?'

'We would. Tomorrow, Brother, I want you to invite those two well-formed ladies here for a little bit of the Brotherhood's hospitality, if you take my meaning?'

Marius' eyes glinted with amusement over the rim of his cup. 'They're big old beasts; it'll take more than me and my two lads.'

'Take Sextus; what he lacks in brains he makes up for in brawn.'

Marius turned to leave, taking his cup with him. 'Right you are, Magnus; I'll have them here by the third hour of the day.'

'Make sure you do, brother; and don't let them see your faces or where you take them.'

'Of course not, Magnus.' Marius opened the door and stepped out.

'Leave the door open; let's get some of this smoke out.'

Servius rubbed his eyes. 'Thanks.'

'We'll be ready to do this first part tomorrow night; how's Tigran doing with his archery practice?'

'He says he's fine; his wound has healed nicely. The last couple of days he's gone out into the country each morning and has been practising shooting at a sack of hay a hundred paces away; he reckons to hit it nine times out of ten.'

'Let's hope it's not the tenth shot tomorrow. Tell him to practise all day and to be here by nightfall. And get one of the lads to purchase a couple of snakes first thing in the morning, but not poisonous ones.'

Servius picked up a stylus and a wax tablet and scratched a note. 'That reminds me,' he said, reading a previous note. 'Cassandros came in this morning; he says he's been doing very nicely with a young lad from the Reds. I'll spare you the details, but the boy enjoys all of Cassandros' little hobbies and can't get enough of one in particular.'

Magnus winced and looked at his hand. 'I suppose that involves a lot of olive oil.'

'I'm afraid it does, Brother. Anyhow, suffice it to say that the lad is very amenable now and Cassandros is sure that he can get whatever information we require out of him.'

'Good; tell him that, when the time comes, I'll want to know the form of the Red teams in the last two races on the first race-day after the calends of March.'

Servius made a note of the race as a figure appeared silhouetted in the doorway.

Magnus rose to greet the new arrival. 'Rufinus, my new friend, good of you to come; I have a little proposition for you concerning the closing of bridges owing to a riot.'

Magnus shivered; his breath steamed in the cold night air as he hunched down on the Servian Wall, keeping low so that his silhouette would not be visible. Next to him, Tigran examined an arrow in the moonlight, checking the fletching was secure and the shaft true; satisfied with his choice he nocked it.

'Juno's plump arse, come on, lads,' Magnus muttered, peering down into the street that ran alongside Fabricius' house, 'what's keeping you?'

Marius and Sextus had delivered the two slaves earlier that day, bound, gagged and blindfolded. Magnus had been truly surprised by their magnitude and had feared for a while that his plan might not work; but after the lads had shown they could lift the women's massive bulk he was happy with it.

After a few more muttered curses Magnus finally heard the noise he had been waiting for: the clatter of hooves and the rumble of iron-shod wheels on stone. Out of the gloom a covered wagon appeared, making its way slowly up the street. As it drew level with the wall of Fabricius' courtyard garden it pulled in as close as possible and stopped. The cover was thrown back by shadowy figures and then two ladders were placed upright in the wagon, leaning against the wall so that they reached its summit.

'Good lads,' Magnus said under his breath. Two of the figures started mounting the ladders with a large, struggling shape between them; underneath, in the wagon, two more figures took the weight of the writhing burden. Eventually they got it to the top and heaved it on to the tiled roof of the garden portico.

'Remember, it's the small skinny man we want,' Magnus reminded Tigran as the second obese slave was hefted up the ladders. 'The first people through the door will be bodyguards; it'll be a fuck-up if you shoot one of them.'

Tigran nodded and took a kneeling position, drawing his compact recurved bow as the second shape was manhandled on to the roof.

'Hoods and gags now, lads,' Magnus muttered, 'and then give them something to make some noise about.'

The two men up the ladders fiddled for few moments with the slave women and then leapt down as shrill screams pierced the night air. As soon as the ladders were removed the wagon thundered off into the night, turning left down a side street and disappearing.

The screeching continued.

Tigran aimed his arrow at the closed garden door of Fabricius' house; light leaked from beneath it. On the roof one of the two slaves started to slide down, increasing the intensity of the shrieks.

'They really don't like snakes down their tunics,' Magnus observed, staring at the door, willing it to open. 'Come on, come on.'

The sliding slave neared the edge and then, with a shriller but suddenly curtailed yelp, fell into the garden.

The door opened and two bulky figures filled its frame.

'Bodyguards,' Magnus whispered unnecessarily.

The second slave continued screaming; the men ran towards her, disappearing from view as an enormous female shape, obviously naked, took their place in the doorway, closely followed by a second and then a third.

Tigran's aim remained firmly fixed on the mounds of female flesh silhouetted against the soft light burning within the house.

A harsh shout from inside caused the three women to turn and move apart; light played on the rolls of fat that draped their forms and wobbled as they moved. A slight man appeared in their midst, pushing them out of the way.

Tigran's bow thrummed.

The man stopped.

The women jumped back.

Tigran's bow twanged again; this time the man jerked, arcing around with his left shoulder raised. The women brought their hands up to their mouths but failed to stifle the squawks that welled up from inside as Fabricius collapsed to the floor with two arrows in his chest.

'Great shooting, Brother,' Magnus said, shaking his head in admiration. 'You've just created a most convenient vacancy.'

'I've made my recommendation,' Gaius informed Magnus the following day as he and a few of his brothers escorted the senator back up the Quirinal from the Senate House.

'And?'

'And the aedile was rather surprised to hear that there was a vacancy, it was the first he knew of it; I assured him that it was the case – one of Fabricius' rivals had finished him off over an argument about positioning in the senators' enclosure. I told him that it wouldn't be worth investigating because whichever one of the other three did it would be sure to cover his tracks.'

'Very sensible advice, Senator; we wouldn't want a man whose time is as valuable as the aedile's wasting it on a pointless investigation.'

'Exactly, especially when he should be utilising it on the far more important task of making sure that there are enough book-makers for the senators to place wagers with next race day.'

Magnus nodded sagely. 'Far more important. What did the aedile think of your suggestion?'

'He took the hundred aurei that you gave me to give him and said that he would send for Ignatius immediately. He then expressed a warm certainty that if Ignatius could come up with a sizeable incentive for the aedile to appoint him it would be confirmed by this evening before any other bookmakers heard of Fabricius' unfortunate end and applied for the position themselves.'

'That's very understanding of him; perhaps you'd like to give him a racing tip as a thank-you? I'm sure Ignatius would be only too pleased to take the aedile's wager after the generosity he's shown him.'

Gaius looked at Magnus and narrowed his eyes. 'Ah! I see: create a certainty, then have people who can afford a large bet lay money with Ignatius and break him. That'll do it; but how does that help Sabinus?'

'We just have to choose the right time to drop his name with someone; but first I've got to create that certainty.'

'How do you plan to do that?'

'By having a nice quiet chat with the Green faction master after the Equirria.'

The Campus Martius brimmed with people in holiday spirits a few days later, making their way to the already packed Trigarium, nestled in the east and south of the Tiber's curve. Having no permanent structures, it was an area ideal for exercising horses; but today it was not mere exercise that the people of Rome were coming to see, it was racing: the Equirria, a series of horse races in honour of Mars.

Magnus barged a path through the heaving crowds towards the Greens' race-day camp on the banks of the river. Although it was not chariots being raced, the factions still entered using their hortatores as jockeys; they would prove to be stiff competition for the noble young bucks who rode their favoured mounts in the gruelling races set over different distances.

'Lucius!' Magnus shouted over the hubbub, spotting his friend checking the girth and saddle of one of the Green horses.

Lucius looked up from his work. 'Magnus, my friend, I was expecting you.' He paused, waiting for Magnus to draw closer. 'I've got good news, but not here, I'll tell you away from the camp.'

A huge roar engulfed the whole Trigarium, signalling the start of the first race. Wearing the colours of their factions or, if they were independent, just a plain tunic, the twelve jockeys urged their mounts at terrifying speeds around the oval course carved through the throng of spectators. With no barriers marking its route, the course itself was a fluid affair, subject to the undulations of the crowd, suddenly narrowing and then widening again as they surged to better see the race. Waving faction flags or ribbons, they cheered on the riders as they negotiated their way around the treacherous track, narrowly missing – or sometimes clipping with disastrous consequences – foolhardy spectators who had encroached on to their path.

Handing the horse's bridle to an attending slave, Lucius led Magnus away from the Green camp and into the heaving mass. 'I heard the faction master telling my uncle yesterday that the mares and geldings will run in two days' time in the second race.'

'And that's for sure?'

Lucius shrugged. 'As sure as it can ever be; there's always the chance of injury during training.'

'And how is their training going?'

'Excellently, my friend. The two teams of geldings would both stand a good chance of winning even without the help of the mares on heat.'

'That's good news. Where can I find your faction master?'

'Euprepes will be in the tent in the middle of our camp; I'll be able to get you in if you want an introduction.'

'Better not, mate, I'll do it myself; it would be tricky for you to be seen associating with me after what I've got to say to him.'

Lucius looked worried. 'You're not going to tell him that you know about the mares, are you?'

'No, my friend, I wouldn't betray your loyalty like that.'

'Euprepes will see no one without an appointment,' the ex-gladiator guarding the tent informed Magnus, cracking both his shoulders in turn to stress the point.

'Oh, but I have an appointment; in fact, I've got a permanent appointment. You tell him that the man who's going to make him richer even than when he was a charioteer driving first for the Blues and then the Greens is here to see him.'

'He won't believe you so I'd fuck off quietly if I was you, mate.'

Magnus squared up to the guard. 'I've got no intention of fucking off quietly – or loudly for that matter. Now you listen to me, matey-boy, I'll get to talk to Euprepes somehow, very soon, and I'll inform him, as he's hugging me to his breast with tears of joy in his eyes and gratitude welling in his heart at my generosity, that his involvement in my proposal very nearly didn't happen because of an over-officious oaf obstinately denying me ingress to his tent. Now, do you want to risk what will happen when he contemplates the magnitude of your error or would you prefer to pop in and tell him that Marcus Salvius Magnus is here with a proposition that will make the prize money from winning nearly two thousand races seem like nothing more than what a dockside whore-boy earns for parting his buttocks for a Syrian sailor?'

The guard's eyes narrowed and his fists clenched, tensing the sculpted muscles all down his arms. However, he remained motionless, weighing up his options for a few moments until he turned, abruptly, and disappeared through the tent's flaps.

Magnus smiled to himself and waited, watching a Green rider bring his lathered horse into the camp surrounded by cheering supporters. 'A Green victory, very auspicious,' he muttered.

'And what makes you think that I would possibly do this, Magnus?' Euprepes asked, stroking his grey-flecked, Greek-style beard and holding Magnus' gaze with surprisingly blue, penetrating eyes.

'Odds of forty or fifty to one?'

'But I'm not allowed to bet on other teams, especially on a Red one-two-three.'

'I quite understand that, Euprepes, and I'm sure that you never break that rule – personally. However, I'm informed that you had a very good day at the last races, when, I believe, the Greens only won once in the whole half-day. I would guess that you had a good friend place the odd, illicit wager on the opposition.'

Euprepes gave a thin smile. 'A man in my position would be foolish not to take advantage of the information that I possess.'

'I quite agree; that would be stretching loyalty too far.'

'Indeed – although, obviously, there is no questioning my loyalty to the Green faction.'

'Obviously.'

'What's your motivation for doing this?'

'I'm a lifelong loyal Green, so what does it matter?'

Euprepes conceded the point with a nod and a wave of his hand. 'Which race?'

'Either the second-to-last or the last in the first race-day after the calends of March.'

'So if I was to give our charioteers orders to let the Reds win how can you guarantee that the Whites and the Blues will also do the same? Have you spoken to their faction masters too?'

'Now that would be letting a few too many into our little circle, I would say. If there were to be numerous people betting on a Red one-two-three in the one race that it actually happens the bookmakers might get a little suspicious.'

Euprepes inclined his head in appreciation of the fact.

'The Whites I can deal with; it's the Blues that are still a problem, but I'm sure that with your help we can guarantee that all three teams will fail to finish.'

'Have my three teams bring them down?'

'Too risky; one might get through and, also, it would look a little strange if the Greens spent the entire race having a go at the Blues whilst the Reds just storm ahead.'

Euprepes considered this for a few moments. 'You're right; we'll just do one.'

'And the other two?'

'A malfunction and a hail of curses?' the faction master suggested.

'Perfect.' Magnus stood and proffered his forearm. 'I knew that a man of your experience would have the answers.'

'So it'll be just you and me who know about this?'

'No, Servius my second knows, as well as a very helpful centurion in one of the Urban Cohorts and also a couple of others who will be betting in the senators' enclosure.'

'So they won't be making our bookmakers suspicious.'

'Exactly; if we spread small bets over quite a few of them we'll clean up without anyone being any the wiser.'

'Thank you for coming to me with this, my friend; let me as a show of gratitude give you a tip for the races the day after tomorrow.'

'A Green one-two in the second race?'

Euprepes' eyes opened wide in surprise; he laughed and slapped Magnus on the shoulder. 'I can see you are very well informed; however, you're not as well informed as I am. I'll give the orders for our first and second teams to cross the line in reverse order so it will be a Green one-two, second team first, first team second.'

'Euprepes, you are a very kind and understanding man.'

'As are you, Magnus.'

Magnus waited on the steps of the Temple of Mars, in Augustus' statue-lined forum, watching the arrival of twelve patrician youths singing and waving long swords in unison in a slow, rhythmic dance. Watched by a solemn crowd, they moved forward with regular leaps in time to the slow beat of the almost unintelligible song. Clad in ancient embroidered tunics of many colours and plain, oblong breastplates under short red cloaks and spiked, tight-fitting leather headdresses, the leaping, armed priesthood of the Salii paraded their sacred bronze shields around the city in celebration of the god of war's birthday. Eleven of the shields, shaped as if two round hoplons had been fused together one on top of the other, were replicas of the twelfth, the original shield said to have fallen from the heavens back in the time of King Numa, Romulus' successor.

'They say that whoever is in possession of the original shield will dominate all the peoples of earth.'

Magnus turned, surprised by the voice so close behind him; he saw Pallas.

'Which is why they made eleven copies; a potential thief wouldn't know which one to steal.'

Magnus tutted. 'In which case, I'd steal all twelve.'

'Yes, I don't think the ancients really thought that one

through. However, my friend, my mistress has thought your request through and is willing to deliver your tip in today's racing to her nephew.'

Magnus grinned in relief. 'That is most considerate of her, Pallas.'

Magnus and his Crossroads Brethren joined in with the rest of the Greens in their corner of the Circus Maximus, screaming themselves hoarse, as the Green second team followed by the Green first team began their last lap with an unassailable lead. Way behind them their nearest rivals, a Red and a Blue, cracked their four-lash whips over the withers of their teams in a vain attempt to squeeze a little more speed from them. Although there was only a prize for the winner, both trailing drivers were well aware that many of their faction's supporters would have the minimum bet of one of their colour coming in the first three at odds of evens or less; neither wanted to upset their supporters by appearing not to be trying.

The two leading Greens, however, did not have that worry; they cut through the dust of the track at a speed that would guarantee a first and second place but would not blow the horses. As their hortatores guided them around the wreckage of their third team, Magnus, for the first time ever, found himself concerned for a horse; he hoped that Spendusa would be cut from the wreck without too much harm done. The ruse had worked very successfully – too successfully as far as the mares were concerned. Two teams of stallions from the White Faction directly behind them in the pre-race procession had bolted in their urgency to get to the mares. The two teams in the starting boxes to either side had smashed their chariots as they reared and bucked in the narrow confines, maddened by nature's compulsive scent oozing in from so close. As the boxes slammed open with high-torsion violence the two teams of Green geldings leapt forward, oblivious to the urgent need to spread seed. The remaining five teams of stallions, however, were not so relaxed; their urge to breed was evident to all in their behaviour and appearance throughout the race until, in a rare breakout of cross-faction harmony, a Red and a Blue charioteer had combined to bring the Green mares crashing down, albeit far too late.

Magnus gave a nervous glance over at the imperial box on the Palatine side of the circus; he could just make out the distant figure of Antonia and he prayed that she had passed on the tip that Pallas had given her, as she had promised she would, to Ahenobarbus. His gaze wandered up to the top of the enclosure; somewhere up there was Ignatius. Magnus smiled inwardly as he cheered his faction on, feeling the thrill of vengeance soon to be had on the man who had publicly cheated him.

The Greens worked themselves up into a frenzy as their geldings crossed the line, which was equalled by the sense of outrage felt by the other three factions at the use of such a ruse.

'Looks like the Reds ain't too happy with us, lads,' Magnus commented as a surge from the Red area, adjacent to the Greens on the Aventine side of the circus, headed towards them. 'That's just as I'd hoped.' Within moments fighting had broken out and blood had been spilt. Magnus looked at his brothers and fellow Greens around him and shouted: 'Let's be having them, lads!' All around, Green faction supporters were having the same idea and a tide of anger began to push towards the Reds.

With Marius and Sextus to one side, Tigran and Cassandros to the other and supported by many more of the South Quirinal Brotherhood, Magnus barged his way through streams of spectators fleeing the violence, knocking men aside in his eagerness to close with the Reds. Bunching his fists he flew at the first person he saw sporting Red colours. Slamming his right into the man's midriff, Magnus knocked the air out of him, doubling him over; he brought his knee sharply up to crunch into the fast-descending face, crushing the Red's nose in a splatter of crimson. Next to him, Sextus, with a straight right jab of his ham-like fist, belted a Red back; blood arced through the air from a shattered mouth as Cassandros caught a knife-wielding hand by the wrist and forced the arm down across his knee, snapping it with such force that a shard of white bone ripped open the skin to the ear-splitting howl of agony. Screams of pain, yells of anger and grunts of exertion replaced the roars of encouragement, shouts of victory and groans of disappointment as the two factions ripped into each other with a venom born of years of mutual loathing and rivalry. Magnus worked his fists with the mechanical precision learnt during his time as a boxer, blocking and dealing blows with rapid jerks and unfailing accuracy, as Marius wrapped the stump of his left arm around a neck and pulled the head forward, bringing his own down abruptly to crack into the face with a sickening, dull crunch.

Above the din came the call of a horn answered by another not far off.

'That's the Cohorts arriving, lads, best be going before they try and introduce us to their iron.' With a well-aimed kick at the genitals of a young man trying to get away he broke off from the fight, turned and sprinted towards the nearest exit that did not contain onrushing units of the Urban Cohorts; his brethren followed.

'I do love a ruck with the Reds – more than anything, Magnus,' Marius puffed as they barrelled down the steps.

'That weren't just a ruck, Brother; that was the means to get a couple of bridges closed.'

'I imagine that you were right in the thick of that,' Gaius Vespasius Pollo boomed, waddling down the steps holding a heavy-looking purse and a scroll.

Magnus took his place with his brothers ready to beat a way home through the crowds for his patron. 'Indeed, but it was more business than pleasure, sir, and very successful it was too; the Reds will be seething with resentment for a good few days. I'm not looking forward to seeing their behaviour on the next race-day if they haven't calmed down by then; it's only four days away. How was your business?'

'Equally successful, I'm pleased to report. I got twenty to one for a Green one-two in the order you told me. This purse contains two hundred in gold and this is Ignatius' promissory note for a further two hundred. Did you profit as well?'

'Very much so; I've sent a couple of the lads back with our winnings.'

'I'm told by an acquaintance that Ahenobarbus was equally successful in the same race.'

'That's gratifying to hear, Senator.'

'Well, yes and no, Magnus. The Lady Antonia sent me a note just before she left the circus: Ahenobarbus is very enthusiastic about the information as he feels that it's impossible for someone of his family to be too rich.'

'A noble sentiment.'

'I couldn't agree more. However, there's one small snag.'

'Which is?'

'Which is that before he lays out such a huge amount on a wager he wants to meet the person who provides the information; he wants to find out just how he intends to fix a Red one-two-three, seeing as no one has ever managed it previously.'

'Ah!' Magnus' face fell.

'Ah, indeed. Antonia said in the note that he expects that person at his house tomorrow morning as soon as he's finished greeting his clients. Obviously there'll be no mention of my name.'

'Obviously.'

Magnus waited in a thin drizzle outside an old and elegant marble-clad house on the east of the Palatine next to the Temple of Apollo. Despite its age the house was well maintained, reflecting the wealth of Gnaeus Domitius Ahenobarbus whose family had first held the consulship over two hundred years before.

With the rain soaking into his toga, Magnus watched the stream of clients come down the half-dozen steps from the front door in reverse order of precedence, calculating that there were at least five hundred – the sign of a very influential man in possession of a very large atrium.

As the last of the clients, a couple of junior senators, came down the steps the door closed behind them. Magnus crossed the street and knocked.

A viewing slot immediately pulled back to reveal two questioning eyes. 'Your business, master?'

'Marcus Salvius Magnus, come at the request of the Senior Consul, Gnaeus Domitius Ahenobarbus.'

The door opened and Magnus walked in, through the vestibule and into an atrium that could easily hold five hundred people.

'Wait here, master,' the doorkeeper requested, 'whilst I inform the steward of your arrival.' He whispered an order to a waiting slave of inferior rank and dress before returning to his post as the messenger walked quickly off.

Magnus studied his surroundings: everything spoke of immense and long-held wealth. Engraved silver candelabras, the height of a man, with eagles' feet of gold; golden bowls on low marble tables polished to reflect the high, brightly painted ceiling. The statue in the *impluvium* was a bronze of Neptune spurting water from his mouth and lifting his trident in triumph. Magnus smiled to himself as he thought of Ignatius seated next to a statue of the same god in the Circus Maximus, the god that was evidently the guardian deity of the Domitii.

'Very auspicious,' he muttered, clenching his thumb in his hand to ward off the evil eye that might be drawn to him by his assumption of a good omen.

'The master will see you now,' a voice from the far end of the atrium informed him. 'Please follow me, sir.'

Magnus did as he was bid and followed the steward through the atrium and to the door of the tablinum.

A gruff 'enter' greeted the steward's knock and he swung open the black and yellow lacquered door soundlessly. Magnus stepped in and the door closed behind him.

A heavy-set, balding man with full cheeks, a small, mean mouth and a long nose that curved up towards its tip stared at Magnus with malevolent eyes. He sat behind a carved, wooden desk; behind him a window looked out on to a damp and dismal courtyard garden waiting for the first shoots of spring. 'Who are you, Marcus Salvius Magnus, that you can fix a race?'

Magnus paused before answering and then realised that he was not going to be offered a seat. 'I'm the agent for the man who has paid to fix a race.'

The eyes bored into him with unsettling intensity as Ahenobarbus slammed both his palms down on the desktop with a hollow crack; colour exploded alarmingly into his cheeks. 'I asked for the fixer to come, not his agent; how dare you disobey me!'

'We are aware of that, Consul, and I've come solely because I'm the one who made all the arrangements and am therefore in a better position to explain to you how it would work.'

Ahenobarbus' small mouth pursed into a tightly clenched moue as he considered this for a moment. 'Very well, tell me.'

Magnus set out his plan, leaving out not the slightest detail; when he had finished Ahenobarbus' mouth remained puckered but the colour in his cheeks had subsided into a less alarming shade.

'That may well work,' Ahenobarbus conceded eventually. 'What's more, if it does it won't look suspiciously like a fix; and I should know because I've tried to arrange the very same thing but failed. My aunt, the Lady Antonia, tells me that you wish me to place a bet with the bookmaker named Ignatius.'

'That is correct, Consul.'

'What amazes me is why she would get involved in something like this; she used all her charm on me to get me to consent; she must be very fond of your benefactor to show such loyalty.'

'It's not something that's occurred to me, Consul,' Magnus replied truthfully, surprised at the thought that the loyalty Antonia had shown had been to him.

'No, of course not, why would someone as lowly as you consider such things? Now tell me why I should place this bet with Ignatius?'

'If you don't we won't tell you which race it's going to be.'

Ahenobarbus laughed; it was a grating sound. 'That's no threat, little man; I could take the information and then place the wager with anyone.'

'But the other three bookmakers in the senators' enclosure have all been in there for a very long time and consequently are very wealthy; even a bet ten times that amount won't hurt them. However, Ignatius has yet to attain such riches as, up until now, he's just been a bookmaker to the masses; if you place it with him it'll ruin him completely and you can get your pleasure in chasing him for every sestertius.'

Ahenobarbus folded his arms and contemplated Magnus. 'Do you think that I derive pleasure from other people's misfortunes?'

Magnus knew that he had to reply with care. 'I've heard that … you like to win.'

There was a brittle silence in the room that was abruptly shattered by another hoarse laugh. 'By the gods below, I do; and, what's more, I like to be sure that I'm going to win. How can we be certain that this Ignatius will accept the wager?'

'His greed; he wants to be as rich as the other three bookmakers in the senators' enclosure and he wants to be so quickly. As you know, one Colour finishing first, second and third is very rare indeed; he'll think that your money is his the moment you show it to him and name your bet.'

Ahenobarbus' eyes narrowed and he compressed his lips so tightly that the skin around them went pale as the blood was forced away. 'The bastard's going to think he's taking me for a fool; no one does that.' Again the palms slammed down on the desk. 'All right, I'll do this. Tell me which race-day?'

'The one in three days' time.'

'Which race?'

'I'll be able to tell you that just after halfway through the programme. Have one of your slaves waiting at the entrance to the senators' enclosure; a man with a missing left hand will come and tell him which race.'

Magnus heaved his way towards Servius through the crowds of Red supporters flocking along one side of the tenement-lined street leading to the Aemilian Bridge. The other side of the road was lined with Whites; as always on a race-day, the Urban Cohorts' heavy presence kept the two sides apart.

'I can't imagine how people get any enjoyment from just watching the teams going to the circus,' Magnus muttered, reaching his counsellor as the final twelve Red chariots of the day came into view to Red cheers and White derision.

'It's good for us that a lot of people expect very little from life, Brother.'

'It is indeed. Where's Cassandros?'

'He'll be along any moment; he had to wait for his flexible little friend to help harness all the last twelve teams before he could slip out and report on their form.'

Magnus took a few moments to scan the crowd and then looked up behind him; he caught the eye of Tigran in a window on the second floor of a plain, rickety brick tenement overlooking the Red crowd. A few windows down from him he discerned the ox-like silhouette of Sextus; Magnus nodded his satisfaction. 'The lads are in position. Did you see Rufinus and his boys?'

'I've just left them.' Servius pointed up the street to Rufinus, who nodded at Magnus. 'He's waiting for your signal; his lads are ready and looking forward to it.'

Magnus slapped his hands together. 'So am I, Brother, so am I.'

The first of the Red chariots, driven by apprentice charioteers, drew level, raising the volume of the crowd all around them.

Marius eased his way through the throng and up to Magnus as the Red teams streamed by, roared on with increasing passion by their supporters. 'They're all ready at the other bridge.'

The last Red chariots drove by and Cassandros finally appeared.

'Well?' Magnus asked.

'Well, of the last four races the teams in the first one are going to be driven by their three best charioteers.'

'No good, Brother, the Whites will put three of their six spare teams in that one and the rest in the next; what about the third race?'

Cassandros grinned. 'If they survive the first race the same three charioteers will drive in the third, and, what's more, the teams have won two of their last eight races and been placed in another four.'

Magnus slapped him on the shoulder. 'That's our one; top charioteers and teams with form. Well done, mate, I know how hard you had to work to get that information. You can have a rest from it now.'

'No chance, Brother, he fits me like a glove.'

Magnus drew the air through his teeth, screwing up his face. 'Literally, I suppose.' Shaking his head to banish the image he turned to Marius. 'Off you go to the senators' enclosure and tell Ahenobarbus' slave: the second-to-last race of the day.'

'Right you are, Magnus.'

'Rufinus has given his men orders to let you across the bridge, just show him your stump and tell him which race. Oh, and Senator Pollo has got one of his young lads waiting there too, tell him the same thing.'

Marius disappeared off into the crowd in the direction of the Aemilian Bridge as roars from the opposite direction indicated the proximity of the final twelve White chariots of the day.

'Cassandros, get back down to the other bridge and tell the lads that we're just about to start.' As Cassandros moved off, Magnus put his arm around Servius' shoulder and guided him away. 'I think we should step this way; some of the lads may not be so accurate.'

'A wise precaution.'

The roaring from the White supporters on the far side of the street intensified as their teams drew closer; at the same time the hisses and cat-calls from the Reds increased in animosity. Here and there small scuffles broke out that were soon dealt with by the men of the Urban Cohorts. Magnus caught sight of Rufinus slapping a miscreant with the side of his sword; their eyes met; the centurion nodded and moved away towards the bridge, taking his men with him.

The White teams came into view, resplendent with tall white plumes adorning their heads and white ribbons decorating their manes and tying back their tails; high-stepping, heads tossing with jangling harnesses and flaccid-lipped snorts, the first team – four greys – came level with Tigran's window as the bays behind them reached Sextus'. Within an instant the Whites' cheers of approval had turned into howls of outrage as they, quite literally, saw red. A tongue of crimson liquid flooded through the air from Tigran's window, expanding as it descended; a second jet of red shot through Sextus' window. For a moment, time seemed to slow as both airborne streams of red paint flowed inexorably towards the leading couple of White teams; with a wet slap and splatter the greys became piebald red and grey whilst behind them the bay team's coats were spattered and their feathers dripped crimson.

The reaction was immediate; enraged that their colour should be so soiled, the Whites charged at the perceived perpetrators of the outrage with the fury of the deeply offended. The Reds responded with equal measure; still smarting from the Greens' ruse four days earlier, they were more than happy to fight anyone. With the men of the Urban Cohorts withdrawn the whole street erupted into an orgy of violence, trapping the White teams who reared and bucked in terror, ripping their traces and smashing their chariots.

'That'll do to start with,' Magnus chuckled as he and Servius hurried away along the back of the crowd before they too were trapped by the fighting. 'A conscientious centurion like Rufinus will have no choice but to close the Aemilian Bridge to everyone in order to prevent the fighting spreading across the river.'

'And it looks like it might go on for a long time,' Servius observed as Tigran and Sextus caught up with them.

'What a shame for the White teams stuck in it; they're bound to miss their races now.'

Sprinting towards the Tiber Island they soon outpaced the spreading riot. As they crossed the bridge Magnus looked back and waved at a second-floor window on the Whites' side of the road. An instant later four streams of green paint spurted out and flew across the street, splattering the Red crowd; four more followed in their wake. It was now the Reds' turn for righteous indignation; covered in the colour of their hated rivals who had cheated them so grievously a few days before they burst over the road and attacked the people who must have been responsible for the deeply offensive insult.

Magnus and his brethren ran on; they traversed the Tiber Island and reached the eastern bank of the river, speeding on towards the Circus Maximus and leaving raucous mayhem in their wake.

*

'I thought I'd come and watch it with you, gentlemen,' Euprepes said, sitting down next to Magnus and Servius as the gates of the Circus Maximus opened to admit the teams competing in the second-to-last race of the day. 'My drivers understand their orders so now comes the moment of truth.'

Magnus shifted uneasily on the stone seating as the three Red chariots appeared followed by the Blues, accompanied by cheers and jeers from the huge crowd. Suddenly his eyes opened wide in astonishment. 'Juno's bald crack! A White!'

Down on the track a single White chariot trailed in after the three Greens to gales of laughter from the supporters of the other three factions.

Magnus looked in alarm at Euprepes. 'I don't call that funny at all. I thought when they only put two chariots into the previous race it was because they only had five spare teams.'

'They must have saved the sixth for a chance in this race. That's Scorpus.'

'The fuckers! He's good.'

'It's all right, Magnus, my lads will deal with it.'

'They'd better, my friend,' Magnus said, thinking of the chances of keeping his eyes, or any other part of his anatomy, should Ahenobarbus lose his money.

The ten hortatores entered the circus whilst the starter drew numbered coloured balls from a barrel; as each team's number was called they could choose which of the twelve starting boxes to occupy.

Once all the teams were loaded, slaves pushed the double doors back against the poles, behind each one, that were inserted into highly tensioned, twisted bundle of sinews. The doors were secured with a wooden bolt placed vertically through two over-lapping iron rings – one screwed to each door; cords of twine, attached to each bolt, ran up to the roof of the boxes and then over, through eyelets, and down the back to the starter's position so that all could be pulled open simultaneously. The hortatores then took up position in a line, fifty paces in front of their teams' respective starting boxes as a slave patrolled the roof, checking each cord, making certain that all could run free.

The crowd went silent with anticipation. From within the dark confines of the starting boxes the teams neighed and snorted; the hortatores' mounts stamped and tossed as their riders struggled to control them.

The presiding praetor – the man who had sponsored the day's racing – stepped forward to the front of the senators' enclosure and held up a white napkin; it fluttered in the breeze. The crowd drew communal breath as he paused for a few moments; then, with a flick, the napkin dropped. The starter pulled on the cords, the doors burst open and, to the delirium of the crowd, the teams sprang forward. Suddenly, from the Blue end of the circus, there came jeers and whistles; Magnus scanned the chariots to see that there were only two of that colour running. Looking back at the starting boxes he saw that one remained shut; of the slave on the roof there was no sign.

'A starting-box malfunction,' Euprepes observed with a look of false concern. 'What a shame for the Blues. Still, it does happen from time to time.'

Magnus grinned. 'Especially if you can get your man on the roof.'

'Now that would be cheating; we wouldn't stoop to that.'

'Never.'

Down on the track the nine remaining teams stormed up the Aventine straight with a Blue in the lead, closely pursued by a Red with a Green outside him.

'The Blue is Lacerta,' Euprepes informed Magnus, 'I've been trying to negotiate in secret with him to come over to our faction.'

Magnus nodded dumbly. With tension constricting his throat, he remained silent as the first corner was rounded with Lacerta ten paces in front. Behind, the Green steered clear of the Red but not so clear as to make it obvious – just a hand's breadth – as both chariots took the corner too fast and skewed out into the middle of the track. Hardly able to look, Magnus watched the next two Reds, battling with Scorpus the White on the inside and the remaining Blue – a Numidian – just behind, negotiate the 180-degree turn. Spraying clouds of fine sand, the four chariots skidded around behind their sure-footed teams, the charioteers all leaning to their left to prevent their vehicles from tipping over to disaster.

They disappeared around the corner mainly obscured from Magnus' vision by the angle of the statues that adorned the length of the spina. A roar went up from the White supporters on the Palatine side of the circus gates as the final two Greens entered the curve.

Magnus strained his neck. 'Fuck! What can they see?'

Glimpses of fast-moving chariots, flashing across the gaps between the statues, tormented Magnus with their brevity.

The Whites' volume grew.

The leading teams raced down the Palatine straight and angle lessened; the gaps grew wide enough for Magnus to see that Lacerta was still in front and also to discern the cause of the Whites' excitement. 'Shit! Scorpus has moved up into second and is gaining; he could fuck this for us. What are your drivers going to do about him?'

Euprepes did not reply but stared intently down at the track, clenching his fists on his knees as the first dolphin tilted and Lacerta started the second lap with Scorpus just five paces behind him; the lead Red was a good twenty paces to his rear.

The supporters of the Blues and Whites strove to outdo each other in the intensity of cheering as the next lap proceeded in a welter of dust and speed. Magnus glanced over at the imperial box where he could make out Antonia; next to her was the brooding figure of Ahenobarbus.

The second and then the third dolphins tilted as Lacerta and Scorpus pulled away from the rest of the field in their own private battle for first place. The leading Red remained third, closely followed by the first Green with the Blue Numidian on his inside. The next two Reds were nigh on fifty paces behind and beyond them the final two Greens were out of the race, over half a length of the track behind the leaders.

Magnus' head slumped into his hands. 'I'm going to have to

get out of Rome, Servius; Ahenobarbus will tear the place apart looking for me.'

The old counsellor looked grim. 'That certainly looks to be the only option.'

Euprepes remained silent, his fists still bunched, glaring down at the track with his jaw jutted out in concentration.

The fourth dolphin tilted and the situation had worsened.

Boys from the factions, based on the spina, threw skins of water out at their racers to quench their thirsts and to wash the dust from their stinging eyes. As the Numidian snatched at a skin aimed at him half a dozen smaller shapes hurtled through the dust from behind a spina statue. They cannoned into his team, catching the inside horse down its flank and on its jaw; the beast slewed to the right, buffeting its fellows and pushing the outside horse's forelegs on to the wheel of the Green chariot next to it. The sharp edge of the iron tyre grated through skin and flesh and rasped the bone; the leg buckled and the horse collapsed to its right, crashing on to the side of the Green chariot, hauling its teammates down with it in a skidding spray of sand. With his team's momentum violently checked the Numidian's chariot arced to the right, snapping it from the central pole, hurling him, splay-limbed, into the air to somersault once before crunching down on his back with lung-emptying force. The Green chario-teer fought to control his team as they veered off to the right; the two trailing Reds swerved to avoid the wreckage, and moved past the Green.

Euprepes fists slammed down on to his knees. 'A hail of curses!'

Magnus inhaled, deeply, suddenly aware that he had been holding his breath for a very long time. 'Very good, my friend; nothing like nail-studded lead tablets to bring a horse down.'

Servius nodded in appreciation, playing nervously with the loose skin on his neck. 'And who's to say who threw them, the track's always littered with them.'

Magnus glanced up at the dolphins as the fifth tilted down. Lacerta pulled his body back on the reins around his waist, slowing his Blue team, taking the bend tightly and allowing

Scorpus to draw level with him as he took the longer route around the outside at considerably more speed; their supporters screamed them both on. They whipped their teams away down the Aventine straight for the sixth time, neck and neck; their hortatores both waved an arm above their heads indicating the position of the Numidian's wrecked chariot. Ahead the trailing two Green teams could just be glimpsed rounding the far turning point.

As the three Reds began their sixth lap, Magnus felt the bile rise in his throat and sweat trickling down his cheeks; he glanced over at Ahenobarbus in despair. 'They'll never catch them; our only chance is that Lacerta and Scorpus bring each other down.' He looked with venom at the trailing Green teams, now almost three-quarters of a lap behind the leaders. 'I never thought I'd say this but: fucking Greens!'

As Lacerta and Scorpus turned into the last lap the last two Green chariots were only halfway down the Aventine straight.

With another quick look at the imperial box Magnus saw that Ahenobarbus was sitting very, very still. 'That's it,' he muttered, getting to his feet, 'I'm off; I intend to be out of the city within the hour.'

Euprepes grabbed his arm and pulled him back. 'It's not over until the final dolphin dives.'

'It is for me.'

Euprepes looked Magnus in the eye. 'Trust me.'

'I was mad to.'

'You weren't; sit back down and watch.'

Magnus did so reluctantly as the trailing two Greens disappeared around the far end of the spina and the excitement of the White and Blue supporters reached a crescendo. Lacerta and Scorpus rounded the turning post with very little between them, more than fifty paces ahead of the Reds, whom Magnus had meant to be triumphant, followed by the third Green.

Now, sure of disaster, Magnus did not care that the top quarter of the Palatine straight all but was blocked from his view; he stared glumly at the first gap that afforded sight of the action, waiting for the inevitable, unable to believe that Euprepes' Green charioteers could salvage the situation from so far behind. They came through, side by side, almost cantering now, having given up hope. Lacerta and Scorpus pounded up behind them hell for leather; their hortatores screamed at the Greens and they parted to let them through as the Red teams rounded the final corner.

Slashing his whip down, Scorpus exhorted his team on, edging just ahead of Lacerta as they neared the gap.

The inside Green charioteer glanced over his shoulder; with an abrupt crack of the whip and a jerk of his right leg, he forced his horses to accelerate. As they sped forward the chariot's right wheel flew off; the crippled vehicle collapsed to one side, dragging the team out to the right and into Scorpus' path, forcing him into Lacerta. The Blue and White teams collided and ricocheted off each other into the Green chariots on either side, slowing abruptly as the terrified beasts shied. Holding his diagonal course, the inside Green forced the rearing White team back into the Blues who in turn remained penned in by the second Green. With bestial screeches – heard only by the charioteers – lost beneath the howls of outrage from the Blue and White factions, all sixteen horses collapsed to the right, fighting against each other in a flurry of equine limbs in vain attempts to stay upright.

Then a new sound rose over the circus: the sound of celebration; Red celebration. Magnus stared, dumbfounded, as first one, then two and then a third Red chariot crossed the line followed, in fourth place, by the final Green. His mouth fell open and his eyes widened; for a moment he sat motionless before springing to his feet and punching both fists in the air with a high-pitched howl of jubilation.

He felt a sharp tug on his tunic and looked down, still roaring.

'A little more discretion would perhaps be appropriate, Brother,' Servius suggested, indicating around with his eyes.

Magnus looked up; he was surrounded by a sea of silent Green supporters staring in incomprehension at the one man in their midst who derived pleasure from a Red one-two-three. Magnus lowered his arms and shrugged apologetically at the nearest Greens. 'We did come fourth.' He sank down, hyperventilating in relief and then tried but failed to suppress the urge to vomit.

Magnus and Euprepes stood under one of the great arches of the Circus Maximus looking out over the Forum Boarium at the Racing Factions packing up for the day. Echoing off the stone all around were the cries of support and howls of disappointment of the people of Rome watching the final race.

'As soon as my lads get back with all our winnings, I'll be off, my friend,' Magnus said, proffering his forearm to Euprepes. 'The South Quirinal Crossroads Brotherhood is four thousand aurii better off from all the bets we spread around. It's been a pleasure doing business with you.'

'And I'm a few hundred thousand in silver better off because of your idea, Magnus.'

'It may have been my idea, but I shall be giving the credit to someone unsuspecting.'

'You give the credit to whomever you want but the fact remains that between us we are the first people to have fixed a one-two-three without anyone noticing.'

'Us with a little help from the gods.'

'Gods? I didn't notice any gods being involved.'

'What about the wheel coming off at the last moment?'

Euprepes raised his eyebrows. 'At just the right time, you mean?'

'Yeah, if that wasn't the gods, I don't know what it was.'

'Mechanics, my friend. The charioteer had a strap around his right foot; a sharp jerk pulled a bolt from the axle and the right wheel came off at just the right time. The other chariot had one too but didn't need to use it.'

'But ...' Magnus frowned, looking puzzled for a few moments, and then his expression gradually brightened in dawning realisation. 'Oh, I see! I'm sorry I doubted you, that's brilliant, Euprepes; those last two chariots were always meant to be last.'

'Exactly. How else could we absolutely guarantee to have two chariots in front of the winners unless they were about to be lapped; and then, when an accident happens ...'

'Like a wheel falling off, for example?'

'That's a very good example, Magnus, it happens all the time. When an accident happens we can't be accused of deliberately crashing into the winners to fix the race.'

'And all bets must be honoured.'

'Indeed. And I didn't have to risk my best horses in a deliberate crash. My worst two teams had no problems being in the right position, almost a lap behind, by the end of the race.'

'You could say they made it look easy.'

Euprepes grinned and turned to go; then he paused. 'Oh, by the way, I'll overlook your mate Lucius giving you highly confidential information.'

Magnus hid his surprise. 'That's very good of you.'

'Next time you want information like that, come directly to me. Even after sparing Lucius, after what I've won today, I'm still in your debt.'

'I don't know if I've mentioned this before, Euprepes, but I consider you to be the kindest and most understanding of men.'

Senator Gaius Vespasius Pollo did not look like a man who had won a lot of money as he waddled down the steps from the senators' enclosure soon after the completion of the last race.

'Did you not get your bet on, sir?' Magnus asked as he and his brethren began the arduous job of escorting him home through the race-day crowds.

'I did, Magnus; I put down all my winnings from the Green one-two the other day on the basis that what I won today would be a sufficiently large bribe to perhaps interest Ahenobarbus in backing Sabinus in the elections. I laid Ignatius' promissory note of two hundred in gold with him and the two hundred in gold coinage I laid amongst the other three bookmakers; they were fine and I have promissory notes from them worth over ten thousand in total.'

'But Ignatius has refused to honour the bet?'

'Worse, my dear man, he disappeared. One moment he was there and then after the three Reds crossed the line he wasn't. No sign of his slaves or bodyguards, just his table was left. I would

117

guess that he took the opportunity to get out of the city very quickly. Now I have only half the amount that I planned to bribe Ahenobarbus with.'

Magnus cursed and bit his lower lip, thinking of Ignatius enjoying his wealth unnoticed in some far-off provincial town. Seething, he took his anger out on the people before him as he barged through the crowd. From the left the crush started to part and, above people's heads, Magnus could see eight fasces – axes wound in rods, the symbol of power – borne by lictors.

Magnus and his brethren stopped to give way for a party of higher status.

'Who could that be?' Gaius mused. 'No magistrate has eight lictors.'

As the walking symbols of Imperium pushed their way past, a grating voice called out: 'Stop!' From behind the last two lictors Ahenobarbus emerged and pointed at Magnus. 'Come here!'

Magnus approached the Senior Consul with trepidation.

Ahenobarbus slapped his arm around Magnus' shoulder and leant in to him in a conspiratorial manner. 'That, Magnus, was spectacular; I'm over two million denarii better off.'

'Two million?'

'Yes, two. I caught the insolent little man smirking as he took my money, taking me for a fool, so I doubled the bet and Ignatius accepted it.'

'But, Consul, I've a nasty feeling that he's left Rome.'

'Left Rome?' Ahenobarbus' mouth pursed in confusion. 'Of course not, although he did seem to be making plans to beat a pretty hasty exit as those three Reds came in. However, I had four of my lictors watching him.' He turned and signalled. His remaining four lictors came forward with a terrified Ignatius in their midst. 'He'll find it very difficult to leave Rome; in fact, he'll find it very difficult to leave my house until he's paid me what he owes. Tomorrow we're going to start auctioning his property and then if that doesn't raise enough we'll auction him at the slave market.'

Magnus gave Ignatius an appraising look. 'Might even buy him myself.'

Ignatius' eyes widened in horror.

Magnus smiled his most innocent smile. 'I expect you're wishing that you paid me my full winnings now, Ignatius?'

'You?' Ignatius blurted. 'You did this to me?'

'No, Ignatius, you did; and, of course, the Fates who contrived to have a Red one-two-three in the very race that our esteemed Senior Consul decided to bet so much on it.'

'Talking of the Fates,' Ahenobarbus said, moving Magnus away from Ignatius, 'who was the particular Fate that organised all this?'

Magnus inclined his head towards Gaius. 'My patron, Consul, Senator Gaius Vespasius Pollo.'

Gaius tried to hide the confusion and consternation he felt but failed as Ahenobarbus clasped his forearm.

'Senator Pollo, we haven't had much contact before but I can see that you are a man of rare ability.'

'I am honoured, Consul, thank you.'

'No, it is I who should be thanking you; what can I do for you?'

Gaius broke into a moist-lipped smile. 'Well, there is the small matter of the quaestor elections coming up soon.'

'Ah yes, such a wide field, so many worthy candidates; it's difficult to choose.'

'Indeed, Consul; but I feel that my nephew, Titus Flavius Sabinus, would be an admirable choice.'

'I think that you may well be right, Senator, I was thinking of backing him myself.'

'It may interest you to know that Ignatius took a bet off me for two hundred aurei in the second-to-last race.'

'Did he now? Were you lucky enough to have the foresight to bet on a Red one-two-three?'

'Like you, I was divinely inspired. I only won a trifling amount, two hundred and fifty thousand denarii, but perhaps, as you strip Ignatius of his assets, you would care to keep it as an aid to your memory?'

Ahenobarbus clapped Gaius on the shoulder. 'The name Titus Flavius Sabinus will be firmly fixed in my mind; in fact, I'll practise saying it every time the subject of the quaestor elections comes up. Good day, Senator.' With a brief nod to Magnus he rejoined his lictors.

Gaius looked at Magnus with delight. 'Promissory notes for a quarter of a million denarii that I can use as a bribe for supporting Vespasian in next year's quaestor elections and the Senior Consul supporting Sabinus in this year's; that should do it.'

Magnus pictured his own considerable winnings; his eyes narrowed in cold satisfaction and a grim smile creased his lips as he watched Ignatius, shoulders slumped, disappear into the crowd at the mercy of Ahenobarbus. 'Yes indeed, Senator; that should do it very nicely.'

THE DREAMS OF MORPHEUS

This story fits in the gap between the prologue of *False God of Rome* and Chapter One of the same book; eighteen months after the first and the month before the latter. It concerns two perennial issues: corrupt politicians and drugs.

Magnus' difficulties revolve around the magistrate in charge of the grain dole in his area defrauding the residents of South Quirinal with short measures of grain. Meanwhile he has done a favour for Senator Pollo – who, in turn, was operating for the Lady Antonia – and stolen the opium that had been a gift from the Parthian embassy, alluded to in the prologue of *False God of Rome*, to Herod Agrippa in gratitude for brokering their mission. It is set to the background of the Festival of the October Horse.

I wrote this a couple of years after *False God of Rome* and had a lot of fun filling in that novel's backstory by getting Magnus, Vespasian and Sabinus into the positions that we find them in Chapter One. I especially enjoyed fleshing out the lives of Magnus and his brethren with those two intrinsic parts of Roman life: the grain dole and the October Horse; as well as getting to know about the weights and measures of ancient Rome.

Opium was not unknown in the Roman Empire but was used for mainly medicinal purposes. It was, however, smoked further afield for recreation and it is likely that the 'Hot Knives' method that I describe was the way of choice; it is, therefore, not beyond reason that this made its way into the empire.

OSTIA AND ROME, OCTOBER AD 34

WITH THE SUDDEN, harsh rasp of flint striking iron, a cascade of sparks penetrated the thick gloom, falling, like a shooting-star shower in minature, into a tinderbox. A quick series of soft exhalations to encourage the dry shreds of cloth and fine woodchippings to start smouldering were successful and soon a tiny flame illumined the scarred, ex-boxer's face of Marcus Salvius Magnus.

One of his two companions, an ox-like man whose shaven head was sheened in sweat, reflecting the tinder's weak glow, handed Magnus a small earthenware lamp.

Magnus held the oil-soaked wick to his flame and in an instant the lamp flickered alight but its radiance failed to reach the walls or the ceiling of the cavernous chamber filled with dark piles of imported goods, other than the corner in which they were standing. Exotic smells of eastern origin pervaded the warehouse's dry, warm atmosphere. 'Thanks, Sextus.'

Magnus listened for a few moments to the constant drone of shouts, laughter, orders, thumping and grinding that came from the harbour of the port of Ostia, just the other side of the building's iron-reinforced wooden double-doors. Satisfied that their presence was undetected, he kept his voice low as he touched his flame to both of his companions' lamps. 'All right, lads, keep the lamps away from the main doors so the guards outside don't see a flicker; keep very quiet and let's find what we came for as quickly as possible. Cassandros, you take the left. I'll do the centre and, Sextus, you search the right-hand side.'

As he stood facing Magnus, Sextus looked at his hands and attempted to work out which part of the warehouse he should be heading to; his forehead creased into a concentrated frown.

'Over there, Sextus,' Magnus hissed, pointing his lamp help-fully to his right as Cassandros moved off.

Sextus looked quizzically at his left hand and shook his head, clearly bewildered. 'Right you are, Magnus.'

'And don't forget that the things we're looking for should be wrapped in sackcloth and are thin, resinous-smelling tablets no more than a foot long and half that wide.'

'Look for tablets in sackcloth; right you are, Magnus,' Sextus rumbled, inwardly digesting his orders as he lumbered off into the gloom, his lamp throwing a Titanesque, flickering shadow of his bulk over the bare brick wall.

'Keep your voice down.' Magnus shook his head, wondering if his subordinate was up to the task, and decided that if the search was unsuccessful, Sextus' area would be subjected to a rigorous second sweep. However, what Sextus lacked in brains was amply made up for in strength and loyalty, which made him a valuable member of the South Quirinal Crossroads Brotherhood of which Magnus was the patronus – the leader.

Magnus began searching through sacks, relying more on his sense of smell than the lamp as the warehouse was evidently the property of a merchant who specialised in the import of Eastern spices, dried fruit, honey and, of course, the objective of their break-in. As he opened yet another sack, this one containing sweet-scented cinnamon bark, Magnus cursed the debt of honour that he owed to his patron, the senator Gaius Vespasius Pollo, which had obliged him to come down to the port of Ostia, the ravenous mouth of Rome. Through that mouth passed every commodity that could be bought anywhere in the world, be it silk from a land so distant that no one was certain of its name, or vividly coloured birds that could talk and seemed to live for ever, or that which Magnus now sought: the resin of an Eastern flower that could unlock the realm of Morpheus.

Just why Senator Pollo wanted this substance that was only used in medicine – and then solely by the few who could afford the exorbitant expense – and exactly why he preferred to have Magnus steal it rather than purchase it on the open market, Magnus neither knew nor cared. What mattered to him was to find it, then climb back up the rope that dangled from a hole in the corner of the ceiling to leave the vicinity as soon as possible before they attracted the attention of the guards outside or of the Ostia Vigiles. Like their counterparts in Rome, the ex-slaves who made up the Vigiles were not known for their kindness or courtesy to thieves.

Magnus rummaged through another sack, this one containing large nuts of a sort that he was unfamiliar with. He was beginning to wonder if the senator's information was correct and the resin really was in this warehouse.

'I've found the right sack, I think,' Cassandros hissed from his side of the building. 'It certainly smells right.'

Magnus made his way over as quickly as the gloom allowed, to find Cassandros examining a collection of two dozen or so dark resinous tablets; a smile cracked his full Greek-style beard which half concealed a vicious scar on his left cheek. He held out the prize as Magnus approached. 'I reckon this must be it, Brother.'

Magnus took the proffered bundle, smelt it and then pinched one of the tablets: it was hard and yet had some give in it. 'I believe you're right, Brother.'

'Are you going to try a bit to make sure?'

'Bollocks I am; I ain't ill so I ain't about to take any medicine.'

'I heard it was good fun, especially if you're enjoying a firm hard body at the same time.'

Magnus grunted as he wrapped the tablets back in the sack-cloth. 'And I heard that it just took your mind off things whilst a doctor sawed your leg off. Anyway, not being Greek, I prefer my bodies soft and giving and I just happen to have one waiting for me back at our crossroads tavern. So, brothers, let's get out of here as I'm keen to test just how soft and giving that body is.'

Magnus' breath came in sharp gasps as he hauled himself up the last few feet of rope to scramble through the hole in the ceiling, into the attic; he felt the strong right hand of the brother waiting there clasp his wrist. 'Thanks, Marius.' He looked through the opening they had knocked in the wall and on into the gloom of the neighbouring attic. 'Any sound from back there?'

'Nothing to worry about, Magnus.' Marius wiped the sweat from his brow with his left forearm; the stump at its end was bound with leather. 'I went back and listened at the side door and whilst I was there it was checked – Vigiles, I assume – but as it was locked they moved on.'

Magnus felt the key hanging from his belt. 'Servius did well to get the copy made.' Magnus knew that was an understatement; exactly how Servius, his counsellor and second-in-command of the Brotherhood, had got a copy of the only key to the side door of the end warehouse in this terrace he did not know, but acquisition and information were his areas of expertise, honed by over forty years of life in Rome's underworld. What Magnus did know was that it had not been cheap; however, Senator Pollo had financed the deal without seeming to care about the price, such was his desire for success and secrecy in this venture.

As Marius hauled Cassandros out of the hole, Magnus crawled into the next attic, holding the lamp up. Ahead, through the beams supporting the terracotta roof tiles, was another wall with a gap punched through it; a couple of rats scurried in the gloom. He looked back. 'Hurry up, Sextus.'

'Give us a hand, Marius,' Sextus quipped as he struggled to squeeze his huge frame through the hole.

'Very funny, Brother. It's still another couple of months to the Saturnalia and yet you're already practising your joke.'

Sextus rumbled a deep laugh as he grabbed Marius' hand and pulled himself clear of the hole.

'Keep it down, lads,' Magnus hissed. 'Pull up the sack and then replace the floor. The senator was very particular about no one noticing there has been a break-in until the theft is discovered.'

Magnus took the sack, unfastened it from the end of the rope and gave it to Sextus, pointing to the heavy tool they had used to dislodge the bricks. 'Bring the sledgehammer as well, Sextus.'

Marius and Cassandros replaced the two wooden boards that ran between the substantial ceiling beams, leaving them unnailed for fear of making unnecessary noise.

Satisfied that the boards had been relaid and their temporary removal would go unnoticed from the warehouse below,

Magnus moved on. Keeping low, he scuttled across the second attic and through the wall, then passed across a third attic to the hole in the floor at the far corner through which they had accessed the space beneath the roof. The head of the military-issue scaling ladder, used for their ascent, rested against the wall just below floor level.

'Down you go, Brother,' he whispered as Sextus joined him, sack and sledgehammer grasped in one massive hand.

With surprising agility, Sextus descended into the dark. Magnus sent the other two brothers down before placing the two loose floorboards on their sides at the edge of the hole. Feeling for the ladder with his foot, he descended a few rungs until his head was just below the level of the floor. He pulled the two floorboards over and shifted them until one fell neatly into place with the other on top of it. Pulling the second board across the remaining gap, he descended another rung, then reached up and, with his fingertips, adjusted the lie of the board until it clicked snugly into the hole.

'Bring the ladder, brothers,' Magnus ordered as he hit the ground. Padding over to the door, he pulled the key from his belt and slipped it into the lock, turning it with a metallic clunk that resounded off the walls with increasing volume but then was drowned by the door's squeak as it swung open a fraction. Magnus grimaced, then peered out towards the harbour just twenty paces away to his right. Even though it was the sixth hour of the night the dockside still teamed with people, silhouetted in the light of hundreds of blazing torches as they unloaded scores of merchant ships that bobbed placidly at wooden jetties. Day and night had no meaning in Ostia. Rome's appetite was insatiable and so, to prevent her from crying out with hunger, the business of landing her sustenance never paused, not even for a moment. He stuck his head round the door and looked left, up the street away from the harbour; no one was too close. Opposite was another door in a brick wall; the mirror image end of another terrace of warehouses. After a further quick glance right, he threw the door wide open. 'Quick, lads, but don't run, it'll draw attention to us.' He stood back so that his brothers could file through and then stepped out into the street, closing and locking the door behind him.

Walking swiftly, Magnus followed his companions left and then right into the street running behind the warehouses. Parallel with the harbour, it was lit only by the dim light oozing from open-fronted taverns and peopled by shadows. Drunken cries and raucous singing echoed up the high walls and the aroma of grilled meat mingled with those of sweat, urine and rotting refuse. Halfway to its end Magnus paused; a group of eight men in silhouette had turned into the street and were marching in two columns up the raised pavement towards him. 'Shit! We can't turn round. It would be too obvious. We brazen it out if we're stopped, all right, lads?'

The brothers mumbled their agreement and followed their leader towards the representatives of the only real law enforcement in Ostia.

Magnus came to a set of three stones set in the road, placed there so that pedestrians could cross to the other side without soiling their feet, and positioned so that carts could still pass between them. 'Marius and Cassandros, drop the ladder and stay on this side. Sextus, follow me.' He crossed the street with Sextus carrying the sack as the Vigiles' optio noticed the ladder discarded by Marius and Cassandros. 'Don't look back, Sextus.' Magnus increased his pace as he heard the optio order his brothers across the street to halt and explain just why they had abandoned a perfectly good military scaling ladder at the sight of him and his men.

Magnus barged through a group of carousing sailors who thought better of taking exception to his manners at the sight of Sextus bearing down on them with a sledgehammer in his hand.

Then there came the sudden shout that he was dreading: 'Halt!'

Magnus walked even faster.

'You! Big man with the sack and your mate, halt!'

Magnus glanced round to see four of the Vigiles break into a run, heading towards him across the stepping stones, pulling their heavy cudgels from their belts whilst their comrades chased after Cassandros and Marius, who had used the distraction to hare off in the opposite direction. 'Run!' He sprinted away with Sextus in train, barrelling down the pavement regardless of other users who, in the main, ended up sprawled in the filth on the road.

Racing down the street, Magnus felt his chest tighten with every urgent pace and became horribly aware of his forty-four years. Very few of his brothers were under forty, most having served their twenty-five years under the Eagles or, as in Marius' case, in the navy. He threw another look over his shoulder and saw that the much younger Vigiles were gaining. 'We'll have to turn and fight them, Sextus.' He looked up and saw the end of the street. 'You go left and then turn straight back at them; I'll go right.'

Sextus nodded, frowning, looking at the sack in one hand and the sledgehammer in the other as he pounded along.

'That way,' Magnus shouted, pointing to the left. He hurtled right, round the corner, then immediately turned and, putting his shoulder down, ran back to it as two of the Vigiles charged round. With a crack of ribs and a stunted grunt, Magnus' shoulder rammed into one of his pursuers' chests, catapulting him back and felling him like a sacrificed beast. The other man sprinted on a few more paces before realising what had happened; he stopped and turned. But Magnus was ready for him and snatched at his right wrist as the Vigile raised his club. Holding it in an iron grasp, he forced it down and round. The Vigile's breath puffed warm on Magnus' face, wine and onion clinging to it, as the man was slowly forced down. His left hand lashed out at Magnus, cracking a tight-fisted punch into his cheekbone that caused light to flash across his eyes and his grip to loosen just enough for the Vigile to raise his arm a fraction. Realising that in a protracted trial of strength the younger man would get the better of him, Magnus jerked his knee up into his genitals and felt the satisfying squash of a testicle. The wind fled from his opponent as his eyes popped and his mouth opened in a silent scream; his legs buckled and he collapsed to the ground, clutching his groin. Allowing himself one stout kick at the man's face as he passed, Magnus picked up his cudgel and ran on to where Sextus was grappling with his second assailant; the first lay staring sightlessly at the night sky, his mouth and nose pulverised by a huge blow from the sledgehammer.

Without pausing in his stride, Magnus slammed the heavy club over the back of Sextus' opponent's head and felt the skull crack; the man went limp in Sextus' arms.

'Time to go, Sextus, my lad,' Magnus shouted as he picked up the sack and pelted towards the crowded port.

'Magnus!' Gaius Vespasius Pollo boomed, looking up from the breakfast he was obviously enjoying, next to the log fire crackling in the hearth of his atrium. He did not rise but indicated with a chubby, beringed hand that Magnus should take the chair opposite. 'You were successful, I trust?' He placed half a hard-boiled egg into his mouth and chewed vigorously, causing his jowls and chins to wobble.

Magnus handed his cloak to the young, blond doorkeeper and crossed the dimly lit atrium; the first signs of dawn could be seen in the courtyard garden through the window. 'We were, Senator.' He sat, accepting a cup of warm, watered wine from another very attractive Germanic-looking slave boy.

'You've not brought it with you, have you?'

'Of course not, sir.' Magnus took a slug of his drink. 'I left it at the Brotherhood tavern. I stopped there before coming over to you for a bit of, er … refreshment, if you take my meaning?'

Gaius chuckled and cast an admiring eye at the boy waiting on them. 'I'm sure I do. How many tablets were there?'

'A couple of dozen.'

'More than expected; I assume you've kept a little something for yourself as commission?'

'Just the one tablet.'

'A fair price; but don't let it be known.' Gaius pulled a ringlet of carefully tonged dyed-black hair from in front of his eyes and fixed Magnus with a hard stare. 'Were you seen?'

Magnus placed his cup down on the table between them. 'Yes and no. We were challenged but only after we left the warehouse; all the lads got away – just. One lad was a bit too enthusiastic with a hammer and brought about an early demise to one of the Vigiles; but that might turn out to be a good thing.'

'How so?'

'Well, we left no sign of a break-in so the prefect of Ostia will only be concerned with who sent one of his ex-slave thugs to meet the Ferryman.'

'Yes, but it would have been better to have had no fuss at all.'

'Granted, but when the theft is noticed, if the owner reports it to the authorities, they'll be too busy looking for a Vigiles' murderer to care that much.'

Gaius raised a finely plucked eyebrow and slipped an olive between his moist lips. 'I very much doubt that; not when they realise who the owner is.'

Magnus felt his insides lurch. 'You said that it was no one important.'

'Well, he's not – in terms of Roman politics, that is. However, he does have some influential friends in the imperial household.'

'Who is he?'

'The Jewish Prince, Herod Agrippa.'

'I heard that he'd fled Rome because of debt.'

'He came back just recently; he managed to organise a very successful embassy of Parthian dissidents, which got him back in favour but not out of debt. The Emperor Tiberius rewarded him by making him tutor to his grandson, Tiberius Gemellus. So, in case the prefect takes a highly placed complaint of theft seriously and on the outside chance that you or one of your lads was recognised, I suggest you move the tablets out of your place to somewhere less obvious.'

Magnus downed the rest of his cup and held it out to be replenished. 'Can't you just dispose of them?'

'I'm afraid not, Magnus; not yet. But I'll send a message soon, telling you what I want done with them.' Gaius heaved his massive bulk up from the chair, his tunic straining to contain copious folds of flesh, and stood whilst a third slave boy – equally as pretty – began draping his toga about him. 'Now, I must greet the rest of my clients and then I've an appointment to see the Lady Antonia before I go to the Senate.'

'She's wanting a favour?'

'No, I need her to return one. I'm hoping that as sister-in-law to Tiberius she can persuade him to grant my nephew, Vespasian, a travel permit to Egypt so that he can do some business there on his way back from Cyrenaica, once he's finished his year as quaestor. As you know, senators are forbidden to enter that bounteous province without the Emperor's permission and he doesn't give that too easily.'

'You'll need to have done something very substantial for her to get that.'

Gaius smiled; his face aglow with firelight. 'I already have, thanks to you, Magnus. What you stole was the very generous commission that Herod Agrippa received from the dissident Parthians for brokering their embassy. Antonia is going to sell it to recoup some of the considerable debt that he still owes her. You may find she's in such a good mood that you'll get a summons.'

'Marcus Salvius Magnus, we have come to you because we hope that as the leader of the Crossroads Brotherhood in our quarter you can right the wrong that is being perpetrated on us.' The speaker, Duilius, an older man in his fifties, whom Magnus knew to be conscientious with his monthly payments to the Brotherhood in return for their protection of his sandal and belt business near the Porta Collina, paused and spread his hands towards Magnus in supplication.

Magnus looked at the crowd of shopkeepers, traders, residents and businessmen before him, all from the South Quirinal. There were a lot of them, more than could fit into the room behind the tavern that he normally used for such meetings; hence they were grouped round the rough tables set outside at the apex of the acute junction between the Alta Semita and the Vicus Longus, both busy with morning trade. Such a large deputation could only mean one thing: it was a serious problem and he would have to solve it for them or lose considerable face, maybe even his position – or perhaps his life.

Magnus felt Servius shift his weight on the bench next to him.

'Do you speak for everyone, Duilius?' his counsellor asked, rubbing the loose wrinkled skin at his throat with claw-like hands.

'I do.'

'Then shall we three retire inside and discuss the matter in more comfort?'

'No, Servius; all should witness the conversation.'

Magnus glanced at his counsellor; his rheumy eyes confirmed that this was indeed a serious problem that could not be ignored. He looked back at the delegation, steepled his hands and, leaning forward on the table, pressed them to his lips. 'Speak, Duilius.'

'For the last month or so we have been in receipt of short measures from the grain dole. We are entitled every market interval to one modius of grain per citizen, which normally fills a tub this big.' He illustrated with his hands a tub about one foot across and not quite as tall. 'However, recently the dole has often been one sextius short; not all the time, you understand, but a significant amount since we noticed and started checking.'

Magnus could see where this was going and he did not like it: he was headed for a clash with someone from the senatorial class. 'You're claiming that the aedile for this area is cheating you out of a sixteenth of your dole?'

'Yes, Magnus. We think that he's had some of the modius measures made smaller because the public slaves who distribute the grain still fill them all to the brim – and yet sometimes the measure is short. We know from acquaintances working in the granaries here in Rome and at Ostia that the stocks are dwindling and, until the first Egyptian grain fleet arrives next year, we are heading for a shortage, which always means higher prices. We believe that Publius Aufidius Brutus is skimming off the top of our dole and hording it for himself so as to sell it when the price inflates next year.'

Magnus nodded, able to see the logic in the aedile's scheme; if it were true that Rome was heading for a shortage there would be fortunes to make in speculation.

'Is this happening in other areas?' Servius asked.

'Does it matter? The fact is that it's happening here, to us.'

Magnus turned to look at Servius. 'Have any of the lads mentioned this to you?'

'No, but if Brutus is clever, as I'm sure he is, then he wouldn't try to cheat anyone that he knew was a member of the Brotherhood; he'll make sure that the altered measures are only used at certain distribution points.'

Magnus grunted. 'Well, he ain't that clever; if he pisses off our people he pisses us off too.'

'I imagine he will try to reach some sort of arrangement with us.'

Duilius cleared his throat. 'That's what we thought he would do, try to buy you off with a small percentage of the huge profit that he's liable to make, then you and he will leave us to suffer.'

Magnus' eyes hardened as he stood, almost pushing the bench over and Servius with it. 'We take your money for two reasons, Duilius.' He pointed to the altar of the Crossroads' lares embedded in the tavern's walls; a flame burnt there constantly, tended by one of the brothers in turn. 'First, to help service our sacred duty to the deities of this area, for the good of the whole community. Second, to protect you from outside interference. If you are being ripped off, then we will see justice done and not be bought off by the perpetrator, whomever it is – even if he comes from a family that has held the consulship. Do you understand me, Duilius? If I ever hear you questioning my honesty again things may not go so well for a few of your slaves and then how would your business be, if you take my meaning?'

Duilius held his hands up. 'Forgive me, patronus; I didn't mean to imply that you would take the bribe. I just meant that I thought you would be offered one.'

Magnus sat back down. 'Very well.' He looked round the crowd. 'Is there anything else?' There were negative murmurs and shakes of heads. 'I'll work out a way of having a private chat with Publius Aufidius Brutus and try to impress upon him the need to desist in this matter.'

'We want more than that, Magnus,' Duilius said. 'We want him to return the grain he has already cheated us out of, or the cash equivalent.'

Knowing the greed of the senatorial classes in Rome – in fact, of all the classes in the city – Magnus felt that would be nigh on impossible; but to say so before he had even tried would be construed as weak. 'Very well. I suggest you all go about your business now as you must have much to do.' Magnus ran his fingers through his greying hair as the crowd dispersed and then turned to Servius. 'Have Terentius come and see me at the eighth hour.'

Servius frowned. 'What use is a whore-boy master in a business like this?'

'It's about the other current issue.' Magnus got to his feet, shaking his head. 'How do I put pressure on an aedile if he ignores my warning, as I suspect he will?'

'Senator Pollo owes us for last night; perhaps he can exert some influence?' Servius suggested, following Magnus back into the tavern.

'I doubt it.' Magnus headed for his table in the corner with a good view of the door; the few early-morning drinkers made way for him and Servius. Cassandros stepped out from behind the amphorae-lined bar to place a full jug of wine and two cups on the table as they sat. 'Senators don't like to squeeze one another unless it's at least partly for their own personal gain. Of course I'll ask the senator but I guarantee he'll say that he has no influence over Brutus, which means that he has nothing to gain by it.'

Servius pushed a full cup across the table. 'Then let's find a way to make Brutus' humiliation of value to our tame senator. I believe his elder nephew, Sabinus, has managed to get himself elected as one of the aediles for next year.'

Magnus froze in the act of putting the cup to his mouth; he thought for a moment, then smiled and pointed his index finger at his counsellor. 'Now that, my old friend, is deep thinking.'

Magnus heaved his way through the crowds in Caesar's Forum with Marius and Sextus to either side of him; all three wore their plain white citizens' togas. None of them spoke as they negotiated a passage through the milling citizenry listening to a case in an open-air law court, or petitioning the Urban Prefect or one of the lesser magistrates who carried out the city's public business every day under the great equestrian statue of the former dictator that dominated his forum.

As they approached the magistrates presiding beneath the Divine Julius, Magnus glimpsed a young man in a senatorial toga, seated at a desk; his almost black hair was oiled and combed forward from the back of his head as if covering premature balding. Magnus stopped to look more closely. 'There's our boy, lads.'

'He looks very pleased with himself,' Marius commented as Brutus stood and grinned, grasping the forearm of an easterner in a white headdress, and slapping his shoulder before taking a scroll from him.

'Business always brings a smile to *my* face, Brother.' Magnus moved forward as the Urban Prefect joined Brutus and his Eastern associate, dispensing back slaps and toothy smiles all round.

'They must be doing a lot of business to be that happy,' Sextus observed in his slow manner.

Magnus waited until the easterner had moved off and Brutus had sat down, unrolling the scroll, before walking up to him. 'Aedile?'

Brutus looked up from the scroll. 'Mmm. Oh, it's you; Magnus, isn't it?'

'You know perfectly well that's my name, aedile.'

'I don't like your tone.'

'I'm not asking you to like it; I'm asking you to listen to what I have to say.'

Brutus sighed. 'You have a right to approach your magistrate; I'm listening.'

'The people of my area believe they are being given short measures at the grain dole.'

'Do they now?' Brutus wrinkled his nose. 'And what makes them *believe* that?'

'They've checked what they receive against what they know to be the correct measurement and they want me to ask you to look into it.'

'I've heard from my sources that a nasty little specimen by the name of Duilius is stirring people up; no doubt it was he who asked you to come here. Well, you've asked me and I can assure you that they are wrong.' Brutus leant closer to Magnus. 'Perhaps, for a small consideration every month to your Brotherhood's coffers, you could reassure Duilius and his friends for me?'

'I'm afraid that won't be possible, aedile; that is exactly what my people expect to happen. And it's out of consideration for your well-being that I would ask you again to look into the matter.'

'Are you threatening me, Magnus?'

'Not at all, aedile; it's just that I wouldn't like to be responsible for your safety walking in an area where the people may have an unfounded grudge against you.'

Brutus scoffed. 'The people know their place; they would never dare lay hands on an elected magistrate.'

'So that's a refusal then?'

'There is nothing for me to refuse; the measures all conform to imperial standards and they all have the imperial stamp on them to prove that.'

Magnus held the aedile's look for a good few moments; neither blinked. 'Thank you for your time, aedile.'

Brutus sniffed and returned to reading his scroll.

'What will you do now, Magnus?' Marius asked as they negotiated a path towards the Senate House in the Forum Romanum.

'Tempt a senator into doing what we want by dangling the chance of patronage in front of him.'

The steps to the Senate House were relatively deserted compared to the bustle of Caesar's Forum behind it. Magnus glanced around at the few senators on their way either in or out of the ancient heart of government of the Roman world. The doors were open so that the Conscript Fathers could be seen at their deliberations by the populace; it was barely an eighth full. 'We'll have to wait, lads; he'll be out soon.'

'Magnus, I could no more ask that of the Urban Prefect,' Gaius confided, 'than invite him for a cosy dinner for two and some fun afterwards with my Germanic boys; it would be presumptuous.'

Magnus walked alongside his patron as Sextus and Marius cleared the way for them. 'I understand that, sir; but if it were to come to his attention that this problem is potentially the cause of serious unrest that could result in him appearing ineffective to the Emperor, then perhaps he would consent to your suggestion in the Senate to order an examination of every modius measure used in the grain dole.'

'Even so, my friend, what would there be in it for me in having Cossus Cornelius Lentulus expose Brutus, other than earning Brutus' and his family's enmity?'

'If every measure in Rome is checked and not just the Quirinal, then Brutus will have no cause to suspect that your recommendation was targeting him.'

'But I'll have made myself conspicuous for no personal gain. They're a consular family, you know.'

'If the Urban Prefect uncovers a scam that's been defrauding a section of the population from their rightful privilege, then the popularity he would gain could reflect well on the Emperor who had appointed him. I'm sure that Tiberius likes to have the people well looked after; and, since he now spends all his time on Capraea, he'll be very pleased with Lentulus for doing such a good job in his absence. That would ensure Lentulus a long tenure of his very lucrative position; he'd be in your debt. Now, I believe that Sabinus is one of the aediles elected for next year ...' Magnus let his voice trail off.

Gaius licked his already moist lips as he made the connection. 'Whose duties are allocated by the Urban Prefect. Lentulus would be particularly well disposed to my family if I had helped him to uncover such a wicked fraud on his beloved populace.'

Magnus nodded, his face composed into the most solemn and understanding of expressions. 'Indeed, Senator; the people whom he lives to serve deprived of the bread of life in such a callous manner, and thanks to your help he could right that wrong. He'll look at you with tears of gratitude welling up in his eyes.'

'I'm sure in that condition he would be willing to grant me the smallest of requests and give Sabinus the most prestigious of all the aedile posts; working with the prefect of the Grain Supply would really bring public attention to him and the whole family.'

'I think it would be the least that Lentulus could do. I believe you would find your credit with him wouldn't be exhausted for some time and that would far outweigh any enmity from a humiliated aedile, even if he does come from a consular family.'

Gaius slipped a pudgy arm round Magnus' shoulders. 'And I believe you may be right, my friend. But tell me, how will you make this issue a potential cause for unrest in order for Lentulus to take it seriously? Riots on the Quirinal might bring a heavy-handed response from the prefect and his Urban Cohorts.'

'My thoughts entirely.'

'So?'

'Well, it's occurred to me that on the Ides of October, in two days' time, an official public brawl is scheduled. It would be a shame if everything started to get out of hand as the residents of the Suburra fight the residents of the Via Sacra for possession of the severed head of the October Horse.'

'You asked to see me, Marcus Salvius Magnus.'

The soft voice just cut through the background chatter in the tavern; Magnus disengaged himself from the plump young whore sitting on his lap, looked up at his visitor and smiled. 'Yes, Terentius.' He removed the whore's hand from under his tunic, adjusted his dress and sent her on her way with a satisfying slap on her buttocks before returning his attention to his visitor. 'Sit down.'

As he sat, Terentius ran his hands down the back of his thighs to control his tunic which was unbelted, like a woman's. He crossed his legs with studied elegance and with a modest smile accepted the cup of wine that Magnus proffered. 'Thank you, Magnus.'

'You're looking good, Terentius.'

Terentius pulled back an errant lock of long, auburn hair, that had come loose from the ponytail into which it was tied, and secured it behind his ear. 'Thank you, Magnus; I try my best.'

Magnus could see that he did. Although he was now in his forties, the whore-boy master certainly looked after his appearance: the pale skin over his high cheekbones remained smooth, his chin and neck were still taut, his lips full and subtly painted and his large eyes bright and interested, despite the life that he had led as first a whore and now a master. *Very nice*, was always Magnus' immediate thought; closely followed by: *if you like that sort of thing.*

Magnus leant across the table. 'How's business?'

'It's very good.' Terentius took a sip before adding, with a raised eyebrow, 'But not good enough to justify an increase in what I pay to the Brotherhood.'

Magnus leant back, laughing, then reached across and laid a hand on Terentius' arm. 'Very good, I take your meaning, old friend. In lieu of that rise I need a favour.'

'Anything for you, Magnus.'

'Yeah, I'm sure. Well, I need something kept safe and secret for a few days.'

With a slight incline of the head, Terentius acquiesced.

'Servius has it out the back; go and find him and he'll have a couple of the lads escort you home.'

Terentius took another sip, placed his cup down and then stood. 'I'll hear from you shortly then?'

'You will.'

Terentius smiled as he turned to go.

Magnus held up a hand. 'Oh, one thing. Have you or your boys been having any trouble with short measures on the grain dole recently?'

'No, Magnus.'

'Any trouble with our local aedile?'

Terentius pouted and shook his head. 'No, Magnus. I make sure that he's very well disposed towards me; I give him free use of my establishment a couple of times a month.'

'Do you now?'

'Oh yes, it always pays to look after those who have power over you; you know that the offer's always open to you too.'

As Terentius walked away, Magnus' gaze lingered on him for just a moment too long for his own liking. He shook his head then looked around for the whore, feeling an urgent need to take her upstairs to the small room that he called home.

Thin, pale fingers of dawn poked through the window shutters as the constant clamour from the street below impinged once more on Magnus' consciousness, hauling it from the realm of dreams.

He lay in the half-light, looking up at the roughly cut ceiling beams, listening to the whore's soft breaths and running through in his mind what he needed to achieve in the next two days; the list was not long but it was tricky.

Once satisfied, he turned his attention to the business of his patron, Senator Pollo, pleased that he had helped to boost his patron's standing with the most powerful woman in Rome, the Lady Antonia.

He was acquainted with Antonia, surprisingly given the vast social gulf between them, but unsurprisingly given her enjoyment for boxing and her penchant for a private round with the after-dinner-spectacle winner once her guests had departed. But that had been ten years or more ago when he had made his living that way after completing his time first in Rome's legions, and then getting a lucky transfer to the Urban Cohorts which meant he only had to serve sixteen years and not the full twenty-five. Once he had fought his way to the position of patronus of his Brotherhood, using the substantial prize money that he had earnt in his two years of gruelling, iron-fisted bouts, he had left the profession and the lady behind. Until, that was, their paths had crossed again after his patron, Senator Pollo, and his nephews, Sabinus and Vespasian, had risen in her favour. Now she summoned him as the fancy took her and because of her status he would be a fool to refuse; he grimaced to himself at the thought of a new summons as she was not getting any younger. He wondered how and to whom she would sell the tablets, and when Senator Pollo would require him to pick them up from Terentius and ... At the thought of Terentius he turned the whore over, putting him to the back of his mind.

*

'Magnus! you get prettier by the year.'

And you get slimmer by the year, Aetius.' Magnus grasped his old comrade's forearm and felt giving flesh where there once had been taut muscle. 'Standards are really dropping in the Urban Cohorts if they allow figures like yours to parade under their banners.'

Aetius threw his bald head back and laughed, placing one hand on his ample belly. 'I haven't stood underneath a banner since they stopped making mail tunics that fitted me which, as quartermaster for the cohorts, was easy to organise.' He swept his arm round his large, well-appointed office complete with mobile braziers, clerks and an oak desk of vulgar proportions. 'When I re-enlisted for a further sixteen years I did so with a nice cosy and lucrative time in the stores in mind and none of that running up and down that the centurions seem so keen on.'

'Quite right, old friend; all that running prevents a man from cultivating a decent paunch.'

Aetius gave Magnus a playful punch to the stomach. 'Still firm; you must be doing a lot of running.'

'Horizontally, Aetius, horizontally.'

'I'm sure. But what can I do for you? I can't recall being in your debt.'

'You're not; but how would you like me to be in yours?'

'That, Magnus, would help me to sleep much easier at nights.'

Magnus pointed to his ear and indicated that Aetius should follow him outside away from eavesdroppers.

They walked out into the bright sunshine of an early autumnal day and crossed the courtyard of the Urban Cohorts' newly constructed stores warehouse near the Tiber; the previous one having burnt down eight years before with, unfortunately, Aetius' inventories and everything within. The fire had been a useful diversion for Magnus and his brothers who had business on the other side of the city and preferred to transact it without the interference of the Vigiles, whose main duty was firefighting. Convenient though it was for the Brotherhood it was a sad loss for the Urban Cohorts. However, having had plenty of warning of the blaze, in that it was Aetius himself who had set it at Magnus' request,

Magnus was very confident that not much of value had remained for the flames – apart from the precious inventories, that was.

They turned left out of the gate in order to avoid the reek of the tanneries along the riverbank; Sextus and Marius, who had been waiting outside, followed at a discreet distance.

As they entered the open space of the Forum Boarium in the shadow of the Circus Maximus, Magnus put an arm round his old comrade's shoulders. 'What's the difference between a civil modius measure and a military one?'

'Not much; both are bronze and both have the inscription acknowledging imperial regulation of weights and measures. The only difference would be that a military one has the legion, cohort and century to which it has been issued engraved upon it.'

'But if it hasn't been issued?'

'Then it wouldn't have a military engraving on it.'

'That's what I thought. I'll take a dozen.'

'A dozen? But these things are tightly regulated; they remain the property of the Emperor. They have to be signed in and out.'

'I wasn't for a moment thinking of having the Emperor's. That could get us into serious trouble; I was planning to have yours.'

'Mine?'

'Yes, why not?' Magnus' grip tightened round Aetius' shoulders. 'I imagine quite a few were sadly destroyed in that fire all those years ago; I just want a dozen of them.'

'I've only got half a dozen left.'

'They'll have to do then. How would you make them one sextius short?'

'Put a false bottom in, of course.'

'How long will that take?'

'I've got a man who could do all six in a day, no questions asked.'

'You sound confident.'

'He's done it before.'

Magnus stopped. 'When?'

'A couple of months ago.'

'Who for?'

Aetius shrugged. 'I don't know; the deal was through a series of intermediaries. I only do business face to face with a very few trusted associates like yourself. There's no way that I can find out who it was, Magnus, unless I jeopardise my anonymity and reputation for discretion.'

'You don't need to, my friend. Have the measures delivered tomorrow morning at the latest, but tell your man not to make too good a job of the false bottoms; I need them to be visible.'

'They're never exact.'

'Good.'

Aetius rubbed his thumb against his fingers. 'And what about, you know.'

Magnus slapped his back. 'Aetius, I believe that your second sixteen years are up very soon and I don't suppose they'll have you back.'

'No, I suspect you're right.'

'So you'll be looking for a safe area from which you can operate discreetly and unmolested?'

Aetius grinned, displaying yellowing teeth. 'Somewhere I can sleep easy at nights?'

'My friend, everyone in the South Quirinal sleeps easy at night.'

It was almost the sixth hour of the day by the time that Magnus, Sextus and Marius reached the baths of Agrippa; but this was a perfect time to run into, as if by accident, the sort of people Magnus needed to see. For all those in the city who followed a regular work pattern, be it trade or political, the working day ran from the first hour to the eighth or ninth. After that there was time to relax before the main meal of the day towards the end of the afternoon. Consequently, after the eighth hour, the baths filled up with a different kind of clientele from those who frequented them earlier in the day. But it was the early arrivals that Magnus wanted to mingle with: the men who did not have a regular working pattern, men who did not do physical trade or politics but, rather, men who dealt in other commodities, the same commodities that Magnus dealt in – fear and protection. Men who could afford to while away the morning in the comforts of Rome's public baths.

Having stripped and handed their clothes to one of the many slaves in the vestibule for safekeeping and received linen towels in return, Magnus led his brothers into the main hall of the baths where men exercised, relaxed, received massages, had their body hair removed and muscles massaged, or just strolled about chatting, scheming or gossiping.

'Have a wander round and keep your eyes out for any members of the Suburra or Via Sacra Brotherhoods, lads,' Magnus muttered as he looked around the throng. 'No pointing, I just want to know who's here and where they are.'

Magnus spread his towel on a leather upholstered couch and settled down to a shoulder massage from one of the many public slaves, while his brothers circulated through the high-domed hall that echoed back, with sharp clarity, the sound of hundreds of voices.

It was after too short a time of oiling, pummelling and kneading that Marius and Sextus returned.

'Well?' Magnus asked, dismissing the slave with a wave of his hand.

'We saw some of those thieving bastards from the Central Suburra,' Marius reported. 'They've just come out of the *frigidarium* and look to be on their way out. The scum from the eastern end of the Via Sacra are exercising over at the weight benches and—'

'Is Dacien with them?'

'Didn't see him. But I did see Grumio with some of his lowlife from West Suburra heading towards the *caldarium*.'

'Did you now?' Magnus got to his feet, picked up the towel and stretched his shoulders with a couple of cracks. 'Time for a sweat, I think, lads.'

Heat stung Magnus' eyes as the heavy wooden door of the caldarium closed behind him; he looked around the dim interior, lit with ambient light from one small window in the wall opposite him, and saw a small group of naked men knotted round a shaven-headed, pot-bellied man of about his own age – in his early to mid-forties. Two slaves stood to either side of the group, fanning the hot air down on to them by vigorously twirling towels above their heads. All eyes in the group turned to Magnus and his two brothers as they approached. Neither party felt threatened as, by convention, there was a truce in all public baths – mainly because the only option in which a naked man could conceal a weapon was not that comfortable.

'Grumio,' Magnus said as he sat down on a stone bench, enjoying the warmth of it on his buttocks.

'Magnus,' Grumio replied, flashing gold teeth in an unconvincing smile.

A slave approached and began fanning Magnus and his brothers; the hot air beating down on them soon caused beads of sweat to prick out all over their bodies.

Magnus put his hands on his knees and lowered his head, ignoring his opposite number from the West Suburra.

Sextus grunted with pleasure with every down beat of the towel.

Marius closed his eyes and leant his head back against the wall, playing idly with the stump at the end of his left arm.

'Word has it that you've got an issue with the aedile,' Grumio said eventually. 'I heard that you had a delegation.'

'You heard right,' Magnus replied without looking up.

'Tricky situation.'

'What's it to you?'

'Just making conversation.'

'If it's conversation that you want, then I heard that we're heading for a grain shortage.'

'Yes, I've heard that too from lads of mine in the granaries.'

'And coincidentally the Via Sacra area is having the opposite problem to the Quirinal; they've got too much grain.'

'I'd not heard that. What do you mean?'

'Dacien at the east end of the Via Sacra and the aedile for the area have been registering false names on the dole list for the past few months.'

'How do they do that? I've been trying for years.'

'Don't know; you'll have to ask Dacien, who will probably deny it. But it's a lot easier, I would assume, if you have an aedile on your side. Anyway, they have, and Dacien and the aedile are stockpiling the surplus to sell at a premium when the shortage hits in the spring before the first grain fleet arrives.'

Grumio hawked and spat. 'They'll make a fortune.'

'They will; but do you want to hear the funny part?'

'Go on.'

'If the aedile were to be caught he'd be banished at the very least and his political career would be over. However, if Dacien were to be caught he would just slip away for a year or two and wait for all the fuss to die down.'

'So Dacien has threatened to expose the aedile? Very sensible. What does he want?'

'Well, quite rightly, he wants his people to be happy, so what would make them happier than this year to win the right to hang the head of the October Horse?'

'They've got to fight us and the other Suburra Brotherhoods for that honour, and they hardly ever win because we outnumber them; how can the aedile fix that?'

Magnus got up and stretched. 'As you know, I used to be in one of the Urban Cohorts and still maintain my contacts there. One of them, and I can't say who for obvious reasons, has told me that the Via Sacra aedile has paid a substantial sum to a couple of the centurions to have their men come in on the side of the Via Sacra.'

Grumio was outraged. 'They can't do that. It's always a fair fight.'

'Of course, and they wouldn't join in if it was just a fight; but if it had escalated into a riot?'

'How are they going to do that?'

'Turn it into a riot? My contact didn't know, but I'm sure they'll have thought of something. I'd be on your guard tomorrow if I were you, Grumio; and just remember that it was me that warned you.'

'I will; but why did you?'

'Let's just say that I like to see fair play when it comes to the October Horse. It would bring bad luck to the whole city if the festival were to be meddled with.' Magnus looked down at his brothers. 'Time to cool off, lads. Let's leave these good gentlemen to contemplate what the Ides of October holds for them.' With a curt nod to Grumio, he headed for the door.

'So who told you that the cohorts were going to side with the Via Sacra?' Sextus asked as they left the baths.

Magnus grinned and slapped his large companion on his broad back. 'I could tell you had a question forming, Brother, you've been chewing your lip for the last hour and frowning more than usual. Tell him, Marius.'

'No one, Brother. Magnus made it up.'

Sextus' frown became even more furrowed. 'How do you think of such things?'

'Because I have to, Sextus. But just because I made it up doesn't mean that it won't become true, or at least partially true. Marius, go and find our old friend, Centurion Nonus Manilus Rufinus, at the cohorts' camp and tell him that I may have an interesting business proposition for him.'

'So what's in it for me?' Centurion Nonus Manilus Rufinus asked, leaning forward over the table in the private room behind the tavern that Magnus used for business. 'If I have my men form up as if they are going to charge the Suburra factions in the fight it'll cause a riot. There'll be a lot of damage and quite a few questions asked; so it has to be worth my while.'

'A noble sentiment, Rufinus.' Magnus walked over to a strongbox in the far corner and slipped a key into the lock. With a dull click the lock turned; Magnus reached in and pulled out a thin, sackcloth-wrapped parcel. 'I think you'll find that this will make it worth your while.' He placed it on the table and unwrapped it to reveal a tablet of dark resin. Taking his knife from its sheath, he cut it in half and pushed a chunk over to Rufinus.

Rufinus stared at it for a few moments. 'What is it?'

'That, my good friend, is worth more than gold.'

'Yes, but what is it?'

'The key to the realm of Morpheus. It's a resin from an eastern flower that transports you to another place. Doctors use it to dull the pain when they're operating; but only on their rich clients because it is very rare. Hardly any makes it into the empire and it's very sought after by the medical profession.'

'How much is that worth?'

'As I said: more than its weight in gold – if you know where to sell it. My guess is that the Praetorian Guard or Urban Cohorts' doctors would be very interested, or perhaps the doctors favoured by the Senate.'

Rufinus picked it up and felt the weight of it in his hand; he whistled softly. 'Magnus, my friend, as always it's a pleasure doing business with you.'

Magnus ripped the sackcloth in half and handed a bit to Rufinus to wrap his resin in. 'Let the fight build up a bit and then threaten as if to join in against the Suburra, but do not make the move. That should be enough to make them attack you and then after that it becomes self-defence.'

Rufinus stuffed his half-tablet down his tunic. 'What if I'm asked why I formed up against the Suburra?'

'You'll say that you thought the fight was escalating into a grain riot.'

'What made me think that?'

'Don't worry, my friend; the evidence will be there. You leave that to me; it'll be flying through the air.'

The Ides of October dawned bright and clear with a golden sun, rising over the eastern hills, slowly drying the dew that glistened on Rome's streets and roofs. The city bustled with an air of anticipation and very little business was attempted; instead, the main part of the citizenry made their way to the Campus Martius, outside the northern walls of the city, to celebrate the most important of the three annual equestrian festivals dedicated to Mars. It was the day when the October Horse would be chosen after a series of two-horse chariot races round a course on the Campus Martius; the right-hand horse of the winning pair would be sacrificed to the god of war and guardian of agriculture in an ancient rite to celebrate the completion of the agricultural and military-campaigning season.

Magnus and thirty of his brothers set out after completing their dawn rituals at the altar of the Crossroads' lares. Both Sextus and Cassandros carried sacks, each containing three of the modius measures that Aetius had delivered during the night. After a short walk they came to the one-storey house of Senator Pollo and joined his clients waiting outside its windowless frontage to escort their patron to the celebrations. Each man held the small bag of coins, their stakes for the day's wagers, which they had received from their patron as they greeted him at his morning *salutatio* – a formality that Magnus was excused from due to his religious obligations at the same time.

Magnus formed up his brothers at the head of the clients, ready to beat a passage for the senator and his entourage through the dense festival crowds. All along the street other parties were assembling, some larger, some smaller, depending on the status of the patron.

The heavy wooden door, the only opening to the street in the plain burnt-ochre-painted wall, opened and Gaius appeared at the top of the steps to applause from the lesser men who relied on his patronage. Raising his hand in acknowledgement, he waddled down to the pavement and made his way towards Magnus, the crowd parting for him, many of them forced to jump down into the soiled street.

Gaius dropped a weighty purse in Magnus' hand. 'May the gods grant you good fortune, my friend.'

'And may they grant the same to you, patronus.'

Gaius chuckled. 'I rather think that our good fortune is down to our own efforts.'

'Yeah, well, it don't do any harm to entreat the gods as well.'

'No, no, my friend, I quite agree; yet the rest of the city is probably entreating away and who will the gods grant good fortune to? I'll tell you: just the bookmakers and the sensible few that bet on form and fitness rather than which racing faction the chariots are in.'

'But these races aren't factional.' Magnus signalled to his brothers to move and the procession headed off down the hill.

'Of course not; none of the four colours can be seen to be more favoured by Mars than the other. But come now, Magnus; you know as well as I that, apart from the young bucks racing for family glory, most of the charioteers are all apprentices of one of the colours – the Reds, Blues, Whites or Greens – and a lot of the horses, rather than being genuine warhorses entered by families of standing, as in ancient times, are, instead, veterans of the wars on the track. Don't tell me that you don't know which chariots belong to your beloved Greens just because they don't sport their colours?'

'It's hard to bet against the Greens,' Magnus mumbled as he hefted the heavy purse in his hand.

'I seem to remember you betting on a Red one-two-three a couple of years ago, and doing very well out of it.'

'That was business.'

Gaius pointed to the purse. 'And so is this; you'll notice that there is considerably more in there than I would normally distribute to you and your lads on a festival day.'

'I was wondering about that; what do you want us to do, sir?'

'Tomorrow, at the second hour, I want you to go to the House of the Moon in the Stonemasons' Street on the Caelian Hill and take with you one of the tablets. Knock four times in quick succession, count three heartbeats and then repeat the signal. When asked to identify yourself say "Morpheus". I don't know how many men will be inside but at least two, I should imagine. You're to go alone; leave the lads that accompany you at the end of the street. You should be quite safe.'

'*Should be quite safe?* That doesn't sound like a hundred per cent guarantee.'

'What is in this life, my friend? Anyway, they will examine the tablet and take a sample. Tell them how many others like it you have and they will name a price. Refuse the first two offers out of hand, then say that you have to consult about the third but you'll have an answer within a couple of hours. Speed is of the essence now that the Urban Prefect has been informed of the theft.'

'He's been what?'

'The theft was noticed yesterday and needless to say Herod Agrippa was apoplectic. He went to both the prefect of Ostia and the Urban Prefect here in Rome and demanded action. I don't know what they can do in reality, but it would be best to conclude the deal and get the tablets out of the city and the money into Antonia's hands as soon as possible.'

'I quite agree; business like this is best done fast.'

'Indeed. Now tell me, how will this other bit of business go today? Am I to be standing up in the Senate tomorrow, urging the Urban Prefect to launch an inquiry into weights and measures, and then proposing a vote of thanks?'

'It'll be fine; my mate, a centurion in one of the Urban Cohorts, will get his men into a provocative position and, with a little help from the lads and me, it should spark the riot.'

'Urban Cohorts, eh? He'll be sticking his neck out a bit; I hope you've paid him well.'

'Don't worry, Senator, I ... Oh shit. I bribed him with half of the tablet that I took as a commission.'

Gaius turned to Magnus in alarm. 'Has he still got it?'

'I don't know; but I suggested who to sell it to: doctors who treat senators, Praetorian officers or Urban Cohort officers.'

'Oh dear. In the circumstances, that's the worst place to go.'

Magnus' ears rang as the people of Rome cheered and whistled, roaring on the twelve teams in the final race of the festival as they hurtled round the temporary track on the Trigarium, the equestrian training ground set in the bend of the Tiber, on the north-west corner of the Campus Martius. Here they had spent the morning enjoying racing of the highest calibre: a dozen heats with twelve pairs of the finest stallions driven to extreme exertion by their charioteers, all contesting the privilege to partake in the ultimate race in honour of the god.

Tens of thousands crammed round the track, ringed by a stout and solid wooden barrier and lined with soldiers of the Urban Cohorts in full military panoply, as the festival took place outside of the *pomerium*, the sacred boundary of the City of Rome. Every vantage point behind the spectators, crammed twenty to thirty deep round the three-hundred-pace-long track with a turning post at each end, had been taken.

As the seven remaining teams still running approached the last lap, flanks and muzzles foaming with sweat, eyes rolling, great hearts pounding, charging forward to the cracks of whips over their withers, the noise escalated to deafening proportions. But Magnus did not notice; he did not cheer. Magnus just stood, unmoving, in the shadow of an equestrian statue of a long-dead patrician, waiting for news from Rufinus. His brothers had scoured the Campus Martius all morning, and had eventually found him and his century at the eastern end of the track. But with the press of people so tight, not even the book-makers' slaves who roamed the crowds taking bets could make it to the front rows. So Magnus had been forced to wait, uncertain whether Rufinus had attempted to sell his half of the resin, and whether it had come to the ears of the Urban Prefect.

The roar escalated to a point that would have competed with the battle-cry of the god himself, and tens of thousands of fists were punched into the air as the winning team crossed the finish line after seven laps of the track. The charioteer leant back on the reins, wrapped around his waist, to slow his victorious stallions – a pair of chestnuts with black manes and tails. The soldiers of the Urban Cohorts stationed at the eastern end of the track, under Rufinus' command, locked shields as they forced a path through the cheering crowd for the victor. Magnus and his brothers shadowed the procession from the edge of the spectators as it made its way towards the altar of Mars at the heart of the Campus Martius where the Flamen Martius, Caius Iunius Silanus, the aged high-priest of Mars, waited, brandishing one of the sacred spears in readiness for the sacrifice. Wearing a fringed cloak over his toga, of double-thick wool and clasped at the throat, his head encased in a leather skullcap fastened by a chinstrap and with a point of olive-wood poking out of its top, he called on the deity to look down kindly upon the sacrifice of the best horse in the city.

Heads tossing, nostrils snorting, and with tails swishing, the two magnificent beasts high-stepped along the path forced for them by punched shield bosses, their hoofbeats and the jangle of their harnesses lost in the tumult. Taken up with the delirium of the moment and aware in some corner of their equine minds that the frenzy was due to their achievement, they held their heads high – skittering occasionally, only to be brought back under control by a sharp tug of the reins – as they progressed slowly through the crowd swirling about them.

Occasionally catching sight of Rufinus' transverse, white-horsehair crest, Magnus kept pace with him, making sure his brothers stayed close, knowing he must wait for his chance to get to the centurion.

On reaching the altar, the right-hand horse was slipped out of its traces and the crowd, sensing the religious significance of the moment, began to hush as it was garlanded with pendants of bread; two priests of Mars moved into position on each side and grasped its reins. The Flamen Martius approached the unsuspecting animal with slow, deliberate, twisting steps so that his cloak fanned around him as he swayed left and then right. With his spear alternatively raised to the sky and then pointed at the October Horse's chest, he repeated forms of words so ancient that their meaning was only vaguely clear to those not schooled in the rituals of Mars. Now, no other voice could be heard other than that of the priest, who was accompanied by the snorts and stamps of his unsuspecting victim.

With a final appeal to the heavens, he brought his spear down and, grasping it in both white-knuckled hands, rammed it, over-arm, into the beast's chest. The priests hauled on the reins as the October Horse screeched and made to rear; they kept it down as two more priests, with folds of their togas covering their heads, grasped the spear and, with a mighty effort, helped the Flamen Martius thrust it home and burst the heart of the gift to Mars. Transfixed on the spear and restrained by its reins, the beast tossed its head, arcing the pendants of bread through the air back and forth as blood flowed from the puncture in its breast; but this soon lessened as the victim's heart, tangled on the iron blade within it, ceased to pump and the pressure dropped. Down came the great beast as its forelegs buckled, cracking its knees on the paved ground already slick with blood; they slipped forward as the Flamen and his assistants hauled the sacred spear free. Released from its supporting prop and with the strength rapidly fading in its muscles, the October Horse rolled its eyes so only yellowish-white was visible and, with an unnatural rattle in its throat, collapsed on to its left side, twitching erratically.

Not a sound could be heard once the last breath had fled the sacrifice; for a few moments all stood still, spellbound by the intensity of the ritual. The Flamen Martius broke that spell by taking an axe from the altar and moving to the rear of the carcass; one of his assistants moved to pull the tail straight and iron flashed in the sun. The tail was severed and then held upright by the assisting priest to prevent the precious blood within from spilling. Holding it aloft, the priest and two colleagues made their way through the crowd, which parted for them as they increased their pace, in order to take the tail to the *Regia*, where the sacred spears and the sacred shields of Mars were housed. There, on the Regia's hearth, the blood would be sprinkled.

The Flamen moved to the front of the carcass, intoning prayers, as his remaining three assistants pulled at the dead head to straighten the neck. A murmur of anticipation spread through the crowd as the time approached when it would be decided where the severed head would reside for the year: nailed to the Regia, if the Via Sacra Brotherhoods won the fight by dragging it there, or to the equally ancient Mamillian Tower in the Suburra if the Brotherhoods from that quarter won.

With a final, hoarse call to the deity, the high priest of Mars brought the axe slicing through the air, over the top of his head, to thump down with the wet, solid blow of a butcher's cleaver, burying itself deep in the neck. With this stroke, the Flamen's job was done and he left it to his younger colleagues to part the head from the body. Once this had been achieved, the garland of loaves was thrown on to the altar to be consumed by fire, and its smoke twirled up in thanks for yet another harvest preserved.

Now it was time to fight for the head.

Ushered by the Urban Cohorts, the crowd dispersed, falling back from around the altar, allowing the massed brotherhoods from the two contesting areas to line up facing each other with a hundred paces between them. Both contingents were several hundred strong, although the Suburra looked to be slightly larger than the Via Sacra; neither side had any obvious weapons other than cudgels and knuckledusters. Magnus saw Grumio in the front rank of the Suburra, looking suspiciously towards Rufinus'

Urban Cohort century and others beyond that had finally been freed from the press of crowds round them. Signalling his brothers to follow him, Magnus moved towards the centurion as the priests began to carry the severed head between the two competing sides, holding it aloft for all to see.

'Have you tried to sell that resin yet?' Magnus asked in a hushed voice as he sidled up to Rufinus.

'Why do you ask?'

'Because the Urban Prefect has now heard about it; it's probably best to keep it hidden for a while.'

Rufinus raised his eyebrows, betraying mild alarm, whilst watching the priests place the head on the ground. 'I've asked an intermediary to make some enquiries.'

'Well, stop him.'

Rufinus nodded as the priests hurried away. 'It's the first thing I'll do once I've earnt it.'

The Flamen Martius raised his spear into the air and called on the deity to bless both sides in their sacred struggle to win through to their respective goals; and to entreat him that, whoever won, Rome would be seen as having discharged her duty to him.

He brought the spear down and with a mighty roar of violent anticipation both sides flung themselves forward to meet head on like two warlike tribes of the most primitive nature.

And the people of Rome cheered themselves hoarse.

Blood, teeth and screams flew through the air within an instant of the collision. The front two or three ranks – if they could be called that – of either side melded into a free-for-all that lost direction so that men fought towards all points of the circle and, with no uniforms or identifying marks other than facial recognition, lashed out at anything standing with brutal intent.

The area where the head had last been seen was more compact and a giant scrimmage had formed; it heaved back and forth as the participants within grappled and wrestled, trying to wrest possession of the head of the once-proud beast that had been declared the greatest horse in Rome.

As he watched, telling himself to concentrate on the business in hand and not be carried away by enjoyment of the spectacle, Magnus slowly led his brothers round the flanks of the Suburra contingent.

The scrimmage eased south, towards the city – the direction of both sides' objectives – leaving a trail of unconscious and wounded participants in its wake. The spectators moved with it, as did the various centuries of the Urban Cohorts in order to keep the fight out of the grand buildings that lined its route through the Campus Martius.

Magnus and his brothers began to infiltrate the Suburra faction, keeping towards the edges.

'Hand me a measure,' Magnus said, holding out a hand to Cassandros.

The brother dipped into his sack and brought out a bronze modius.

Magnus weighed it in his hand and smiled with narrowed eyes. With a straight arm, he hurled it high into the air over the Via Sacra contingent. He did not see it land but he knew it would cause grievous injury or maybe death. Looking to his right, he saw that Rufinus had brought his men closer. 'Right, lads, five left; hurl them all at Rufinus' boys.'

Within a few moments five bronze missiles had landed amongst the Urban Cohort century, bringing two down, despite their helmets, shields and chainmail, and cracking the bones of a couple more. The response was instant. Shields came up, lines formed and swords were drawn, and left legs stamped forward as they faced the source of the attack: the Suburra faction.

A shudder went through those of the Suburra closest to Rufinus' century as they saw the threat just paces from them.

Magnus signalled his brothers to withdraw, filtering back through the looser edges of the melee as, with a change of timbre to the roars, a section of the Suburra split off to attack the century that had formed up as if on the side of their opponents – just as they had been told it would.

And, just as Magnus had expected, the century took two paces forward, stamped their left feet down and slammed the bosses of their shields up and into the faces of their attackers, driving them back, bloodied and broken, before following up with the hilts or the flats of their swords to crunch down on the crowns of unprotected heads. Seeing their comrades under attack, other units of the Urban Cohorts came to the aid of Rufinus' men, protecting their flanks so they would not be swamped as violence repaid violence in a sudden escalation that fed upon itself.

'That should do it,' Magnus muttered to himself as he watched the scrimmage for the severed head split off from the newly instigated riot in the direction of the city walls. He turned to his brothers. 'Right, lads; we split up and walk away from this nice and slow, disgusted that such a sacred occasion should end in an attack on the city authorities.'

Pleased with his day's work so far, Magnus walked up a set of three stone steps and rapped on an iron-studded, wooden door; an erect phallus painted above it advertised the type of business transacted within. A viewing slot slid back and the cold eyes of a man whose living was earnt by the threat of violence stared through.

'Evening, Postumus,' Magnus said. 'Me and the lads are here to see Terentius.' He indicated back to Marius and Sextus who stood on the pavement; behind them the street was choked with wheeled vehicles, banned from the city by day, taking advantage of the fall of dusk to make their deliveries.

The door ground open; Magnus and his brothers entered past a hulking man who grinned with broken teeth. 'I'll send one of the apprentices to find him for you, Magnus.' He closed and bolted the door before leading Magnus through the vestibule into a sweetly perfumed and subtly lit atrium. 'Galen, the master's steward, will look after you whilst you wait.' Postumus indicated a middle-aged man of refined, well-preserved looks that were obviously enhanced with cosmetics.

'Masters, you are welcome; please, follow me.' Galen led them off as Postumus called a small boy of eight or nine to him and sent him on an errand.

Delicate chords of two lyres, ascending and descending in slow rhythm, thrummed in the background over the gentle patter of the fountain in the centre of the impluvium at the heart of the chamber, beneath the rectangular opening in the roof. Around the pool were set many couches upon which languished scantily dressed youths, each of a different combination of skin tone and hair and eye colour, but all possessing a beauty and allure not to be ignored, and Magnus found his eyes roving as the steward led them to a group of tables at the far end of the room.

'Some wine, masters?' Galen suggested as he bid them recline at a free table. 'And perhaps some pastries?'

'Just wine.' Magnus set himself down, glancing left and right at the other tables; they were occupied by groups of men sipping from finely worked bronze and silver cups and nibbling at small delicacies laid out on platters before them, whilst examining from a distance the merchandise for hire. Here and there a client had a youth reclining next to him for closer perusal or to ascertain areas of expertise before coinage changed hands.

'You won't have time, Sextus,' Magnus warned with a grin as his brother gawped, open-mouthed, at the feast of lithe flesh displayed all about. 'We're just here to make a pickup and then we're back to the tavern; you can have a whore or two there if you fancy.'

Marius took a cup from a tray proffered by an effete man in his late twenties, who had evidently outgrown the desires of most of the clients and been relegated to waiting upon them. 'We don't really have to hurry back, do we, Magnus? I mean, well, I'm surprised by, er … how nice some of them look. Not all of them, mind you.'

'No, no, of course not.' Magnus took a large swig from his cup. 'But I'm afraid this is far too refined a place for you two to frequent, lads; Terentius wouldn't like you soiling the goods, Marius, and he certainly won't be best pleased if our oversized friend, Sextus, caused unpleasant damage to one of the boys in his enthusiasm.'

'I'm sure they'll treat my boys with the greatest respect, Magnus.'

Magnus looked up; Terentius stood before them, hands clasped at his chest. His long, auburn hair had been dressed and woven in intricate coils on top of his head, held in place by jewelled pins and partially covered by a woman's crimson palla; gold earrings dangled almost to his shoulders, exposed by the extended neckline of his ankle-length, pleated midnight-blue stola. He smiled, his painted lips contrasting with whitened teeth and his eyes peering out through rims of kohl. *Very nice,* Magnus mused, *if you like that sort of thing.*

'They're welcome to enjoy themselves as my guest, Magnus, whilst I offer you some hospitality in my private chamber and discuss a business proposition with you.'

Magnus looked back at his two brothers and shrugged. 'Well, if you really are interested, lads?'

Marius and Sextus nodded with ill-concealed eagerness.

Terentius signalled his steward to join them. 'That's settled then. Galen will help you make your choices; he'll know just what is best if it's your first time.' He leant down and took the cup from Magnus' hand. 'You can have something of a far superior vintage if you follow me.'

Leaving Marius and Sextus to make their choice of entertainment with Galen, Magnus followed Terentius as he sashayed from the atrium, out into a surprisingly large courtyard garden imbued with the scents of damp, autumnal vegetation, then on round the colonnaded walkway, past curtained-off doorways that blocked the sights if not the sounds of passion, and finally to a set of double doors at the far end.

Terentius ushered Magnus into his private domain, which was everything that could be expected of a successful master of a respectable male brothel: a fine mosaic floor depicting numerous positions of male congress; frescoes of a similar nature but with famous lovers of Greek antiquity as their subjects, and furnishings of a lavish, but not vulgar, disposition.

'Make yourself comfortable, Magnus.' Terentius plumped up the cushions on a white-linen upholstered couch.

Starting to wonder as to his true motives in coming here, Magnus settled on the couch, resting an arm on its raised end and enjoying the fumes of whatever it was that had been sprinkled on the mobile brazier nearby.

'Leave us,' Terentius ordered as he poured two glasses of wine from a deep-blue glass decanter whose elegant long neck seemed too fragile to support its bulbous belly.

Magnus turned in surprise and saw an old slave leave the room; he had no recollection of noticing him as he entered.

Turning back, he accepted a goblet of matching glass to the decanter from Terentius who then sat in a high-backed, wicker chair draped with a deep-red damask cloth; he adjusted his palla so that it fell to either side in a manner that any Roman matron would have approved of.

'To us and business, may the gods of this house look down kindly on us.' Terentius raised his goblet and poured a small libation on the floor and then another on to the brazier before taking a sip.

'Us and business,' Magnus repeated. He tasted the wine, fragrant with fruit, rich and full as it assaulted his palate with a succession of flavours and hints of more, and he knew that although it was wasted on his rough tastes, Terentius had not misled him: it was one of the finest of vintages. 'Very nice.' He immediately regretted such a crass remark and covered his embarrassment by taking a whole-hearted gulp. 'So, Terentius, what business have you in mind?'

Terentius ran his finger round the rim of his goblet, looking at Magnus as if trying to decide how best to approach the subject. He crossed his legs and raised his finely plucked eyebrows. 'The tablets that you gave into my safekeeping.'

'What about them?'

'I know what they are, Magnus, and I know what they are used for.'

'So?'

'I also know what they can be used for; the potential that they have. I don't mean their medical potential; I mean their potential in furthering the art of love.'

'The art of love?'

'Yes, Magnus. The resin in those tablets can unlock realms of pleasure known only to Morpheus himself; realms so large that a man could lose himself there for days on end.'

'Really?'

'Really, and I want to purchase some from you. With those tablets I could offer an experience so intense that no man having undergone it would want to seek his pleasure anywhere else but here. I would make a fortune and you would share in it, Magnus.'

Magnus drained his goblet and held it out for a refill. 'What do you mean?'

Terentius picked up the decanter and poured. 'I have heard stories from the East, from beyond the empire, of how to augment the senses by using this resin. It's not how our doctors use it, made into a potion or just chewed; it's a different and far more efficacious method.' He placed the decanter back on the table, rose and walked over to a chest at the far end of the room. He removed one of the sackcloth-wrapped tablets and two broad-bladed knives before returning to his chair. 'I'll show you.' He exposed the edge of the tablet, shaved off a sliver and then put the points of both knives into the brazier.

Magnus watched with interest as Terentius worked the sliver into a ball, rubbing it between his thumb and forefinger. He then handed it to Magnus and removed both knives from the fire. He held one out. 'Put the resin on the tip of the blade.'

Magnus obeyed; Terentius pressed the second blade down on it. Immediately fumes spiralled up; Terentius leant over and inhaled, pulling the smoke deep into his lungs. 'Your turn,' he said with a tight, almost choking voice.

Magnus opened his mouth and sucked in the white trail emitting from between the blades. He felt a harsh rasping in his throat and a warmth in his chest.

'Hold it in,' Terentius said, his voice higher from having held his breath.

Magnus did so for as long as he could, then exhaled a thin stream of smoke. He looked at Terentius. 'Well?'

'Give it time, Magnus; Morpheus needs to be woken from his slumbers before he will show you his realm.'

Magnus took a sip of wine and waited, contemplating the beauty of the glass. And it was beautiful, intensely blue in a way that he had never seen before; the bluest of blues. And yet, where the reflections of the brazier's red glow played on it, the blue deepened into purple, flickering across the surface, picking out the fine engravings of grape-laden vines; imperial vines, he mused. He smiled to himself, enjoying the thought, then realised that red grapes were often purple in hue and was about to make a connection with ... but then the goblet's stem caught his attention: thin blue glass, so blue, but right at its heart a very fine line of purple; again, that must be a reflection from the fire. He looked across at the brazier, still smiling, yes, it was glowing; so comforting. His eyes rose to meet those of Terentius; they were wide open but their pupils had contracted to pinpricks, and he too was smiling. Magnus was about to say something but then the calm of the moment prevented him; it would be wrong to break so peaceful an atmosphere with harsh talk. His gaze drifted down. He discerned, with a widening of his smile, that the blue of Terentius' stola matched that of the goblet – if it was held at certain angles. He experimented with the position of the goblet, looking between it and the stola. He noticed Terentius rise and walk past him; he heard the door open just as he discovered a fascinating new angle at which to hold the goblet. Then voices, followed by the soft click of the door reclosing. Terentius swished past him, a blur of blue motion – so beautiful, blue. The decanter glided towards him, it tipped; the glug of pouring wine so slow and regular. The taste of the wine, sublime. He looked up to thank Terentius; Terentius smiled down, his hands touching Magnus' shoulders. His palla was gone; there was no crimson, only blue. And then there was no blue, just cream flesh, and Magnus understood. He heard the door creak open and soft voices approached from behind him; he felt his belt being unfastened. He raised his goblet and finished the last of the wine; it was taken from him as he sluiced the liquid around his mouth and allowed his tunic to be pulled over his head. A soft hand on his chest eased him back on to the cushions on the couch – soft, smooth and warm, so warm. He felt the hand stroke his hair and he opened his eyes; Terentius stood over him, his skin sheened with the glow of the brazier, and then he sat, revealing two more figures, lissom and delicate, one blond and one dark – both naked. One held out the knives; Magnus sucked in the spiralling smoke, holding it deep. As he laid his head down, feeling the sweet touch of multiple caresses, he saw the gates to the realm of Morpheus open and, with absolute calm and contentment, he floated forward to sample the dreams therein.

A damp cloth, warm and fragrant, dabbing his brow brought him back. For a while he did not open his eyes, content to enjoy the sensation of being cleansed.

'What did you think?' Terentius whispered.

What *did* he think? He cast his mind back: the images, the colours, the acts, the abandon, the release, the pleasure; all as he had never experienced before. 'Well, it weren't natural and yet it seemed to come so easy, if you take my meaning?'

'I do, Magnus; and now do you see how so much money could be made out of this?'

'Fortunes.' Magnus opened his eyes; Terentius was dressed and his hair pulled back into a ponytail. 'But I doubt that you'd be able to afford even one tablet.'

'How much are they each?'

'I don't know exactly, but more than gold. I'm going to—' He sat up and looked around; early light crept in through the window. 'What time is it?'

'Halfway through the first hour of the day.'

'Shit! Where are my clothes? And get me one of the tablets. Are Marius and Sextus still here?'

Terentius handed Magnus his tunic, belt and loincloth. 'Yes, I've had them woken and they've been served breakfast.'

'Served breakfast? They don't have time for that.'

Within moments Magnus had dressed, strapped on his sandals and, with a tablet wrapped in sackcloth under his arm and Terentius following behind, was walking at a rapid pace through the garden. 'Come to the tavern at dusk and I'll have a reasonable idea as to how much the tablets are worth; meanwhile, you work out how much you think you can make from each one; then we'll know whether it's viable.'

'I'll be there,' Terentius confirmed as they passed through into the atrium.

'No time for that, lads,' Magnus said, grabbing a hunk of bread from the table at which Marius and Sextus were breaking their fast in delightful company. 'We're almost late.' He hurried on through the room and into the vestibule. Postumus opened the door and Magnus stepped out into the street with his brothers following. As he headed at a brisk walk towards the Caelian Hill and the meeting at the House of the Moon in the Stonemasons' Street, he addressed Marius and Sextus without looking at them. 'I think it would be best all round if we didn't mention where or how we spent last night.'

Finding the House of the Moon had been easy, with a carving above the door of Luna, the divine embodiment of the moon, cloak billowing behind her in the shape of a crescent moon as she rode in her oxen-drawn chariot. What had not been easy was concentrating on business and Magnus found his mind wandering as he sat opposite a brown-skinned man in his thirties with a thin face and lips, a sharp nose and tight curly black hair; Egyptian, Magnus had assumed when the man introduced himself as Menes.

Menes sniffed the tablet and looked across the table at Magnus, his dark eyes glinting with barely restrained greed. 'How many these you say your patron had, my friend?'

Magnus hauled his attention away from some vivid images of the night before and focused on one of the two thickset bodyguards standing behind the Egyptian. 'I didn't.'

Menes grinned in a manner that totally failed to convey any charm or warmth. 'So, my friend, how much you want for this?'

Magnus took a moment to register the question. 'Offer me a price.'

'How can I make an offer when I don't know how much is for sale? If I take a lot you make me special price.'

'There is no special price, *my friend*; whoever makes the highest offer gets to purchase as much as they want at that price. No discounts, understand?'

Menes' grin widened into an obnoxious leer, which, by his manner, he evidently deemed to be a winning smile. 'My friend, I make you good offer: three thousand denarii a tablet.'

Magnus almost choked with shock at such a high figure, but managed to transform it into a growl of indignation and, grabbing the tablet from Menes, pushed back his chair. 'If you start so low, then I've wasted my patron's time in coming here.'

Menes was on his feet quickly, his hands in the air, palms towards Magnus, laughing, cold and forced. 'My friend, my friend, I see you are serious man of business; sit, please, sit, we have wine?'

'No wine, Menes,' Magnus said, pulling his chair back to the table, 'and no jokes, just the right price.'

'Yes, yes, right price.' Menes sat down again and made a show of thinking for a few moments. 'Three thousand, five hundred denarii.'

'That's enough of this nonsense.' Magnus got to his feet, toppling his chair.

'Five thousand!'

Magnus paused and looked at Menes. 'Five thousand a tablet?'

'Yes, my friend.'

'There are twenty-three more.'

Menes' eyes widened with unbridled greed. 'I take them all, one hundred and ten thousand denarii; I can have the money in gold by dawn tomorrow.'

'I need to consult my patron; you'll have the answer by tonight.' Magnus turned to go. 'If you try to have me followed, the deal will be over as will be your life. And, my friend, there's no special price. It's one hundred and twenty thousand for all twenty-four; which in gold aurii is ...' He did a quick mental calculation, dividing by twenty-five. 'Four thousand eight hundred.'

'There is no doubt in my mind that this outrage was sparked by a growing mistrust within the more ignorant sections of the city's population of the trustworthiness of the measures used in distribution of the grain dole.' Gaius Vespasius Pollo was adamant and the force with which his right arm sliced down from above his head on the final word emphasised the fact. 'Why else, Conscript Fathers, would the Urban Cohorts be attacked with bronze modius measures? Modius measures that had been fitted with false bottoms to make them one sestius short. We are all aware how much grain could be skimmed off and hoarded if just a tenth of the modius measures in the city were a sixteenth light. Not that any member of this house would organise such a thing, Conscript Fathers, for by the sacred law of the ways of our ancestors we in the Senate are forbidden to partake in trade.' Gaius looked around the Senate House, his face flushed with exertion and righteous ire conjured up for the moment; many of the senators seated in rows on either side of the house nodded in agreement at this timely reminder of the ways of the ancestors. 'But the equestrian class is not so tied and for a very few of them the making of money is a pursuit that they follow with no consideration for the consequences.' He puffed himself up. 'And we saw the consequences yesterday at the Festival of the October Horse!' This time his right arm soared above his head, fist clenched, excess fat on his upper arm wobbling. 'Conscript Fathers, we cannot allow the Emperor's peace to be disturbed so. We must beg Cossus Cornelius Lentulus, the prefect of Rome, to organise an inspection of every modius measure in the city; only he can avert the oncoming crisis.' With another powerful rhetorical gesture and a flurry of spittle, Gaius underlined the final word. 'And I move that we write to the Emperor and thank him for his wisdom in appointing Lentulus to the post.' With a final, outraged glare round the chamber, he walked back to his place, to the rumble of agreement, and sat down on his folding stool, which strained beneath the pressure of his ample behind. His colleagues surrounding him patted him enthusiastically on the back, congratulating him loudly – all, no doubt, jealous that they had not taken the opportunity to so ingratiate themselves with the Urban Prefect.

The chorus of agreement continued as all eyes turned to Lentulus. He rose slowly and Magnus, watching from the Senate House steps through the open doors, noticed a grateful nod in Gaius' direction.

'Conscript Fathers, I am indebted to Senator Pollo for his expression of confidence in me and I shall do everything in my power to head off this crisis before it takes root,' Lentulus declaimed as Magnus turned away with a satisfied expression, walking back down the steps to await his patron.

'Do you trust Menes?' Gaius asked as he and Magnus walked through the Forum, preceded by Sextus and Marius.

Magnus' look was answer enough.

'Nevertheless, we'll proceed with the deal. That's roughly what was expected, a very good price; that should help even Antonia's score with Herod Agrippa. It should please her greatly, far more than my speech pleased your friend Brutus; you should have seen the way he looked at me. And then, as I was leaving just now, he sidled up to me and said I've made my last speech before my natural death. What do you think he meant by that, my natural death? How would he know when that will be?'

'I don't know, sir, but I would consider it to be a threat; I'll have a couple of the lads posted outside your house, just to be safe, if you take my meaning?'

'I'm afraid I do; I've made a bad enemy there.'

'But a good friend of the Urban Prefect,' Magnus pointed out.

'That's very true; it was a good morning's sycophancy for me and I trust that it'll solve your problem, Magnus. But what's more, it will get me noticed by the Emperor and make him more disposed to grant Vespasian that entry to Egypt when he sees the transcript of the day's debates tomorrow morning.'

'Has Antonia asked him yet?'

'Yes, she added the request to a letter that she despatched that day. Hopefully, she'll have an answer when you take the money for the sale to her.'

'What do you mean? I thought I just had to do the negotiation.'

Gaius slapped a chubby arm round Magnus' shoulders. 'I can't be seen soiling the Senate's reputation with such a grubby transaction and the Lady Antonia certainly can't.'

'What about Pallas, her steward?'

'Oh, he's chosen the location for the meeting and he'll be close by to ensure safe delivery of the four thousand, eight hundred aurii back to the Lady, once you've completed the transaction.'

'Four thousand, six hundred,' Magnus corrected.

'How so? There are twenty-four of the tablets.'

'We negotiated a special price; the full deal was five thousand denarii each, but twenty-four tablets for the price of twenty-three.'

Gaius squeezed Magnus' shoulder and looked at him sidelong. 'I'm sure Antonia won't fuss about two hundred aurii here or there. Get a message to the purchaser that the exchange will be at dawn tomorrow at the Temple of Asclepius.'

Magnus was about to argue but then paused and nodded slowly in approval. 'Marius, go to the House of the Moon and tell them dawn at the Temple of Asclepius on the Tiber Island.' As Marius ran off Magnus inclined his head to his patron. 'That's very clever of Pallas, sir; if I have my lads covering both bridges, Menes will find it very difficult to double-cross us and get away.'

'We've a big problem on our hands,' Servius announced, not looking up from the abacus and the scrolls of accounts he was working on as Magnus walked through the door of the tavern, refreshed from a few hours at the baths. 'Our aedile has evidently not taken too kindly to the city-wide inspection of measures.' He pointed over his shoulder to a man slumped in a dark corner of the bar.

Magnus approached him, frowning. 'Duilius?'

There was no reply.

'It *was* Duilius,' Servius informed him, still not looking up as the abacus clicked rapidly, 'until about an hour ago.'

Magnus cupped Duilius' chin and examined the face; there were no marks of violence. A swift perusal of the rest of his body showed no wounds, bruising or blood. 'There's not a mark on him! How did he die?'

'We're meant to believe that he died of natural causes; we found him—'

'Natural causes?'

'Yes. We found him sitting on the pavement just outside with his head between his legs as if he was being sick. Nobody can remember seeing him left there, although a drunken rabble did pass by just before, so it must have been them with arms round Duilius' shoulders as if he was insensible with drink.'

Magnus examined the body again with a grudging respect. 'What do you make of it?'

'It's a declaration of war; this is about who has authority in the South Quirinal. We may have managed to manoeuvre the Urban Prefect into an inspection of every measure in the city, forcing Brutus to quit his scam or face being exposed and humiliated; but in return he has shown us that he can get his revenge without attracting suspicion and accusations of murder. I would guess that Duilius won't be the only sudden natural death around here.'

Magnus sat down, still looking in fascination at the unmarked corpse. 'I think you may be right, Brother; Brutus threatened our senator with a natural death very soon. I promised a guard round his house; have half a dozen stationed up there. If there is going to be another natural death, then it ain't going to be us or Senator Pollo; and what better way to get rid of a magistrate with no questions asked. How was it done?'

'Ah! It took me a while, but I think I've worked it out.'

Terentius walked through the tavern door as the sun slid into the west; Magnus rose from his table and indicated that he and Servius should follow him through to the back room.

'Well?' Magnus asked as they sat.

Terentius placed a wax writing-tablet on the table. 'Each tablet weighs two and a half libra; with twelve uncia to a pound, that's a total of thirty. Each one of those little balls weighs an obolus, which is forty-eight from each uncia, so from a tablet that's one thousand, four hundred ...'

'... and forty from each tablet.' Magnus whistled softly. 'How much do you think you could charge your clients for one?'

'For that luxury and including the boy, ten denarii easily.' Terentius pointed to the writing-tablet. 'It's all in there, Magnus.'

Servius picked it up and read it quickly. 'How much can you get a tablet for, Magnus?'

Magnus shook his head, unable to believe his luck. 'I've just got one for free plus the half I have already, that's—'

Servius flicked some beads on his abacus. 'Twenty-one thousand, six hundred denarii or eight hundred and sixty-four aurii.'

'But it'll take some time to realise that money; at least a year, probably more,' Terentius pointed out.

'With no initial outlay to cover, that doesn't matter, my friend,' Magnus said, leaning back in his chair and beaming. 'You take as long as you like and we'll go fifty–fifty, five denarii each per sale.'

'That's generous, Magnus.'

'I'd say it's fair. You provide the boys and the premises and I'll provide the resin; you can settle up once a month with Servius. In the meantime I would be very grateful if you could ensure that Aedile Brutus samples the new pleasure next time he frequents your establishment; in fact, encourage him to have two of those balls and then send me a message at whatever time of day or night it is.'

Terentius looked quizzical. 'Certainly, Magnus.' He stood to leave.

'I'll send a couple of my lads back with you to pick up the rest of those tablets.'

'Of course, Magnus; will I see you later?'

Magnus was aware of Servius' eyebrows raising a fraction and shook his head, waving a hand in dismissal. As the door closed behind Terentius, he turned to his counsellor. 'Well, I had to sample the goods before I could decide whether to invest in them or not.'

'Very wise. And what do you think?'

'I think that it's wasted on doctors; it's much more than just a medicine.'

'Will we really make that sort of money?'

'Oh, yes, my friend; once those who can afford it try it, they'll find it hard not to go back for more.'

'And you?'

'Now I know how good it is I daren't have it again; not if I want to get things done, if you take my meaning?' Magnus got to his feet, stretched and yawned. 'Have all the lads assembled here two hours before dawn; wake me then.'

*

'Magnus, wake up.'

Magnus roused himself and opened an eye to see Servius standing over him, holding a lamp. 'Are all the lads downstairs?'

'No, there're still a couple of hours to go yet.'

'Why wake me then?'

Servius indicated with his head to the door.

Magnus sat up in bed and squinted, trying to focus. 'Rufinus! What are you doing here?'

'Yesterday, after the festival, I went to tell my intermediary to stop making inquiries about selling the resin.'

'Good. And?'

'I couldn't find him.'

'Shit!'

'It's worse than that; he was found about an hour ago. It was all round the cohort very quickly because of the state he was in.'

'Go on.'

'He'd been tortured before they cut his throat. It was made to look as if they wanted to get the keys for the stores off him because some stuff was missing, but not enough in my opinion to warrant murder. Besides, I know Aetius—'

'Aetius? Of course, who better to act as an intermediary; he can buy or sell anything.'

'Could. But he wouldn't have risked his life for a set of keys.'

'But he would have risked it to keep his reputation for discretion.'

'I'd asked him to approach a couple of doctors to see whether they would be interested.'

'And one was the Urban Cohorts'?'

'Exactly.'

'Who went straight to the Urban Prefect, who immediately had a little chat with Aetius and, because he was killed having been tortured, we can assume that he gave them what they wanted.'

'Yes, Magnus; they know my name.' Rufinus handed his half-tablet of resin to Magnus. 'This is no good to me; I need cash. I'm disappearing until all this dies down.'

'Very wise, my friend.' Magnus took the half-tablet, calculating its intrinsic worth, and knew that he could be very generous in buying Rufinus' silence. 'Servius, give the centurion twenty-five aurii.'

Rufinus' eyes widened at the equivalent of two and a half years' pay for an average legionary. 'That's good of you, Magnus.'

'I'll always help a friend. There'll be another twenty-five for you if you haven't mentioned my name by the time the fuss dies down. Now get going.'

'Thank you, Magnus.'

Servius paused in the doorway as he followed Rufinus out. 'There was a message from Antonia's steward, Pallas. He'll be at the river steps below the Temple of Asclepius half an hour before dawn.'

'Are all your men in position, master?' Pallas enquired as Magnus walked down the steps from the Temple of Asclepius to the Tiber; the groans of scores of sick slaves, left to die in the precinct of the god of medicine by masters refusing to pay for their treatment, blended with the gurgling of the river.

'They are, Pallas.' Magnus looked at the full-bearded Greek, aware that he was a slave, but in awe of the fact that with one question he had taken complete control of the operation; but he was used to it. In the course of his numerous contacts, in various capacities, with the Lady Antonia's steward, he had developed a respect for Pallas' judgement and discretion; Magnus knew him to be more than a mere slave. 'I've got ten covering each bridge and a further ten round the temple; all with orders to keep out of sight. Plus I've ten of my best lads with me to guard the tablets and then transport the cash. Menes won't be able to leave without handing over the money.'

'Unless he tries to go by boat, which is why I took the precaution of bringing mine.' Pallas stepped out of the six-oared river craft that had ferried him to the island. 'We will return by river once the transaction has taken place. Get into position; I'll be waiting here.'

Magnus nodded and picked his way back up the steps through the huddles of dead and dying slaves.

'Looks like them,' Marius announced as the first rays of dawn sun hit a high altitude cloudbank, accentuating ripples on its grey surface with highlights of deep red. 'I'd say there are at least a dozen round that cart.'

Magnus watched the group cross the Fabricium Bridge from the Campus Martius, then turn off the main street bisecting the island and pull into the forecourt of the Temple of Asclepius.

'My good friend!' Menes exclaimed, walking towards Magnus with open arms as if it were a reunion of acquaintances of many years' standing after an unreasonably long period of absence; the expression of joy on his face, however, registered as a rictus contort.

Not wishing to cause offence, Magnus subjected himself to the embrace which was nothing more than a clumsy attempt to frisk him for hidden weapons, which he returned; Menes was unarmed.

'You have tablets, my friend?'

'Naturally.'

Magnus indicated the cart. 'Four thousand, eight hundred aurii?'

Menes inclined his head. 'In twenty-four bags of two hundred.'

'Take one of them away; my patron is only selling twenty-three of the tablets.'

Menes attempted to transform his expression into one of shock and deep disappointment, but succeeded only in gurning like a tragic actor's mask. 'My friend, we had a deal.'

'For two hundred aurii a tablet; my patron has just decided to keep one for himself. Now, let's do this. Sextus!' The brother lumbered forward, holding a bulging sack. 'Put them down here. Menes, have the money stacked next to them and then all our men will withdraw twenty paces whilst you and I check the contents.'

Menes eyed the bag as Sextus placed it down, his smile returning, before shouting in his own language. The tarpaulin was pulled back from the cart and half a dozen of his men began unloading the weighty bags concealed within. When twenty-three were piled next to the tablets, Magnus and Menes nodded to one another and gave the order for their guards to withdraw back into the tangle of sick slaves who were too ill to pay attention to events around them. Once they were alone in the centre of the forecourt, Magnus pulled a square piece of leather from his belt, spread it on the ground and, choosing a bag at random, poured the contents out.

With practised fingers, the contents were soon counted and, after three more random selections revealed totals of two hundred aurii for each bag, Magnus felt satisfied that Menes was not trying to cheat by underpaying. Magnus eyed the Egyptian in the growing light as he finished examining the last couple of tablets. He found it hard to believe that the man's blatant greed would not tempt him into a double-cross.

'Very good, my friend,' Menes announced, rewrapping the final tablet. 'Now we go, yes?'

Magnus nodded and called his brothers back. 'Marius, have the lads take the sacks down to the boat.'

Standing opposite Menes, who was grinning furiously as if to convey a feeling of calm and normality, Magnus kept his eye on the Egyptian's men as they turned their cart round and loaded the tablets under the tarpaulin.

It was no more than an anxious twitch of Menes' eyes towards the cart, followed by an almost imperceptible tensing of his leg muscles in preparation for a quick sprint, which alerted Magnus; he dived to the left, putting Menes between him and the cart as a fletched shaft hissed through the air where his head had been. 'Down!' he bellowed as three more bows just grabbed from beneath the tarpaulin thrummed arrows towards his lads, felling two.

More sleek missiles spat through the dawn air, thumping one brother to the ground, the bag he carried bursting open in an explosion of dull gold.

Menes' men, now all armed, ran forward, arrows nocked and bows drawn as they aimed at the chests of Magnus' brethren.

'Put the bags down, lads, and step back,' Magnus ordered, edging towards Marius but keeping his eyes on Menes.

The Egyptian's grin had morphed into a triumphant gloat. 'Now we go, yes? But we take the money as well, no?'

Magnus looked round at the twelve bow-armed men covering his surviving brothers. 'You can try, but I warn you: if you leave now without the money, you can keep the resin; if you don't leave the money with us, you'll all die.'

Menes croaked a cackling laugh. 'Oh, you funny man, my friend. You hand over the money or *you* all die.'

Magnus shrugged and pointed to the last few bags on the ground by Marius' feet. 'There's a few, my lads have got the rest.'

Menes shouted in his own language and his men moved forward cautiously, stepping over recumbent slaves to retrieve the sacks.

'Stay calm, lads,' Magnus called. 'Put the sacks on the ground and let them take the lot; it's not our money so it's not worth dying for.'

'Very sensible, my friend,' Menes said, hefting up a bag from the ground.

All but three of Menes' men were obliged to shoulder their bows in order to pick up the coinage. Magnus' brothers watched in silence as they carried the heavy bags away, taking care not to trip over the recumbent forms that lay moaning in the thin light.

And then a hand grabbed an ankle and a dull, shimmer of a blade was forced up into an unprotected groin, severing a testicle and releasing a cascade of blood on to a man who had hitherto been overlooked as too sick to be of consequence. More blades flashed up from the ground, more blood flowed, and Magnus' brothers who had lain amongst the dying rose to life. Two went back down immediately as arrows thwacked into them, before the three remaining bowmen were despatched in a flurry of blades and blood.

Menes reacted instantly and fled for the cart, abandoning his men to be slaughtered in vengeance for brothers lost. Magnus smiled to himself and, indicating to Marius and Sextus to follow him, walked after the fleeing Egyptian as the cart driver urged his horse into action, clattering out of the forecourt and then turning right towards the Fabrician Bridge. Magnus did not rush; he knew there was no need to. As he stepped on to the main street the cart began to traverse the bridge. Midway it stopped.

'Thank you, Cassandros,' Magnus muttered, prowling forward as the cart attempted to turn a hundred and eighty degrees; behind it a line of silhouettes blocked the bridge.

The driver whipped the horse without mercy, trying to reverse it in order to complete the turn, but to no avail. The beast reared in the harness as its chest scraped against the brick parapet and sharp whip-inflicted pain seared along its back.

Menes leapt from the vehicle, grasping the sack of tablets, his head jerking left then right, like some demented bird, as if the situation might change at any moment and a way off the bridge would miraculously present itself.

'Where were you going, my friend?' Magnus called.

Menes froze and then cranked his mouth into the widest of grins. 'No problems, no problems, my friend, no problems.'

Magnus stopped five paces from the Egyptian. 'You see, that's the funny thing; there *is* a problem. You killed a few of my lads and took a lot of money.'

Menes laughed as if it was a matter of small import that could easily be cleared up over a cup of wine.

'I'm going to kill you slowly for that, Menes, and then there'll be no problem.' Magnus lunged forward; the Egyptian stepped back, turned and leapt on to the bridge's parapet, hurling himself into the river below, the sack clutched in his hand.

'Shit!' Magnus exclaimed, rushing to look over the edge. Menes was struggling with one hand to keep himself afloat, whilst still holding the sack with the other, as the river swept him away. He looked back up at Magnus, laughing, as he shouted in his own tongue. But in his triumph at escape he failed to see the danger that whistled in from the river steps. His face contorted into a grin more pronounced and rigid than he had ever concocted before as an arrowhead burst out of his right eye-socket, the eyeball skewered on the bodkin. The feathered shaft vibrated, embedded in his crown, and a few paces away Pallas, his expression passive, set down his bow and sent his oarsmen diving into the river as the dead Menes finally gave up his hold of the tablets.

'It would seem that you've had a very successful morning, Pallas; keeping the tablets was an unexpected bonus,' Antonia conceded, looking at the pile of moneybags and the wet sack of tablets on the mosaic floor of her private office at her residence on the Palatine. She looked at Magnus, her green eyes showing life in them that belied her seventy years but matched her high-cheekboned, fading beauty that still needed little cosmetic augmentation. 'And I have much to thank you for too, Magnus. I will pay the blood money for your men. Pallas.' She indicated to the bags.

Pallas picked one up and gave it to Magnus.

'I think that should cover it.'

'Thank you, domina,' Magnus muttered.

'What's the matter? You don't look overly thrilled.'

Magnus looked at the bag and then down to the tablets. 'Well, begging your pardon, domina, but I was wondering what you intend to do with them.'

'I shall inform the Urban Prefect that they've fallen into my hands and that I shall return them to their rightful owner, so he needn't concern himself about them any more. Then I'll restore them to Herod Agrippa for the pleasure of watching him control his expression as I demand a substantial finder's fee. I think that'll be the point when he realises I was behind the theft and that it might be a good idea to pay off the debt he owes me to avoid further inconvenience in the future.' She smiled at the thought.

'If that is the case, domina, could I swap the aurii for one of the tablets?'

Antonia looked at Magnus, frowning. 'And why would you want to do that?'

'Let's just say I know a use they can be put to that is worth far more than two hundred in gold.'

'How?'

'Well, it … er … if you inhale the fumes when it burns, it takes you to a place where pleasure has no bounds if you share it with another, if you take my meaning?'

'I think I do, Magnus.' Antonia smiled again and looked at Pallas. 'Leave us.'

Magnus tried but failed to hide his alarm as the steward left the room.

'Show me.'

Magnus walked through the tavern door soon after dusk, clasping a tablet under his arm and fit to drop; it had been a long day, although much of it was now a blur. He looked across to his table in the corner and saw Servius bent over his abacus; next to him sat a youth of notable beauty.

Magnus sat down, looked at the youth and then at Servius. 'Is this what I think it is?'

'Tell him,' Servius growled, clacking his abacus.

'The master says to tell you that everything is prepared in the matter that you spoke of.'

The fatigue fell away immediately. 'Run back and tell him I'll be there very soon.'

'I'll come with you. I had already sent Marius, Sextus and Cassandros up there about half an hour ago when the message arrived.'

'Thank you, my friend.' Magnus brandished the tablet. 'I need to drop this off with Terentius anyway.'

Servius' eyes glinted in the lamplight. 'Another thousand or so aurii; just a fraction of that will reimburse our people for the grain that Brutus cheated them of. It's been a good day.'

'Indeed; and it's just about to get better.'

'Well, well,' Magnus ruminated as he looked down at the recumbent form of Brutus, lying on the couch in Terentius' private room. 'You look to be enjoying yourself, aedile.'

Brutus looked up with unfocused, drooping-lidded eyes and stared at Magnus for a few moments, with no sign of recognition, before returning his attention to the genitalia of the writhing youth straddling his hips and riding hard.

Terentius signalled to a second youth busy flicking one of the aedile's nipples with his tongue whilst caressing the other; he removed the two knives from the brazier and pressed them to either side of a small ball of resin on the table next to it. Smoke immediately spiralled up and the youth offered it to the aedile; even in his engrossed state, Brutus noticed the source of pleasure nearing him and turned his head to suck greedily at the smoke.

'He certainly has developed the taste for it,' Magnus observed as the door opened and Servius entered holding a rope; behind him came Marius, Sextus and Cassandros, struggling with a large tub of water.

Servius pointed to the floor next to the couch. 'Set it down there.' He looked down at Brutus who lay back with a fixed grin on his face. 'Is he ready?'

'He's far too deep into Morpheus' realm to notice anything,' Terentius assured him. 'Leave us, boys.'

The writhing youth eased himself off Brutus and, picking up his tunic from the couch, scurried, giggling, out of the room with his colleague.

'Get him on his knees in front of the tub, lads,' Servius ordered, throwing the coiled rope on to the couch.

Sextus and Cassandros raised Brutus to his feet.

'All forgotten, I've forgotten,' the aedile mumbled as they lowered him on to his knees over the tub. 'Ah, water; so much water.'

'Head in and hold it there; but be very careful not to bruise him. Once he's dead we hang him upside down to get all the water out, then dry him off and dress him and he'll seem to have died of natural causes.'

As Brutus' head disappeared beneath the surface Magnus turned to Terentius. 'It's probably best if you don't witness this; the last time you saw him he was still alive.'

'And in such capable hands,' Terentius added with a smile as he walked away.

Magnus watched him go for a few moments before turning back to Brutus just as the convulsions started.

*

'Natural causes?' Gaius was shocked; he leant forward across the desk in his study, almost spilling an inkpot. 'At his age? He couldn't have been more than thirty-five or six.'

Magnus contrived to look equally shocked. 'I know, sir; but there it is. He was found near the Viminal Gate soon after dawn this morning, in the Via Patricius. Not a mark on him so it is assumed that he just dropped down dead after some mighty exertions in one of the brothels along there.'

'There'll be an investigation.'

'I'm sure there will.'

'And if they find that it wasn't natural causes can they trace it to you?'

'I very much doubt it. He was found on the Viminal; not my area.'

'Because if they can I might be implicated as well. How did you do it?'

'You don't need to know, sir; other than it was the same way he would have killed you.'

'How do you know?'

'Because my client who made the original complaint against him was found dead of natural causes yesterday, soon after Brutus had threatened you. I think he was starting a spree of natural revenge.'

'Yes, well, I suppose I should thank you, Magnus.'

'Yes, I suppose you should, sir.'

'But even so, I think that you should get out of Rome for a while whilst I try and persuade the Urban Prefect that young men of his age drop dead all the time of natural causes.'

'Lucky that he's in your debt.'

'Yes, but I think this will use up the last of the favours he owes me; he did grant my request to make Sabinus the Grain Aedile next year now that he's back from serving as quaestor in Judea. But I'm sure that the Lady Antonia will emphasise the unfortunate tragedy of the thing; especially as she failed to get me that imperial permission for Vespasian to enter Egypt.' He picked up a wax tablet from his desk and looked at it ruefully. 'She sent me the message this morning.'

'Then it would seem that I'm the right man to go to Cyrenaica and tell Vespasian the bad news.'

'Yes, my friend, it would seem that you are.'

Magnus stepped out of Gaius' carriage on to the quayside at Ostia, helped by an extremely attractive groom. He ignored the youth's languid eyes and coy smile and looked, instead, with a sinking heart at the hulking merchantman in which he was to spend the next half a month or so; her sides were stained with age and she exuded an unpleasant smell of rotting refuse.

'I'm sorry, Magnus,' Gaius said, 'but it was all that I could get at such short notice; the sailing season's over and there're very few making the crossing at this time of year.'

Magnus glanced back at the terrace of warehouses in which, just six nights previously, he had organised the break-in that had somehow led to his enforced exile; he cursed vociferously.

Gaius smiled in sympathy as he gave him a handful of scrolls. 'Letters for Vespasian.'

'I'm sure he'll be very pleased to have them.'

'Yes, well, I should be getting back; the Lady Antonia has invited me and the Urban Prefect for dinner. I'm sure that by the time you return this matter will be completely forgotten.'

Magnus took his bag from the groom. 'I'm sure it will, Senator.'

'Just mention my name to the trierarchos; I've paid in advance so there'll be no problems.'

'Thank you.'

'Will you be all right?' Gaius asked, his eyes lingering on the groom's legs as he climbed up next to the driver who was equally as lissom.

Magnus grinned and slung his bag over his shoulder. 'I've got nothing to do for the next fourteen or fifteen days, sir.' He patted a small lump concealed underneath his tunic. 'So don't worry about me, I'll put that time to good use; I've got a whole realm to explore.'

THE ALEXANDRIAN EMBASSY

This story comes between *False God of Rome* and *Rome's Fallen Eagle*. It concerns the Jewish Embassy to Rome, led by Philo, the brother of Alexander, the Alabarch of Alexandria, to protest to Caligula about the violence perpetrated upon the Jews of Alexandria that we witnessed in *False God*. Vespasian was a praetor at the time so, therefore, could very likely have been involved somehow with the diplomatic mission. Amongst his many works, Philo wrote an account of the embassy; it is the only extant description of Caligula by someone who actually met him and conversed with him. All the interaction with Caligula in this tale is therefore taken from a first-hand account – he really was interior decorating whilst he received the embassy!

I had always wondered how I was going to cope with the relatively boring – to my mind – time taken up by Vespasian's term as a praetor and had already come up with the idea of writing a short story to cover the period; however, once the Magnus shorts had started to take shape it seemed much more appropriate to take the incident from his point of view, rather than Vespasian's. And so, set against the backdrop of the Mercuralia, Magnus is dragooned by Senator Pollo to fix up the security for the embassy that has become Vespasian's responsibility; at the same time he has difficulties of his own in completing an illegal arms deal and getting one over his old enemy, Sempronius of the West Viminal Brotherhood, as well as an unscrupulous arms-dealer – it was ever thus.

Vespasian's obsequiousness to Caligula in thanking him for a splendid dinner is a matter of record and gives us a good insight into how he managed to survive such a dangerous time.

ROME, MAY AD 39

Marcus Salvius Magnus did not look impressed; far from it. His pugilist's face was crowned with a heavy frown; dark eyes stared grim from above a battered nose at the suave man across the desk as his index finger took out his aggression on one of his cauliflower ears, drilling it deeply. 'I've not come all the way here, Tatianus, to be told that the shipment hasn't arrived and, in fact, may never arrive.'

Tatianus shrugged; the two thick gold chains around his neck glinted in the lamplight. He flicked away a fly that had had the temerity to land on the sleeve of his fine-spun pastel-green tunic and then met Magnus' hostile gaze. 'I'm afraid, Magnus, that it looks rather as if that's exactly what you've done because it's not here. I do, however, think that you're exaggerating when you claim that I said it may never arrive. I believe that I told you that it would not arrive in the near future.' With his little finger extended, he took an elegant sip of wine from a silver cup and swilled it around his mouth; his eyebrows creased and his lips puckered in appreciation of the vintage.

Magnus struggled to keep his temper; he had never liked this smooth middle-man but, unfortunately, when it came to acquiring certain items, he was forced to do business with him. 'And what do you mean by that?'

'By the near future I mean today and tomorrow, so, by process of deduction, my statement means that the earliest your order will arrive is in two days' time.'

Magnus' fist slammed down on the desk causing his untouched cup of wine to disgorge some of its contents on to the waxed walnut-wood surface. 'You promised me that it would be here by two days before the Ides of May, and that is today.'

The room was not large and Magnus' voice filled it, causing Tatianus to wince. 'My dear Magnus, shouting at me is not going to make the slightest difference to the speed with which your order gets past the Urban Cohort guards on the city's gates. A consignment of fifty swords or a dozen re-curved Scythian composite bows are one thing: they can be hidden beneath a load of vegetables or suchlike, but a Scorpion? That's a very big piece of kit to conceal. And bearing in mind that it is illegal for all but the Praetorian Guard and the Urban Cohorts to carry swords within the city, just imagine how much more illegal it would be to be caught in possession of a legionary bolt-shooter?' Tatianus raised his eyebrows. 'I've resisted asking but now my curiosity has got the better of me: what in Hades' name do you want a Scorpion in the city for? It's not as if you can reassemble it anywhere public without it being noticed.'

'I'll tell you what I want it in the city for, Tatianus. I want it in the city for the thousand denarii that I've paid you up front, and the balance of a thousand that I've brought with me, that's what I want it in the city for.'

'And you shall, Magnus, you shall; but not today. The centurion with whom I have a close financial understanding won't be on duty at the Capena Gate on the Appian Way until the midnight of the Ides; as your delivery is coming up that road in three different carts, we'll get them through then in the early morning. You can bring back the balance at the third hour of the Ides; I'll be out until then.' Tatianus raised his shoulders and spread his hands in a conciliatory gesture. 'Unless, of course, you would prefer to leave it here for safekeeping rather than risk walking back to the Quirinal with such a large amount at night?' He gestured to the formidable-looking iron-reinforced wooden door with many locks, behind him. 'I have the most secure strongroom.'

'Leave you the money before you give me the goods? Bollocks! I've brought five of my lads with me; we'll be fine.'

'Just trying to be helpful, that's all,' Tatianus muttered, taking another sip of wine. 'Remember, I only hold on to the items for a few hours. If you don't come with the money quickly then I offload it to the first comer and your deposit is forfeit. It's all one to me.'

Magnus checked himself, swallowing a string of invective, and then looked around the painted and gilded items of furniture in Tatianus' study. The tables and sideboard bore the trappings of a wealthy but tasteful man: exquisite coloured glass vessels, their rich umber and turquoise hues warm in the flickering light, were interspersed with many small, delicately sculptured figurines of gods; more gods, in fact, than Magnus had ever seen in one room. Lining two of the walls were shelves full of scrolls, almost all of them contracts, for Tatianus liked to keep his business close to hand in the only room in which he would discuss it. Tatianus visited no man. All who required his services had to come and pay court to him; he would have it no other way, and all of Rome's underworld knew it and accepted it. 'Very well,' Magnus conceded, calming somewhat and getting up, 'I'll come back on the Ides and it had better be here or ...'

'Or what, Magnus?' Tatianus leant across the desk and steepled his hands as if his interest had been exceedingly piqued. 'What would the patronus of the South Quirinal Crossroads Brotherhood have to threaten me with? A drubbing in a dark alley or an arsonistic visit to my home, perhaps? The latter's more your style, from what I hear. Or you might even skewer me with a Scorpion bolt if you could find someone else who could supply you with that particular item; but of course, you can't, can you?' He sat back in his chair and gave Magnus a pleasant smile. 'So it's "or nothing", isn't it, Magnus? And if you ever say "or" to me again it will be the last word you will ever utter in this room because my services will be closed to you. Understand?'

Magnus closed his eyes and grimaced; Tatianus was a man he could not afford to alienate. 'I apologise, Tatianus, I meant nothing by it. I'm sure you will do your best to get my order here as quickly as possible.'

'Of course, my friend; of course I will.' Tatianus, suddenly all affability once more, rose and walked around the desk and, clapping an arm around Magnus' shoulders, guided him to the door; he was a full head taller than his guest. 'It's been a pleasure as always.' He opened the door and slapped Magnus' back so hard it propelled him out of the room.

The door slammed closed leaving Magnus, seething inside at the humiliation of being dismissed in such a patronising manner, standing in a brightly lit, marble-floored corridor, staring at two grinning henchmen. With as much dignity as he could muster he barged his way past the two heavies and stomped back down the stairs and on through the house to the atrium.

'Where do we take this, Magnus?' Marius, a tall, shaven-headed crossroads brother, asked, pointing the leather-bound stump of his left arm at a strongbox on the floor.

Magnus shook his head at the five crossroads brothers who had accompanied him with the money from the Quirinal to the Esquiline Hill. 'Put it back on the cart, lads; we're leaving empty-handed.'

The largest and most oxen-like of the brethren turned his hands over and stared at the half-eaten onion in his right palm.

'It's an expression, Sextus,' Magnus snapped, venting his frustration on the slow-witted brother as he headed into the vestibule and grabbed his cloak from its hook. The doorkeeper performed his role with alacrity and Magnus stepped out into the drizzle-laden gloom of an overcast, but warm, May night. Pulling his hood over his head, he kicked the slave belonging to Tatianus who had been keeping watch on the handcart, shouldered him into the gutter – the man's head narrowly missing the wheel of a passing wagon – and then walked at pace straight down the raised, ill-lit pavement, forcing other pedestrians to stand aside for him. His five brethren scurried after their patronus, placing the strongbox under a pile of rags on the cart, pushing it out into the constant delivery traffic that plagued Rome's streets at night and shoving the filth-splattered slave back down into the gutter as they did so.

'So he didn't have it then, Magnus,' Marius asked as they finally managed to catch up with their leader as they passed the Temple of Juno Lucina towards the base of the Esquiline and in the shadow of the Viminal.

'No, he didn't have it,' Magnus growled, kicking at the corpse of a dog.

'Then what will we do?'

'We need to get on to the roof in order to break in through the ceiling. We can't get the rope across without a Scorpion, and therefore if we don't have a Scorpion until the night of the Ides we'll just have to do the job then. So let's not moan about it and find something to occupy ourselves with in the meantime.'

'Right you are, Magnus.' Marius grinned. 'We could always stop at one of the brothels on the Via Patricius on our way back.'

'No, I ain't going to go into the West Viminal Brotherhood's territory with this amount of cash on me; that would be asking for—'

A cry of agony cut him off.

Magnus spun round to see three figures hacking at the two brothers pushing the handcart whilst Sextus fought off another couple of assailants, smashing at them with ham fists; the fifth brother, who had been pulling the cart, was struggling to relieve the ever tightening grip of vice-like fingers around his throat. As one, Magnus and Marius pulled their knives from the sheaths on their belts and crashed back into the fray as more attackers materialised out of the night. Leading with his left shoulder, as if he bore a shield, Magnus cracked into the ribcage of the nearest shadowed threat, stamping his left foot down on the man's own, fracturing many bones, as he thrust his knife forward, military-style, underarm and low, with a short, powerful jab. Blood slopped over his wrist as the breath rattled out of the assailant. Magnus twisted the knife left and then right, shredding groin muscles and drawing a satisfying howl from the core of his victim's being, as next to him Marius punched his leather-bound stump into the mouth of his adversary, shattering teeth and pulping his upper lip as he slashed the point of his blade to his right, taking one of the men hacking at the brother pulling the cart in the back of the neck, severing the spinal column; down he went like a stringless puppet.

Magnus wrenched his weapon free of the tangle of ripped tissue, releasing the foul faecal stench of evisceration; he thrust his dying opponent aside and spun, one hundred and eighty degrees, his forearm raised, to block the downward stroke of a new entrant into the fight. The blow thwarted, he let his arm give a little, allowing the man to close with him, before jamming his knee up between his legs, rupturing a testicle, and doubling him over with a strangled intake of breath as three more shadowy figures emerged from the crowd – watching but making no attempt to intervene – and headed directly for the cart. Magnus felt the wind of a thrown knife hiss past his right cheek and instinctively ducked in the opposite direction as a blade from behind stabbed at the place his head had been an instant before; he turned to see a squat man staring cross-eyed at a knife juddering in the bridge of his nose. A sharp flick of Magnus' right wrist opened the man's throat as Marius crunched his forehead into the face of one of the new attackers, crashing him back with blood spurting from his nose; with one look at his mates he turned and ran. Sextus, with a bull-like roar, picked up his last surviving assailant and hurled him after the rest who were now, suddenly, all beating a hasty retreat.

Magnus looked around. No one else threatened them and the crowd had begun to disperse, none of them wishing to get involved in a matter that was plainly not of their concern. On the ground dead, amongst the bodies of six of their attackers, lay two of his brethren; a third knelt, coughing drily as he massaged his bruised throat. 'Are you all right, Postumus?' Magnus asked, hauling the brother up as Marius restrained a bellowing Sextus from chasing after their attackers.

'Just about, Magnus; and you?' Postumus wheezed.

'I think so.' As he drew breath, Magnus suddenly turned and rushed to the cart; the rags had been brushed aside. 'Juno's puckered arse!' he cursed as he stared at the empty bed of the cart. 'The bastards got it; they must have known what we were carrying.' Marius and Sextus joined him, both still panting hard; they looked forlornly at where their strongbox had been. A groan from the ground distracted Magnus; he glanced down to see the man with the shattered mouth trying to crawl away. Catching him by the collar, Magnus cracked his head down on the paving stone, knocking him unconscious.

'Here, lads,' Magnus snarled, holding the limp body up, 'get him on the cart and cover him with rags. Let's get to our tavern before the Vigiles turn up and try to prevent us from asking matey-boy here a few very tricky and painful questions, if you take my meaning?'

The questions were far less tricky than they were painful; in fact, they were very simple and remarkably few.

'I'll ask you again,' Magnus said in a convivial manner, smiling down at the prisoner and patting him in a kindly fashion on the cheek. The man wriggled in fear at the sight of a red-hot poker in Marius' gloved hand as he hung naked, suspended by his ankles, from a ceiling beam in a room deep in the rear of the tavern building that served as the headquarters of the South Quirinal Brotherhood. 'Who do you work for and how did you know what we were carrying?'

The man's eyes widened as Marius grinned at him over Magnus' shoulder, showing him the glowing iron and repeatedly raising his eyebrows in ill-concealed anticipation. His swollen mouth, however, remained sealed as he struggled against the rope binding his wrists behind his back.

'Tch, tch.' Magnus shook his head in exaggerated disappointment as if he were a *grammaticus* having received the wrong answer from his most promising pupil. 'I'll tell you what: I'll ask you the questions for the third time, just in case you misheard before. Who do you work for and how did you know what we were carrying?'

The prisoner shook his head, screwing up his eyes.

Marius made a show of putting the poker back into the mobile brazier that, along with an oil lamp on a table next to it, lit the chamber. Sextus' bulk lurked in the shadows by the door, under which flickered the dim light from the adjoining corridor; Postumus stood behind the prisoner to prevent him from rotating.

'Perhaps he's lost his voice,' Magnus mused, scratching his chin. 'Why don't you check, Marius?'

'Right you are, Magnus.' He withdrew the poker, its tip now orange. Within an instant the stench of burnt flesh was accompanied by a piercing shriek that brought a happy smile to Magnus' face.

'His thigh doesn't look too nice but I can't hear anything wrong with his voice,' Magnus observed, turning back to Sextus, 'can you, Sextus?'

'What's that, Magnus?'

'I said: can you hear anything wrong with his voice?'

'Er … no, Magnus; it sounded fine to me.'

'I thought so. What about you, Postumus, did you hear anything wrong?'

'It sounded sweet to me, Brother.'

'In which case it's time to stop being nice. Hold the gentleman's buttocks apart for him, would you?'

Postumus grinned with genuine enjoyment at the prospect. 'My pleasure, Magnus.'

Magnus squatted down and thrust his face close to the prisoner's as Postumus pulled his legs apart. 'Now listen, you piece of rat shit. I'm in a very bad mood and I don't give a fuck how much or for how long I hurt you. Two of my brothers are dead and a lot of my money is missing so I'll do whatever it takes to redress those facts. Answer my questions and Marius here won't use your arse as a scabbard for his poker.'

Still the man shook his head, his eyes bulging at the sight of the glowing terror coming towards him.

'That's a silly decision.' Magnus nodded at Marius. 'Just in the crease and then, Postumus, squeeze.'

The red-hot tip was placed between the man's buttocks as Postumus pushed them together. Smoke rose to the hiss of burning hair and skin and, after a moment's delay, the prisoner issued a scream that made his last effort seem pathetic in comparison; on it went, rising in timbre and getting rougher as it grated, drying in his throat.

At Magnus' nod, Marius withdrew the object of torment and pressed it back into the brazier; the prisoner started to hyperventilate.

'He's going to have to be careful how he sponges his arsehole for a few days,' Magnus opined, peering at the damage before squatting back down and grabbing the prisoner's chin. 'Now how would you like that done to your scrotum, maggot? I can assure you that we'll all enjoy watching and listening.'

The man's chest heaved and tears rolled down his forehead; his swollen lips drew back to reveal shattered teeth. 'Se ... Sem ...'

Magnus put his ear closer to the man's mouth. 'Who?'

'Semp ...' He struggled for breath for a couple of moments. 'Sempronius.'

The name came out as a wheeze but it was clearly audible; Magnus' face darkened. 'Sempronius,' he growled, chewing on the word. 'He of the West Viminal Brotherhood?'

The prisoner nodded feebly, his eyes closed.

'How did he know about the cash?'

'I don't ... I ... I don't know; he just ...' He winced and spat some blood from his ruined mouth; a globule rolled into his nostrils. 'He just told us to track you back from the house on the Esquiline and attack you as you neared our territory so we'd not have so far to go with the box.'

'So he knew about the box?'

The man nodded, his eyes still closed.

Magnus stood, his face set grim. He paused for a few moments in thought and then wrenched the glove from Marius' hand, pulled it on his own and grabbed the iron from the fire. 'As you've been a good boy and answered the questions as best you can I'll make good my promise: Marius won't use your arsehole as a scabbard for his iron.' He pushed Postumus aside and, brandishing the searing bar in his right hand, he exposed the man's anus with his left. 'But I will!' With a jerk he forced the poker into the sphincter and thrust it, with the palm of his hand, as deep as it would go. With a howl that would have drowned out both the previous ones combined the prisoner convulsed, almost doubling up, so that his face stared, eyes brim with horror, over his scrotum, directly at Magnus for an instant, before slumping back down, swinging limply, dead from shock, pain and horrific internal injuries.

'Cut him down, Marius,' Magnus ordered, heading out of the room, 'and then dump him on the West Viminal's border; you can use Sextus and Postumus for the job.' Magnus walked through the door and then put his head back round. 'And make sure that the poker is pulled out a bit and clearly visible. I want Sempronius to know exactly what I think of him.'

'Your tame senator sent a boy round,' an old man with gnarled fingers and a sagging throat said, not taking his eyes off the scroll that he was perusing in the light of two lamps.

Magnus took a seat next to him at the table in the corner of the tavern with the best view of the door through the fug of the crowded room. 'Which one, Servius?'

'Which boy? I don't know, I didn't ask his name.'

'No, you old goat; which senator?' Magnus took the cup and wine jug brought to him by the man serving behind the bar. 'Thanks, Cassandros.'

Servius looked up, his eyes awash with milky patches. 'Oh, the older one.'

'Senator Pollo?'

'Yes.'

'And?'

Servius looked back at his scroll. 'It's no good, Magnus; I'll be blind before long. Already everything is vague and dimming.' He shook his bald head and placed the scroll down on the table. 'I didn't want to disturb you whilst you were … in conference but the senator is very keen that you should attend his *salutatio* in the morning and then accompany him to the Senate House; his nephew, Vespasian, has a job for you.'

'What sort of job?'

'The boy couldn't say but Senator Pollo said that you were to keep the next three days or so free.'

'Three days?'

'Or so.'

Magnus kicked the nearest stool. 'Shit! Just when things are getting busy.'

With a fold of his plain white citizen's toga covering his head, Magnus crumbled a flour and salt cake over the flame of the small fire that was kept continuously burning on the altar of the Crossroads' lares, embedded into the tavern's exterior wall. The upkeep of these shrines was the original reason for the formation of the brotherhoods all over the city, centuries earlier. In the intervening time, however, the function of the brotherhoods had expanded to looking after the interests and welfare of the local community, for which they received remuneration from the locals commensurate with the amount of protection they needed. Their word, therefore, was law in the area in which they held sway.

As the crumbs flared in the flame, Magnus muttered a short prayer to ask the gods of the junction of the Alta Semita and the Vicus Longus to hold their hands over the area. That done, he raised a bowl and poured a libation in front of the five small bronze figures that represented the lares, promising the same offering that evening should they keep their side of the religious bargain. Pulling the toga from his head, he patted the brother, whose turn it was to tend the fire, on the shoulder before heading off down the wakening Alta Semita, with the first indigo glow of dawn to his back and with Cassandros and a bearded, betrousered easterner, both of whom carried staves and sputtering torches, to either side.

It was but a short walk to Senator Gaius Vespasius Pollo's house and, although Magnus arrived there just shy of sunrise, there was already a goodly crowd of the senator's clients waiting outside for admittance to his atrium in order to wish a good day to their patron, receive a small largesse, enquire if there was any way that they could be of service to him that day and, perhaps, occasionally take advantage of the symbiotic relationship and ask a favour of the senator themselves.

'Cassandros and Tigran, you stay here.' Magnus did not care for order of precedence and pushed his way through the crowd to the front door, leaving his two companions waiting on the fringe of the gathering. No one objected to his progress as all were aware that this battered ex-boxer, although low on the social scale, was high in their patron's favour.

As the sun crested the eastern horizon, bereft of yesterday's clouds, bathing the Seven Hills in a spring morning glow, the door was opened by an exceedingly attractive youth with blond hair, the length of which was countered by the shortness of his tunic. Magnus was first through the door.

'Magnus, my friend,' Gaius Vespasius Pollo boomed, not getting up from the sturdy chair set in the centre of the atrium in front of the impluvium with its spluttering fountain. He brushed a carefully tonged ringlet of dyed black hair away from his porcine eyes glittering in a hugely fat face.

'Good morning, sir; er … you require a service, I believe.'

'Yes, yes, but I'll talk to you about it later. In the meantime my steward will give you a list of Jewish requirements and customs.' Gaius gestured to a slightly older version of the youth on the door who bowed his head to Magnus. 'Oh, and he'll also have one of my lads read it for you seeing as you, well, you know.'

'Can't read,' Magnus said, his confusion plain upon his face.

'Indeed,' Gaius replied, already looking to the client next in line.

'Philo!' Magnus exclaimed as he walked beside Gaius, processing with his two hundred, or so, clients accompanying him down the Quirinal. 'You mean the brother of Alexander, the Alabarch of the Alexandrian Jews?'

'The very same,' Gaius puffed; although he had set a sedate pace he was already sheened with sweat. His jowls, breasts, belly and buttocks wobbled furiously to different rhythms beneath his senatorial toga as he waddled behind Cassandros and Tigran with their staves at the ready to beat a path for him should the way become too crowded.

'What's he doing in Rome?'

'He's been here since the start of the sailing season. He's heading an embassy of Alexandrian Jews to the Emperor to complain about the way Flaccus, the Prefect of Egypt, handled the riots between the Jews and the Greeks in Alexandria last year.'

'I saw them, I was there with Vespasian, stealing Alexander's breastplate from his mausoleum for Caligula because Flaccus refused to hand it over.'

'Of course you were; so you know what the riots were like, then?'

'Well, according to Philo, they were an outrage because, how did he put it? The Jews were scourged with whips by the lowest class of executioner as if they were indigenous country dwellers, rather than with rods wielded by Alexandrian lictors as was the entitlement of their rank.'

'What?'

'Yes, that was his main complaint. Forget the fact that his sister-in-law had to be put out of her misery by her own husband because she had been flayed alive and had no chance of survival, or that gangs of Greeks dragged Jews off to the theatre to crucify them and then set fire to the crosses. No, he was more concerned about the etiquette of beating and how some of his acquaintances were not accorded the dignity of the rod, as he put it. An arsehole, as far as I could make out, and a pompous one at that.'

'Yes, well, he is the arsehole, pompous or not, that Vespasian wants you to ... look after, shall we say, for the next few days.'

'Why?'

'Because no one else will. He's either refused or got rid of, on religious grounds, everyone that Cossa Cornelius Lentullus, the Urban Prefect, has provided for his safety. Not wanting to take the blame should something happen to Philo and his embassy, Lentullus passed on responsibility to Corbulo, the Junior Consul, who in turn immediately passed it down the line to Vespasian, in his capacity as one of the Urban Praetors this year. Corbulo is well aware that Vespasian has a relationship with the family from his time in Alexandria and therefore perhaps has some influence over Philo. So Vespasian, naturally, is anxious that Philo should not wander around the city unattended as he is likely to cause offence wherever he goes.'

'Well, that's for sure. Why doesn't someone just bundle him on to a ship and send him back to Alexandria?'

'Because, after keeping him waiting, Caligula has decided that he will receive him and his embassy and is looking forward to it; which is why no one wants to be responsible for disappointing our divine Emperor by allowing Philo to get himself killed. Apparently Caligula's curious as to why the Jews don't accept him as a god.'

Magnus scowled. 'Well, they don't accept anything as a god. That's what the Greeks used as the reason for the riots: they didn't see why the Jews should have equal status with them if they weren't going to behave like equal citizens and make a sacrifice to the Emperor when they took their annual oath of allegiance.'

'Which is, I believe, the very question that Caligula wants to put to Philo: why should the Jews have equal status if they don't behave like everyone else in the Empire?'

'Tricky.'

'Yes, so just make sure that he's kept alive to answer it. Caligula is on his way back from Antium and Vespasian is accompanying him; they should be back in a day or so as Caligula's keen to get his campaign in Germania under way.'

Magnus grunted; he did not look enamoured of the commission. 'If you say so, sir.'

'I don't *say* so; it's just a small favour that I'm asking.'

'And in return, sir?' Magnus asked as they went through a colonnade that opened out into the Forum built by Augustus.

Gaius looked askance at his client and raised a knowing, plucked eyebrow. 'Yes?'

'Have you heard of a man named Quintus Tullius Tatianus?'

'An equestrian from an unfashionable branch of the Tullian *gens*?'

'I think so.'

'He who can get hold of any weapon you care to name and get it through the city gates?'

Magnus hid his surprise at a senator being aware of the existence of such a shady figure. 'That's the one; what do you know of him?'

'Just that, there's nothing he can't get hold of and smuggle into the city for the right price: Scythian composite bows, Thracian rhompheroi, Rhodian staff-slings and the correct lead shot, throwing axes from the barbarian North, Jewish sicari daggers, you name it and he can get it. Oh, and he only ever does business at his house and on his own terms. Why do you ask?'

'I was going to ... well ... enlighten you, if you take my meaning?'

'He's upset you so you were going to report his illegal enterprise to me in the hopes that I would take it to the Urban Prefect or some such thing?'

Magnus was disappointed. 'But you already know what everyone else knows?'

'If by "everyone else" you mean the criminal underbelly of Rome who seem to have an insatiable demand for novel ways of despatching one another, then yes.'

Magnus thought for a few moments as Gaius hailed other senators also making their way through the Forum of Augustus. 'But how come you know about him as well?' Magnus asked once he had Gaius' attention again.

'Anyone who has been a praetor knows about him. He's well known to all of us who've had a responsibility for law and order in Rome.'

'And yet nothing's been done about him?'

'No, we leave him alone.'

Magnus could not conceal a look of astonishment. 'You mean the authorities let him continue in business.'

'Naturally. We never touch him, which has led him to become so complacent that he thinks that he can trade openly from his own study.'

Magnus' astonishment morphed into incredulity. 'The authorities just let him bring weapons into the city with impunity?'

'Of course.'

'Why?'

'Now, Magnus,' Gaius said with a concerned frown, 'you sound as if you're in danger of becoming an upright and outraged citizen. It makes absolute sense to let him carry on undisturbed: if he disappeared who would take his place and how long would it take us to find out? And, actually, would it just be one person? Tatianus guards his trade very jealously so that anyone who encroaches on his business normally finds themselves the victim of their own merchandise. He polices it very nicely for us; rather like your crossroads fraternities are tolerated because you keep the crime down in your areas even though you're a bunch of criminals yourselves. It's a most peculiar paradox.'

'Now, sir, you're not being entirely fair.'

'Really? Well, if you say so.' Gaius looked amused as they passed into Caesar's Forum where the Urban Prefect could be petitioned in the shadow of an equestrian statue of the onetime dictator. He pointed to Lentullus at his desk perusing a scroll. 'We could go and tell the Prefect all about Tatianus now and he would just laugh. If it wasn't for Tatianus he would have no idea of how much weaponry was in the city and who possessed it so that every so often he can send the Urban Cohorts round and have a collection.'

Magnus' mind was reeling as they came out into the Forum Romanum where Cassandros and Tigran were forced to begin using their staves to clear a passage through the morning crowds. 'You mean that Tatianus tells the Prefect about every shipment he brings in?'

'Of course not; how could we trust him? No, that would be a silly idea; he's completely unaware of our interest in him. Much simpler just to find out who's in his pay and then threaten nasty mishaps to their loved ones if they so much as forget one item that comes through. At the moment Tatianus seems to be using a certain Urban Cohort centurion who's part of the Capena Gate detail.'

'Who happens to be on duty on the Ides.'

'Ah! So that's when your shipment is coming in, is it?'

'Now, I didn't say that I had purchased anything, sir. I just said … well, I didn't really say anything, did I?'

'No matter, Magnus; but you can be sure that the Urban Prefect will know about anything illegal that does come through the Capena Gate tomorrow within an hour of its arrival. Then he has only to watch who comes and goes from Tatianus' house to have an idea as to where the shipment is destined.'

'Pluto's slack sack!' Magnus realised the seriousness of his position should he take possession of his order. 'And then depending on what it is he will act accordingly; is that how it goes?'

'Very much like that, Magnus.'

'So if I were to go to his house soon after a very illicit item comes in, I could expect a visit from the Urban Cohorts and have some serious explaining to do.'

'Precisely; and even I would find it hard to assist you in that situation. Has that helped you?'

'Thank you, sir; that is interesting. Naturally I'll keep this to myself.'

'Magnus, the day that either of us betrays a confidence will, I'm sure, be the last day of our very mutually beneficial relationship.'

They stopped at the base of the Senate House steps; Gaius bade farewell to the majority of his clients as all around other senators did likewise. He then gave instructions to the few clients he had asked to remain behind concerning the lobbying favours he needed them to carry out for him that morning in the Forum. Once he had dismissed them he turned his attention back to Magnus. 'Vespasian will be in contact when he returns to the city, probably tomorrow, provided Caligula doesn't decide to dispense his bizarre forms of imperial justice at every town along the Appian Way. Hopefully he can persuade the Emperor to see the Alexandrian embassy soon and then we can hustle them onto a ship in Ostia and be done with them. Keep Philo out of trouble until then.'

Magnus grimaced at the thought of at least a couple of days with Philo. 'I'll do my best, sir. Where will I find them?'

'Ah, didn't I tell you that? Well, the delegates are all staying at a villa in the Gardens of Lemia just outside the Esquiline Gate.'

'And Philo?'

Gaius nodded towards the base of the Capitoline Hill. 'He's in there.'

'What, in the Tullianum?'

'Yes, although he's not in the cell, he's with the gaolers. The Urban Prefect had no option but to imprison him until he could find someone who would be able to restrain him from spitting at every statue of our gods he passes. As you've met him, and his family is, to a great extent, in yours and Vespasian's debt, that someone appears to be you.'

'It's an outrage!' Philo was quite clear on this point; it was the fourth time he had made it to Magnus, growing more vehement on each occasion. 'Me, the leader of the embassy from the Jews of Alexandria to the Emperor of Rome, locked up like a common criminal as if I were from the lowest order; of no more account than you, Magnus.' Philo's long grey beard stuck out at a strange angle from his chin, wobbling up and down as he sucked in his lower lip, working it furiously in his disgust. His heavy brows creased and uncreased in time to the blinking of his eyes, one of which was surrounded by a purpling bruise. 'Does the Urban Prefect not know who I am? Is he unaware of the dignity of my rank? Doesn't he know the extent of my literary achievements? Is he not cognisant of the fact that my brother, Alexander, is the Alabarch of the Alexandrian Jews? The Alabarch, I tell you; not some vague title such as head of the Alexandrian Jews, or leader, or foremost Jewish citizen, but Alabarch. *The* Alabarch! And I, the brother of *the* Alabarch and leader of the embassy, was forced to share the company of gaolers so uncouth that I doubt that even you would find them suitable company, Magnus. Do you see just how I have been insulted when all I was trying to do was to give alms to the Jewish beggars who live amongst the tombs on the Appian Way? It's an outrage.' He adjusted his white turbanesque headdress to further emphasise the point.

Magnus tutted in sympathy. 'To be treated as if you were me; I can't imagine anything worse for you. But I'm sure that it was all nothing more than a misunderstanding based on you just clearing your throat at the wrong time, whilst you were passing a statue of Mars. I'm positive that any phlegm you deposited on the god's foot was due to misaiming, and the outraged citizens who attacked and beat you were overreacting to what was no more than a rogue globule of mucus.'

Philo pulled his black and white patterned mantle tighter around his shoulders. 'Yes, and to be set upon by common people and beaten by their unwashed hands was a shame that was almost too much to bear; not one person of the equestrian rank amongst them, let alone a senator. None of my attackers had the quality to lay a finger on me and yet here I am, cut and bruised by the lower orders.'

'Yeah, well, I'm afraid that there's never been much thought for relative status when it comes to people taking exception to the actions of others, even misinterpreted actions. On the other hand ...' Magnus tried to think of something with which to change the subject as they headed, with Tigran and Cassandros, towards the Esquiline Gate and the gardens just beyond, but nothing came to mind and instead he had to endure the whole diatribe again from the beginning, spiced with added outrage and pepped-up indignation. He prayed to the gods of his crossroads that the messenger that Senator Pollo had promised to send to his brethren at the tavern had completed his errand and that there would be four other brothers awaiting them at the gardens and he could delegate the unpleasant duty to Tigran and them.

'Don't allow them to leave the garden complex, Tigran,' Magnus ordered as Philo was reunited with the other members of his embassy, each one a greybeard and each one looking very much like the next, dressed as they all were in white, ankle-length robes, black and white mantles and wound cotton headdresses. He took the list of Jewish requirements that Gaius had supplied him with and handed it to Tigran. 'And this is a list of what they won't eat and when they won't do stuff – it's quite long. You can read, can't you?'

Tigran smiled as he looked at the scroll. 'Yes, Magnus, Servius taught me. He's a good teacher,' he added pointedly. 'No shell-fish! Why ever not?'

'Who knows and who cares? And don't try and eat with them as they don't share the table with people not of their religion, apparently. Not that I suppose you were planning on making friends with them.' He looked over at Philo who had seated himself beneath a pergola in front of the villa, at the garden's centre, and was greeting each of his companions in turn and telling each one, at length, of his ordeal. 'Have the lads guard the gate to the gardens. I've explained to Philo that they should stay here for their own safety and warned him that the common people are still angry with him and he faces fresh humiliation at the unwashed hands of the hoi polloi until I can talk to their leaders and clear up the misunderstanding that sparked it all off.'

'Are you really going to do that?'

'Bollocks I am. No, I've got business with Sempronius to pursue and a patronising middle-man to pull down from his perch.'

'Postumus disappeared a couple of hours before they found the body soon after dawn,' Marius informed Magnus when he arrived back at the tavern at midday. 'They pulled the poker out and took it back to Sempronius who was sacrificing at their lares altar. He left as soon as he'd finished the ritual and arrived back at his headquarters looking as if he wouldn't mind heating up the poker and using it on someone himself.'

Magnus took a deep draught of the warm, spiced wine that he was cradling in both hands and reflected for a few moments. Servius shuffled his accounts scrolls on the table next to him. 'So, what happened to Postumus?'

Marius shrugged. 'We smelt fresh-baked bread, so I gave him some money to go and get a couple of loaves and some hot wine but he never came back. I reckon he spent my money in a brothel on the Vicus Patricius; he was very aroused after the poker episode.'

Magnus nodded in agreement. 'He'll turn up and you can shake him for the money. As for Sempronius, I reckon that we can expect a revenge attack. We should double the lads watching our border with the West Viminal and give them some speedy small boys to run messages. Meanwhile, I need Sempronius to come into possession of a piece of information that will, I hope, be too much for him to resist.'

'What's that, Brother?'

'I want him to find out that I'm doing business with Tatianus and that I owe him an outstanding thousand denarii for a delivery that is due to arrive tomorrow, but since the theft of that money I'm struggling to raise the cash in time. Tatianus has said that he will sell the item to the first comer with the correct coinage even though I've already put down the deposit of a thousand.'

Servius rubbed his clouded eyes. 'Tatianus has been known to do that before. He always says that the deposit only guarantees that he will keep the consignment for a few hours and after that he'll sell to the first person with the right money so that he doesn't compromise himself by having illegal goods on his property for too long.'

'Exactly; we have a precedent so Sempronius will believe it. And I'll bet he would love to get hold of what I wanted to buy just to prevent me from having it. Plus, to do that using my money would please him greatly.'

'But what's he going to do with a Scorpion?'

'Doesn't matter, the point is that he'll think he's stopped us doing whatever we were going to do with it and it will have cost him nothing in real terms.'

'And what happens if he gets it?'

'Then he'll be the one who has to explain himself to the Urban Prefect.'

'But then the job will be off.'

Magnus took another sip of wine. 'What I've just learnt from Senator Pollo means that the job's already off at the moment unless I can do some deep thinking to retrieve it. I'm just trying to make the best of the situation and make things uncomfortable for Sempronius and inconvenient for Tatianus. But first I need to plant the seed.'

Servius wheezed a weak cough. 'It goes without saying that the best place to plant your seed is where you want it to grow.'

Magnus frowned and drained his cup. 'Are you trying to be philosophical, because if so that was a pretty poor attempt. Of course I need to plant it with Sempronius.'

'But that's not where you really want it to grow, is it?'

Magnus looked at his counsellor, considering his remark. Over the fifteen years that he had been the patronus of the South Quirinal he had come to value his second-in-command's advice based on an encyclopaedic knowledge of the inhabitants of the dark underbelly of Rome. 'You're right, Brother: Tatianus is where I want that notion to take hold. If he thinks that I can't come up with the money then he'll start trying to offload the shipment as quickly as possible.'

Servius essayed a smile which appeared as more of a grimace on his wizened face. 'Precisely; and provided you also plant the idea that Sempronius would be a likely alternative purchaser then the whole matter should take care of itself very quickly.'

'But how do I do it without having a formal meeting and then mentioning Sempronius by name? Tatianus is bound to tell him that I suggested him and then he's bound to suspect it's a trap.'

'Where does Tatianus go when he's not doing business in his house?'

Magnus thought for a few moments. 'The normal places: the baths, theatre, games and all that sort of thing.'

'Yes, but what else? What did you notice about him? About the decoration in his room?'

After a brief pause to recollect, Magnus pointed his index finger at his counsellor. 'The statuettes of the gods; he has a lot of them.'

'Yes, he's a very religious man so he does all the things that religious men should do.'

'Such as observing all the festivals, and tomorrow is the Ides of May.'

'Indeed, and we shall be celebrating the Mercuralia in honour of Mercury, the god of merchants and commerce, amongst other things; and what do all merchants do on that day?'

Magnus grinned and shook his head slowly in awe at the way his counsellor's mind worked. 'They sprinkle their heads, merchandise and places of business with water taken from the well at the Capena Gate, and because they have to draw the water themselves we can guarantee that at some time tomorrow Tatianus will be at the Capena Gate. In fact, he said that he wouldn't be home until the third hour that morning so he'll be at the gate first thing. I've just got to work out how to take advantage of that.'

Night was three hours old but the streets of Rome were none the quieter for it. Magnus, with Marius and Sextus for company and protection, watched a group of half a dozen men make their way up the Vicus Longus. All were hooded and all had the bearing of men used to violence; a couple had limps from old wounds and one was missing three fingers on his left hand. One had a bulging sack slung over his shoulder.

'The lads watching the West Viminal were sure that they came from that brotherhood's headquarters?' Magnus asked Marius, raising his voice to make himself heard against the rattle and clatter of mule- and ox-drawn carts and wagons.

'Yes, Brother. As soon as they appeared to be heading in this direction they sent one of the errand-boys racing up here with the news. There's no doubt about it: they're out to do no good in the area.'

'Well, they don't look like they're on a shopping trip, that's for sure. But there're not enough of them to threaten the tavern; so what do they want?'

All three turned away and leant against the open bar of a street wine-seller's establishment as the six heavies approached.

'There you go, Magnus,' the owner said, placing a jug of wine and three earthenware cups on the counter. He then turned to the old slave working with him. 'Come on, Hylas, you lazy sod, get a move on with those victuals.' He looked apologetically at Magnus. 'I'll get you some bread and roast pork as soon as my idiot slave wakes up; no charge, obviously.'

'Thanks, Septimus,' Magnus said, edging his head around to try to get a closer look at the intruders as they passed close by but their hoods were too deep. 'Have you ever seen any of them before up here?'

Septimus looked at the men as they passed and waited until they were out of earshot. 'Hard to say, Magnus, I couldn't see their faces; but there were a couple of strangers hanging around earlier today, big lads who had the look of ex-gladiators about them. One of them had a limp and his mate was missing a few fingers, I seem to remember when I served him; although how many and which hand I don't recall.'

'Did you catch any of their conversation?'

'Not really, we were very busy at the time and, what with Hylas being about as dozy as a slave can get without actually dropping down dead, that means I'm rushed off my feet and have very little time for chit-chat or eavesdropping.'

'Pity.'

'I did notice that they were always looking up the hill in the direction of your tavern and after they'd had a couple of jugs of my roughest they moved off in that direction. That's the lot, I'm afraid, Magnus.'

'Don't you worry, Septimus my lad; that may be very helpful. About what time was this?'

'The third hour or so.'

Magnus turned to Marius and Sextus. 'They found poker-boy's body soon after dawn and took the implement to Sempronius, who would have seen it at the end of the first hour. The timing fits.'

Marius nodded whilst Sextus, judging by his strained expression, struggled to get to grips with such advanced arithmetic.

Magnus downed his wine and then grabbed some pork and a hunk of bread as Hylas placed the plate of food in front of him. 'Come on, lads, let's follow the bastards and see what they're up to.'

Keeping a dozen paces behind the suspicious group, Magnus and his companions tracked them along the Vicus Longus as it made its way up the Quirinal Hill. Just before they arrived at the junction with the Alta Semita, the intruders stopped and took a deep interest in a reinforced door out of sight of the main street at the end of a recess, a couple of paces deep, in the wall. 'That's one of the back doors to the tavern,' Magnus hissed as they watched the men from a distance. 'How do they know about that? We haven't needed to use it in ages.'

Having tested it with a crowbar extracted from the sack and found it to be solid, the intruders moved on up the hill.

'I think they're planning to give us a painful shock by taking us in the rear, lads, if you take my meaning? My guess is that they're heading for the back door on the Alta Semita to see if they can force an entrance there. If we hurry we could be there to meet them.'

The group carried on up the hill, past the tavern's south wall, skirted around the tables and benches set outside the building at the apex of the forty-five-degree junction and then turned left along the Alta Semita.

Magnus stayed in the shadow of the south wall as he watched the intruders disappear behind the northern wall. 'Quick, lads!'

He ran through the outside tables, signalling to the brothers drinking and playing dice to follow him, and pounded through the tavern's front door, causing a lull in the raucous atmosphere within. On he went, through the gradually widening room as it expanded, following the diverging courses of the two roads encasing it, and then out through a curtained doorway and right into an ill-lit corridor. 'Break out the weapons box, Sextus,' Magnus ordered as he turned left into the room at the far end of the corridor in which he conducted brotherhood business.

'Break out the weapons box; right you are, Magnus,' the brother replied, digesting his orders and then picking up a heavy box from just inside the door as Magnus ran to a further door on the far side of the room, its key already in the lock in preparation for a quick getaway. He turned the key, opened the door, crossed another, longer corridor and rushed through the dark chamber, infused with the lingering smell of burnt flesh, which had been the scene of the previous night's brutalities.

Here Magnus slowed and, signalling to the men racing behind him to do likewise, he listened. From the adjoining room could be heard the distinct sound of wood being worked on by metal. 'Dole them out, Sextus,' Magnus said, nodding to the weapons box clasped in the huge brother's ham fists. 'And close the door behind us, Marius.' The one-handed brother quietly pushed the door to, shrouding the room in almost complete darkness.

Taking the first sword from the box, Magnus crept forward to the door at the far left side of the room and put his ear to it. Listening, he slid his hand over the wood and found the key, again ready in position should this escape route be urgently required. 'They're almost in, by the sound of it. There's only one way out of that room and it's through this door; let's make it easy for them.' He turned the key and the lock clicked; a moment later came the sound of splintering wood from the room beyond. 'Keep tight against the walls, lads,' Magnus hissed at the eight or so brethren veiled by gloom. 'Let's try and get all six of the arse-sponges.'

Magnus pulled back into the corner opposite the door as the handle was tried from the other side; there was a dull clunk and then a tall thin chink of dim light materialised as the door was slowly pushed ajar. The chink widened and then was filled by the silhouette of a bulky man; he paused and listened – none of Magnus' brethren dared breathe.

After what seemed like an age, the intruder stepped through into the room, his mates close behind. 'We go through this room and then across a corridor,' he whispered as he trod gently forward and the last of the shadows passed through the door.

'No you fucking don't!' Magnus shouted as he ground the tip of his blade into the nearest silhouette, rolling his wrist as it punctured flesh and muscle; a roar of pain, guttural and prolonged, was his reward. His brothers took his lead and descended on the shadowed figures from all angles, hacking and stabbing wildly in the dark at the surprised and confused intruders who, despite their disadvantage, very soon rallied with the three remaining on their feet managing to get back to back. Weapons clashed with ringing reports and men grunted and cursed in the blackness as a wounded intruder moaned pitifully somewhere on the floor. The three survivors, swiping their blades before them to discourage their attackers from closing with them, edged back the way they had come. Slowly they retreated, their forms indistinct in the gloom, defending every assault with lightning-swift ripostes that gave credence to Septimus' assumption that they were men trained for the arena.

'Easy, lads!' Magnus shouted as he realised that there would be no way that they could break through the gladiators' guard in the near absent light. 'Pull back and let the bastards go.'

His brethren obeyed the order as the three survivors stepped back through the door and then, after a brief pause, turned as one man and ran off, out into the street and on into the night.

'Minerva's dry dugs, they were good,' Magnus puffed as he slammed the remains of the shattered back door closed behind the fleeing intruders.

'What do you want us to do with the wounded one, Brother?' Marius asked, kicking the moaning, prone form and eliciting a cry of pain. 'Would you like me to heat up my poker?'

'No, Brother, we know where he came from; just make sure he doesn't go back there, if you take my meaning?'

The wet sound of honed iron slicing through muscle and carti-lage was followed by a protracted gurgling as Servius and another brother entered the room with an oil lamp each, illuminating the dying man as he drowned in his own blood, his throat a gaping gash.

'Is everyone all right?' Magnus asked as Servius knelt down and pulled the sack from the intruder's weakening grip.

His brothers examined themselves for wounds and to their surprise found none.

'We've got a couple of problems, Servius,' Magnus said.

'No back door,' the counsellor replied, rummaging in the sack.

'I'll have that mended and reinforced before morning; Marius will see to that. No, it's more that we haven't got a back door that isn't known about.'

'Then you'd better make another one.'

'Where?'

'In a different place.' Servius nodded to the wall opposite the ruined door. 'What's on the other side of that?'

Magnus scratched his head and frowned. 'I imagine it's just a deserted courtyard full of shit and stuff. Perfect. I'll have the lads knock a door through.'

Servius shock his head. 'People can see a door; just have them remove the mortar from the bricks so that a couple of blows from a sledgehammer will knock them down.'

'That's a nice idea, Brother. I'll have them do the same in a couple of other places too. What have you got in there?'

Servius tipped the contents of the sack on to the floor; an earthenware jar, about the size of a man's head, fell out wrapped in bundles of rags. 'It looks like they were planning on torching the place.' He picked up some rags and held them to his nose. 'Oil.' Then he pulled the stopper from the jar, immediately releasing a pungent scent that Magnus did not recognise. 'I'll wager that, whatever this is, it can burn fiercely; I'll have a little play with it somewhere safe.' He refitted the stopper and then looked up at Magnus. 'You said that we've got a couple of problems?'

'Yeah; the other is how did the leader of those bastards know his way through this building in the dark? I heard him say: "We go through this room and then across a corridor." How did he know that without someone telling him?'

'Or without having been here before?'

'True, Brother, very true. And that's an even more disturbing thought.'

The Capena Gate was busy the hour before dawn the following morning; scores of merchants and traders pushed and shoved each other to get to the well at the foot of the Caelian Hill, sandwiched between the city walls and the line of the Appian Aqueduct, to the left of the gate. Each one was keen to draw the water with which Mercury was sure to bless their business ventures and each one wanted to complete the task as quickly as possible so as not to be away from those ventures for longer than necessary. In the cut-throat world of Roman commerce, time definitely was money and therefore manners came into little consideration when it came to waiting one's turn in the scrimmage that passed for a queue. The priests of Mercury, standing on a dais overlooking the well, in torchlight, offered prayers to their favoured deity as his special day dawned; even their presence did nothing to help restore a semblance of order to this thoroughly un-reverential scene. Just to the right of this chaos, the centurion of the watch had the men of the Urban Cohort under his command inspect every cart coming through the gate. Most were given a cursory search but occasionally, at random, one was given a rigorous frisking much to the annoyance of the carter, who knew that he had only an hour to make his delivery and get his vehicle out of the city before the daytime ban on beast-drawn vehicles came into effect – unless, of course, he had access to expensive stabling within the walls.

'I suppose he knows which ones not to search too carefully,' Magnus commented as he and Marius watched the centurion point to a cart loaded with leather buckets. 'Mind you, I imagine our order is already through.'

Marius yawned and grunted something unintelligible but to the affirmative. They stood beneath an arch of the Appian Aqueduct where it crossed from the Caelian Hill to the Aventine, running within the Servian Walls.

Magnus nudged his brother with the amphora he carried. 'Try and keep awake; you're not going to be much good at playing your part if you're continually dropping off and starting to snore.'

'Sorry, Magnus. I didn't get much sleep tonight or the night before either, what with the poker work and then getting rid of the body and all.'

'Yeah, well, everyone has to work hard sometimes and our business is no exception. Now, keep your eyes open and look for Tatianus.'

'Right you are, Magnus,' Marius said, repressing another yawn and blinking.

Even Magnus was struggling to stay awake by the time the sun had risen for an hour and its rays had begun to penetrate down into the busy thoroughfares, lanes and alleyways of Rome, but his vigilance was rewarded by the sight of a tall man surrounded by four bodyguards.

'That's him, Brother,' Magnus hissed, nudging Marius again and jolting him from semi-consciousness. 'Come on.'

They nipped out from under their archway and jogged up to the well so that they arrived just before Tatianus. The crowd had died down to only two or three deep by this time as most of the worshippers who wanted to take advantage of the god's benefi- cence but not lose any working time by doing so had now departed, leaving the well clearer for the devotees of Mercury who, perhaps, took a slightly less mercenary attitude to the festival.

'We could really do with the god's help for our business this year, eh, Marius?' Magnus said in a loud voice.

Marius looked at him bleary-eyed. 'What?'

Magnus gestured at his brother and made encouraging move- ments with his eyebrows as Tatianus stopped just behind them to wait his turn.

Marius finally took the hint. 'Oh, right. Er ... Yes, Magnus, we could really do with all the help that Mercury can give us this year, what with having all that money stolen the other night. Do you think it was Sempronius?'

Magnus nodded with exaggeration, his face turned to Marius so that it was in profile to Tatianus behind him. 'The patronus of the West Viminal Brotherhood? Definitely, Brother; he heard what we were trying to buy and wanted it for himself. He hopes that having stolen the money from us we wouldn't be able to raise enough at short notice to replace it.'

'And can we?' Marius asked as they shuffled forward.

'It's not looking good, brother. The Cloelius Brothers' banking business in the Forum refused me a loan yesterday and the rest of the Brotherhood's cash is tied up at the moment. I'll have to go to Tatianus and ask him as a favour to hold on to our item for a day or so.' Magnus got to the well and handed the amphora to Marius who held it steady as Magnus took the draw-bucket and slopped water into it.

'Do you think that he'll do it?'

'He might, seeing as I don't suppose many people would want to buy what we've ordered for the price that we're prepared to pay for it, that is; except, perhaps, Sempronius, who would do it just to spite me and enjoy watching me lose my deposit and spending the money he stole from me on an item that I was going to pay for with it.'

'That would be nasty.'

Magnus jammed the stopper into the amphora. 'It would, Brother; but highly unlikely. How would Tatianus ever make that connection? After all, he ain't that bright.'

'That's what I heard too,' Marius agreed as they moved off, restraining themselves from looking back at Tatianus and enjoying what they both imagined would be a look of deep outrage on the middle-man's face.

The sudden blare of horns cut across the general chatter at the well. Magnus looked towards their source at the Capena Gate to see the upheld axes wrapped in rods, the fasces, which were borne by lictors. Someone important was coming through the gate.

'Let's get out of here before we're obliged to stay and applaud whoever it is,' Magnus said. 'I never like being too close to anyone with lictors, just in case I get noticed and come under strong scrutiny.'

Marius nodded and rested the amphora on his shoulders. 'I quite agree, Brother; besides I'm curious as to whether Servius has found out anything about the contents of that jar.'

They turned away from the incoming dignitary and stopped abruptly.

'Ah, Magnus, how nice to see you.' The voice was smooth and affable and laced with genuine pleasure.

Magnus feigned surprise. 'Tatianus! I'd have thought that you were far too busy to have time to come to festivals like this.'

Tatianus was all smiles and teeth. 'On the contrary, my dear Magnus, I am very fastidious in my worship of all the gods, especially Mercury. I always ask him to hold his hands over my business and I'm usually rewarded for my piety; in fact, he has helped me already today.'

'I'm very pleased to hear it, Tatianus. As a fellow devotee of Mercury it does me good to see that he bestows his favour on such a deserving gentleman of business.'

'Indeed. I look forward to seeing you at the third hour so that we can conclude our deal on such an auspicious day.'

Magnus sucked his teeth. 'Ah, Tatianus, there's a bit of a problem there. I stupidly didn't take up your kind offer to look after my money in your strongroom the other night and, unfortunately, it was stolen on the way home.'

Tatianus' expression of concern would have done credit to the most practised dissembler. 'I'm so sorry to hear that, Magnus; how awful for you.'

'Yeah, well, it's my fault. So I was wondering if you would give me a little time to raise the money?'

'I don't normally discuss business outside my study, Magnus, but as it is Mercury's day and seeing as he has already favoured me I shall make this an exception. Come tomorrow.'

Magnus' look of gratitude was deep and filled with relief. 'Thank you, Tatianus.'

'Don't mention it, Magnus, my friend.' With a hearty slap on the shoulder, Tatianus moved on as from the gates came the first shouts of 'Hail Divine Caesar!'

'Shit!' Magnus spat as he turned towards the gate. 'If that's the

Emperor we'd better stay and cheer him; nasty things can happen to people seen walking away from Caligula. Besides, he did save my life once by stopping Tiberius hurling me off a cliff in Capreae.'

'How did that come about, Brother?' Marius asked as a litter, high and wide and borne by sixteen slaves, four at each corner, came through the gate. Bearded Germans of the imperial body-guard lurched to either side of the litter, preventing any of the cheering citizenry from getting too close to their master to whom they showed complete devotion.

'Some other time, Brother, some other time. Hail Divine Caesar! Hail Divine Caesar!'

Caligula waved his right hand with regal dignity, reclining within the sumptuous cushionage of his litter. With his high fore-head, thinning hair and deeply sunken eyes underlined with insomniac's dark smudges, Caligula would have looked inconse-quential, had it not been for his golden Mercurial costume that did little to hide a magnificent erection with which he toyed with his left hand.

'Hail Divine Caesar! Hail our star, our rising sun! Hail Divine Gaius!' the crowd called out with unfeigned enthusiasm, praising the giver of largesse and holder of games so spectacular that none could recall their like or imagine them being bettered.

Caligula raised himself as the shouts grew with more and more people coming to line the street, genuinely happy that their Emperor had returned to Rome and hoping that he would cele-brate the fact with impromptu chariot racing at the Circus Maximus whose soaring, arched bulk overshadowed the Capena Gate. With a sudden movement he thrust his right hand into a bulging purse and then threw dozens of golden coins into the air to shower down on his adoring subjects. The cheering turned into screeches as everyone tried to get a gold aureus, the equiva-lent of almost six months' wages for a legionary. Another expansive gesture released more of the golden rain as Caligula began to work his erection with increased urgency. 'There, my sheep, there's your fodder. Feed, my flock, feed,' Caligula called as he dispensed his largesse. 'Take your blessings from your god, my sheep, and live under my hands.' He smiled with benign calmness as he surveyed the chaos caused by the contents of his purse; and then his expression clouded and his head twitched. 'Stop!' he screamed, causing his bearers to halt immediately. The crowd froze in whatever position they were in and looked to their Emperor; Caligula pointed a shaking finger at a couple of beggars, with filthy, wound headdresses, scrabbling on the floor and evidently unaware of the change of atmosphere. 'Pick them up,' he ordered the nearest of his Germanic bodyguards.

The German pushed his way through the crowd to the two beggars and hauled them up by the grimed collars of their tattered robes. As they realised their predicament, the beggars ceased groping for coinage and stared with wide eyes at the Emperor, terrified by the wrath on his face.

'Bring them here,' Caligula hissed.

The German hauled the two men forward and then threw them to their knees before the litter. They mumbled entreaties for mercy into their long, ill-kempt beards, in heavily accented Latin.

Caligula surveyed them for a few moments and then addressed the crowd: 'Look at their noses, look at their headdresses. They take the money I dispense and yet they refuse to recognise me for what I am.' He looked down at the beggars and sneered in disgust. 'What are you?'

'B-b-beggars, Princeps,' one replied, not raising his eyes.

'I know that! But what sort of people are you, what religion?'

'We, we are Jews, Princeps.'

'Jews! I knew it. Call me by my title.'

'I have, Princeps.'

Caligula smiled a smile that would have frozen Medusa herself. 'Vespasian,' he called, not taking his eyes from the two visibly shaking beggars now grovelling piteously.

A stocky man in a senatorial toga stepped forward from the entourage of senators and Praetorian officers following the litter. 'Yes, Divine Gaius.'

'They seem to think that I don't notice their lack of respect for my godhead.'

'Indeed, Divine Gaius; they must be amongst the most stupid of your sheep.'

Caligula frowned as he considered this statement. 'Yes, they must be. Remove any coinage they might have gathered and have them thrown out of the city. I'll not have unbelievers amongst my flock. It's time to get a proper understanding of these people's way of thinking. Have the Alexandrian embassy brought before me after I have received the welcome of the Senate.'

As Vespasian obeyed his god and Emperor's orders, Magnus caught his eye. 'Philo and his mates are being kept out of trouble, sir.'

'Thank you, Magnus. Meet me at the Senate House in a couple of hours.'

'Put it down there, Marius, and don't get too close,' Servius advised as Marius put down an earthenware bowl in the middle of the floor of the backroom in which Magnus transacted the brotherhood's business. 'You'll notice, Magnus, that there is nothing in this bowl but wet rags.' Servius pulled out a dripping bundle just to emphasise the point. 'Not the sort of thing that you would normally expect to burn.'

'That's a fair point, Brother,' Magnus said, leaning back on his chair and folding his arms. 'But, no doubt, you're going to surprise me.'

'How did you know?'

'Because you wouldn't be making such a fuss about damp rags not burning otherwise.'

Magnus' counsellor's lined face took on a disappointed aspect as he opened the jar taken from the intruders' sack. 'I was hoping to astound you, not just surprise you.' He took a single wet rag and dipped it into the jar; it came out smeared with a dark, viscous substance that seemed to be halfway between solid and liquid. He dropped it into the bowl and then took a dry rag and dangled it over the flame of an oil lamp. As it caught fire, Servius threw it after the impregnated rag. There was an immediate puff of flame and within an instant the damp contents of the bowl were burning as if they were tinder-dry.

'I am astounded,' Magnus affirmed. 'What is it?'

'It comes from the East but it's very rare here in the Empire and therefore very expensive. The contents of this jar, if it were full, would have cost as much, if not more, as what we were prepared to pay for the Scorpion.'

'That is impressive. What's it called?'

'I've heard it called the River-god's fire but what its real name is I don't know. However ...' Servius looked at his patronus and raised an eyebrow.

'Ah!' Magnus exclaimed, understanding.

'We know someone who does,' they said in unison.

Magnus stood, as was every citizen's right, at the open doors of the Senate House watching, with wry amusement, senators struggling to outdo one another in outrageous flattery as they welcomed their Emperor back to Rome. The fact that he had only been absent for ten days did not seem to dampen their enthusiasm for their reunification with their divine ruler.

'Senator Titus Flavius Vespasianus has the floor,' Gnaeus Domitius Corbulo, the presiding Consul, announced, looking down his long nose that dominated an equinesque face.

'My thanks, Suffect *Junior* Consul,' Vespasian said, rising to his feet and bringing a smile to Magnus by stressing the full title of Corbulo's rank. Corbulo bristled in his curule chair, adding to Magnus' amusement for he considered him to be even more pompous than Philo. 'I would also like to make my joy at the Emperor's safe return to Rome a matter of record. Although I have had the good fortune to be escorting him on his journey and, therefore, never far from his radiance, it is still a relief for me to know he is back at the heart of the Empire in his rightful place, guiding our lives. And I hope that he will spare us as much of his precious time as he can before he sets off on his divine conquest of Germania.' Vespasian turned to Caligula ensconced on his litter, which had been placed in the centre of the chamber. 'On a personal note, I would like to thank the Emperor for the splendid dinner he invited me to only last night. The food was exquisite, the music sublime, the conversation riveting and the entertainment highly amusing.'

Caligula shrieked a high-pitched laugh at the memory. 'Yes, it was fun; we should do it again this evening. Cancel the Alexandrian embassy later – I'll see them in the morning at the fifth hour – and have a dozen condemned prisoners brought up to the palace.'

'Indeed, Divine Gaius.'

Magnus could see Vespasian straining to keep a delighted expression on his face.

Caligula's anticipation of the evening revelries was evidently enough to distract him from the business of being flattered and he signalled his bearers to set about their duty. 'You will come, Vespasian?'

'With utmost pleasure, Divine Gaius.'

'Excellent.' He turned to Corbulo. 'And perhaps you too, Corbulo? Wait, no, no, what am I thinking? You're far too dull.'

Dullness was, plainly, an attribute that Corbulo in this instance was very grateful for, Magnus assumed, judging by the expression on the Junior Consul's face.

Caligula was swept from the chamber before the senators could even hold a vote on whether to commission another bronze statue in thanks for his safe return.

'Thanking the Emperor for inviting you to dinner,' Magnus said as Vespasian and Gaius joined him at the bottom of the Senate House steps, next to Vespasian's lictors, 'that was sycophancy of the highest degree.'

'Yes,' Gaius agreed, 'and very good it was too. And you managed to get yourself another invitation for this evening. Excellent work, dear boy.'

Vespasian closed his eyes and massaged his temples with a thumb and a middle finger. 'There is nothing excellent, Uncle, about dining with a living deity who finds the dismembering of criminals amusing entertainment between courses.'

'Then you shouldn't have said it was amusing,' Magnus observed.

'Magnus, have you any idea what it's like trying to please the Emperor just so as to stand a chance of still being alive at the end of the day? Sometimes I think that the only reason I've escaped his purges is because he doesn't consider me rich enough to execute.'

Gaius' jowls wobbled in agreement. 'Yes, poverty, or at least the appearance of it, can be a life-saving condition.'

Vespasian scowled at his uncle, ordered his lictors to proceed to the Palatine and then turned back to Magnus as they started to move. 'So, have Philo and his embassy escorted to the Palatine tomorrow just before the fifth hour. I'll meet you there – if Caligula doesn't confuse me with a criminal and I survive dinner, that is – and, hopefully, by then I'll know where Caligula will receive them.'

'I'll be there,' Magnus affirmed. 'In the meantime, sir, I've got a favour to ask in return.'

Vespasian looked wary but could not refuse his friend. 'What is it?'

'Well, as one of the Urban Praetors could you use your influence with the Urban Prefect to take some action over a highly illegal piece of equipment that would have recently come to his notice?'

'What have you done, Magnus?'

'Now that's not fair, I ain't done nothing. No, it's Quintus Tullius Tatianus …'

'He who can procure any weapon ever conceived and have it smuggled into the city?'

'That's the one,' Magnus said, shaking his head. 'You all seem to know about him. Well, I believe that he is just about to supply Sempronius, the leader of the West Viminal, with a Scorpion. I mean a bolt-shooter, not those nasty little things with a sting in their tail.'

'That would be a very illegal transaction. When did the item arrive?'

'Last night.'

'Then I assume that the Urban Cohort centurion has already informed Lentullus, wouldn't you say, Uncle?'

'Undoubtedly, dear boy; unless he's grown tired of his wife and children.'

Magnus shook his head again. 'Ain't nothing secret?'

'Not when it comes to a dangerous man like Tatianus,' Vespasian said. 'So what would you like me to get Lentullus to do?'

'Well, I assume that now he knows about the Scorpion he will take steps to confiscate it?'

'I'm sure he will.'

'In which case could you ask him to do it at the third hour tomorrow morning?'

'Why so precise?'

'Let's just say that I'll be in conference with an interested party at that time and that type of information would be exactly the sort of thing that I could use to bring him down a bit.'

Vespasian sighed. 'So I'm supposed to get the Urban Prefect to enforce the law at a time that suits your criminal agenda, is that it?'

'Well, if you put it like that then I suppose so, although there's nothing criminal about it.'

'I doubt that very much.'

'And then, what happens to things like Scorpions when they're impounded?'

'That's up to whoever is in charge of the raid.'

'The centurion?'

'No, a centurion will lead it but a magistrate will oversee the whole thing.'

'An Urban Praetor, perhaps.'

Vespasian raised his eyebrows. 'It has been known. I'll see what I can do. You just make sure that Philo's there at the fifth hour.'

'That I will, sir,' Magnus said, taking his leave. 'I wonder what the punishment is for being caught in possession of a Scorpion? Whatever it is it'll give Sempronius quite a sting, if you take my meaning?'

'There they go,' Magnus said, looking down at a wagon being unloaded by torchlight in a narrow side street off the Vicus Patricius. 'I knew the bastard would do it.'

'Do what, Magnus?' Sextus asked, pulling his cloak tighter around his shoulders as the temperature fell with the deepening of night.

Magnus did not bother to answer his bovine brother as he felt sure that the short answer would prove too baffling and a longer explanation would be beyond his attention span. Instead he counted the number of components brought out from beneath the leather covering of the wagon until he was satisfied that it was indeed the Scorpion being delivered to the back door of the West Viminal Brotherhood's headquarters.

Magnus eased the weight off his cramped buttocks, which had transferred most of their heat to the flat, tiled roof on which he and Sextus had been concealed for their three-hour vigil, and then ran his eye over the building that housed his bitter rivals. Unlike the South Quirinal, the West Viminal chose not to base themselves in the tavern built at the junction of the Vicus Patricius and the Carpenters' Street, the road leading to Magnus' territory, but, rather, in a four-storey building built around an inner courtyard some fifty paces from the crossroads. It was a wise decision, Magnus conceded: apart from the minor inconvenience of the Crossroads' lares altar not being a part of the building, it was far better situated than his own tavern as it only had one wall facing the main street, with the other three backing onto narrow side streets, in one of which the wagon was being unloaded. This meant that it was that much harder to attack as the narrow streets on three sides could be blocked to prevent access, leaving only the possibility of attacking through what would be a very well-defended front door. As he rued the ease with which his defences had been breached the previous night something stirred within Magnus' scheming mind and he raised his gaze to the roof of the building, some ten feet higher than his position: it was, like the one that he was crouched on, flat. However, there was a structure built atop it, a structure that Magnus knew to be solid because it was where the West Viminal liked to keep their captives. 'Unless one had a Scorpion,' Magnus muttered to himself.

'What's that, Brother?' Sextus asked.

Magnus smiled in the dark. 'I meant, Sextus, that I've just seen a less lucrative but more satisfying use for a Scorpion.'

'I didn't think we had one any more on account of the money being nicked and such.'

Magnus began to ease his way back, keeping low so that his silhouette would not rise above the parapet. 'Never you mind,

Brother; you just kill who I tell you to and leave the thinking to me.'

'Kill who you tell me to and leave the thinking to you,' Sextus said, digesting the suggestion as he followed. 'Right you are, Magnus. I've always found that to be the best course for me.'

'Good lad, Sextus, good lad.'

'You know my policy,' Tatianus said, shrugging his shoulders and opening his arms as if he were helpless to change something of his own making. 'If you don't come with the money within a few hours of the item being on my premises then I sell it to the first one who does. And you were meant to come at the third hour yesterday, not today.'

'But, Tatianus, you said to come today when I told you that I'd had the money stolen.'

Tatianus bared his teeth in what would have been a smile had it not been so triumphant. 'Yes, I did, didn't I? However, I made no promise as to whether or not your Scorpion would still be here, did I? It's just such a pity for you that you took it for granted that it would be; you're evidently not very bright.' Tatianus' triumphant air wavered somewhat as Magnus leant back in his chair and entwined his fingers behind his head, serenity on his face and looking for all the world like a man who had just won a long-odds bet at the Circus Maximus on an unfancied chariot in a fixed race.

'What do you think the Urban Prefect will do when his men, who are raiding Sempronius' headquarters as we speak, find the Scorpion that you sold him yesterday?'

Tatianus could not conceal his surprise. 'How did you know?'

'Because I planted that seed in your head, at the well, remember? I think it's you that isn't very bright; oh, but I said that yesterday too, didn't I?' Magnus stood, ready to take his leave. 'Now, Sempronius is very implicated, but I can keep your name out of this or I can keep your name in it; it'll be up to you.'

Tatianus sneered. 'How can you have any influence over the Urban Prefect?'

'I think the River-god's fire would get his attention, don't you?

Come and find me when you've decided and bring my deposit with you.' He turned and made for the door.

'Wait,' Tatianus called, his voice higher through tension, 'we can discuss this now, Magnus, my friend.'

'Sorry, Tatianus,' Magnus replied without turning back as he went through the door, 'I don't have the time just now; I've got to take a Jewish embassy before the Emperor.' Leaving Tatianus with a baffled look on his face, Magnus grinned at the two henchmen in the corridor. 'And a good day to you too, gentlemen.'

'It's an outrage!' Philo declared as he walked between Vespasian and Magnus down the Palatine.

'It's the Emperor's will,' Vespasian reminded him.

Philo gestured to the members of his embassy following behind, escorted by Tigran and a few of the brothers. 'But we've been waiting for months to present our case to him; we've paid the right bribes, but nothing, no. And then Isodorus arrives with an embassy from the Greek citizens of Alexandria and gets to see the Emperor within two days. Two days, I tell you; and what's more he gets to see the Emperor at the same time as us, denying me the advantage of putting our case first, which would be only just as we are the injured party and have also undoubtedly laid out much more in bribes.'

Magnus, by now, was unsurprised that Philo was the injured party; he was more than tempted to add to his injuries himself, but refrained from mentioning it.

'I'm afraid there's nothing to be done, Philo,' Vespasian said, exasperation barely concealed in his voice. 'It's the Emperor's idea of saving on his valuable time to see you both together before he sets off for Germania. From his point of view it makes perfect sense.'

'But Isodorus is a villain of the very lowest stock; even Magnus would look down on him.'

'He must be rough,' Magnus opined, shaking his head and sucking air through his teeth in disbelief.

'He is and it's an outrage that he gets treated with the same dignity as me. Me! The brother of the Alabarch of the Alexandrian

Jews; a literary figure of great renown having to share an audience with the Emperor of Rome along with a common criminal, a murderer, a ... a ...' Such was his outrage that words failed Philo at this point.

'A man of lower birth than even me?' Magnus suggested helpfully.

'Exactly! And to make matters worse we are not even being received at the palace as a personage of my rank would expect. No! We are being taken instead to the Gardens of Maecenas – why is that?'

'Again, I'm afraid that it's the Emperor saving on his time,' Vespasian informed him. 'He has decided to do some improvements to the gardens and the villa within them and so will see you as he goes around the house and the grounds.'

'So I will acquaint the Emperor with the injustices perpetrated on the Jewish citizens of Alexandria whilst he does some interior decorating and consults with his gardener?'

'Something like that.'

'It's an outrage!'

The Gardens of Maecenas were richly laid out, as would be expected of that cultured intimate of Augustus who had risen to power by providing the first Emperor with canny political advice. He had been Augustus' brains as Agrippa had been his muscle, and his reward was great wealth. It showed in the beauty of the terraced gardens that he had created on the Esquiline Hill, along the Servian Wall between the Esquiline and Viminal Gates. However, that had been almost fifty years before and since his death little had been done to maintain the villa in their midst. Not even Philo could argue that the place was not in need of refurbishment as they waited on one side of the atrium whose frescoes had seen better days. On the other side stood a collection of hard-looking men, bearded and garbed in the Greek fashion and murmuring amongst themselves whilst casting threatening glares across to the Jews.

'And this is too miserable for words!' Caligula's voice, loud and pitched quite high, preceded him and all in the atrium turned towards the tablinum whence it came. 'The frescoes are scenes from the *Aeneid*, ghastly! I want to be portrayed in congress with my fellow gods and goddesses.'

'Yes, Divine Gaius,' a small, balding Greek said, making a note on a wax tablet whilst scuttling behind the Emperor as he emerged, on spindly legs, into the atrium. 'What sort of congress?'

'I leave that to you, Callistus; whatever seems appropriate with each god. You can imagine that there is a world of difference between congress with Venus and then Neptune.' Caligula stopped, his sallow face lit up with inspiration. 'Of course! Depict the victory that I'll have over Neptune later in the year after I've subdued the Germanic tribes. I intend to lead my legions into the Northern Sea and thrash him there and then carry on to conquer Britannia.'

'Very good, Divine Gaius,' Callistus said as if Caligula had just announced that he was to take a longer bath than usual.

'Ah! The god haters.' Caligula's eyes alighted on the Alexandrian embassy.

Philo immediately prostrated himself; his fellows followed. 'Hail Gaius Caesar Augustus.'

Caligula frowned and cocked his head as if he feared that he had not heard correctly. 'You see,' he said, looking at Vespasian and Magnus and gesturing with an outstretched arm at the Jews who were now getting back to their feet. 'Not one mention of my divinity.'

'Indeed not, Divine Gaius,' Vespasian replied as Magnus mumbled his discontent at the omission.

'Indeed not, Vespasian; and Magnus, isn't it? Would you deny that I am a god, Magnus?'

'How could I, Divine Gaius? You saved my life.'

'There you have it: I can both give life and take life. Which one shall it be with yours, I wonder?' Caligula walked up to Philo and peered at him as if he were looking at a strange and puzzling phenomenon for the first time. 'You are god haters inasmuch as you don't think that I'm a god; I, who am already confessed to be a god by every nation but am refused that appellation by you.' He then raised his hands to the heavens. 'One fucking god! Are you mad?'

The Greek embassy broke into applause at this performance and began showering Caligula with divine honorifics, much to his obvious delight.

As the Emperor bathed in the godly flattery, the evident leader of the Greeks stepped forward and bowed deeply, his expression oozing subservience. 'Divine master, you will hate with just vehemence these men that you see before you and all their fellow countrymen if you are made aware of their dissatisfaction and disloyalty to yourself.' The Greek's tone was honeyed and his gestures flowery and as he spoke he smirked. 'When all other men were offering up sacrifices of thanksgiving for your safety, these men alone refused to offer any sacrifice at all. And when I say "these men" I mean also the rest of the Jews.'

'My Lord Gaius! Princeps!' Philo cried. 'We are falsely—'

Caligula cut him off with a sharp gesture and then pointed to the floor. 'Callistus, the mosaic is far too pastoral. Have it re-laid with a more martial theme: me vanquishing the Germans would do it. Vespasian, come with me.' He looked back at Philo. 'Continue your whingeing!' With that he hurried off along an airy corridor with high windows, running off the atrium, with Callistus and Vespasian accompanying him and Magnus in close attendance.

'We are falsely accused, Princeps,' Philo called out as he and his embassy, now bereft of any semblance of dignity, scurried after their Emperor with the Greek delegation in hot pursuit. 'We did sacrifice, many times. We didn't even take the flesh home for our tables as is our custom but, rather, committed the victims entire to the flames as burnt offerings.'

Caligula turned into a high-ceilinged room, bare apart from a few faded upholstered couches and a couple of statues, one of Augustus, the other, Agrippa. One look at the second statue caused Caligula to shriek: 'Get rid of it! And have the place scoured for any more likenesses of that ... that ...'

'He doesn't like to be reminded of his grandfather,' Vespasian whispered to Magnus. 'He came from an unknown family.'

'And, Callistus, have my statue replace it but make sure that it's bigger than Augustus. The room needs to be lavishly furnished in the—' Caligula stopped mid-sentence and looked back at the door in which Philo stood with the bobbing heads of Jews and Greeks alike trying to see over his shoulders. 'How many?'

Philo looked puzzled. 'How many what, Princeps?'

'How many times have you sacrificed?'

'Three, Lord Gaius: once on your accession, once when you recovered from your illness, and a third time, recently, in hope of your victory over the Germans.'

'Greek style, Callistus,' Caligula said, barrelling towards the door and causing Philo and all those jammed within it to retreat in disarray. Callistus, Vespasian and Magnus followed him through, further disordering the two delegations. 'Grant that all this is true,' Caligula said, waving a pointed finger in the air as he disappeared on down the corridor, 'and that you did sacrifice, you sacrificed to another god and not to me.'

'But we sacrificed on your behalf, Princeps,' Philo called from within the throng barging each other to keep pace with the Emperor.

'What good is that to me?' Caligula stopped suddenly and swung round, causing both delegations, now hopelessly mixed together, to halt as if they had slammed into an invisible wall. 'You sacrifice to me, not for my sake!' He spun away and the Greek delegation cheered a point well made whilst Philo and the rest of the Jews looked downcast and rubbed their beards.

'They'd have done better staying home in Alexandria,' Magnus observed as he and Vespasian followed Caligula into the next room.

'Not enough red,' Caligula said and doubled back causing Magnus and Vespasian to part for him.

Callistus scribbled a note as he chased his master out.

'Philo was under the misapprehension that the Emperor had the same grasp of justice as a learned Jew would,' Vespasian muttered. 'I would guess that his reaction to the reality would be ...'

'Outrage?' Magnus suggested. Vespasian tilted his head indicating agreement with Magnus' assessment.

'Why won't you eat pork?' Caligula asked, much to the vocal amusement of the Greeks.

Philo's mouth opened and closed a couple of times. 'Er, well, Princeps, different nations have different laws; there are things of which the use is forbidden to both us and our adversaries.'

'Ha! That's true,' Caligula said, causing the Greek mirth to subside.

Philo pressed his point. 'There are many people who don't eat lamb, which is the most tender of all meats.'

Caligula laughed. 'They are quite right for it's not at all nice.'

Philo beamed with relief that he had finally got the Emperor to accept a point.

'Perhaps you're not so backward,' Caligula mused. 'What principles of justice do you recognise in your constitution?'

'So did they find the Scorpion?' Magnus asked as Philo launched into an in-depth analysis of Jewish law, failing dismally to capture the Emperor's attention.

'They did,' Vespasian replied with a half-smile. 'Sempronius is currently languishing at the Urban Prefect's pleasure whilst he decides whether to condemn him to the arena as he deserves.'

'And?'

'And they took the Scorpion away.'

'Obviously. But where did they take it?' Magnus asked as they entered a huge hall at the heart of the villa.

'As it happens, I had them deliver it to my house.'

Magnus looked at Vespasian, astounded.

'It's too cold in here, Callistus; have all the windows filled with glass pebbles so the light can still get in.' Caligula moved onto the next room as Philo continued his monologue on all aspects of Jewish law, unattended by the imperial ear.

'How did you manage to do that?' Magnus asked once he had digested the information.

'In very much the same way as Lentullus hoisted responsibility for Philo's embassy, when the Emperor took an interest in it, onto Corbulo's shoulders and then he onto mine so that any mistake could be construed as my fault, not theirs.'

'Ah! You told Lentullus that the Emperor was involved.'

'Yes; I said the Emperor had heard a rumour, as he came up the Appian Way, that something was to be smuggled into the city using his arrival at the Capena Gate as a diversion and he had asked me to look into it. Lentullus, naturally, couldn't pass on all responsibility to me fast enough.'

'I'm sure.'

'So I used the centurion who had let it through the gate to search Sempronius' place, explaining to him that since he knew what it looked like, having been bribed to let it through the gate, it would make it much easier for him to find it again before forgetting he had ever heard of it in the first place.'

'Very sensible.'

'What are you saying?' Caligula asked abruptly, bringing Philo's speech to a sudden halt.

'I was saying, Princeps—'

'Bring my father's pictures that he brought back from Syria and install them in here,' Caligula said, his attention now on the small, intimate library he had just entered rather than on Philo.

'Yes, Divine Gaius,' Callistus said, making another note.

Caligula contemplated the ceiling for a few moments before turning to Vespasian. 'These Jews don't appear to me to be wicked so much as unfortunate or foolish, in not believing that I have been endowed with the nature of God.'

'Indeed, Divine Gaius,' Vespasian replied, the solemnity of his voice matching his expression.

'Princeps, may we now put our case?' Philo asked.

'Case? What do you think you've been doing for the last half an hour? You've put your case to me and I've decided that you are misguided in your attitude to my divinity and not malicious and therefore can be allowed to live. You may go.' He turned on his heel and headed off with Callistus padding behind him leaving Philo straining, with every fibre of his being, to swallow his view on how he had just been treated until Caligula was out of earshot.

'Gentlemen,' Vespasian said, amusement on his face, 'it's time to go home now. We'll take you to Ostia tomorrow to find passage back.'

'It's an outrage!' Philo finally burst out.

'If you mean your still being alive, Philo, then you may find some that would agree with you. However, if I were you I would get on a ship back to Alexandria and thank your god that you caught the Emperor in a merciful mood.'

'But we were here to complain about our ill-treatment.'

'No, Philo; you were here to defend your ill-treatment of the Emperor and in his magnanimity he forgave you.' He steered Philo around; the rest of the Jewish embassy followed to the jeers of the victorious Greeks.

'About that Scorpion,' Magnus said as they retraced their steps.

'Yes?'

'Would you happen to know exactly where it is in your house?'

'No,' Vespasian said unhelpfully.

'Oh.'

'But I can tell you that at the fourth hour of the night it will be on a wagon in the yard behind my house, totally unattended.'

'Now that is a very foolish place to leave it.'

'Not if you want it to be stolen and never to hear of it again. I'm sure the Urban Prefect will rest much easier if he knows the whole thing has disappeared and is completely out of his hands.'

'And I'm not someone to disturb such a great man's rest, if you take my meaning?'

'I do, Magnus; so when you've done whatever you plan with that Scorpion, destroy it and we'll consider ourselves equal for the favour that you did me in keeping Philo out of trouble until the Emperor could decide his fate.'

'Now tie that off with a good tight knot, Sextus, and then secure it with a nail that doesn't go all the way through.'

'A good tight knot and nail it; right you are, Magnus.'

As Sextus carried out his instructions Magnus looked with admiration at the Scorpion, now reassembled in the moonlight on the roof opposite the West Viminal's headquarters.

'She's a beauty, ain't she, Magnus?' Marius said, stroking his hand along the groove in which the two-foot-long bolt would rest.

'She is indeed, Brother,' Magnus readily agreed, examining the wound torsion springs, made of animal sinew, in which the bow arms were set. 'There should be ample power in these for our purposes. Are you ready, Tigran?'

The easterner grinned and slipped off his tunic leaving only his trousers and a small sack hanging from his belt. 'The less weight the better, I would say, Magnus.'

'You're the lightest we've got and you'll be fine, Brother; the pace with which this thing will thump into that wood over there will make it impossible to dislodge the bolt. I've seen these things pass through two barbarians in a row before getting stuck in a third. Very pleasing to the eye it was too.' He tested the stability of the weapon standing on four splayed legs as if perched atop a pyramid. 'Perfect. All right, Cassandros, wind her up.'

The Greek attached the engine's claw to the bowstring and then wound a pair of winches at the rear of the weapon to ratchet it back tight against the counter tension of the torsion springs.

'Sextus, the bolt,' Magnus said as the weapon reached maximum draw.

'Right you are, Brother.' Sextus picked up the two-foot wooden bolt, as thick as his thumb, with a vicious-looking iron head and three leather flights at the other end. Tied to it, with a good tight knot, was a hemp rope; a nail was driven into the bolt just behind the knot.

'The sharp end goes at the front,' Magnus said helpfully when Sextus appeared confused. 'And make sure that the nail is upright.'

The bolt in place, Magnus looked along its length, sighting it up towards its target. He made a couple of adjustments to the weapon and then, when satisfied, hit the release mechanism.

With a crack that echoed off the surrounding buildings, the two bow arms, set in straining sinew, blurred forward and whacked into the restraining uprights, sending the bolt fizzing through the night, pulling the fast-uncoiling rope behind it. An instant later a resounding hollow thump announced its piercing of the wooden structure on the opposite roof, closely followed by the vibrating thrumming of the missile juddering, lodged firm in its target.

Magnus took hold of the rope and gave it a couple of test tugs before putting all his weight against it; it held. 'Tie that off with a nice tight knot, Sextus.'

'If you don't mind, Brother, I'll do it myself,' Tigran insisted. 'Then I've only myself to blame if I end up splattered all over the street below.'

'Fair enough,' Magnus said as Tigran fastened the rope to a roof beam exposed by the removal of a couple of tiles.

When all was secure, Tigran dangled himself from the rope upside down with his legs curled around it. He shifted his weight; the rope bounced slightly but held. 'No time like the present.' He grinned and began to move his hands one over the other, hauling himself up the gradient. As he came to the edge of the roof he muttered a short prayer before pulling himself out over the void whence came the rumble of night-time traffic and the jollification of drunkenness.

Magnus held his breath as he watched the silhouetted figure ease along the rope, taking care not to make it swing and loosen the bolt. Little by little he progressed over the twenty-foot-wide drop until, with a suddenness that caused Magnus' throat to constrict so that he almost chocked, Tigran let go of the rope and fell a few feet on to the other roof.

'Done it,' Magnus blurted in relief.

A few moments later the rope slackened off as Tigran detached it from the bolt. The tension came back to it as he fastened it to something more secure.

'Good lad,' Magnus muttered. 'Now open the door.' The cracking of wood being worked at with a crowbar confirmed that that was indeed what Tigran was doing, and very shortly Magnus could see the door to the West Viminal's private gaol swing open and a couple of shadows stalk out. 'Well, they can either stay or come over here, it makes no odds to me,' Magnus informed the brothers watching with him.

Both the men, having by now been acquainted by Tigran of his objective, decided to risk the crossing rather than stay where they were. As the first man climbed on to the rope, Magnus saw orange glimmers come from inside the wooden structure; soon it was a constant glow. By the time the first man had made it over, flames flickered from the structure and, Magnus hoped, would be now catching on the roof beams beneath the tiles that Tigran had, hopefully, removed from the floor of the gaol with his crowbar.

The fire grew and Magnus rubbed his hands together. 'Sempronius will never suspect that it was us who started it; he'll think that the prisoners did it somehow – if he escapes being condemned to the arena, that is.'

The second man was halfway across when Tigran came racing out of the gaol and back to the rope, flames sheening his naked torso. 'Hurry up, you bastard.' The escaping prisoner quickened his movement; as soon as he dropped down on to Magnus' roof Tigran clambered onto the rope and all but slid back down.

'Eh? Look what we have here, Magnus,' Marius said, grabbing the newly escaped prisoner by the wrist. 'You little bastard, where's my money?'

'Ah! So that's how they knew the way through our tavern,' Magnus said, recognising the man's face. 'Did they hurt you, Postumus, or did you just offer free directions to be friendly, like?'

'I'm sorry, Magnus, they caught me in one of their whore-houses; I was stupid to go in. They chucked me in their gaol and Sempronius threatened me with a red-hot poker, he did. I didn't like it.'

'You liked it well enough the other night.'

'Not to be on the receiving end, though. Anyway, I didn't think that telling them the layout of the tavern would do much harm; it was only directions they wanted.'

One flick of Magnus' head was enough for Marius and Sextus to lift a screaming Postumus up. Marius looked briefly down into the street before nodding at his brother. With a diminishing howl Postumus hurtled streetwards to slap on to the stone as Tigran arrived safely back with the roof ablaze behind him.

'What happened to him?' the easterner asked as he handed the jar of the River-god's fire to Magnus.

'He's been giving people directions that he shouldn't; so we gave him directions for the quick way down to the street. The rest of you lads had better join him but I recommend using the stairs, even though it takes slightly longer.' He took a rag and smeared the Scorpion all over with the remains of the jar's contents. 'Quick as you like, Cassandros.'

With a few deft strikes of his flint, Cassandros got a cascade of sparks falling into his tinderbox which, coaxed with gentle breaths, caught into a small flame. Lighting his rag from the kindling, Magnus lobbed it at the Scorpion's feet. Flames jumped from the wood and raced up to the main body of the weapon, along the bolt groove and then left and right to the bow arms and up and down the torsion springs.

Magnus looked at the raging Scorpion with regret. 'Pity, but it would be unwise to break a promise to Vespasian, however expensive.' Beyond it the West Viminal's roof was an inferno and shouts of panic issued from the building as the flames spread. 'Still, she did a good job. Time to go, Cassandros.' Cradling the empty jar so that it was safe, Magnus turned and sped down the stairs. From across the street came the crash of the first roof beams collapsing onto the floor below.

'On a grain ship? Me? It's an ...' Philo began spluttering, his outrage such that he could not even spit the word out as he stared in horror at the hulking monstrosity of the flagship of the Egyptian grain fleet.

'It's all that's available,' Magnus replied, trying not to show his irritation. 'The first grain convoy of the season has almost filled the harbour, and of the few other ships berthed here, none is destined for Alexandria. Take it or leave it, but that's what the port aedile said.'

'Then we shall wait until a vessel more suitable to my standing arrives.'

'I wouldn't advise that, Philo,' Vespasian said from his seat on a folding chair set beneath a makeshift awning. 'Firstly, you don't know how long you might have to wait for so fine a ship, and secondly,' he indicated around the crowded, bustling port and the clogged streets leading off it, 'where would you stay? I doubt that you'd find anything that you would consider suitable here.'

'We'll go back to the Gardens of Lamia.'

'No you won't, Philo. I can't allow you back into the city.'

'Why not?'

'Because I can't guarantee your safety, and because of my friendship with your brother I would not wish to put you at risk.'

'But yesterday the Emperor ...'

'What the Emperor does one day bears no relation to what he might do the next. Indeed, if he did hear that you were back in the city he might very well forget that he has already questioned you as to why you don't recognise his divinity.'

'Then I'd have another chance to put the case against Flaccus and the Greeks to him.'

'No, Philo, you won't; but Caligula might come to a different conclusion than he did yesterday. So forget Flaccus, forget all the outrages that you have been subjected to and get on that ship.'

'But—'

'No buts, Philo,' Vespasian said, rising to his feet to emphasise his earnestness. 'Just get on board, go back to Alexandria and write to Caligula protesting about Flaccus. Meanwhile, if I get the chance, I will remind the Emperor that Flaccus would not hand over Alexander's breastplate to me and mention to him how rich Flaccus has become whilst serving as prefect of Egypt. That's the best way to deal with a god who needs all the money he can find for his Germania campaign.'

'But he's not a god.'

'Yes he is, Philo, and you'd be wise to remember that. If the Emperor, who has the power of life and death over us all, considers himself to be a god then a god he is, and I for one will be the first to keep up that pretence.'

'So you don't really believe that he is a god.'

'What I believe is irrelevant. Now go.'

Philo stroked his beard, considering his position. 'Very well, I'll take your advice.' He signalled to his fellow ambassadors to board the waiting vessel and then approached closer to Magnus and

Vespasian. 'I would thank you for the help that you have both given us – me. I have found it hard not to be treated according to my rank and that has led to a few outbursts of frustration, so that you haven't, perhaps, seen me in the best light.' He produced a weighty purse from inside his mantle. 'As a token of thanks and in anticipation of what you will do to aid us in bringing Flaccus down I would like to give you the last of the money we have set aside for bribes.' He offered the purse to Vespasian. 'Take it, there are a hundred and fifty-three aurei in it.'

Vespasian pushed it away. 'I can't be seen to take money off you in public like this, but there is absolutely no reason why Magnus should not accept the gift and we'll share it out later.'

'Very good,' Philo said, handing the purse to Magnus who took it with a grave face. 'I bid you both farewell and will carry your greetings to my brother and his sons.'

'Do that, Philo,' Vespasian said with feeling, 'and tell him that someday Magnus and I will come back to Alexandria and he can repay the debt he owes us with hospitality.'

Philo bowed and then turned and walked up the gangway.

'Did I hear you right, sir?' Magnus asked as they watched him go. 'I could have sworn that you said we'd share the money out.'

'I did. I thought a third for you and two-thirds for me.'

'Fifty-one aurei – that's very generous.'

'Not really; it just puts you back into my debt, which is where I like you to be.' Vespasian turned away. 'Come on, let's get back to Rome – if there's any of it still left standing, that is.'

'What do you mean, sir?' Magnus asked, feeling the comforting weight of the purse in his hand.

'I mean that I heard that a chunk of the Viminal burnt down last night. Oddly enough it was the same building that the Urban Cohorts raided the day before.'

'Ah, yes. Well, it's amazing just how viciously a Scorpion can burn.'

'I hope that I never have the opportunity to find out, and so does the Urban Prefect, if you take *my* meaning?'

'I do, sir; and I can promise you that no one will ever get one into the city again and life will go back to how it was.'

'Good. Make sure that *everyone* understands that.'

'Oh, he will, sir, he will.'

'Tatianus, what a lovely surprise,' Magnus said in a voice that conveyed the exact opposite; he did not get up as the middleman was shown into his room at the rear of the tavern by Marius. Servius sat next to him. 'This must be a social visit as I know you never discuss business outside your establishment.'

'In normal circumstances that would be the case,' Tatianus said as he sat opposite Magnus and placed a strongbox on the table between them.

'But not today; why's that?'

Tatianus bared his teeth in a snarl. 'You know perfectly well why that is, Magnus, so let's stop the play acting and get down to business: you said that you have the power to keep my name in or out of this Scorpion and the River-god's fire affair. Well?'

Magnus leant forward and rested his elbows on the table, pressing the tips of his steepled fingers to his lips. 'Hmmm. Tricky. After all, you did swindle me.'

'No I didn't; I just used my normal business practice and you well know it.'

'Well, Tatianus, I'll tell you what I know: the Urban Cohorts did raid Sempronius' place yesterday and they did take away a Scorpion as well as Sempronius himself. The Urban Prefect knows all about your business but turns a blind eye because he can control it much better if he knows how and when items arrive in the city. However, a Scorpion was a step too far and he's a bit cross, to say the least, and if I was to give the jar of the River-god's fire to my patron to pass on to him then your days would be up, if you take my meaning?'

'I do. So what do you propose?'

'I propose that you give me back the deposit that you cheated me out of and in return I'll give you back the jar. And then, secondly, I've been asked to convey this message: you undertake never to bring in anything more dangerous than swords, slings, bows and those sorts of things, and then the Urban Prefect will be very happy and let you carry on in business.'

'That's easy enough.'

'There is one exception, though.'

Tatianus eyed Magnus across the table. 'And that is you, I suppose.'

'Indeed, Tatianus. You will bring me anything I ask for – except for a Scorpion, of course – because I'll be able to get it into the city without the authorities finding out.'

'And how's that?'

'That's what tame senators are for.'

Tatianus looked down at his strongbox and then pushed it across the table to Magnus. 'You have a deal. One thousand denarii paid in gold.'

Magnus opened the lid and counted the coinage. 'Fifty aurei, very nice, Tatianus. Servius, give the gentleman his jar back.'

Servius leant down and produced the jar from under the table; Tatianus took it greedily and then pulled the top off. 'It's empty!' His eyes squinted accusingly.

Magnus shrugged and leant back in his chair. 'Of course it is. The deal was for me to give you back the jar; I made no promise as to whether or not the contents would still be in it, did I? It's just such a pity for you that you took it for granted that it would be. Sempronius has that, or at least, he had it smeared over his roof beams until someone carelessly dropped a flaming rag on them. Now he's just got a gutted shell of a building which is going to cost him a lot more than the thousand denarii he stole from me if the Urban Prefect ever lets him go.'

'You fire-raising bastard!'

Magnus' smile got nowhere near his eyes. 'I may well have kept enough of the River-god's fire to prove that statement right on your house, Tatianus. As you said, I am known for my arsonistic tendencies. You can go.'

Tatianus picked up the jar and hurled it across the room to shatter on the far wall. Without a word he turned and stalked out.

'I'll call for you when I need you,' Magnus shouted after him. 'I much prefer doing business here, on my terms.' Magnus grunted with satisfaction as he listened to Tatianus stomp down the corridor. He tipped the fifty aurei onto the table and then looked at Servius. 'Fifty aurei from him and fifty-one from Philo; it would seem, brother, that we're one aureus up on the deal.'

'I'll record that in my ledgers.'

'You do that, Brother; and meanwhile I'll try and work out another way of getting into Tatianus' strongroom without using a Scorpion.'

THE IMPERIAL TRIUMPH

This story comes between *Rome's Fallen Eagle* and *Masters of Rome* and covers what Magnus was doing in his trip back to the Imperial city after the initial invasion of Britannia and the reason why he had to leave Rome in a hurry and return to Vespasian.

Set against the backdrop of Claudius' Triumph for his 'subjugation' of Britannia the story concerns the ramifications of the tumbling price of slaves due to the market being flooded with so many Britannic captives. Both Magnus and Senator Pollo have their own concerns in the run-up to the Triumph and once more work together to their mutual interest.

Again, it also has modern themes, in this case property speculation and gerrymandering. It also provides the explanation as to how Vespasian came to own the house in Pomegranate Street that Suetonius tells us of; I was very interested to learn about Roman property law!

I wrote this after I had written *Masters of Rome* and *Rome's Lost Son* and thoroughly enjoyed tying in all the loose threads and setting up the backstory to Magnus finally relinquishing control of the South Quirinal to Tigran.

The opportunity to describe Claudius' faux-Triumph was too much to resist even though I had already written about Plautius' Ovation and knew that I still had Vespasian's and Titus' joint Triumph to come. The idea that most people knew that Claudius had done next to nothing, personally, during the invasion and yet everyone went along with the conceit that he conquered the whole island almost single-handed leaving only the odd mopping-up operations amuses me still; but that is the art most dictators use for holding on to power; just look at North Korea.

ROME, SEPTEMBER AD 44

PITILESS WAS THE roar that greeted the condemned as they were herded, naked, on to the arena sand. Pleading for their lives – or at least for another mode of death – the ragged formation clung to one another; the whiplashes of the overseers rained down upon men and women alike, forcing them out into the open and, at the same time, drawing blood from their shredded backs that would inflame the hunger of the beasts waiting below the Flaminian Circus on the Campus Martius.

A few final cracks of supple leather across the shoulders and haunches of the rearmost were enough to make them clear the line of the gates, which were then drawn closed as the overseers darted back inside. The fifty-thousand-strong crowd raised their volume even more as they toyed with themselves and salivated at the prospect of the coming slaughter.

In their midst, in the imperial box, Tiberius Claudius Augustus Germanicus, Emperor of Rome and conqueror of Britannia, struggled to his feet, his head twitching so that the stream of drool hanging from his chin swung back and forth – although all those close enough to see affected not to. Claudius raised an unsteady hand, stilling the crowd so that only the wailing of the prisoners could be heard; it was ignored by all. 'P-p-p-people of Rome; I, your emperor, in honour of the seventh and last day of the Roman G-Games, give you a foretaste of what is to come in three days' time when I celebrate my T-T-Triumph, voted to me by the Senate as a mark of distinction for my crushing victory over the c-c-c-combined tribes of B-B-Britannia.' Claudius paused to allow the crowd time to laud his boast of military prowess, even though most of them could tell from their emperor's unmartial appearance that it was nothing more than that: just a boast; the real fighting had been done by real soldiers. Again he raised a juddering arm and quietened the mob. 'There, in the arena, stand some of the wretched p-p-prisoners that I took in my final victory before the gates of Camulodunum; the rest, who number in their thousands, will be paraded in my Triumph and then will either be auctioned off or exhibited for your entertainment as gladiators. Until that time let us enjoy ourselves with these miserable creatures, fit for nothing other than the jaws of beasts.' With a flourish he gave a signal to the gatekeepers; the iron-reinforced wooden doors swung open.

There was a communal gasp as, from the darkness within the bowels of the circus, there came a chorus of bestial bellows followed by the appearance of a dozen of the strangest-looking animals with long necks and an odd hump on their backs. Ungainly, the creatures trundled out into the open and looked around with an air of haughty superiority whilst masticating in a leisurely manner, causing the audience to fall about in fits of mirth at their appearance and allowing the condemned a brief moment of hope.

Back in the thirteenth row, to the right of the imperial box, there was one man who found it impossible to join in the hilarity: Marcus Salvius Magnus sat with his chin upon his hands and his elbows resting on his knees; his face a study of a man wrestling with a problem. It was a problem that had plagued him for the half a moon that he had been back in Rome, having returned from Britannia to re-establish his command over the South Quirinal Crossroads Brotherhood after almost three years' absence.

'Look at those things!' a huge man next to Magnus shouted, jumping to his feet. 'What are they, Magnus? I ain't ever seen anything so ugly and cumbersome in my life.'

'Then you ain't never scrutinised yourself in a mirror, Sextus. They're camels and they smell about as bad as they look. They don't put up much of a fight but they make people laugh.'

'Too right, Brother, I'm going to love watching them rip the—' Sextus stopped mid-sentence; his countenance took on a strained aspect, as if he were dealing with a troublesome stool.

Having known his companion since signing up to serve under the Eagles on the same day, over thirty years previously, and then joining the same brotherhood upon their return to Rome, Magnus recognised the signs. 'You're thinking, aren't you, Brother? You're wondering how the camels are going to despatch the prisoners if they don't put up much of a fight.'

Sextus' expression became even more pained. 'How did you know?'

Magnus suppressed an exasperated sigh. 'A lucky guess, and the answer is that they can't.' He pointed down onto the arena floor as two oblong holes appeared to reveal the tips of ramps leading up from the dank cells below. 'But here come some things that can.'

Whether or not the score or so of the sleek cats, some spotted, some black, growled with hunger as they emerged into the light could not be heard beneath the rapture of the crowd and the terror of the victims as they viewed the animate instruments of their deaths. Only the camels seemed unconcerned by the appearance of such ruthless hunters – the camels, that was, and Magnus who furrowed his brow and lowered his head, running his fingers through his thinning hair.

'You're missing this, Brother,' Magnus' neighbour to his other side shouted over the din, nudging his shoulder with the leather-bound stump of his left arm and pointing to the victims. 'They're pissing and shitting themselves.'

Magnus sucked the air through his teeth and shook his head. 'Nah, you enjoy it, Marius, I just ain't got the heart for it today. I'm not in the mood to be entertained, not when I've got to work out how to get us out of this fix.'

'Why did you come then?'

'Because I can get a lot more thinking done here rather than back at the tavern with that old bastard, Servius, continually nagging me to come up with a solution in quick time.'

'Well, he is in charge of the Brotherhood's finances so you can't blame him – whooa, look at that, they've surrounded the humans and left those strange things alone – and we have to address the situation without putting up what we charge the local traders in the neighbourhood for our protection.'

Magnus grimaced as the crowd's noise reached a crescendo and Sextus, to his other side, started masturbating with vigour. 'I know, Brother; and it was me what made the purchase that got us into this mess so it'll be me that sorts it out; I just need time to think.'

Marius punched his stump in the air. 'Oh yesss! They've split the pack up; they're running all over the place.' The crowd made a communal low noise of awe. 'It just took her face right off with one bite; lovely! Ohhh, and look at that, those two are fighting over that fat bastard.' Marius burst out a short laugh. 'You've got to see this, Brother; they're ripping them apart and the strange things are starting to get very distressed, by the looks of it.'

'Yeah, yeah.'

'Look, Magnus, it weren't your fault that soon after you made what we all thought was a very good deal in purchasing that batch of Germans on your way back from Britannia, Claudius announces that he's going to be selling off all the captives from Britannia here in Rome immediately after his Triumph.'

'But I should have seen it coming. The price of household slaves has plummeted; and as for gladiators, you can't get even half the amount that I paid for those Germans with a view of selling them on to one of the training schools when I got back here. Prime specimens, ten thousand sesterces each and I'll be lucky to get three, thanks to that drooling fool flooding the market. That's a loss of almost a hundred thousand.'

'They've gone for one of them, them ... what are they, Magnus?'

'Camels, Brother, camels.'

'Well they've got one down and that's sent the rest into a stampede around the ... gods below, they just trampled that cripple; you're missing the best show of the whole games.'

But Magnus was not interested, nor had he been for the entire Roman Games. He had received a crushing blow upon entering the city with what he thought were a dozen superbly built potential gladiators, only to find, a few days later, that the emperor intended to auction off over ten thousand captured Britons, more than half of them warriors, in Rome, rather than sending the greater amount for sale in the markets around the provinces. The move had deflated the city slave-market to such an extent that many of the slave-dealers had gone out of business or been forced to move to the fringes of the Empire where the disastrous effect of Claudius' policy was little felt.

For Magnus, however, that was not an option and he was left with a dozen healthy men of fighting age who were not only unsaleable, without taking a massive loss, but were also very hungry; unless he wanted their worth to depreciate even more he was forced to feed them copious amounts of fodder every day. It was not the situation that he had expected to find himself in when he had bought the slaves from his friend Vespasian's parents' estate at Aventicum in the lands of the Helvetii in Germania Superior on his way home. The sale had been forced by the death of Vespasian's father three years before and the subsequent removal of his mother, Vespasia Polla, back to the house of her brother, Senator Gaius Vespasius Pollo, in Rome. Vespasia had decided to liquidate her assets and had sold off the entire estate; Magnus had purchased the slaves for a relative pittance of a deposit on the understanding that he would pay the balance upon his arrival in Rome. And thereby lay the problem: he was a client of Vespasia's brother, Gaius Vespasius Pollo, and it would be unthinkable not to honour a debt to his family.

He had been back in the city for nearly half a month now but had kept low so that the senator was not aware, yet, of his return; but he knew that this state of affairs could not go on and that in the morning he could delay it no longer: he would have to attend the dawn *salutatio* of his patron. Senator Pollo would, doubtless, enquire as to the whereabouts of the hundred thousand sesterces that was owing to his sister and Magnus would have to tell him the unpalatable truth. It was a situation that could lead to a disastrous rupture between

Magnus and his patron who had, in the past on many occasions, used his influence to stop the full force of the law from falling upon Magnus and his brotherhood.

And as the unfortunates down in the arena were ripped to shreds and devoured for the delectation of the people of Rome, Magnus just could not bring himself to enjoy the spectacle; such was the weight he felt at the prospect of explaining that he had not got the money nor would he be likely to have it in the near future. With a sigh, he decided upon his course of action. 'Come on, lads; let's get going back,' he shouted, getting to his feet and barging past Sextus who was grunting his relief and leaving splattered stains on the back of the cloaks of the man in front and his wife. 'We've got work to do.'

'But it's a public holiday, Brother,' Marius protested.

'Which is for the public; but we're not the public, we're the South Quirinal Crossroads Brotherhood and we shit on the public and do things in our own way, and today, just now in fact, I've decided to call a meeting that will convene in a couple of hours.'

Marius looked longingly at the action in the arena. 'But it's the mutilations next.'

Magnus pointed at where Marius' left hand had been severed. 'I'd have thought that you would have had enough of mutilations. Now come on and do as I say. I want to talk to Servius before I address the rest of the brothers.'

'One of the traders from further down the Vicus Longus is here to see you, Magnus,' a gnarled old man with milky eyes informed him as he entered the tavern that served as the headquarters of the South Quirinal Crossroads Brotherhood situated on the sharp junction of the Vicus Longus and the Alta Semita. 'I told him to wait by the back door.' He gestured with a blind man's vagueness to a man sitting in the far corner of the bustling parlour, hazy with the smoke from a cooking fire behind the bar.

Magnus squinted at the man; it was too gloomy to make out his features. 'What does he want, Servius?'

'Normal: a favour.'

Magnus sighed. 'Not now, I've got too much to think about.'

'I know; we're deep in shit but that doesn't mean that we neglect our duties to the neighbourhood. If it got around that you're not looking after your own then Sempronius and those West Viminal cunts will be all over us within days; you know how much he would love to expand his brotherhood into our patch. And Primus, his new number two, is very hungry to prove himself.'

Magnus slumped down on to the chair opposite his counsellor and second-in-command. 'You're right, Servius; but first I need a drink.' He signalled to the brother serving behind the bar who acknowledged him with a nod. 'And whilst I have one I want you to have messages sent to all the brothers to assemble here in a couple of hours. Before that we'll meet this trader; what's his name?'

'Quintus Martinus.'

'Marcus Salvius Magnus, I come to you as the patronus of the brotherhood of the area in which I live, in the hope that you can prevent me from being wronged.' Quintus Martinus wrung his hands, ingrained with dirt and covered in burn scars, and lifted his head so that he looked directly into the dark eyes of Magnus and then into the sightless orbs of Servius; both were sitting, cups of wine in hand, behind the desk in the back room of the tavern, used for transacting brotherhood business. 'I have always paid you my dues on time and in full and never before have I required a service from you; so now, after twenty years under your protection, I beg you to grant me this one favour.'

Magnus took him to be in his late forties by his appearance but guessed that the sallow skin, white hair and gaunt expression were the result of a hard life of constant work and struggle rather than age and he was in reality ten years younger; he indicated to a chair. 'You may sit, Martinus, and ask your favour.'

The trader smiled in gratitude as he took a seat. 'My thanks, patronus. My problem is with the landlord of the tenement block where I live with my family and have my chainmaking business, on the corner of the Vicus Longus and the Chainmakers' Street.'

Magnus was instantly uninterested, but refrained from showing it. 'He's putting your rents up?'

'No, patronus, just the opposite: he told me today that he's evicting us with three days' notice.'

'One could consider that generous.'

Martinus shrugged. 'I suppose so; it could have been with immediate effect.'

'Why's he doing it? Are you behind on your rent?'

'No, Magnus; business is good at the moment. With all the prisoners here for the Triumph the price of chains and manacles is going up.'

'I'm pleased to hear it. So why is he evicting you?'

'He hasn't told me.'

Servius took a sip of his wine. 'There's no reason why he has to give an explanation.'

'I know,' Martinus agreed.

Magnus tugged at one of his cauliflower ears that, along with his broken nose, were testament to his time as a boxer. 'What's this man's name, Martinus? I'll send a couple of the lads to have a quiet word with him.'

'That's just it, patronus, I don't know.'

Magnus frowned as if questioning what he had just heard. 'You don't know what?'

'His name, Magnus. I've never known it since he bought the property from the previous landlord a couple of months ago. He communicates with his tenants by sending a slave round with a message.'

'And the slave won't divulge his master's name?'

'Exactly.'

'What about the other tenants in the block?'

'No one knows his name and we're all being evicted.'

Magnus paused for a few moments' reflection, uninterested no longer. 'Why would he want to do that, I wonder? He's doing himself out of all the income from the block. Getting rid of you alone I can understand, Martinus, in that he may well have found someone who would be willing to pay more for your business premises. But getting rid of all the tenants living there, that's a different matter.'

'We think that he wants to tear the building down and put up a new one.'

Servius shook his head slowly, staring vacantly at the wall behind Martinus. 'He wouldn't do that; no landlord in his right mind would rebuild a block that hasn't fallen down of its own accord. Why go to the expense if you don't have to? Mind you, I've heard that there've been two similar incidents in our area in the last month but in those cases the tenants went quietly, without coming to us, so I didn't bother you with it, Magnus; but I'd be interested to know if there is a pattern.'

Magnus refreshed his cup. 'Well, if we're going to find out then the first thing we've got to do is ask that slave as politely as we can just who his master is, if you take my meaning? Servius, have a couple of lads stake out the place and grab him next time he appears.'

'Of course.'

'If I'm too late to prevent your eviction, Martinus, I'll ensure that you have an alternative.'

Martinus rose. 'My thanks, Magnus, you're a fair man.'

Magnus gave a grim chuckle as Martinus left the room, closing the door behind him. 'That's the first time I've ever been accused of being fair – have you ever heard anyone call me that, Servius?'

'No, Magnus, plenty of other things, but never that.'

'So, Brothers,' Magnus concluded at the end of his explanation, 'that is the situation. Whilst the price of slaves remains so depressed I have no choice but to go to Senator Pollo and ask what he will accept in lieu of the debt or whether he could see his way to postponing payment. Either way, I'll have to come up with a lucrative money-making scheme very shortly, which I will.' He looked around the faces of the fifty or so brethren to see if he could spot any signs of discontent at his leadership. Although he had not admitted that the predicament was his fault and had blamed the emperor's policy, he was more than aware that the brighter of the brethren would construe that he was rash to buy slaves so soon after the conquest of a new province, no matter how good the bargain could have proven to be.

'I have a question,' said a brother with a dyed, pointed beard, sporting a pair of embroidered trousers and a knee-length, eastern-style tunic.

'Yes, Tigran.'

'Would you say that you've shown good judgement in this affair?'

Magnus stiffened; it was a well-phrased question from one of the more ambitious of his brethren. To answer truthfully would be to invite a challenge to his position and yet how could he bluff it? 'I bought those slaves at a good discount; we will see a profit from them yet.'

Tigran's eyes hardened just a fraction. 'But not for some time; meanwhile, we're not much better than paupers.'

Magnus thought he detected a low murmur of agreement but couldn't be sure. 'As I said: we will make our money and, in the meantime, I will put the slaves to work in the most profitable way possible. When this is over then perhaps that will be a good time to ask me if I consider my judgement to be sound.'

That got the support of the vast majority of the brethren, forcing Tigran to back down with an eastern bow, hands across his chest.

Magnus took a deep breath as he felt the threat recede. 'Sextus and Marius, you'll both come with me in the morning; I want to be at the senator's house before dawn.'

'Magnus, my friend, you're back,' Senator Pollo boomed as Magnus took his turn to greet his patron, along with a couple of hundred other clients of the influential ex-praetor, in his atrium. 'How good it is to see you.' With jowls and chins wobbling, Senator Pollo heaved his bulk up from his chair and did Magnus the honour of grasping his forearm in welcome, to the obvious envy of many in the room.

'It's good to be back and to see you, sir.'

'Yes, yes.' Senator Pollo cuffed away a tonged ringlet of dyed black hair from a heavily kohled eye. 'I was wondering when you were going to turn up because there is a bit of business that I need you to do for me.' He turned to an extremely attractive flaxen-haired youth, brandishing a stylus and a wax tablet and wearing a tunic that would have had difficulty fitting a boy two or three years younger than him. 'Siegimerus, I'll see Magnus last of all, as we've much to discuss.'

'So why has it taken you almost half a month to present yourself at my *salutatio*, old friend?' Senator Pollo leaned across his study desk; both his carefully plucked eyebrows were raised quizzically. A tray of freshly baked honeyed cakes filled the room with a mouth-wateringly sweet aroma.

Magnus swallowed. 'I ... er ... how did you know, sir?'

'Oh, come on, Magnus. First of all I get letters from Vespasia's steward in Aventicum telling me the deal that you and he have reached over a dozen Germanic slaves; he writes to me because I'm dealing with my sister's affairs in the absence of Vespasian and Sabinus in Britannia. So I knew when you left Germania Superior and, therefore, roughly when to expect you in Rome. Then, of course, when you do get back it's not too easy for you to keep a low profile on the Quirinal, and seeing as this is my neighbourhood also – although I do frequent higher circles, I grant you – the return of the leader of the local brotherhood will always reach my ears.'

Magnus cleared his throat and prepared himself for the unpalatable truth.

'But don't worry,' Senator Pollo continued before he could speak, 'I know exactly what the problem is and it's all to do with Claudius flooding the slave-market, isn't it?'

'Er, yes, sir, it is and I'm fucked, I ain't got the money.'

Another chuckle sent quivers through the excess skin around the senator's neck. 'Well, you should have come to me earlier, old friend, because I'm sure there is a way that we can resolve the situation to mutual gain.'

'You think so?'

'I know so because I find myself in a delicate predicament. You see, the Imperial Triumph in a couple of days has a lot of other ramifications other than just the tumbling price of slaves – which, incidentally, will correct itself within a few months as we all know how much Claudius likes to see generous amounts of blood spilt in the arena. But the captives aren't the only things that will be paraded: there'll be all the booty as well, including skins, furs, grain, hunting dogs and gold, silver, tin and iron from the mines.' The senator paused to reach for a honeyed cake and bit into it with obvious delight. 'Now, all these things will be sold off, apart from the precious metals, which will go to the treasury to help pay for what has been a very expensive campaign; the person in charge of the sale will, naturally, be our old friend Pallas, the imperial secretary to the treasury.'

'That makes sense,' Magnus said with a creeping smile. 'And I suppose you have had a quiet word with Pallas?'

'We've had much to discuss recently, I will admit. One of the points of mutual interest was what would happen to the wagon-loads of weapons, helmets and shields that are going to be paraded as they're of little use to anybody, apart from the best examples, which will be lodged in the Temple of Mars.'

'And you suggested to Pallas that you might be able to do him a favour and take them off his hands.'

'Not surprisingly there were quite a few people offering to help but in view of the past connection between Pallas and our family he agreed that I was the obvious choice to take receipt of all that iron – for a small consideration of the profits, naturally.'

'Naturally.'

The other half of the honeyed cake disappeared between moist lips. 'So after the Triumph more than a few wagons will fall into my hands, filled with thousands of blades of no use to anyone unless they're reforged into legionary swords and daggers and sold to the army quartermasters back in Britannia, who are desperate for new equipment considering the hard campaigning that's still going on there.'

'And no doubt Pallas, as chief secretary to the treasury, will facilitate a favourable deal for the sale.'

The senator took on a solemn countenance and reached for a replacement cake. 'He is ideally placed to do so; I'm fortunate to have him as a business partner.'

'What about the helmets and shields?'

'Mainly iron and some bronze that needs to be sorted and then melted down so that we can sell it, again through Pallas' good services.'

Magnus began to comprehend where he fitted in. 'But ...'

Senator Pollo's porcine eyes glinted in the lamplight. 'Oh, Magnus, you understand so well. But, indeed; and it's a big but ...'

'But senators aren't allowed to participate in trade or at least be seen to participate in trade.'

'There you have it, Magnus: I need someone I can trust to dirty their hands in my place and I believe that you would be an ideal choice as this has to be done with secrecy. I don't want it to get out that I'm about to produce thousands of swords and daggers as well as plenty of iron bars and bronze ingots and we have the same resulting crash as with the slave-market.'

'I can see the point, sir; I'm certainly your man.' Magnus adjusted his face into what he took to be an innocent countenance. 'And as to my little problem ...'

Senator Pollo waved a conciliatory hand. 'I don't think that we need to worry ourselves unduly about that until we've processed all this weaponry, for which you'll be needing a business premises and quite a large one; preferably close to here so I can look in on it.'

'The closer the better. Any suggestions?'

'Not that I would know but I wouldn't be surprised if there's an empty house just around the corner in Pomegranate Street; it has two shops to its front, one of which used to be a blacksmith's, and would be easy to convert into a foundry that could deal with the volume of metal; the other shop I'm sure you could do the same with, obviously with a little more effort involved. And then the very spacious living accommodation behind we could use to store all the weapons and resulting ingots. It also has a large stable yard to its rear that would be perfect for discreet loading and unloading. I believe it's owned by a certain Lucilius Celsus, an equestrian of questionable integrity and unquestionable greed.'

'A businessman then. I shall look into it on my way back to the tavern, sir.'

'Good, Magnus. Secure it by the morning of the Triumph and hire me a couple of blacksmiths who have worked as military armourers.'

'I don't know, Magnus, we haven't seen him for some time,' the baker at the corner of Pomegranate Street and the Alta Semita informed Magnus.

'And your rents are collected by an agent, are they, Anistius?'

'That's right; and even if I were interested in Lucilius Celsus' whereabouts I doubt the rent-collector would tell me.'

Magnus looked back up Pomegranate Street to where Marius and Sextus were examining the security of the boarded-up property, standing empty just fifty paces away; tables were being set out, by public slaves, at various intervals up the hill in preparation for the feast after the Triumph. 'How long have the two business premises been empty?'

The baker scratched his head and frowned. 'Well over a year; probably more than two, I should say. One was a blacksmith and the other made candles; both moved out when Celsus' agent put up the rents.'

'Why didn't they come to see me about it? I could have explained how things are to this Celsus.'

'You were in Britannia so they took the problem to Servius, your counsellor, but he couldn't do anything about it because Celsus was away on business at the time and the agent said he didn't have the authority to go back on his master's ruling – even after Servius had him roughed up.'

'Hmm, I see. Well, thanks, Anistius. Business been good?'

The trader grinned. 'Not good enough for you to justify a rise in what I pay in protection.'

'But with all the people coming into the city for the Triumph it's sure to get much better.'

'It is. The Triumph is going to be good for everybody.'

Magnus scowled. 'Not necessarily, Anistius, not necessarily.' Tucking the fresh loaf of bread under his arm and calling to Marius and Sextus to follow, he stalked off.

'I couldn't get a thing more out of him, Magnus,' Servius confirmed as they sat on a bench outside the tavern enjoying the warm, September midday sun. Sextus and Marius were feeding the fire kept constantly burning on the altar of the lares of the crossroads, whose worship was the original reason for the formation of the brotherhoods, centuries back. Up and down the Vicus Longus and the Alta Semita more public slaves were hard at work making ready for the celebrations, setting up kitchens, decorations and awnings; all around the carnival atmosphere grew with country folk coming through the Porta Colina, just two hundred paces away, to grab their share of the emperor's largesse. 'I believe he told us all he knew.'

'So, Celsus let his house on the Esquiline before he left for Gaul, a year before the invasion of Britannia, in order to supply army sandals to the legions?'

'That's all he knew; even with a couple of broken fingers.'

'Hmm.' A distraction in the street caught Magnus' eye; he nodded to a young brother playing dice at the table next to him and pointed to a wealthy-looking family progressing down the Alta Semita. 'Festus, go and introduce our services to those good people who seem to have come to the city unaccompanied by bodyguards. I think they look like they can afford a denarius a head to avoid any nasty accidents, if you take my meaning?'

The young brother beamed with pride at being given the task. 'I do, Magnus.'

As Festus walked off, Magnus signalled to a late-middle-aged brother, bearded in the Greek style, with a gash down his left cheek. 'Go and make sure that he doesn't fuck it up, Cassandros.'

'My pleasure, Magnus.'

'And keep your dirty Greek hands off him.'

Cassandros grinned and flexed his fingers. 'And out of him?'

Magnus shuddered, shaking his head. 'Nasty Greek habits; it ain't natural.'

'You need to watch him, Magnus,' Servius said, lowering his voice, 'he showed some sympathy for Tigran's point of view last night.'

Magnus looked at the useless milky eyes of his counsellor, confused. 'How could you know?'

'I may be blind but other senses sharpen. There was a short, low murmur of agreement with Tigran last night; very slight, I agree, but nonetheless it was there and to me it sounded like Cassandros.'

Magnus looked over to the Greek as he stood behind Festus, leering with menace at the waylaid family; money was changing hands. 'I'll keep my eye on him.' He scratched his head to bring himself back to the discussion before he had been distracted. 'So this Celsus hasn't been heard of since?'

'What?' Servius took a moment to return to the subject. 'No, he hasn't. I'm surprised he isn't back for the Triumph; only a fool would miss the opportunities of such wealth flowing into the city.'

Magnus clapped his second-in-command on his shoulder. 'Well, he ain't, so we'll just have to take matters into our own hands.'

'Magnus!'

Magnus turned in the direction of the shout; Quintus Martinus was running up the Vicus Longus. 'What is it, Martinus?'

'The two lads who you posted at my tenement sent me to get you. They're holding the landlord's slave.'

Magnus took one look at the slave sitting in the corner of Martinus' workshop with a sack over his head and his hands and feet bound and then turned on the two brothers who had caught him. 'What the fuck are you doing holding him here?'

The men glanced at one another confused and then looked around the workshop, hung with lengths of chains and tools, trying to find fault with it or its décor.

'Servius told us to grab him the next time he came,' the

older of the two explained, jutting out his chin in defence of his actions.

'And where did he tell you to keep him, Brother, eh?'

'Close by; but we thought that—'

'Thought? When was the last time anyone trusted you to think? Servius chose you for your muscle not your intellectual capacity, which is so limited that even Sextus might stand a chance at outsmarting you.'

The brother lost a bit of his defiance; his head lowered and his face furrowed into an injured scowl. 'That ain't fair, Magnus; we did as we were told.'

Magnus tensed as if he were about to launch an attack and then took a deep breath and spoke with exaggerated patience: 'That's the second mistake.' He pointed to the prisoner. 'Now he knows my name; so he might as well know yours, *Laco*.' He walked over to the slave and ripped the sack off his head. 'In fact, he might just as well know what we all look like, for that matter; what difference would it make now?'

Laco looked down at the frightened slave who was barely out of his teens. 'Well, none, I suppose, seeing as I did mention your name, Magnus.' He looked at his patronus, contrite. 'I'm sorry; that was stupid of me.'

'Yes, it was, but not as stupid as keeping him here in Martinus' workshop as he will report back to whoever owns him that Martinus was involved, which was why Servius told you to keep him close by.'

'I won't say anything, master, I promise,' the young slave protested. 'Just let me go and I won't mention it to my owner.'

'Oh? And who might that be?'

The slave paused and then decided that he had nothing to lose. 'Lucius Favonius Geminus.'

'Who's he?'

'He's a wealthy businessman who invests in properties all over the city.'

'Oh yes? Where does he live?'

'Down on the coast at Antium.'

'Doesn't he have a house in Rome?'

'Many, master, all around.'

'So which one does he stay in when he's in town?'

'That depends; they're all rented out so he stays with one of his tenants, most of whom are also his clients.'

Magnus thought for a few moments and then pointed at the slave. 'Where do you live then, if not with your master?'

'I've got a small room in one of his tenement blocks.'

'And he sends you messages there, telling you what he requires?'

The slave nodded, his eyes still wide with fear. 'Yes, he sent me a message this morning, asking how the eviction is going; I'm due to reply at the second hour of the night.'

'Someone will come round and pick up your reply?'

'Yes, master.'

'Where's your block?'

'In the Subura; on the Fullers' Street. It has a tavern, with the sign of the moon on its door, on the ground floor; my room's just behind it.'

Magnus nodded and scratched the back of his head. 'Right; Laco, deal with him.'

The slave tried to leap to his feet but his bonds constrained him and he tumbled onto his face. 'But, master, I've helped you!'

'I know, but I can't let you go. Blame Laco; he sentenced you to death the moment he decided to keep you here. Be kind to him and do it quick, Laco; and try to dispose of the body without fucking up.' Magnus spun on his heel and walked out of the workshop deep in thought.

The thoroughfares of Rome were filling up as night began to creep over the city. The carnival atmosphere prevailed and was reflected in the amount of vomit and urine in the streets as the country folk spent their savings in the many drinking establishments, all of which had taken care to stock up for what they knew would be the busiest few days for many a year. Magnus leant against the open street-bar of the Moon tavern, sharing a jug of wine, a plate of roasted pork and a loaf of almost fresh bread with Marius and Sextus. Resting on his right elbow he kept his eyes on the shabby entrance of the four-storey tenement block in which the tavern took up half the ground floor; he sipped his wine constantly to help counter the faecal reek that pervaded the dimly lit street.

'We need to find a couple of blacksmiths good with blades,' Magnus said, never taking his eye off the entrance door.

'Blacksmiths? Right you are, Magnus,' Marius replied through a mouthful of pork as Sextus frowned, confused.

'They're people who work with iron, Sextus,' Magnus informed his brother before turning back to Marius. 'We've a few in our area. Find out tomorrow which of them have done weapons-work for the military and of them who owes us the most favours; have them stand by to do quite a bit of forging after the Triumph.'

'Right you are, Magnus.'

Magnus glanced at Sextus, who seemed even more confused. 'It would take too long to explain to you, Brother; you just concentrate on your wine.'

Sextus found immediate intellectual relief in his cup.

A figure, just over Sextus' shoulder, caught Magnus' attention. 'Don't look back but there's a freedman opening the door to the tenement.'

Magnus watched as the man, wearing a *pileus* – the felt cap of a freedman – went in, leaving the door open behind him. 'Walk past and see if he's gone to the back room, Marius.'

With a nod the one-handed brother put down his drink and sauntered, in a casual manner, to the door, looking in as he passed. After a half-dozen paces he turned and wandered back. 'He's gone in.'

'Well, he'll find it as empty as we left it.'

A few moments later the freedman reappeared and looked up and down the street; seeing nothing of interest he took to pacing around in an impatient fashion, constantly straining his eyes to see if the slave he had come to meet was about to arrive for the rendezvous.

Magnus and his brothers finished their food and wine at a leisurely pace as the freedman became more and more aggravated at the non-arrival of his contact. Eventually he stomped off.

Magnus pulled his hood over his head. 'Keep it to a decent distance, lads. I'll trail him first, then, Marius, you come and take over and then Sextus; we'll swap every five hundred paces.'

Keeping the quarry always between ten and twenty strides ahead of him, Magnus followed him through the human stew of the Subura, ignoring the calls of whores of both sexes, the beseeching of cripples for alms and all the other cries and distractions of the tightly packed realm of the poor in which quality of life was judged in terms of lack of misery rather than abundance of happiness.

On they went through narrow streets and alleys, continually changing the lead man as the freedman started to bear north and climb the Viminal Hill heading towards that area's main thoroughfare, the Vicus Patricius. Magnus swore to himself, conscious that they were approaching the area ruled by his rivals in the West Viminal Brotherhood.

Soon he came to that street, renowned throughout Rome for the profusion and variety of its brothels, and turned right in the direction of the Viminal Gate, beyond which stood the Praetorian Guard's camp. Magnus pulled his hood further over his face to prevent it from being recognised in the torchlight that illuminated the entrances to whorehouses to either side. After another couple of hundred paces the freedman turned right into a wider street populated with houses of an impressive size. As the object of the tail reached the fifth house on the right-hand side, Magnus drew up and cursed again as he watched him say something to the two very imposing guards, one of whom then knocked on the door. He turned immediately and walked back in the opposite direction to where Sextus and Marius were.

'Fuck, Brothers; that's all I can say. Fuck! Fuck! Fuck!'

'What is it, Magnus?' Marius asked as he turned about and fell in step with him.

'I say "fuck", Brother, because it looks as if Lucius Favonius Geminus is staying as a guest of the new number two of Sempronius' West Viminal Brotherhood: Primus.'

*

'Fuck!' Servius said as Magnus finished recounting the evening's events. 'That ain't at all good.'

'I know, Brother; someone connected to Sempronius is trying to meddle in our area.'

Servius shook his head; the flame of the oil lamp on the table between them reflected in his blank eyes as they gazed sightlessly around the crowded tavern. 'That's not the half of it, Magnus; do you know who Lucius Favonius Geminus is?'

Magnus thought for a few moments and then shrugged, waiting for the benefit of his counsellor's encyclopaedic knowledge of Rome's underworld. 'I've never heard of him; should I have?'

'No, that's just the point; very few people actually know what he does.'

'What does he do?'

'He's a gerrymanderer.'

'A whatywhaterer?'

'He specialises in gerrymandering.'

Magnus grunted and looked none the wiser.

'I'll start at the beginning. Geminus made a fortune as a tribune in the Vigiles as, more often than statistically probable, he managed to arrive first at the scene of a fire.'

'Ahh. Are you saying that he would start them?'

'I wouldn't accuse him personally of doing that but I would accuse him of knowing where and when quite a few fires started well in advance. Anyway, foresight, as we know from fixing chariot races, is a very useful thing, and being on the scene with his team of Vigiles ready to put out the blaze as soon as the owner has agreed a price, no matter who is being burnt alive within, is a profitable position to be in.'

'Yeah, well, that's standard practice. The Vigiles never put out a fire unless they get well rewarded for it. I mean, why should they risk themselves if they're not being paid? Stands to reason, don't it?'

'And I quite agree with you: a little remuneration for a dangerous task undertaken is absolutely understandable. But he went further than that; much further.'

Magnus scratched his chin as he began to understand. 'He did a Crassus.'

Servius chuckled and leant forward. 'No; further even than him. Crassus had his own private fire-fighters before the Vigiles were formed and, rather than negotiate a fee for putting out the fire he would instead negotiate a selling price for the property and consequently became the biggest landowner in the city.'

'How can you go further than that?'

'Because if the owner of the building refused to sell, Crassus would just shrug and walk away saying that if he wanted his property to burn to the ground then that was his lookout. Meanwhile all the locals would be fighting the blaze with whatever means at hand in order that they didn't lose everything if the fire spread; sometimes with success but mostly not. Anyway, Crassus died a century ago at Carrhae and no one seemed to think about being quite so mercenary with incendiary incidents again, especially after Augustus created the Vigiles as a fire-fighting night-watch.'

'Until Geminus?'

'You have it, Brother. Geminus admired Crassus' methods but thought that they were a little too prone to chance: there was no way of knowing where the next fire was going to be and the owner of the property could always refuse to sell.'

Magnus rumbled an agreement. 'Looking at it that way it does leave a lot to Fortuna.'

'Indeed, so Geminus made a slight refinement, apart, that is, from, shall we say, *predicting* where the fire would start: he would offer a selling price to the distraught owner and, then if he refused, rather than walk away with his Vigiles, he would have them put out the fire on condition that the owner help them. Now, naturally, working so close to a blazing building is very dangerous and not one owner who refused to sell managed to survive helping the Vigiles put out the fire in their property. Word gradually got around and Geminus started to buy every building that he wanted that caught fire on the Viminal and Esquiline.'

Magnus whistled softly. 'Fortunes.'

'Yes; but he was clever. He only went for the buildings on

the borders between brotherhoods so that when he rebuilt them the brotherhood in whose area it was would be willing to pay a premium for its people to live there; and, of course, the brotherhood whose area it bordered on would also want to pay a premium for its people to live there in order to expand their influence. Gerrymandering: weighting the power of one group within an area by moving more of its members to live there. He was responsible for the West Viminal taking two whole streets off their eastern rivals back in Sempronius' early time as patronus, before he fell foul of the Urban Prefect over that business with the ballista and was almost rewarded with a starring role in the circus had he not managed to get a massive bribe together.'

Magnus saw the danger. 'Did Geminus ever do any gerry-whatsit here on the Quirinal?'

'No, Brother; which is probably why you ain't ever heard of it. His Vigiles Cohort's jurisdiction was over the Viminal and Esquiline districts only. Anyway, his methods got a bit too strong even for our esteemed Urban Prefect, Lucius Volusius Saturninus, and he was given the choice of retiring to private life or explaining to the emperor at the time, Caligula, who as we know was always very keen on cash, just how he had come about his stash and how much he was willing to contribute to the treasury. Naturally he retired, giving the Urban Prefect quite a hefty commission for ensuring that his wealth never came to the emperor's attention in the last couple of months before his assassination.'

'But he's still very well off, no doubt.'

'Very; well off enough to purchase tenement blocks in our area straight, for cash, without having them burning as an inducement for the owners to sell. But it's not just in our area; it's right on the border and—'

Magnus sucked the air between his teeth. 'And you said that there've been two similar evictions in the last month.'

'I did and, thinking about it, they were both close to Martinus' block.'

'Evicting everyone in the block?'

Servius nodded.

'All of whom pay – or, should I say, paid – us for protection?'

'Correct; and I think even Sextus would be able to guess who the new tenants will be.'

'I think you could be right, Brother; Sempronius and Primus will be paying him to put their people on our patch.'

'Yes, and when you realise something about him, it's obvious why.'

'Why?'

'What's Primus' full name?'

Magnus thought for a moment and then made the connection. 'Of course! Marcus Favonius Primus.'

'Exactly, Primus is the eldest and Geminus is his twin; by no means identical but twins nevertheless. It was Geminus' cash that secured Sempronius' freedom as part of the deal reached between Geminus and the Urban Prefect at the time of his *retirement.* Sempronius repaid the favour by making Primus his counsellor and leaving the way open for him to become the patronus of the West Viminal when he steps down, which will be soon. Geminus is evidently ensuring that his twin will have a lot of local influence.'

'They're an ambitious pair.'

'Very.'

'And now they've set their eyes on us.'

'It looks that way. But the real problem is that one or two tenement blocks at the bottom of the Vicus Longus is not going to make a huge amount of difference; we might lose influence in half a street or so.'

'Fuck! How many has he bought?'

'Fuck, indeed, Brother, because I don't know; but what I do know is that he can afford a lot.'

'So how do we find out?'

'We don't; but we have a tame senator who can.'

'It entirely depends upon what form of law Geminus took possession of the properties with,' Senator Pollo informed

Magnus as he progressed with his entourage of clients down the Quirinal Hill the following morning.

Magnus looked blankly at his patron; Sextus, Marius and four other brothers strode in front of the group, brandishing poles with which to beat a path through the crowds already gathering in anticipation of the next day's festival.

'Well, there are three ways to transfer ownership of property: you can do a formal transfer whereby you and the transferor make a verbal contract in front of five citizens as witnesses. Or you can do it in front of an aedile whereby you claim title to the property and the transferor admits it and then the aedile makes a judgement in your favour. Or, finally, if you have been in possession of the property for two years, provided that it wasn't acquired by theft or violence, and you're not a tenant, it's yours.'

Magnus gave a grim chuckle. 'That last one is ruled out; so which of the other two is more likely to suit his purchasing methods?'

Senator Pollo mopped the sweat from his brow, which, despite the cool morning and leisurely pace, was accumulating in some quantity. 'Either. In the first case the five witnesses could have been some of his Vigiles as, being all freedmen, they would have been citizens and therefore it could have been done there and then. But that's equally the case if the local aedile was in on the scam and travelled with Geminus to each site.'

'That's more than possible; I don't think that I've ever heard of an honest local aedile.'

'Which you have found to be very useful on numerous occasions, if memory serves me correctly.'

'Yes, well, one has to make do with what one has.'

'That's always been my view, too.'

'But anyway, it's not so much how many properties he bought whilst he was a Vigiles tribune that I'm interested in; it's how many properties he has bought recently in my patch of the Quirinal that's concerning me.'

'Then you need to go and have a little chat with the local Quirinal aedile; he at least will be able to tell you if he's witnessed any property transfers recently.' The senator stepped his large bulk aside to avoid a copious dog turd, which was immediately crushed by one of his following clients.

'I rather suspect our local aedile is too busy with the Triumph at the moment,' Magnus commented as the man slipped and ended up sitting in the offending pile whilst the rest of the clients filed past him, 'far too busy to want to talk about recent property deals with the likes of me without a good reason, if you take my meaning?'

'I do indeed, old friend. I'm almost certain to bump into him in the Senate this morning; I'll mention it and see if I can coax anything out of him. I'm sure there must be something he wants of me in return. How are things going with my little issue?'

'Well, it turns out that Celsus let his house on the Esquiline before he left for Gaul to supply the invasion force with footwear but hasn't yet returned.'

'Let his house? Why would he do that?'

'I suppose he planned to be away for some time.'

'But he still needs somewhere to come back to; no one in their right mind would want to live in Britannia for a moment longer than it takes to make a fortune out of the natives.'

'Quite right and Servius reckons that, having done his business in Britannia, he will be arriving in the city in order to take advantage of the business opportunities that the Triumph will present and will ... ahh ... of course.'

The senator stopped in his tracks, causing more chaos behind. 'Oh dear; I see where you're heading, my friend: he's going to move into Pomegranate Street. We can't allow that to happen. He must be made to sell; I need that property.'

Magnus paused for reflection and then, after a few brief moments, his countenance brightened. 'Don't worry, Senator; what you just told me was very interesting. I think I might have an idea but it'll cost an aureus, if you could see your way clear to forwarding me such a sum.'

The Forum Romanum was splashed with an abundance of decoration. The statues, already painted in lifelike colours, had been crowned with leaves and swathed in red, white or golden cloaks; bright banners of many hues were draped from the coloured frontages of the public buildings; ochres, reds, umbers and resonant blues assaulted Magnus' eyes. Senator Pollo dismissed his clients and made his way up the steps of the Curia with scores of his peers, each carrying a folding stool, ready to lavish praise on the emperor in advance of his Triumph and to compete with one another in lauding the martial skills of one who could not help but twitch and drool as he shambled along on weak, malformed legs.

But such worthwhile usage of time was not the lot of Magnus and a handful of his brethren. They made their way across the Forum, past the gangs of public slaves erecting the wooden barriers, normally used as animal pens on market days in the Forum Boarium, to keep back the tens of thousands of spectators expected on the morrow for the spectacle. The air of anticipation at the centre of the Empire was palpable and the one topic of conversation that could be heard throughout the entire complex was of the Triumph and the largesse that would flow at the mere expense of barbarian savages far to the north.

Except, of course, for one group; they had far more important things to discuss. 'We need to go all over our border area with the West Viminal asking the residents of each building whether they know if its ownership has changed hands within the last few months,' Magnus said as they approached the House of the Vestals. 'Marius, you take the lads through systematically; it's vital that we don't miss one.'

'Right you are, Magnus.'

'Start with the streets adjacent to West Viminal territory and then work in three or four hundred paces. And have one of the lads keep a lookout on the house in Pomegranate Street; I want to know if old matey-boy turns up before I get back. I'll see you there when you've finished.'

Marius nodded his understanding of his task. 'Will do, Brother.'

'Good lad. Sextus, you come with me.'

'Come with you,' Sextus rumbled, slowly digesting his orders. 'Right you are, Magnus; where're we going?'

'Now if I told you that, it wouldn't be a nice surprise for you, would it?'

Sextus' face gradually brightened. 'I like a surprise, I do.'

'That's just as well with a memory like yours,' Magnus observed, walking off in the direction of the Forum Boarium and the Aemilian Bridge at its far end.

The crowds swarming across the Aemilian Bridge into the city could have made the passage in the contra direction a time-consuming affair but for Sextus' bulk and both his and Magnus' forbidding looks. Their path was hardly impeded; the few unfortunates who did cross them soon realised the foolishness of their ways – one from the depths of the Tiber itself.

Having taken a couple of turns left and then right in the tangle of alleys that made up the less than salubrious quarter of the city known simply as Trans Tiberim, Magnus stopped at a door that he had passed through on half a dozen previous occasions. Having knocked, he waited a few moments before a viewing slat opened and he was subjected to the scrutiny of a dark eye.

'Oh, it's you,' the owner of the eye muttered before pulling back the bolt and creaking open the door.

'Hello, Laelia,' Magnus said to the bent old crone revealed by the door, 'you're keeping well by the looks of you.'

Laelia spat on the floor. 'If you think that flattery will get you a better price, Magnus, then you're sadly deluded; I'm very aware that I'm well past my best and deteriorating rapidly with every succeeding day. What do you want?'

Magnus stepped into the gloom of the interior, trying to ignore the pungent stench of old and ingrained urine that emanated from its occupier. 'Your services; what does anyone want if they come to you?'

Laelia closed the door. 'My prices have gone up.'

'I'm sure they have, what with so many people in the city for the Triumph.'

'What Triumph?'

Magnus peered at Laelia but could see no trace of guile or humour. 'You really don't know, do you?'

Laelia gestured towards the outside world and shuffled off into the depths of the house; one candle burnt within. 'What goes on out there is no concern of mine.' She led Magnus and Sextus into a shadow-filled room crammed with earthenware jars and bunches of dried, hanging herbs; the table at its centre was covered in dishes and jugs and in the middle was a massive mortar and pestle. A pot steamed on the cooking fire in the corner. 'Who's the target?'

Magnus waved a dismissive hand. 'I don't want one of your potions, Laelia; I'm here for the keys.'

'I don't give them out, you know that.'

'Nor would I expect you to.'

Laelia looked at her steaming pot and then at the contents of the mortar. 'I'm busy.'

'When can you come?'

'About four hours' time.'

'I'll expect you at midday then. I'll leave Sextus to escort you to Pomegranate Street on the Quirinal.'

'What needs opening?'

'Three doors; one domestic and two workshops. The house dates back to Sulla's time.'

Laelia tutted. 'I don't know what you're up to but it had better be worth it; that'll cost you a gold aureus.'

Magnus grinned, despite the exorbitant price, and reached into his purse, pulling out the coin in question. 'That's exactly what I thought you would say, so I came prepared.'

'And ...' Laelia indicated with her head towards Sextus.

'I also knew that would be a part of the price and again I came prepared; Sextus will do whatever you tell him to whilst your pot boils, if you take my meaning? Won't you, Sextus?'

'Er, do whatever she tells me to.' He paused for a moment to digest this but the full implications did not seem to sink in. 'Right you are, Magnus.'

'Good lad, Sextus, good lad.' Magnus held out the coin. 'I'll see you at midday.'

Laelia took the gold, bit it and then looked appreciatively at Sextus; fire rekindled in her aged eyes. 'I'll be there an hour after midday.'

Magnus fretted at the delay as he made his way back to the Quirinal but knew there was nothing that he could do to speed up Laelia; she always worked at her own pace and could afford to: as the Keeper of the Keys – the largest set of skeleton keys known to the Roman underworld, each one of which she had made in her youth with her father – she dictated her own terms and timetables. It was said that there was not a door in Rome that could not be opened by one of her keys.

'You were very favoured if she agreed to come today,' Servius said after Magnus had told him the timescale on his arrival back at the tavern. He nodded to two men sitting over a jar of wine in the centre of the room. 'They're the two blacksmiths; they both owe us favours for various reasons, not least because we dealt with the man who raped the daughter of the one on the right.'

'Did we? What did we do?'

'The normal.'

Magnus winced and signalled the two men to approach his table.

'Orfityus,' the right-hand man said, introducing himself.

'Minos,' the other, bearded, smith announced with a strong Greek accent.

'Well, lads, I'm pleased that you're ready to honour your debt to the Brotherhood. Have you ever done military work, swords and the like?'

Both men assured him they had.

'I'll need you to be on Pomegranate Street at the beginning of the eighth hour with your tools and slaves. Now, I believe that there already is a blacksmith's forge in one of the shops of the property we're taking over but it's not going to be big enough; how easy is it to set up another forge?'

'It depends how big, Magnus,' Orfityus replied as an attractive young slave with long flaxen hair entered the tavern and made his way over to Servius.

'Big enough to re-forge loads of blades into military-quality ware and to melt down more iron than you've ever seen in one go into bars,' Magnus said as the slave whispered into his counsellor's ear and then turned and left.

'Why don't we just work in our own forges?'

'Because, my friend, this has to remain discreet; no one must know that this amount of iron is going to come on the market, otherwise we'll have exactly the same situation with the price dropping as with the slaves.'

The two smiths looked at each other and then back at Magnus. 'If we could have a couple of days,' Minos ventured.

'So a day and a night would do it then?'

'Er ... I suppose so, Magnus.'

'Good, then see it done as the iron will be arriving on the evening of the Triumph. Be prepared for it to be a time-consuming job, but you'll be recompensed.'

The two men nodded their agreement and were dismissed with a wave of Magnus' hand.

'Well?' Magnus asked Servius.

'That was one of Senator Pollo's boys.'

'I know, I can see ... ah, sorry, Brother.'

'Yeah well, it would seem that the good senator has had a word with the local aedile this morning and reported that in the past three months he's witnessed seven transfers of ownership of tenement blocks in our area; all of them were at the bottom of the Vicus Longus near our border with the West Viminal.'

'Jupiter's slack foreskin! Fuck!'

'Fuck indeed, Brother; fuck indeed.'

'No one has been near it, Magnus,' the brother watching over the house in Pomegranate Street reported as Magnus arrived shortly after midday.

'Well, that's a bit of good news, Laco. Any sign of Marius?'

'Yes, Brother; he and some of the lads were here not long ago and have just gone to the nearest tavern for a wet and a fill. He said they won't be long.'

'Fair enough. How did you do disposing of the body of that slave yesterday?'

'It's done; a Tiber job and the head down a sewer. I'm sorry about that, Magnus; I weren't thinking.'

'That's the trouble: you were thinking and it's best you didn't; just follow your orders. It was a bad mistake to make, Brother; he would have been more use to us alive than dead as I think he knew a lot more than he let on.'

Laco mumbled another apology but was saved from further embarrassment by Marius' arrival.

'The news ain't good, Magnus; not good at all,' the one-handed brother announced as he led his lads up the hill.

'Don't tell me – you've found seven tenements that have changed ownership.'

'Seven? No, Brother; more like ten and all of them have been served eviction orders in the last day or so and all of them have to be out by tomorrow. It looks like we're under attack.'

'I'll say so, Brother; and it's time to start fighting back. But first we've got to get this bit of business going. Where's Sextus got himself to? It was must be an hour after midday.'

Sextus, when he arrived, surprised Magnus, for not only did Laelia have a serene expression on her aged face but so too did the bovine brother. 'She knows a few tricks, Magnus,' he admitted upon being questioned closely on the subject. 'If you close your eyes so you don't see her and try to ignore the smell then it's quite a thing what she can do. A high-class, two-denarii whore couldn't match her for invention and would certainly have more teeth.'

Magnus winced as he looked at the bent figure of the crone and tried not to imagine her mid-tryst but failed, having himself been subjected, on one occasion in the past, to her voracious attentions as it was always a part of her price. Since the first time he had used her services he had always taken care to have the physical part of her fee covered by one of the brothers; Sextus was the first to have fully appreciated her skills to the point of enjoyment. 'I'm sure you're right, Sextus, but I'd appreciate it if you keep your opinions to yourself on that subject; for me it's rather raw, if you take my meaning?'

Sextus did not but refrained from further observations as he gazed in wonder at the old woman rummaging in the leather bag slung over her shoulder.

'Which door is it, Magnus?' Laelia asked, producing a prodigious bunch of keys from the bag.

'Come with me, Laelia,' Magnus said, pleased to have his thoughts distracted from the disturbing images that had clouded his mind. He turned to the rest of his brothers. 'Stay here, lads; we don't want to attract too much attention.'

'If you need my services again, Magnus,' Laelia said as she shuffled up the hill after him, 'then Sextus has to be a part of the price. He's very amenable; strong and hard, just like a man should be.'

Magnus muttered something incoherent and kept any other thoughts to himself as they approached a two-storey house with shuttered shops to either side of the front door; dark blue paint peeled from it to expose the wood underneath. 'This is the one.'

Laelia bent down to examine the lock, her eyes no more than a hand's breadth from it. After some close scrutiny and comparison with a few of the keys on her bunch, she looked up at Magnus. 'The house might have been built in the time of Sulla, but this lock is more modern; it's the work of Blassus of Tusculum from around the time of the beginning of Augustus' rule.'

'Does that mean that you can open it?'

'Of course; but not with these.' She put the keys back in her bag, pulled out an even bigger collection and began thumbing through it. She paused at a key with three evenly spaced, thin teeth, each with a small horizontal extension at differing heights. 'This should do the trick; I made this with my father after we had studied over a dozen of Blassus' designs. The common theme was always the three teeth.' She slipped the key into the lock and, to Magnus' relief, it turned with a satisfying metallic clicking as the teeth did their job.

Laelia grinned at Magnus, exposing her toothless gums as she pushed the door open and then moved on to the two shops, both of which she opened with different keys after a short inspection. 'If you want to change the locks, send Sextus to me with twelve denarii and a couple of spare hours and I'll give him three new ones with two extra keys each.'

'That's a very good idea; he can pick them up when he escorts you back.'

She looked at Sextus, waiting with the rest of the brothers at the end of the street. 'No, he'll have to come again tomorrow, Magnus. The locks won't be there when we get back this afternoon; I need to fetch them.'

'Ahh! I take your meaning, Laelia. What time would suit you best?'

'First thing is always good; sets one up for the rest of the day.'

'He'll be there, but send him back as soon as you've finished with him this afternoon; he's got work to do.'

Laelia cackled, her eyes gleaming as she turned to go. 'I know he has, Magnus; oh yes, don't I know it.'

'It'll do,' Orfityus said to Minos as he looked at the large furnace in the right-hand corner of the street-side wall of the black-smith's shop; a metal flue guided the smoke out through a hole in the bare-brick wall above it. Two years of dust and draping spiders' webs attested to the building's abandonment. 'We can set up a second furnace in the other corner with another flue through the wall to take its smoke and then do the same thing in the shop next door.'

'And you can have all that done by sundown tomorrow and the place cleaned?' Magnus asked in a tone that brooked no negative response.

'Yes, Magnus,' Minos affirmed; he indicated to four burly slaves standing in the doorway. 'They're good workers; they all know their job as they've been with us for over five years now.' Behind the slaves, a stream of Magnus' brethren were going in and out of the main house carrying in furniture, boxes filled with household goods and all the other items essential to furnishing a home.

Satisfied, Magnus made for the door. 'Make it so then, lads; there will be a lot of iron to process over the coming days.' The slaves parted for him as he stepped out into the street. 'Marius! Send one of the lads back to the tavern and have Servius organise bringing the Germanic slaves up here; we're going to have a look at these tenement blocks.'

'These four on the left, the three opposite them and then three from the corner in the Chainmakers' Street,' Marius explained as they reached their boundary with the West Viminal's territory towards the bottom of the Vicus Longus.

Despite the holiday atmosphere, enhanced by decorations and the setting up of street kitchens for the public feasts, there was a sombre feel to this part of the road. Handcarts loaded with possessions stood outside each of the three-storey tenement blocks that Marius had pointed out as the dispossessed piled everything they owned on them; all around children cried and babies wailed, sensing that the patterns of their already hard lives were about to change for the worse.

Magnus surveyed the scene, sucking the air through his teeth and slowly shaking his head. 'We're being made to look stupid; even the ones who don't get evicted would willingly acknowledge the West Viminal once they've moved their people in, seeing as we seem to have nothing to stop them.'

'Well, it's happened so quickly, Magnus.'

'I know, Brother; but they won't see that as an excuse. We're meant to look after our own and that is something that we plainly haven't done in this instance.'

'What are you going to do?'

'Well, we're too late to stop the evictions now and, besides, Geminus has the right to do whatever he wants with the property and if he wants to fill it with West Viminal people there's little we can do to stop it; he won't bow to our threats.'

'So we're buggered, then?'

'As the situation stands at the moment, yes we are, Brother; soundly buggered. But things would be a lot better if either we owned the buildings or they didn't exist, if you take my meaning?'

*

'Buying them is out of the question, even if Geminus would consider selling them to us, which, of course, he wouldn't,' Servius said as the Germanic slaves shuffled into the house on Pomegranate Street, their chains clinking and scraping on the stone pavement. 'Which leaves us only one option.'

Magnus screwed his face up in disappointment. 'That's the way I saw it too.'

'But, we could take advantage of the timing.'

Magnus frowned. 'In what way?'

'The Triumph.'

Magnus' face lightened. 'Of course, it'll be chaos tomorrow.'

'And for the next few days.'

'Our local Vigiles are going to be very hard-pressed.'

'And with all the public feasting there will be so many obstructions in the roads.'

'Many more than normal.'

'Indeed, Brother. It'll seem like there're barricades all around the area; it'll be very difficult to get their pumps through quickly.'

Magnus' face brightened still further. 'Very difficult; especially if they've been partaking of the dozen or so amphorae of the strongest wine we can find that we, as a brotherhood, will present to our local Vigiles tomorrow first thing, in honour of our beloved emperor's Triumph.'

'And what a very generous gesture that would be, Brother; one worthy of the great tradition of philanthropism for which the South Quirinal Crossroads Brotherhood is renowned throughout Rome. I'll organise it as soon as I get back to the tavern.'

'And I'll prepare the lads for a warm day's work tomorrow, which I imagine will end in a bit of a toe-to-toe once Geminus, Sempronius and Primus hear of it. Send word to Martinus to cut a few lengths of chain and leave them in his workshop.'

The morning of the Triumph dawned cold and Magnus' breath steamed from him as he waited outside Senator Pollo's house with the rest of the senator's clients. The chatter was excited as the togate crowd discussed what largesse they might receive from their patron in honour of the greatest day seen in Rome since Caligula celebrated his Triumph over Neptune, having soundly defeated the god in the sea to the north of Gaul and brought back cart-loads of shells as proof. As the first rays of a red sun hit the underside of the sparse cloud coverage, the door was opened and the extremely attractive door-boy stepped back to allow ingress. In order of precedence they went in, and in that same order they filed past Senator Pollo wishing him health and joy of the day as he bestowed purses of coinage of differing size according to the station of the client.

'Ah, Magnus!' the senator boomed. 'I'll need to talk with you in private after the *salutatio*. We've got quite a day ahead.'

'Pallas will separate the weapons carts from the rest of the booty once the parade has returned to the Campus Martius; that will happen inside the Flamian amphitheatre. He'll give you a pass for each vehicle so that the guards don't search them as you take them back through the gates after dark; you don't want to be caught smuggling weapons into the city.'

'We know what happens to those who have been caught; poor Sempronius getting caught with that ballista, such bad luck. But I'm sure that you can use your influence if we do fall foul of the Urban Cohorts; as his benefactor did.'

'Let's hope it doesn't come to that. I want as much profit from this as possible.'

'And rightly so. We'll use the Gate of Salus on the Quirinal; we should be able to avoid the most crowded areas and get them to Pomegranate Street without too much fuss.'

'Good. There'll be six carts in all so bring covers for each of them. Get them unloaded as quickly as possible and start work immediately; the sooner it's finished the sooner I can make money. Is everything ready in the house?'

'It is.'

'No sign of the owner?'

'None so far.'

'Good. I'll be down the morning after to see how you're getting on.'

'We'll be fine, Senator, provided you can furnish me with a letter and a certificate.'

'What do you mean?'

The senator's well-fleshed face creased into a florid grin as Magnus told him. 'Oh very good, Magnus; I do most certainly take your meaning. I'll do the letter immediately and you'll get the certificate when you pick up the wagons after the Triumph.'

The Triumphal Gate – used only for this sacred procession and the lesser version: the Ovation – swung open, shortly after the second hour later that morning, to a fanfare of horns and the deep percussive resonance of massed drums. At a sedate walk, matching the beat, the musicians entered the city. A roar of gargantuan proportions erupted from all those within view that transmitted itself along the crowds lining the entire route, as a flame follows a trail of oil. Soon, the whole city was cheering the Triumph of the man who laid claim to the conquest of an island whose strategic worth was negligible and financial value negative. But despite that, still they cheered and waved the colours of their racing factions, Red, Green, White and Blue, for they cared not for such lofty considerations; their main concerns were their stomachs, their purses and their loins – although not necessarily in that order.

And then, following the musicians, came the captives, ragged rank after rank of them, weighed down by chains and misery, to be paraded in front of a crowd of hundreds of thousands whose collective martial prowess was noticeably less than the ten thousand once-proud warriors whom they jeered. But at their head was no king nor great chieftain; only a few of the lesser nobility from minor sub-tribes were destined for ritual strangulation later that day, for the Triumph was a sham as many of the tribes of Britannia fought on still, resisting the Claudian invasion with every drop of their blood. Caratacus, their leader, was by no means subdued. But that did not bother Magnus and his brethren as the captive women and children, in their wailing masses, began to stumble through the gate in the wake of their menfolk, for Magnus had business to attend to that was made easier by the distraction of the farce being played out throughout the city.

'You take the Chainmakers' Street with your lads, Tigran; we'll do this one,' Magnus said as he and a dozen of the brothers pushed four handcarts down the Vicus Longus. Apart from the public slaves working in the newly set-up kitchens, the road was virtually deserted; just cripples and drunks remained and they were too preoccupied with their own conditions to care over-much about the passing of the brethren. Magnus stopped next to the temporary kitchen at the junction with the Chainmakers' Street. 'Remember, Tigran: just the middle house and then make sure that a kitchen is moved right outside it. We'll meet up at the Flaminian Circus with the rest of the brothers after the Triumph.'

The easterner nodded his agreement and led Cassandros and two other brothers into the narrow street where more kitchens and tables were set out, bedecked with the colours of the Blue racing faction; Magnus hawked and spat at the sight of the banners. 'Marius, you lads do the centre one of the three on this side and we'll see to the middle two of the four over there.'

'Right you are, Magnus. Good luck on getting Sextus to concentrate what there is of his mind on the matter in hand.' With a grin at the bovine Sextus, evidently still in the thrall of his early-morning visit to Laelia to pick up the new locks, the one-handed brother led his three lads to the property in question past the kitchen on the pavement outside where slaves were butchering sides of pork ready for the grill.

'This way, lads,' Magnus said to Sextus, Laco and a third brother, crossing the street to the second of the four tenement blocks. Whereas on a normal day the two business premises – one a tavern, the other a bakery – inbuilt into its ground floor to either side of the entrance would have been open and bustling, today they were firmly shut; who would want to spend their money on food and drink when there would be enough for all for free? And besides, the new tenants were yet to take up their residencies as there were far greater attractions to occupy them this day. Magnus walked towards the building unremarked.

'Get them moved closer, Laco,' he ordered, pointing to public slaves stoking the cooking fires in the kitchen on that side of the road, bringing them up to temperature.

He disappeared into the tenement; Sextus, his expression still wistful, followed with his cart and the third brother.

The hallway was dank and dark, no light other than what seeped through the door reached into its depths; its reek was almost physical in the suddenness of its violence. A stairway, with the steepness of a ladder, punched up through the low ceiling into the first floor, which was a realm of gloom whence no light escaped, just the sound of dripping fluid.

'Put it there,' Magnus said, pointing to a shadowed corner to the left, just inside the door.

Sextus swivelled the cart and pushed it to where he had been ordered, pulled back the leather sheet covering it and then, along with the other brother, took a couple of handfuls of rags from within and scattered them on the floor all the way to the front door.

Magnus took an amphora from under the remaining pile of rags in the cart and lobbed it up the stair to hear it shatter on the first-floor landing. 'That should do it, lads; time to nip next door.'

Laco had terrorised the public slaves into moving their kitchen further up the hill as Magnus came out the first building. 'Bring your cart, Laco,' he ordered, pushing past one of the slaves repositioning an awning.

The interior of the adjacent building was much the same, the only noticeable difference being the dead dog that must have crawled in there to die during the night having come a poor second in a fight. This time Magnus led them on through the creaking passage to a rear door and then out into the relative freshness of a dingy courtyard no more than twenty paces square, backing on to both buildings. Moss covered much of the walls and crept up the trunk of a long-dead tree whose branches touched the upper storeys' shuttered windows of either tenement. 'Over there, Laco, next to the tree, between it and the wall.'

Laco did as ordered and again they spread some of the rags around the cart and again Magnus removed an amphora from the remaining pile left within; this time, however, he also pulled out some twine. He handed both to the third brother, a slim lad not yet out of his teens. 'Up you go, Lupus.'

Using Sextus' hands as a step, Lupus shinned up the tree into the upper branches and secured the amphora so that it dangled directly above the cart; removing the waxed stopper he made his nimble way back down.

'Good lad,' Magnus said, adjusting the handcart a fraction. 'Come, Brothers, time to go and see just what it is that we'll be taking delivery of later.'

The tail of the three-mile trail of slaves had just reached the Via Sacra by the time that Magnus and his brethren had shoved their way to a vantage point. The whips cracked down on the last ranks of weeping women and their wailing offspring and the crowd's catcalls and jeers turned to whistles and cheers as the first of the tableaux trundled into view. The cheers were expressions of wonderment as the invasion fleet was depicted in the form of four quarter-scale triremes with oars, operated by slaves, beating in time, each on its own carriage pulled by heavy oxen. On their decks, actors, dressed as legionaries, struck heroic poses and in the prow of the first stood a representation of the emperor boldly leading his men to the mysterious island across the water.

'I was there at the landing,' Magnus shouted to his brothers above the din of the crowd, 'and I can assure you that he was not.'

And then came the depiction of the landing itself. Terrifying tribesmen waved fearsome swords at legionaries seemingly stuck in the sand as yet another representation of Claudius battered down a chieftain resplendent in a winged helm. Again it was another piece of political spin that had absolutely no basis in reality: the landing had been unopposed.

More and more tableaux laboured past, each depicting a phase of the conquest: the first contact as the legions had marched west between a line of hills and the Tamesis estuary and swept the tribes back thanks to Claudius' bravery; the death of Togodumnus, the brother of Caratacus, defeated in single combat by the emperor; the battle to cross the Afon Cantiacii in which Claudius singlehandedly built a bridge. On it went: the crossing of the Tamesis led by the emperor, the routing of the final resistance, the fall of Camulodunum and the surrender of the kings and chieftains. Only in this last event did Claudius actually participate, but even this was exaggerated as it implied that every king on the whole island had presented his sword to the emperor. But the crowd did not care and cheered themselves hoarse nonetheless, applauding the most martial of the Caesars ever, if the floats were to be believed.

And then came the real proof of the matter, and Magnus wondered if he had agreed to do something for his patron that he would just not be able to see through, for the wagons containing the weaponry of the vanquished were brim full; six of them, each twenty feet long and six feet high. 'They'll take a month just to unload, let alone process,' Magnus observed as he felt his heart sink.

'We don't have to unload them all at once, Magnus,' Marius pointed out. 'They could all just about fit into the stable yard if we unharness the oxen and wheel them in.'

'I suppose so, Brother; it's just that I didn't really appreciate the magnitude of what the senator wants us to do for him ...' He paused as a thought struck him. 'But then I don't suppose Senator Pollo did either. Now that is an interesting point that I think I might bring up with our patron at a suitable moment.' With an inkling of how to resolve one of his present difficulties Magnus relaxed and turned his mind back to the parade as the rest of the booty was driven past: wagons piled high with furs, ingots of tin, silver and gold, cages filled with huge, barking hunting dogs, chests of jewellery and other riches ripped from the most recent people to have been raped by Rome.

With the booty seized in the invasion now completely displayed, the tone changed: out went the martial music of horns and drums to be replaced by massed lyres plucking sweet chords in harmony as the trilling of many pipes soared above in descant.

And then, enveloped by this melodious sound, came the victors: first, the senate, over five hundred of them in their chalked-white togas edged with thick, purple stripes; each man wearing whatever honours he was eligible to display: military crowns, Triumphal Regalia and other baubles of the elite. Waddling in their midst, sweating profusely, was Senator Gaius Vespasius Pollo, doing his best to look dignified, displaying his Triumphal Regalia that he, along with the hundred other senators who had accompanied Claudius to Britannia, had been awarded, thus considerably downgrading its worth. Each senator currently serving as a magistrate was preceded by his due of lictors; incense carriers belched out clouds of sweet-smelling smoke so that the stench of the vanquished before them did not offend their sensibilities. At the sight of the Senate the common people of Rome not only raised the level of their vocal appreciation but also demonstrated it in a physical form: fronds and flowers soared into the air to fall on the parade as a multi-coloured rain that intensified as, following the long line of senators, the object of this day's adulation came into view mounted in a four-horse chariot. Crowned with laurel, wearing the purple and gold *toga picta* and shod in red boots with his face painted the same colour in honour of Jupiter Capitolinus came the twitching, drooling form of Claudius. He acknowledged the acclaim of the crowd with shaky waves with one hand whilst holding the reins in the other; but that was just for show as each of the horses that pulled the quadriga had a groom holding its harness so that there was no danger of the beasts bolting and turning what was already a perceptual farce into a physical one.

Fronds, flowers and now rose petals rained down upon the emperor and on to the mounted officers riding behind him – few of whom had actually served in any of the legions that had done the fighting, but they were not going to let that detail prevent them from sharing a modicum of the glory. Only the two lumbering white oxen, following behind them, had a genuine reason for being there and the sacrificial ribbons tied around them advertised their purpose. Finally, through the floral rain, dressed in the plain white toga of citizens appeared the victorious emperor's troops, bellowing out marching songs with cheeky lyrics addressed to Claudius that carefully omitted any mention of the disabilities that afflicted him. Yet more flowers and fronds were strewn as the women of Rome called out their admiration for such martial men, some baring their breasts to emphasise the point whilst the cohorts of whores in the crowd lifted their tunics to show what could be purchased with the largesse that would be distributed to the legionaries; and the faces of many of the men showed that they too thought that this would be a very worthwhile transaction.

And so passed the soldiery, but there were far fewer of them than would normally expect to be parading in a Triumph as none of the men actually serving in the legions of Britannia could be present due to the fighting still raging in the province. The legionaries receiving the people of Rome's acclaim were drawn from the Praetorian Guard, parade-ground soldiers in the main who had accompanied Claudius to the island and had taken part in a staged battle so that the emperor could, with a certain degree of truth, claim to have led an army in anger. But, again, these considerations were brushed aside as the city embraced the holiday and the Triumph rolled by to the accompaniment of the musicians, incense and cheers topped with the rich aromas of roasting meats from the hundreds of kitchens throughout the city.

As the last rank of legionaries passed followed by the final phalanx of musicians combining, in a crescendo, the earlier martial beats of drums and horns with the melodic strains of the lyres and pipes, the crowds turned to follow the route to bear witness to the sacrifices and pageantry in the Forum.

'Time to go, lads,' Magnus said, turning in the opposite direction, 'the head of the parade will be arriving back on the Campus Martius by now.'

*

The rest of the South Quirinal brethren were gathering near the Flaminian Circus as Magnus and the brothers accompanying him pushed and shoved their way through the chaos of the Campus Martius. All the elements of the Triumph were being dispersed to their various holding places. Slaves, many of them now naked, were being herded into pens to await the mass auctions that were to take place over the following few days; the tableaux were being dismantled whilst the wagon-loads of booty were drawn into the arena of the circus itself.

'Any sign of Pallas?' Magnus asked Tigran, arriving at the open gates as a wagon of howling hunting dogs trundled through.

Tigran indicated with his head to the tunnel exposed by the gates. 'He's through there; he said to find him as soon as you arrived.'

'We'll go together, we need to talk.'

The easterner nodded and followed Magnus into the gloom of the passage leading beneath the seating and out onto the sand.

'You don't have enough support, Tigran,' Magnus said in a conversational tone.

'What do you mean, Brother?'

'Don't play dumb with me; you know precisely what I'm talking about, and if you carry on then you might find yourself not needing any support at all, if you take my meaning?'

'Are you threatening me, Magnus?'

'No, Brother; I'm just pointing out the facts as I see them: you openly criticised me the other night and the only person who showed open support was Cassandros. When it comes down to it he and I go back a long way; we served in the legions together and, ultimately, I think I can count on his loyalty whatever you might have offered him. I know he's ambitious, as are you, but now is not the time to try and push me aside.'

'Who said that I was trying to do that?'

'No one said it but questioning my judgement is the equivalent to asking whether or not I'm fit to be the patronus of our brotherhood. I've waited until this time to have a word with you about it because I now know that by tomorrow all our problems will be solved and any silent support you may have thought you had will have melted away.'

Tigran rubbed his hennaed beard between his thumb and forefinger but said nothing.

'So you have three choices, Brother: support me completely, or leave Rome, or carry on muttering and end up with your body floating downriver to Ostia and your head sinking in shit in one of the sewers.' Magnus smiled – it did not reach his eyes – and put a friendly arm around Tigran's shoulders. 'But we don't want it to come to that, do we, my friend? There'll be time for you yet but it ain't now.' With a squeeze, Magnus let go as they came out into the light of the arena crammed full of wagons, bellowing oxen and busying people. 'Now, what's it to be?'

Tigran answered immediately: 'I stay, Magnus.'

'Good lad for not hesitating. Now, I ain't stupid and I know that when a man is hungry the best thing to do is feed him. So, Brother, I shall give you more responsibilities, which will in turn lead to greater financial benefits. Never let it be said that I don't look after my own.'

'Thank you, Magnus.'

'Good. Well, I'll leave you a couple of dozen lads; you can start by being in charge of this shipment that we're about to take possession of. You take it through the gates after dark, get it into the stable yard behind the house and start unloading and get the smithies working. I'll see you at Pomegranate Street once I've attended to our business on the Vicus Longus.'

'You can rely on me, Brother.'

'I know I can – now; and there's the man we have to rely on to help us get them back into the city.'

'Ah, Magnus,' Pallas, the imperial secretary to the treasury, said, his voice flat and his expression behind his full Greek-style, silver-flecked beard, unreadable; his pale blue tunic, under his toga, was of the finest spun wool. 'These passes will get the vehicles through the gate after sundown.' He handed six wax tablets to Magnus, who passed them on to Tigran. 'Have you got covers for them?'

'They're with the lads outside,' Tigran replied.

Pallas nodded his approval. 'Good, because as soon as it gets dark those wagons have to disappear.'

'Won't people see us taking them out of here, though?'

'Indeed they will and that's why they have to believe that they're seeing something else.' Pallas indicated to a substantial pile of clothing lying nearby; its reek was palpable. 'I had many of the prisoners stripped; scatter the captives' clothes over the wagon covers.'

Magnus chuckled. 'Perfect. No one's going to look twice at that let alone want to rummage in that stinking pile.'

'Quite.' Pallas pulled out a scroll from within the fold of his toga. 'Senator Pollo told me that you needed this.'

'That's, er ...'

'It's a certificate stating the date that you took possession of a certain property in Pomegranate Street on the Quirinal.'

'And it's, er ...'

'Yes, it is, signed and dated by the aedile who would have dealt with that at the time.'

'It's amazing how such a document can turn up after being mislaid for so long.'

'I thought so too; but with a little pressure on the man who's very anxious to follow up his aedileship with a praetorship in the very-near future his memory was soon much improved; he went into his study and very quickly managed to find not only the relevant document but also his duplicate copy should it ever be needed in court.'

Magnus unrolled the scroll and perused it. 'Not that I can read at all but to me this looks to be the exact same document that he gave me – and I have since lost – to confirm that we had not taken possession of an abandoned house illegally. Give him my thanks, Pallas.'

'I already have. Now, Magnus; get these weapons processed as quick as you can and you will find yourself well rewarded.'

Magnus transformed his face into a mask of solemnity. 'My patron's gratitude is reward enough.'

'Shall I tell him that?'

'Er, no; best we keep that to ourselves.'

Pallas almost smiled and then turned to go to oversee the offloading of the heavily guarded bullion carts into strong boxes.

'Well, Tigran,' Magnus said, looking over to the malodorous pile of old clothes, 'it's always best to lead from the front; enjoy disguising the carts whilst I'll take the rest of the lads over to the Vicus Longus.'

The feasting had already begun and chaos abounded in the streets of Rome. With the greed of the deprived offered limitless sustenance for free, the people of Rome glutted themselves on the bread, wine and roasted meats that were their reward for glorifying their emperor. And they seized it with gusto as if it were their last night in this world – which, for more than just a few, it was – gorging themselves without care, vomiting and fornicating freely; and, as the sun went down over Rome and the city's shadows lengthened into night, all sense of law and order began to dissipate.

'Perfect,' Magnus muttered to himself as he and thirty of his brethren arrived at the junction of the Chainmakers' Street and the Vicus Longus; the public slaves manning the kitchens were still cooking meat and baking bread whilst others distributed amphorae of wine to an increasingly inebriated populace. The pairs of soldiers of the Urban Cohorts that had been assigned to guard each kitchen were fast losing their discipline as the temptations of the evening began to outweigh their sense of duty. Whores plied their trade openly without shame, as to take a client away to find privacy would lead to precious time being wasted in which a few more small bronze coins could be earnt. 'Marius, take a dozen lads and freshen up the trails; if you need more oil there're always the kitchens.'

Marius grinned. 'Right you are, Magnus; they won't be having much use for it very soon.'

'Ain't that the truth, Brother; When you're done meet us at that kitchen a couple of hundred paces up the hill.'

With a cheerful wave, Marius disappeared into the mayhem as Magnus turned to Sextus. 'You stay here with Laco and half

a dozen of the lads and discourage anyone who tries to interfere. I imagine that a lot of these are the new West Viminal
tenants, seeing as they think that this is already their territory
and I don't recognise many of them.'

'Discourage West Viminal interference: got you, Magnus.'

'But don't stop any of them running off; I want news of this
to spread quickly.'

There was a slight pause as Sextus took this in. 'It's to spread
quickly; got you.'

'Good lad; when it's done, you wait by Martinus' workshop.'

This proved slightly too complicated for Sextus to digest
immediately but eventually he got there and nodded slow
understanding to his patronus. 'Got you, Magnus.'

Satisfied, Magnus slapped Sextus on the shoulder and then
led the remaining brethren up the Vicus Longus, barging their
way through the crowds who were now beyond recognising the
leader of the local brotherhood and giving way to him.

'Help yourselves, Brothers; just wine, no food,' Magnus said as
they reached a kitchen further up the hill. He pulled aside a couple
of drunks leaning for support on the trestle table and signalled to
the slaves to pass a few amphorae from their store to his waiting
brethren; the Urban Cohort guards raised their cups to Magnus
and slurred a greeting, the effort of which caused one to stagger
and grab his comrade's shoulder to prevent a total collapse.

The wine was quickly distributed, more amphorae were
requisitioned and, by the time Marius had made it back up
the hill, half an hour later, the members of the South Quirinal
Crossroads Brotherhood were feeling the effects of drinking on
empty stomachs.

'Perfect,' Magnus again muttered to himself as he surveyed
his men enjoying the juice of Bacchus.

'All done, Magnus,' Marius reported, taking the full cup that
Magnus offered him.

'Then let's get on with it, Brother.' At the top of his voice he
broke into the most popular of the marching songs that had been
sung about Claudius that day. It was an old song, concerning
the necessity of locking up one's daughters as the Triumphal

general, who has the reputation of a billy-goat, returns; it had been made popular by Julius Caesar's men back in his day but had had many lives since – although the subject of this incarnation was perhaps the most unlikely. But that made no matter as the tune was rumbustious and the lyrics boorish, perfect for alcoholically refreshed men, many of whom had served under the Eagles and, therefore, knew it well.

Bellowing out the tune and pumping the air in time with his fist, Magnus began to lead his brothers back down the hill. As they progressed, other revellers took up the refrain, roaring out its many stanzas whilst slapping their thighs and rocking their cups back and forth in time to the beat and then making the requisite lewd gestures to the chorus. On down the hill Magnus led the impromptu choir, their number growing all the time as more and more joined in this homage to the generous provider of the day's bounty. And who could deny that it was not appropriate? For was it not the most natural song to sing at the feast celebrating a Triumph? The raucous crowd grew and began to sweep all aside; drunks were flung back into doorways; couples, mid-tryst, were scraped from walls and tumbled over; dogs, brave enough to scavenge for scraps, were kicked aside and kitchens were pushed over, crashing to the pavement in a shatter of amphorae accompanied by showers of sparks flung up from overturned ovens and braziers. But that did not deter Magnus; quite the contrary. He sang even louder and pumped his fist in the air even stronger and, as they approached the junction of the Vicus Longus and the Chainmakers' Street, he moved to the left, then stopped and let the crowd surge around him as he watched the destruction of the kitchen Laco had moved to outside the two tenements that he had visited that morning.

And it was immediate and spectacular. Down went the brazier, spilling its many red-hot coals onto the ground, a ground already slick with a viscous fluid; a flash, pale blue, then it travelled away, flickering as it ran, towards the door of the nearest tenement; through it went and then orange light began to glow within as the rags that they had scattered now caught.

With a puff of flame the pile in the handcart flared and within a few heartbeats the stair was aglow, closely followed by the first-floor landing. With a feeling of great contentment, Magnus looked to the other side of the street and made out, above the heads of the singing mass still passing by, the unmistakable glimmer of nascent flame in the tenement opposite.

It did not take long and when it came it was a joy to hear. The first shout of 'Fire!' was sudden and shrill, like the crack of a slingshot ricocheting off an iron helm; rapidly others took up the cry and the ribald song was soon forgotten. Then, as the first flames began to lick out of the windows and rise into the air, panic seeded itself in the crowd and, apart from Magnus' brethren, it began to disintegrate; some ran forward and others back but a large majority funnelled their way left, along the Chainmakers' Street. Narrow as it was, the street was soon bottlenecked and the final kitchen was kicked to the ground causing yet more panic as it too spawned flame in the tenement that Tigran had visited that morning and Marius had refreshed just recently.

'Back up the hill, lads!' Magnus shouted once he had seen the tell-tale glow emerging from the Chainmakers' Street. And back up they pelted along with many others, unremarked in the mass, as near neighbours of the affected buildings called for the Vigiles. But the Vigiles were, as yet, nowhere to be seen for the streets were congested beyond normality, and, besides, Servius' gift had been put to very good use, making their reaction time less than acceptable.

By the time the fires had really taken hold Magnus, looking back down the hill, could see by their light what he was waiting for. 'Off we go, lads; and with a sense of urgency expected of a civic-minded organisation like ours.'

Back down he led his brethren at a run to arrive as if it had been the first time they had been on the scene that evening. 'Quick, Marius!' Magnus shouted, the earnestness in his voice mightily exaggerated. 'Find buckets and get the lads to form lines.'

'Who are you?' a voice close by shouted.

Magnus turned to see a middle-aged man who would have been deemed to be expensively attired had it not been for the state that his evident consternation had brought him to. 'I am the man trying to put out these fires: Marcus Salvius Magnus, the patronus of the local brotherhood; who are you?'

'I'm the man who owns these buildings: Lucius Favonius Geminus.'

Magnus did his best impression of a surprised man. 'Well, that is fortuitous. How much are you willing to pay me and my lads to put out these three fires seeing as the Vigiles seem to be otherwise engaged?'

Geminus stared at Magnus in horror. 'Pay you? Just do it, otherwise the whole neighbourhood will go up and it's your area, your responsibility.'

Magnus made a show of thinking for a few moments. 'You're right, Geminus: it's more important to save the area than to try and squeeze a little profit out of a desperate owner.' He turned to see Marius running up to him with a few lads with buckets. 'That ain't going to be enough, Brother; there's no way we can do all three with that. We're going to have to take drastic action: firebreaks. We've got to tear down the buildings to either side and stop the flames spreading.'

'Right you are, Magnus; what do you suggest?'

'There will be plenty of stuff we can use in the Chainmakers' Street: chains with grappling hooks, crowbars, you name it. Get the lads to break the shop doors open.'

'You can't be serious,' Geminus cried as Marius ran off to do as he was bid.

'It's the only thing to do to save the area, as you pointed out.'

'But I own the buildings to either side too!'

Magnus looked incredulous. 'All of them? All six buildings either side of the three ablaze?'

Geminus nodded, his eyes wide.

'Well, that is unfortunate; but what can we do?'

'You can stop acting so innocent for a start, Magnus,' a new voice said. A huge figure emerged out of the night behind Geminus with the shapes of many more beyond him.

Magnus' eyes narrowed at the sight of the West Viminal patronus. 'Sempronius! What are you doing on South Quirinal territory?'

'I might ask you the same question: what are you doing on West Viminal territory?'

'This has always been South Quirinal.'

'Until my brother bought these tenements.' Primus stepped from Sempronius' shadow, all bulging muscle and furred with body-hair. 'Tenements that you've just torched and will now pay for.' He reached under his cloak, unsheathed the knife he kept in the small of his back and then spun it in the air, catching it without looking; its blade gleamed gold with flame.

Magnus took a glance over his shoulder to see that his brethren were now gathering. 'If you prefer to fight rather than try and save the area, then that's fine by me; as a matter of fact, this is exactly what I was hoping for.' He turned to Marius, who now stood next to him. 'Are we ready?'

Swinging a heavy length of chain before him, the one-handed brother gave a grim smile. 'Not one missing link, Brother.'

'I take your meaning, Brother; very good, very good indeed.' Laco handed him a three-foot length of chain; he took it and wrapped one end around his fist. 'I think we're ready, Primus; what about you, Sempronius?'

The patronus of the West Viminal baulked at the sight of more than thirty adversaries suddenly whirling chains, glinting in the firelight, and retreated a couple of paces behind Primus. But Magnus was not going to let Sempronius' hesitation spoil a well-laid trap; he leapt forward and, swinging low, caught Geminus around the shin. With a brutal yank, he pulled him off his feet.

The brethren of the South Quirinal Crossroads Brotherhood surged forward, flailing fearsome weapons about their heads as Magnus slammed his chain-entwined fist into the side of Geminus' head, knocking the senses from him.

As the first heavy links thrashed into the faces and bodies of the West Viminal, jaws cracked and skulls dented; an eye, trailing dark gobbets of blood, flew, silhouetted, across the ever-rising flames as cheeks were gashed asunder to expose the stumps of broken, bloodied teeth that parted, revealing frothing gorges whence howls of pure agony issued. Without qualms they slashed into their foes, sending them back or down in a welter of blurred violence that none could withstand; Sempronius slunk further back behind Primus and then ran. Magnus bounded up from the prone body of Geminus towards his twin; Primus stood, rooted to the spot, aghast at the scale and suddenness of the violence that had erupted. Having never before faced lashing chains he knew not how to defend himself; his knife was certainly not up to the task. He turned and fled in the footsteps of his patronus; but as he did so Magnus flicked the chain so that it no longer encircled his fist and swung it above him, letting go as the flaying end aligned with Primus' head. Round it went, hissing horizontally through the air, revolving around the centre of its own axis, heavy in flight, to wrap itself about Primus' skull with a dull clacking of chain-links furling. Primus screamed and, with arching back and arms flying, fell forward to hit the street, knees first with the rest of his body crumpling after; with one bounce he was still.

His brethren could take no more and they fled, leaving the dead and unconscious behind.

'Call the lads back, Marius! Get them fighting the blaze!' Magnus shouted above the victors' roar as from up the hill a new force appeared on the scene. 'Ah! I wondered when they would finally get through.' Picking up a discarded chain he knelt down beside the unconscious form of Geminus as ten groups of eight Vigiles jogged down the hill, wheeling a few hand pumps and pushing equipment carts. He slapped Geminus about his bloodied face a few times and stirred him back into lucidity. 'Now, you gerrymandering cunt, you've got a choice: either accept my offer of a hundred denarii per tenement block, which is generous seeing that they're all going to be either burnt to the ground or pulled down by our gallant friends in the Vigiles, or to never have any need for money again, if you take my meaning?'

Geminus looked at Magnus, his eyes slowly focusing as Marius began to marshal the brothers into fire-fighting teams. 'You bastard!'

'Me the bastard? I ain't the one trying to muscle into another brotherhood's area. Now, what's it to be? If I understand property law correctly, a verbal agreement made in front of five citizens is a legally binding contract; or would you prefer a casual slash around the head with this rather heavy chain?' Magnus raised the item in question.

Geminus looked at the links dangling just in front of his eyes and sighed. 'All right, I'll do it. Two hundred, though.'

'Just a hundred. But I'll be generous.' He pointed at the building to the left of the tenement that gave access to the courtyard; neither yet burnt. 'There's one building that we perhaps can just save, and even with the Vigiles arriving we're going to be hard-pushed fighting all the fires, seeing as we wasted so much time in arguing. If you can help us save it, I'll let you keep it and I'll give you a nominal ten denarii each for the other nine fire-damaged plots.'

With the resigned look of a man trying to retrieve something from a terrible situation, Geminus raised himself up onto his elbows. 'Agreed.'

'Marius! Get over here with the Vigiles centurion and four of the brothers, now!' Magnus pulled Geminus to his feet as Marius got the witnesses together.

'We're going to wansht paying, you knowsh,' the Vigiles centurion informed Magnus; he frowned and looked closer. 'Oh, itsh you, Magnush.' He signalled to his men to begin work. 'Another amphorash or two of that wine will go down a treat, though.'

'And they shall be yours, Densus; but bear witness to this first. Marcus Favonius Geminus agrees to sell me, Marcus Salvius Magnus, his seven properties on the Vicus Longus and his three on the Chainmakers' Street for a hundred denarii each or ten denarii each should we save a building intact, which he would then keep in lieu of the balance. Do you agree, Geminus?'

'I do.' Geminus went on to repeat the exact terms of the deal and the witnesses affirmed their presence and understanding as the frenetic action of pumping water into the flames and attaching ropes to the buildings to be demolished carried on apace.

The legal deal done, Magnus wondered how Rome had not completely burnt down in the days of Crassus continually extorting property at knock-down prices from the unfortunate owners watching their buildings burn, as he rushed to the tenement with the courtyard; ropes were already being tied onto the upper storey. Smoke had started to spout from the front door and a couple of windows but, as yet, there was no tell-tale orange glow.

'We need to get this one down quick, Densus! You carry on here and we'll get some ropes on the back.' He ran through the door with Marius following, pulling Geminus along with him. Through the passage they went, keeping their heads down and squinting against the sting of smoke. Out into the courtyard they burst; flames licked out of the next-door building's windows and smoke swirled all around; the upper reaches of the tree were charring and some twigs were alight. Magnus stopped as Marius held on to Geminus.

Geminus looked around. 'What are we doing here? Where're the ropes we need?'

The cold look on Magnus' face told the story.

'But we had a deal!'

'I know, a lovely one and it's all legal now – whatever happens.'

Geminus did not see the knife come up through the smoke, punch into his chest just under his ribs and then plough on through into his heart; but the pain in his eyes as he stared at Magnus showed how much he felt it.

'You know how it goes, Geminus; you did it enough in your time. I just made one more refinement to your scam in that instead of the ones who refuse to sell ending up dead, like you used to do, the ones that sell also end up dead once the deal's been witnessed.' Twisting the knife left and right, he pulled it out; blood slopped to the ground.

Geminus slumped, the life fading quick in his eyes. Marius let him go and, with a shove, pushed him onto the pile of rags in the handcart; the first sparks started to fall from the tree as the fire spread from the twigs along the branches. Magnus picked up a smouldering brand and blew on it; it glowed. He stuck it into the pile of rags and, within a few moments, they burst aflame.

Looking up through the smoke, Magnus could see that the fire had caught the branch to which the amphora of oil was tied. As he watched, the flame crept along and reached the rope; it started to burn. 'Let's go!' He sprinted back into the corridor with Marius close behind; both were wafting the smoke away to increase visibility. Out they raced into the flame-lit night and the pandemonium of fire-fighting as more and more of the local residents came to help stop the blaze spreading to their properties.

'We can't pull him out!' Magnus shouted to Densus.

'Who?'

'Geminus! A branch has fallen on him. I need to borrow a couple of your men.' As the last word passed Magnus' lips a dull whoopff made him turn in time to see an explosion of flame burst through the door as the oil-filled amphora fell and shattered on the body of Geminus. 'Too late!' he shouted, slamming his fist into the palm of his hand, before adding, under his breath: 'Just in time.'

'Well, Magnus,' Senator Pollo boomed, 'this all looks very good; very good indeed.'

They were standing in the now well-furnished atrium of the house on Pomegranate Street the following morning; all around there was ordered activity as a couple of manacled Germanic slaves shuffling in leg irons, closely supervised by Tigran and Cassandros, brought in armfuls of weapons from the carts parked in the stable yard and stacked them in the rooms off the atrium; here, under Marius and Sextus' eyes, three more slaves stripped the blades of any leather, wood or bronze before two more slaves took them to the forges in the two shops out front whence came a steady heat and the acrid smell of super-heated iron.

'It was Tigran that got it all going; I was otherwise engaged.'

'My thanks will be forthcoming, Tigran.'

Tigran bowed his head. 'I look forward to it, Senator.'

'Show me the rest.'

Tigran led Magnus and the senator to the workshops past a couple of slaves bringing back well-formed swords and daggers. Here the blacksmiths and their slaves were re-forging the weapons into army issue; twisting white-hot blades together, combining them, they hammered ceaselessly, strengthening the metal from the softer type produced by the Britannic tribes into biting Roman iron.

'Very good, Magnus,' Senator Pollo boomed again over the clanging of hammers on anvils; sweat poured down his face. A figure beating away at smaller pieces of metal in the corner caught his eye. 'What's he doing?'

'Martinus? Ah, he's a chainmaker. He's putting the off-cuts to very good use seeing as there seems to be a shortage of chainage in the city; what with all these prisoners and all, the price is going up.'

The senator wiped the sweat from his jowls with a large handkerchief – it was a losing battle – as he waddled to the door. 'Excellent! How long do they reckon to process the whole consignment?'

'Ah, well; that's just the trouble, you see, Senator: the smiths are estimating four months. I don't think neither you nor me realised just what was involved – how much there was, if you take my meaning?'

Senator Pollo paused and looked knowingly at Magnus. 'I think I do; what do you want?'

'Now, sir; no, no. Nothing for myself. It's just that there was a fire in my area last night on the Vicus Longus and also in the Chainmakers' Street.'

'Go on.'

'Well, three of the buildings were destroyed in the Vicus Longus and a couple more had to be pulled down. However, they managed to put out the fire in the Chainmakers' Street before it did too much damage to the adjoining buildings.'

'Yesss?' the senator said, more as a question as he stepped out into the street covered with the debris of a public feast not yet cleared up.

'Well, the workshops along that street are all chainmakers –
forges, in other words; one of them belongs to Martinus. With
some money I could get them working again and we could use
them to melt down the metal from the helmets and shields; we
could take it all down at night to keep it all very discreet. It'll
speed things up considerably.'

'Ah! I see. So you want …?'

Magnus shrugged. 'A thousand should do—'

'Just what the fuck is going on here?'

Magnus looked round to see a balding man wearing an
equestrian tunic and toga edged with a thin purple stripe. 'And
who's asking?'

The man's face was puce with indignation. 'Lucilius Celsus,
that's who; the owner of this house.'

'I'm afraid you're completely mistaken. I took possession of
this abandoned building over two years ago and have a certificate from the aedile at the time to prove it was acquired legally
and not through theft or violence.'

'You what?'

Gaius stepped forward. 'I don't know if you laid claim to
the ownership of the building before but if you do you should
be ashamed of yourself: once you abandoned it the house
started attracting the most insalubrious characters. As a
concerned resident I informed Magnus here – I believe he still
has the letter – as the patronus of the local brotherhood and
he did his civic duty and expelled the riff-raff and selflessly
took on the expense of the property.'

Magnus gave his best cold-eyed smile. 'I did.' He pointed
through the open front door into the well-furnished atrium. 'As
you can see it has been lived in for some time; over two years,
in fact.'

Senator Pollo ruffled himself up to look his most magisterial.
'Which means in law … sorry, I didn't catch your name?'

'Lucilius Celsus!'

'My dear Celsus, the property now belongs to him. You're too
late.'

'I want to see these documents.'

Gaius nodded; sweat dripped from his chins. 'Of course you do; who wouldn't in your position? I was just saying to Pallas, the other day, that if the original owner would ever turn up—'

'Pallas? Marcus Antonius Pallas, the imperial secretary to the treasury?'

'Yes, the very same; he was here because we're doing some business together. He said that if the original owner ever did turn up he was sure that he could in some way recompense him seeing as the building has suited our purposes so well. Would you like me to arrange an interview with the man who controls the proceeds of the Triumph, or would you prefer to squabble over the ownership of an insignificant house?'

Celsus looked unconvinced. 'How can I trust that you have any influence with him?'

'You can't; but neither could you win the argument about who legally owns this house. My name is Gaius Vespasius Pollo; I live in the next street. Come to my *salutatio* in two days' time and I shall have procured you that lucrative interview. Now go, before I decide not to be so helpful.'

Celsus' indignation had not abated but it was overruled by the possibility of preferment by the man with control of the Empire's finances. 'Two days' time, then; I'll be there.' Issuing threats and oaths in equal measure as to what he would do if he were thwarted, Celsus stormed away past Servius coming up the hill guided by Lupus.

'Will you get him into Pallas?' Magnus asked the senator.

'Yes, Pallas owes you a favour for the discretion you've shown in this matter.'

'Speaking of which: about that thousand?'

'You shall have it if it speeds up the work.'

'It'll be finished in under two months.'

'Excellent!'

'Not everything is excellent, I fear, Magnus,' Servius said.

'What's wrong, Brother?'

'Unfortunately the Urban Prefect has been looking into the cause of the fires last night.'

Magnus shrugged. 'Let him look; we're in the clear.'

'If only, Brother, if only. But it would seem that two Urban Cohort men saw you start the singing and lead the mob down the hill; then the public slaves on the kitchens that caused the fires have all testified under torture that they were told to move their kitchens and some described you as the instigator.'

'Just supposition.'

'Would that it were, Brother, would that it were. Unfortunately the Vigiles centurion, Densus, in having to explain to his tribune the state his watch were in last night admitted that it was us that gave them all the wine and then placed you as being already at the scene upon his arrival. Now that in itself could just about be dealt with. However, he's also told of witnessing your property deal with Geminus shortly before you took him into a building whence he never returned; and as I told you, the Urban Prefect has done business with Geminus and knows all about that sort of thing. I think that when he hears of that he might well be very interested in having a little chat with you.'

'Ah!'

'Ah, indeed, Brother.'

'Perhaps I should … er?'

'I think perhaps you should.'

'I'll do what I can to sort out the misunderstanding,' the senator offered.

'That's very kind of you, sir. I suppose it's back to Britannia for me in the meantime, then.'

'The safest place for you, Magnus.'

By the look on Magnus' face he was not entirely convinced. 'And the little matter of the money I owe your family for the slaves, Senator?'

'My dear Magnus, do not trouble yourself with details like that. They are doing a fine job in there; I'll take them off your hands and we shall call the matter quits. You lose the deposit you paid, that's all.'

Magnus smiled inwardly, knowing that he was not going to be without his deposit for long. He gave his best impression of a look of innocence – it was not that convincing. 'And what about the house?'

'What about it?'

'Well, sir, it would seem that in law I own it.'

'Now, just a moment; I was—' Senator Pollo stopped mid-flow and reconsidered. 'You're right I suppose; only you could use that certificate in the courts. I'll tell you what I shall do: in return for my silence on the matter we'll sell it and split the proceeds fifty-fifty once the job is finished.'

'That should just about cover our rebuilding of the tenements destroyed in the fire; it's a deal. Give the money to Servius, he'll sort it out for me. Any idea who we could sell it to?'

'As a matter of fact I do: my nephew, Vespasian, will be needing a house when he returns from Britannia and I said that I'll find him one; this'll suit him perfectly.'

'That's ideal.'

'It is, but when you see him back in Britannia there's no need to mention that he's purchasing it off us, otherwise, knowing him, he'll be wanting a large discount, and we wouldn't want that, would we, Magnus?'

'No, Senator, we wouldn't want that; not at all.'

THE SUCCESSION

This Magnus romp through Rome takes place a month before the prologue of *Rome's Lost Son* and is set against the festival of The Punishment of the Dogs; a rather cruel event – to our modern way of thinking – punishing our canine friends for sleeping through the Gallic attack of the Capitoline Hill in 390 BC, an action that was thwarted only by the vigilance of the geese who, no doubt, thoroughly enjoyed the annual festival.

Astrologers were purged from Rome by successive emperors due to their sensitivities about having the Imperial charts read; no emperor could countenance the fact that the time of their death could be public – or even private – knowledge. However, the people of Rome's innate willingness to believe in astrology and mankind's illogical need to give credence to charlatans must have meant that there were many backstreet or underground Astrologers willing to risk life and limb for exorbitant fees.

It struck me that it would be a good thing to link the final tussle between Magnus and Tigran as they fight for supremacy of the South Quirinal Brotherhood with the similar battle for the succession going on at the same time on the Palatine Hill. And so in this final Magnus story we find him physically weakened, having lost an eye in Britannia, but still mentally sharp as he ensures his survival after he steps down as patronus – a courtesy that he did not extend to his predecessor.

I thoroughly enjoyed my annual foray, every October, into the underbelly of Rome and came to love Magnus and his brethren even when they were at their most badly behaved – although, I'm sure that I would not have felt the same way had I come up against them in real life – so I hope that you, dear reader, enjoy reading the Magnus romps as much as I delighted in writing them.

ROME, AUGUST AD 51

'Marcus Salvius Magnus, it has been a long while since I last begged a favour from you as the patronus of my local brotherhood.' In her early twenties, the supplicant stood, wringing her hands, before Magnus' desk in the back room of the tavern that was the headquarters of the South Quirinal Crossroads Brotherhood. Even in the dim light of an oil lamp suspended from the ceiling, and another on the desk, next to a jug of wine and three cups, it was obvious that she had a black eye and a cut to her lower lip.

Smoke from the lamps made the already stuffy atmosphere unpleasant but Magnus was not about to open a window, even at the height of summer, for fear of someone on the street outside eavesdropping on brotherhood business. He wiped the sweat from his brow with the back of his hand and gestured to the chair opposite. 'Sit down, Tacita.'

Stepping forward, Tacita did so and nodded in gratitude, automatically checking her raven hair, piled high on her head and studded with cheap jewellery in imitation of the coiffure of the rich; her attire similarly aped her betters, although her palla and stola were cut from cloth of lesser worth. With her coming further into the light, Magnus could see that her face had a pleasing, girlish quality despite the liberal application of make-up, again in an attempt to raise her perceived status.

A woman to whom appearance is everything, Magnus mused to himself, mentally stripping her and admiring her curvaceous, womanly figure with his one good eye, the other being a glass imitation, and not a very good one at that, that seemed to have a mind of its own.

Shaking his head to rid himself of the agreeable thought, Magnus took a sip of wine and then glanced at the old man sitting next to him, his eyes milky and his fingers gnarled with arthritis. 'What have we done for Tacita in the past, Servius?'

Servius, wheezing with every breath, scratched the loose skin hanging beneath his chin as he cast his encyclopaedic mind back. 'Four years ago last May we arranged for the then aedile of the Quirinal Hill to clear her husband, Tuscus, of the accusation that he was a practising astrologer.'

'Yes,' Tacita agreed, 'and he swore an oath never to practise again. Since then he has built up a candle-making business, which has become a great success, with high-profile clientele such as the current aedile himself and many of the senators and equites living on the Quirinal. Again, it was thanks to you, Magnus, for recommending the business to such people.'

'I did?' The question was directed more at Servius who, as his counsellor and second-in-command, knew all the Brotherhood's affairs.

'You asked Senators Pollo and Vespasian as well as the imperial freedwoman Antonia Caenis to have their stewards purchase from Tuscus as he is the only candle-maker in our territory. People of quality from the Quirinal and also the Viminal, as the business is close to our border, have joined the fashion, thereby boosting Tuscus' income and thus the contribution he makes to us, which is over ten denarii a month.'

Magnus scratched at the stubble on his battered, ex-boxer's face and looked back at Tacita. 'So trade is good then?'

Tacita nodded. 'Very good; but maybe that's the root of my problem.'

Magnus leant forward, resting his elbows on the desk and his chin on his fists, staring with his one good eye at Tacita as the glass replica in his left socket looked blankly over her head. 'Go on.'

A series of rasping, painful-sounding coughs obliged Tacita to pause as Servius' chest heaved. As his gaunt frame shook, Magnus was forced to hold his shoulders to prevent him from falling off the chair. After a few more convulsions Servius hawked up a large gobbet of phlegm into his hand.

'That's got blood in it,' Magnus said, looking at the resulting mess.

'I know, Brother; I can taste it.'

'Here,' Tacita said, handing over a rag handkerchief that she produced from within her palla.

Magnus took it and wiped the gunk from Servius' hand. 'How long have you been coughing up blood, Brother?'

'The last few months, but it's been getting worse recently.' Servius took a large swig of wine and swallowed with evident relief. He gestured in Tacita's direction. 'I'll be all right; carry on.'

Tacita looked to Magnus, who nodded. 'Well, since my husband's business has become successful he's naturally had quite a bit of spare cash once he's paid the rent for the premises and our accommodation, as well as making his contribution to the Brotherhood, of course.'

'And a very fine contribution it is,' Magnus acknowledged, 'which is why we will be more than happy to help you both out in any way we can.'

Tacita did not look suitably pleased by this statement. 'Yes, well, it's for myself alone that I'm here, not on behalf of my husband, as he's the reason why I've come. You see, with all this spare cash he has, rather than save it so that we could buy a new slave to help with the business, he fritters it away on whoring and wine along the Vicus Patricius on the Viminal.'

Magnus spread his hands and tutted in sympathy, despite being of the opinion that this was a very sensible and worthwhile expenditure; although, he would have preferred that Tuscus frequented the brothels under his own control, but he refrained from mentioning it.

Tacita suppressed a sob. 'We haven't yet been blessed with children. I haven't given up hope but he's paying less and less attention to me, no matter how much effort I make, and when I try to talk to him about it he gets aggressive and shouts at me; and then, last night, when he came home drunk and reeking of stale whore, yet again, he, well, when I complained, he did this.' She pointed to her black eye and split lip.

Magnus again tried to demonstrate his sympathy, though with less success this time. 'Why have you come to us about this? It's a domestic matter; what goes on between a husband and his wife is for them alone and nothing to do with the Brotherhood. You are legally his property and he has the right to treat you as he will; he can kill you if he so wishes. I'm sorry but I have no reason to interfere.'

Tacita was unable to keep her sobs in; she held her face in her hands. 'But you must help me, Magnus; you're the cause of this.'

Magnus sat back in his chair, unsure whether or not he had heard her correctly. 'What? You're saying that I'm responsible for your husband beating you after he's been out drinking and whoring?'

'Of course. It was you that persuaded all those important people to patronise his shop; if you hadn't have done that then—'

'Your trade might have struggled, we wouldn't have got so much from it and you'd be poor.'

'I'd rather be poor than live in fear of my husband.'

'And not wear those nice clothes and have your hair and make-up done so you look much more than what you are?'

'That's my right; it's not my husband's right to hit me when I complain that he doesn't give me enough money to dress really well because he spends it all on his cock.'

'Ah, so that's the real problem, is it? Not enough pretty things.' Magnus had had enough; he got up, walked around the desk to the door and opened it. 'Sextus, show the lady out.'

'Show the lady out,' Sextus repeated, as always digesting his orders slowly, as his huge, lumbering form darkened the doorway. 'Right you are, Magnus.'

Tacita sprang to her feet, hissing and spitting and flinging herself, nails clawing, at Sextus as he approached her. 'I'll not go! I'll not go until you've promised, Magnus!'

Sextus recoiled at first at the ferocity of the attack, his heavily muscled forearms scratched and bleeding, before clamping his bear-like hands on Tacita's upper arms and lifting her off the ground so that her legs now became her main weapons. Magnus managed to grab them before they had done too much damage to Sextus' shins. Struggling with the writhing woman, now shrieking like a lunatic, Magnus and Sextus manhandled her through the door and then right, out into the dim passage at whose end lay a staircase leading upwards, opposite a leather-curtained door on the left, beyond which came the sound of laughter and alcohol-fuelled chatter. Still grappling with the woman's legs, Magnus pushed his way past the curtain and into the tavern. All eyes turned to him and conversation died as he barged through the crowded bar.

Magnus looked at a man of Eastern appearance, with a hennaed beard and embroidered trousers. 'Tigran, clear a path.'

Tigran ran to the doorway and shoved a couple of freedmen out of the way, who had been lounging against it. Picking up speed with Tigran clearing people before them, Magnus and Sextus hurried along with their thrashing burden screeching like a harpy; through the open door they went and out, under the baking August sun, into the tabled area and then beyond that to where the Alta Semita and the Vicus Longus met at a sharp, acute angle. With little ceremony, Magnus and Sextus dumped Tacita in the road. Her hair awry and her eyes wild she sat, looking up and sobbing. 'You must help me, Magnus; you must!' She picked up a handful of filth and hurled it at Magnus, only to miss and splatter, instead, Tigran's finely embroidered knee-length tunic. Without pausing to think, Tigran drew his knife, carried as much for fighting as for eating, and walked with intent towards the wailing woman.

Magnus clamped a hand on his shoulder. 'Don't!'

Tigran shook it off and turned to Magnus. 'She threw shit at me; no one does that and lives.'

'And nobody kills anyone in my territory without my permission, and in this case that is withheld.'

They locked eyes.

'Do I really need your permission?'

'Be careful, Tigran; don't forget I've made you very rich over the past few years. Don't spoil it.' Magnus felt the strength of the easterner's pride wrestling with the knowledge that if he went against his patronus in public he would not last out the hour. Tigran backed down and jammed his knife back into its sheath. Looking over his shoulder he spat at Tacita and then walked away along the Alta Semita. No one followed him.

Magnus looked down at Tacita, wiping the saliva off her face. 'After that display I'm of a mind to completely sympathise with your husband and I can only marvel at his forbearance in giving you just the one black eye and splitting only your lower lip. I'll do the rest of his work myself should you come back in here, if you take my meaning?'

'Sempronius of the West Viminal wouldn't let a woman down so, and his territory starts at the bottom of my street.'

Magnus sneered. 'Sempronius of the West Viminal would take exactly the same attitude as I have, and what's more he would have dragged you back to your husband and told him exactly what you have just done because, unlike me, he's a real bastard. Now piss off!'

Magnus looked over to a table with four men seated around it playing dice. 'Cassandros, make sure she stays clear of our property and pisses off in good order.'

A brother, in his early sixties like Magnus, with a silver-flecked full beard, Greek style, growing ragged on the left cheek due to a livid scar, stood grinning. 'My pleasure, Magnus. I always enjoy slapping a bitch about.'

Magnus glared at him. 'You will not slap her about; you will just make sure that she doesn't step on to our property. If you slap her about, I'll pay the next boy you bugger to bite your bollocks off.'

Cassandros held his hands up. 'All right, all right, Magnus, I was just joking.'

Magnus swallowed a caustic remark as he saw a wealthy-looking couple walking along the Alta Semita ostensibly unguarded. 'Lupus!' he growled at a younger brother in his early thirties. 'Just what the fuck do you think you're doing? Why aren't you offering our services to that man and his good lady? We wouldn't want anything nasty to happen to them on South Quirinal territory, would we? Get to it, and make sure your South Quirinal Brotherhood amulet is showing so they understand just who they're dealing with. If you come back with less than five denarii, it'll be your arse that Cassandros gets his hands on next.' Feeling thoroughly aggravated, Magnus watched

Lupus approach the couple, pulling out the wolf pendant that advertised his allegiance, and then stop them as other brothers gathered around. Satisfied that trade was proceeding as normal, Magnus stomped back into the tavern, glaring at anyone who so much as glanced at him; few did, sensing his mood.

He kicked open the door to the back room. 'What's wrong with everyone today? It must be the heat, Brother.'

Servius' clouded eyes stared at him but his counsellor declined to comment.

Magnus grabbed a cup and drained its contents before pouring himself another. 'That woman – what a fucking handful. Makes you wonder why some men are foolish enough to get married, eh, Brother? Unlike people like us who very sensibly keep romance to a simple cash and bodily fluid transaction.' He tossed the contents of his cup down his throat and wiped his lips with the back of his hand, feeling calmer. 'So, Brother, what do you reckon: should we tell her husband that she's been here complaining about him or do you think that we should just keep out of it?'

Servius still made no reply.

Magnus squinted with his one good eye, leaning forward. He reached out a hand and touched Servius on the shoulder, shaking him. 'Brother?'

With a suddenness that made Magnus jump back, Servius toppled forward, crashing on to the table, sending the wine jug tumbling to the floor to smash into jagged fragments. 'Servius? Brother?' Magnus put his fingers on his counsellor's neck, closing his eyes and feeling for a pulse. There was none. 'Oh fuck, Brother, why did you have to go and do that just now?'

'So, brothers, I have come to this decision,' Magnus announced to a packed tavern the following morning, after Servius' dawn funeral; his audience of over sixty brethren was spilling outside but all were able to hear him as the bar was open to the elements. 'I know that there are a couple amongst you who can claim longer service, but I'm sure they will understand.' He caught Cassandros' eye and then Sextus'. 'It's not a case of length of service but, rather, aptitude for the job that I deem to be the most important, and so I choose Tigran to succeed Servius and be my counsellor and second-in-command of our brotherhood.'

Magnus got down from the chair and embraced Tigran.

'That was a very wise choice, Brother,' Tigran whispered.

Magnus pulled back, holding Tigran by the shoulders; they smiled at one another, cold and stony-eyed. 'Wise or self-preservatory, my friend?'

Tigran's false smile broadened. 'Both.'

Magnus slapped his new counsellor's shoulders. 'I'll move aside soon. In the meantime you can have Servius' old room; I like my second to live on the premises.'

'So you can keep an eye on them.'

'No, Brother – so you can keep an eye on the others and be there when I need your advice.'

Tigran nodded and then turned to be acclaimed with a series of cheers.

'And why wasn't it me?' Cassandros asked in Magnus' ear. 'We go all the way back to the Fifth Alaudae together; we've fought shoulder to shoulder in the front rank against all sorts of savages.'

'I know, Brother, and so has Sextus.'

'Yes, but Sextus would have trouble counselling himself to sponge his own arse after a good shit.'

'I don't doubt it, which is why I didn't even consider him for the position like I did you.'

'Then why didn't you give it to me instead of that easterner? He only arrived in Rome, when was it?'

'Twenty-five years ago, Brother, and he's been a member of the Brotherhood ever since so he can't be accused of not having the right to be patronus. What's more, he's started to challenge my authority, such is his ambition; something you well know because you supported him when he asked if I thought that my judgement had been right when I bought those Germanic slaves just before Claudius flooded the market with Britannic captives soon after his Triumph.'

Cassandros looked outraged. 'I didn't support him.'

Magnus shook his head. 'You did, Brother, and don't try to deny it. I heard a small mutter of agreement from the crowd and so did old Servius. It was him that identified your voice; being blind he had sharper hearing. So what had Tigran offered you, eh? To be his counsellor? Was that your ambition?'

Cassandros' face betrayed the fact that Magnus had hit the mark.

Magnus put his hand on Cassandros' arm and steered him towards the door. 'Well, Brother, that's what I thought and that's why I couldn't make you my second for your own safety. Had I done so, then for Tigran to get to be patronus of the South Quirinal he would not only have to kill me, but you too.'

Cassandros looked at Magnus in alarm. 'He's going to kill you?'

Magnus nodded as they paused outside by the shrine of the Crossroads' lares, whose upkeep was the Brotherhood's official reason for existence; a flame constantly burned on the altar, tended by a brother whom Magnus now gestured to move away. 'Of course he is. Now that Servius is dead he knew that I would have no choice but to make him my counsellor as it was obvious from his ambition that he would kill anyone else I nominated. He's just one step away from his goal. I've just told him that I'll move aside soon and allow a smooth succession, but he's too greedy to wait for that.'

'Then kill him first.'

'And lose a ruthless patronus who will keep the South Quirinal sharp and hungry for more territory? No, my friend, he's going to have the job but I just want him to serve some time as my second as he'll be better for it.'

'What are you going to do, Magnus?'

'Do? Why, stay alive, of course, Brother.'

Shouts and whistles cut in over the cheering for Tigran. Magnus pushed his way to the street to see a contubernium of eight Vigiles running down along the Vicus Longus; his curiosity was aroused as they did not seem to be chasing anyone, nor were they pushing one of their hand-pumps as if they were racing to a fire.

He signalled to Cassandros and Sextus to follow him and strode down the hill, at a leisurely pace, after Rome's firefighters and city watch. It was into Red Horse Street, just before the border with the West Viminal, that the Vigiles had turned; they had stopped outside a shop that Magnus knew well and his concern began to grow. 'He's gone and disobeyed me, the eastern cunt!' He ran forward and barged his way through the crowd standing around the shop entrance. 'What's going on here?'

The Vigiles optio turned to him. 'Oh, it's you, Magnus. We've got a body and the aedile seems to be taking it very seriously for some reason.'

'Where is she, Cordus?'

'She? What do you mean she?'

'Tacita. This is Tuscus' shop, isn't it?'

'Yes, but we've got Tacita at our depot; she reported the murder just now. She said it happened sometime last night.' Cordus pointed to a body slumped on the floor, lying on its back, half hidden behind the counter. The legs were definitely male. 'It's Tuscus.'

Magnus looked over the counter and into the dead eyes of Tuscus. Blood was everywhere: puddled and sticky on the floor, soaked into his tunic and splattered over his face. His head lay at an unnatural angle and his throat gaped where it had been slit, good and deep from ear to ear.

'Did Tacita do this?'

Cordus shrugged. 'As I said, she reported it and swears that she didn't, although that could just be a bluff; but the whole neighbourhood heard them fighting last night and then he turns up dead.'

Magnus walked around to the other side of the counter and squatted down by the body. There were no other wounds that he could see.

'Don't touch it,' Cordus cautioned. 'The aedile's orders. When he questioned Tacita he got very agitated and doesn't want the body moved until he's had a look himself. Although I can't see why. What's Tuscus to him?'

'Perhaps he liked his candles.'

Cordus took the suggestion seriously. 'Do you think so?'

'Never mind.' Magnus looked around: the door of the cupboard beneath the counter caught his eye as it was ajar, the lock evidently forced. He pulled it open and peered inside; it was empty.

'What have you found?' Cordus asked, coming to stand at the counter with Cassandros and Sextus.

'Whatever was kept in here has been removed.'

'Tacita could have done that to put us off the scent.'

'She could well have.' But Magnus' attention was drawn to a small hole, the width of a finger, in the floor of the cupboard. He probed it and pulled. A piece of wood detached to reveal a hiding place; inside was a scroll. He unrolled it and perused the circles within circles, divided up into twelve equal sections filled with symbols that he could not decipher, even if he had been able to read and write. But he did not need to read to recognise it for what it was. 'So Tuscus still practised on the side, did he?' he muttered to himself.

'What have you got there?' Cordus asked, leaning over the counter to get a better view.

Magnus rolled up the chart. 'Nothing to worry yourself about; just a list of his prices. I'm going to take a look to make sure that he was paying us our due.'

Cordus frowned and glanced about. 'So what do you think, Magnus – did Tacita do it?'

Magnus smiled to himself; he knew exactly what he thought. 'I don't know. I'll ask around, pull in a few favours.'

'That would be great, Magnus.'

Magnus took a satchel that hung on the back of a chair and slipped the chart into it. 'We can't have this sort of thing happening in our area, can we, Cordus? It looks bad for all of us.' He turned to Cassandros and Sextus. 'Come on, lads, we need to show this to someone who can read.'

'Ahh, Magnus!' Senator Gaius Vespasius Pollo boomed as he came down the steps of the Senate House to where Magnus, Cassandros and Sextus waited amongst the crowd in the Forum Romanum. 'That was quick.'

Magnus was confused. 'Quick, Senator?'

Senator Pollo waddled forward, stomach, breasts and jowls all wobbling furiously to a variety of rhythms. 'Yes, I've just sent a message up to the tavern to fetch you. I've been speaking to our aedile on the Quirinal who consulted me as the most senior resident on the hill. We've got a slight problem – well, more than a slight problem, really – that your brotherhood may be able to help us with. Indeed, it would be in your interest to do so.'

'I'm sure that we can be of service, Senator. I in turn am here to ask you a favour.'

Senator Pollo clapped a pudgy arm around Magnus' shoulders and steered him towards a clutch of magistrates, one extremely ancient, talking, with obvious urgency, in hushed tones. 'I'm sure we can find a course of action that is for mutual benefit. But first listen to what the aedile has to say, if I can get him away from the Urban Prefect.'

'And this is what many of us find most disconcerting,' Publius Vestinus Barbatus asserted after giving Magnus a brief outline of the facts, as they strolled through the Forum crowds with Cassandros and Sextus clearing a path for them, 'that this Tacita claims this was a robbery to get hold of Tuscus' duplicate charts and that she saw the two robbers and could identify them, provided we keep her safe. However, she and Tuscus had a major fight last night, and not for the first time by any means, so the local Vigiles tell me. Now, if she's right and it was a robbery, then who's got all the horoscopes and what do they plan to do with them? And if she's lying and she did kill her husband and then took the horoscopes to make it look as if it were a robbery, then what has she done with them?'

'And more to the point,' Senator Pollo put in, breathing deeply despite the leisurely pace, 'what does she intend to do with them now?'

Barbatus looked downcast. In his mid-thirties, pallid and prematurely balding with a downturned mouth and bags under his eyes, this was not difficult. 'Exactly. There are a lot of people who would rather it didn't come out that they have consulted an astrologer. I've heard that Sextus Afranius Burrus, the new Praetorian prefect, has been making discreet enquiries as to the whereabouts of astrologers; no doubt with another purge in mind.'

Magnus scratched the back of his head. 'I've never understood what's considered so bad about astrology.'

Senator Pollo pushed a black-dyed ringlet of hair away from a kohled eye. Sweat began to line his brow. 'It's the emperors; they don't like the idea that someone might enquire about their deaths. That's why Tiberius expelled them all from Italia, apart from Thrassylus, his personal one, of course.'

'Of course. I met him on Capraea with Vespasian when Tiberius was about to throw me off a cliff for his own amusement.'

'Yes, he used to love doing that sort of thing to his guests. Anyway, astrologers have started to come back to Italia; however, if they're caught practising in Rome, they're prosecuted and face banishment. But if they admit it, as did Tuscus four years ago, then they're allowed to stay provided they swear an oath never to practise within Rome again.'

'And he went back on that oath and you all carried on consulting him anyway?'

Senator Pollo looked sheepish and glanced around to make sure no one was walking close enough to them to overhear the conversation. 'Well, he was extremely good and it's always very tempting to take a look into the future. He told me that I would die in my own house at a great age. I find that very comforting considering the arbitrary nature of justice these days. It strengthens my opinion that having no opinions is the best way to survive in politics. But, for him to make secret copies of all our charts was an outrageous breach of confidence and very dangerous; and now that we know of their existence but not their whereabouts, it is, well, it's very concerning.'

'I wouldn't worry, Senator.'

'Why not?'

Magnus grinned as they passed the Cloelius Brothers' banking business in the Basilica Aemilia, diverting around the large queue outside it. 'Well, no harm is going to come to you because of it, as you're going to die at home a long time in the future. Tuscus told you so himself.'

Senator Pollo was not reassured. 'But what if he were wrong? What if these charts find their way to the Emperor? I don't know how many there are.'

Barbatus looked equally concerned. 'Tacita couldn't say exactly how many but she reckons over a hundred in the four years.'

Magnus was shocked. 'A hundred? Just how much does he charge?'

Senator Pollo and Barbatus shared a look as a couple of stray dogs ran past, chased through the crowds by a group of public slaves with nets.

'Two hundred denarii a consultation,' Barbatus admitted.

'Two hundred? That's outrageous! That's twenty thousand denarii he's hidden from the Brotherhood; we've missed out on two thousand. The bastard, I'm going to ... Ah, no need, someone already has.' Magnus paused to compose himself. 'So what do you want me to do?'

Barbatus cleared his throat. 'We could try to extract the information out of Tacita, but if she genuinely doesn't know who has the charts then we gain nothing. Neither can we risk eliminating her just in case she has the horoscopes and has made arrangements for them in the event of her sudden demise.'

'I see the problem.' Magnus walked in silence for a few moments, assessing the situation. 'And then at the same time if she really didn't murder Tuscus and take the charts, then who did kill him and did they take the charts and can Tacita really identify them? Or did Tacita take the charts after she found the body, knowing their value with an eye to making a fortune later on?'

'Exactly. So the only way we can narrow it down is to kick her out of the depot and see if someone tries to kill her; if they do then she's telling the truth and we need to catch the murderer in the act and that's the priority.'

'Not keeping Tacita alive?'

Barbatus waved the thought away. 'No, and actually it would be more convenient if we didn't. I want your lads to watch her once we release her and, if there isn't an attempt on her life, see where she goes and who she talks to.'

'That's no problem. And the other issue?'

'Ask around your area to see if anyone had any bad blood with Tuscus.'

'And see if anyone local knew that he was still drawing up horoscopes or whether it was just people of your classes: senators and equites?' Magnus suggested as they approached the Temple of Vesta. A veiled priestess was being helped into a litter at the foot of the steps.

Senator Pollo turned towards Barbatus. 'Now that is a very good angle that we had not thought of.'

Barbatus stopped, bringing the group to a halt. 'Do this well, Magnus, and you won't regret it.'

'That seems a little vague to me, aedile.'

'What do you want? Money?'

'No; it'll be a favour.'

'What?'

'I'll think of something when the time comes.'

'That seems a little vague to me, Magnus.'

'I guarantee that you won't lose anything and no one will get hurt.'

Barbatus looked at Magnus long and hard. 'Very well, seeing as Senator Pollo vouches for you and you seem to keep the crime rate down in your area; this is the first murder of note for a while. Have your lads outside the Quirinal Vigiles depot in half an hour.' He turned to Senator Pollo. 'Good day, Senator.'

Magnus gestured to Cassandros. 'Go with him, get a couple of brothers and keep an eye on Tacita when he releases her. My guess is she's lying and she'll head straight home to retrieve the charts from wherever she's hidden them. I'll see you there as soon as I can.'

'Right you are, Magnus.'

Magnus watched Barbatus and Cassandros walk away before turning back to Senator Pollo and pulling the chart out of his satchel. 'What do you make of this?'

Senator Pollo took the proffered scroll and unrolled it. His face paled. 'Well, it's a horoscope, obviously. Where did you get it from?'

'Tuscus' house.'

Pollo could not conceal his surprise. 'You've been in there? You never said.'

'You never asked.'

'But you might have mentioned that fact to Barbatus.'

'Why? And tell him that I found a scroll?' Magnus winked; it did not work too well with just the one good eye, the other having been lost in a brush with Myrddin, the immortal druid of Britannia, some years previously. 'No need to share information until I know just how valuable it is.'

'I thought that all Tuscus' scrolls had been taken.'

'They had, except this one. It was in a hidden compartment underneath where he must have kept the rest.'

Senator Pollo looked in alarm at the document. 'Oh dear, oh dear me! I don't like the sound of that at all.'

'Can you read it?'

'I'm glad to say that I can't; far too dangerous. I used to let Tuscus read them for me.'

'I think we should find out whose chart this is, because it may well be what the robbery was really all about. Who do you think will be the best judge of that?'

'I don't know of any other astrologers, so I suppose we could try Caenis – she used to consult Tuscus as well. I'll meet you there in an hour, after I've eaten.'

'Fair enough, Senator; but make it a couple of hours as I've just thought of a little business I need to do while I'm on this side of the city.'

'Where're we going, Magnus?' Sextus asked for the fourth or fifth time as yet more dogs raced past with public slaves in full pursuit, nets waving above their heads.

As on the previous occasions, Magnus kept his counsel. He led Sextus through the Gate of Fontus, following the Flaminian Way on to the Campus Martius. It was at the market in the

Saepta Julia, on the left-hand side of the street, that Magnus halted and looked around its long colonnades. Conceived by Julius Caesar and completed by Marcus Vipsanius Agrippa, eighteen years after the dictator's assassination, it had been originally used for voting and so had become redundant with the advent of the Empire and had been converted into a market as well as being used for occasional gladiatorial fights.

'Who are you looking for, Magnus?' Sextus asked as he cast his eyes about the bustling market stalls.

'It's not who but what, Brother,' Magnus said. He began to make his way north, along the considerable length of the building, past stalls piled high with tunics, sandals, hats, as well as foodstuffs, spices, wine, garum, live animals in cages and much else; most things could be had here and most races from all over the Empire and beyond were represented. 'We're looking for a stall selling Eastern stuff.'

Sextus' countenance was vacant, the face of a man who had given up trying to make sense of it all and had resigned himself to following.

'That should do us,' Magnus mused as he headed towards a stall-holder whose appearance was far from Western.

'I give you best price, noble sir,' the stall-holder, a wizened little man with brown skin and eyes to match, promised as Magnus began to peruse his wares. 'Very good, all genuine,' he assured him, tugging at his pointed and curled beard.

Magnus picked up a curved-blade dagger with an ivory handle topped with an engraved silver pommel; it was sheathed in a casing of bronze inlaid with silver of the same pattern as the pommel. 'Where does this come from?'

'A very fine choice, noble sir; I see you are a man of the finest taste.'

'In that case your eyesight is piss-poor. I asked you where it came from not what you misguidedly think of my taste.'

The stall-holder put his right hand to his heart and bowed his apologies. 'Indeed, noble sir. The blade is Damascene steel, the finest money can buy. Touch.'

Magnus slipped the blade from the sheath; it glinted in the

sun with a hue that had more than a tint of blue. He ran his thumb across the blade. 'Like a razor.'

'Better than a razor, noble sir; a razor needs regular sharpening whereas this keeps its edge for a long, long time.'

'So it's from Damascus?'

'No, noble sir; the blade was forged there but the dagger itself is from the highlands of Cappadocia.'

'Is that quite close?'

'Indeed, noble sir; it's to the north. I compliment you on your knowledge of the region I come from. You must be a man of vast geographical knowledge.'

'Again you are mightily mistaken. How much?'

'Oh. For such a thing I would be a fool to myself to let it go for less than twenty denarii.'

Magnus was outraged and dropped the dagger back on to the table. 'A legionary's monthly wage for that. You must have been out in the sun for far too long in your life. The most I'll give you is four and that's my last word.'

Warming to the task, the stall-holder picked up the dagger, feigning horror. 'Four! Four? How can I expect to feed myself if I let it go for that when it cost me four times that amount? Sixteen is as low as I can go and that is special price for the noble sir.'

Magnus turned to Sextus. 'We're wasting our time here. Come on.'

'I meant fourteen.'

Magnus put a hand to his ear. 'Did you hear something just then, Sextus?'

The bovinesque brother frowned and cupped his ear with a look of deep concentration.

'Twelve is my final offer.'

Sextus' face brightened. 'I think someone said: "Twelve is my final offer", Magnus.'

'Did they now?' He turned back to the trader. 'Six and that's that.'

'Eleven and I get no profit.'

'Seven is as high as I'll go.'

'Ten and I've robbed myself.'

'Eight it is.'

'We meet at nine.'

Magnus turned back to Sextus. 'You know what we're looking for now, Brother. Go around the stalls and see if you can find something like it and don't pay more than seven for it; I've had enough of this.'

The stall-holder held up his hands. 'Eight shall be the price, noble sir, although please don't tell my wives.'

Magnus grunted, having no intention of meeting the good ladies in question, and pulled out a purse hanging around his neck. Taking eight silver coins he handed them to the Eastern trader, who examined every one.

Once satisfied, he handed the dagger to Magnus. 'It was a pleasure selling to you, noble sir. Please, I hope to see you again soon.'

'That depends.'

'On what, noble sir?'

Magnus leant in close. 'On whether you can get hold of a horoscope chart.'

'Babylonian? Egyptian?'

'Anything that looks like it could have been cast here in Rome. And bear in mind that I won't be paying more than three denarii for it.'

The stall-holder nodded. 'Come and see me tomorrow, noble sir. It shall be here and the price will be six.'

'Four it is then. I'll probably send one of the lads.' Magnus turned to go.

'It shall be a pleasure. Until then. And please forgive my assertion that you were knowledgeable and a man of good taste, noble sir; it was very rude of me and I shall never make that mistake again.'

Magnus looked over his shoulder to see the stall-holder bowing deeply. He frowned to himself and pulled at one of his cauliflower ears, wondering whether he had been insulted.

'So what's it for, Magnus?' Sextus asked, pointing at the purchase as Magnus slipped it into his satchel.

'That, Brother, is my insurance policy.'

Sextus looked none the wiser.

'Never you mind, brother. You get back to Red Horse Street and tell Cassandros that I'll be longer than I thought I would; he's to act on his own initiative.'

Sextus did not move.

Magnus tried again. 'He's to do what he thinks is best.'

Antonia Caenis dismissed the slave girl once she had filled three pale-green glass beakers, all of them decorated with various wild fowl, from a matching pitcher filled with pomegranate juice. The courtyard garden, with its cooling fountain pattering at the centre, the soft breeze slipping over the tiled roof of the colonnaded walkway and the gentle rustle of crickets, was an oasis of calm compared to the relentless hustle of Rome's streets. Magnus' pleasure at being seated in the shade of a mature walnut tree made up for the disappointment that there was nothing stronger than fruit juice on offer. Despite the cooler temperature of the garden, Senator Pollo still sweated profusely; his ringleted hair clung in lank clumps to his head and the kohl outlining his eyes left grey streaks down his cheeks.

Caenis served her guests, passing each a drink across the round, marble table in the middle of which lay the scroll. 'Are we wise to be getting involved with this, Gaius?'

The senator shrugged as he took a sip of juice. 'I don't see how we have any option, Caenis. We've both consulted Tuscus, along with most people of rank on the Quirinal and probably the neighbouring Viminal as well. It's pretty sure that copies of the charts he cast for us are amongst those missing.'

Caenis pointed at the scroll. 'And you think that this was the real object of the theft, Magnus? Assuming this woman is telling the truth and it was a robbery.'

Magnus stopped eyeing his fruit juice as if it was about to attack him. 'It was well hidden.'

'Or it could be just a coincidence.'

'I don't believe in coincidence.'

Caenis smiled. 'Very wise, Magnus; neither do I. In a case like this, facts have meaningful connections. Let me have a look.'

Magnus leant over and pushed the scroll across to Caenis. She set her glass down and unrolled the chart flat on the table.

Magnus closed his eyes, enjoying the peace, and began to daydream about the sort of place he would buy himself with his not inconsiderable savings once he finally retired from the brotherhood.

'Well?' Senator Pollo asked eventually, dragging Magnus from a world of cool gardens, populated by generously built water-nymphs, where fruit juice was banned.

Caenis looked up from the chart; her normal composure, for which Magnus had always admired her, was not quite so apparent. 'This is a death sentence for anyone who has seen it.'

Senator Pollo's jowls wobbled in consternation. 'Then we had better destroy it.'

'Destroy it, Gaius? That would be rather a hasty action, I think. Why would you want to destroy the horoscope of someone who could become our next emperor?'

'Emperor!' Magnus and Senator Pollo exclaimed in unison.

'Yes. This is the horoscope of Claudius' natural son, Britannicus; at least, I assume it is as it's forecasting the life of someone born two days before the ides of February, ten years ago, at the third hour of the day. But far more interesting is the date that it was done.' She pointed to the bottom right-hand corner of the scroll. 'Look at that very small writing; this was drawn up last month. And then this.' She moved her finger along. 'This is the initials of the person who paid for it to be done: JAA. Since last year Claudius has allowed her to use the title. This stands for Julia Augusta Agrippina.'

'The Empress! We should definitely destroy it.' Senator Pollo drained his drink, forgetting that it was not restorative wine.

Magnus smiled as he realised why Caenis was reluctant to destroy the horoscope. 'That is a powerful weapon to have.'

Caenis agreed and, rolling up the scroll, handed it back to Magnus. 'Yes, the Empress enquiring into the future of her step-son, the only serious rival to her own natural son, Nero. She's very ambitious for him and has already started manoeuvring for the succession; it was her who got Sextus Afranius Burrus appointed as one of the Praetorian prefects.'

Senator Pollo winced at the thought. 'So that's why Burrus was enquiring after astrologers. It was not for another purge; it was so that Agrippina could get this chart done discreetly. And since she managed to get Lucius Annaeus Seneca recalled from exile to be Nero's tutor, it's rumoured that he's preparing the young brute for the Purple. But we all know that Agrippina will be the real power. It is the height of folly to come between an ambitious, megalomaniacal woman and her objective.'

'I quite agree, Gaius; or at least don't be seen to come between an ambitious, megalomaniacal woman and her objective,' Caenis said. 'Use it well.'

Magnus could not hide his surprise. 'You don't want it?'

'No, Magnus, you found it, you keep it. Besides, I would have trouble trying to use it against anyone other than Agrippina, which, as Gaius says, would be very dangerous. Whereas you—'

'Could use it against anyone I wanted; I just have to let the relevant authorities know.'

'Precisely. And that way it could come to the attention of someone who perhaps has fewer scruples than Gaius or myself and thereby find its way to the Emperor, who might be very interested as to the plans his wife has for the succession.'

'She came out of the Vigiles' depot about an hour ago and came straight here,' Cassandros reported to Magnus as they stood in the entrance of Red Horse Street not long after. 'I got the distinct impression that she didn't want to leave the depot; they practically had to throw her out and then she all but ran home. Cordus' men wouldn't allow her back in as it's still sealed off until the aedile has time to inspect the scene of the murder himself.'

'Does Cordus have any idea when that might be?'

Cassandros shook his head. 'He doesn't know.' He looked at Magnus with a furrowed brow. 'Just what is all this about, Brother? Why is the aedile getting himself all upset about one little murder?'

'It's not the murder that has got the quality so upset; it's the possible motive and the end result.' Magnus looked back down the street to Tuscus' house. 'So, where is she now?'

'In her neighbour's place. I've got Lupus covering the back entrance with a boy to run a message should she leave by that method; Sextus is up the other end of the street.'

'Good lad. I'll wait with you until either she moves or Barbatus comes along.'

Barbatus arrived first, soon after the beginning of the ninth hour. 'Well?' he asked Magnus, without bothering to stop. 'Did anyone try anything?'

Magnus fell into step next to him. 'No. She's in the house next door. She spoke to no one on her way.'

Barbatus grunted and walked on up the street. Magnus kept pace with him.

'Where are you going?' the aedile asked.

'I was coming with you to have a look at the body.'

'Why would you want to do that?'

'We might learn something.'

'Only that he's dead with his throat cut, I should think.'

'I just thought that if you want me to help clear up this rather delicate matter, I should take every opportunity I get.'

Barbatus grunted again but did not gainsay Magnus as they walked up to Tuscus' house, past a guard of two Vigiles.

'No one has been in since Magnus left, aedile,' Cordus replied to Barbatus' question.

Barbatus turned in surprise to Magnus. 'You've been here already?'

'This morning when Cordus arrived. I came as the concerned patronus of the local brotherhood.'

'Why didn't you say?'

'I didn't think it was important.'

'Magnus found Tuscus' price list,' Cordus said in an attempt to be helpful.

'A price list?' Barbatus stared at Magnus. 'What sort of price list?'

'Oh, just for his candles; nothing of interest.'

With another grunt Barbatus walked over to the body. It was exactly how Magnus remembered it, only the blood had congealed even more and word had got around the local flies of a feast to hand. Barbatus knelt down and looked closely at the wound. 'A single slash, cleanly done; I don't think a woman could have done this.'

'Professional?' Magnus asked.

'That wouldn't narrow it down much; I expect more than half of Rome could neatly slit a throat. Still, this looks to have been done from behind as he's lying on his back as if he has been laid down, rather than crumpled to the floor if he'd been slashed from the front.'

'Fair point,' Magnus said, not really understanding or caring what the aedile meant but very pleased that he had said it. 'In which case, shall we turn him over to see if there are any wounds to the back?'

'Good idea. Give me a hand.'

Magnus rummaged in his satchel as Barbatus turned his back for a moment to get up to the head end. With a deft movement, Magnus pulled out the curved blade and, bending down to grab the corpse's thighs, slipped it beneath them, taking care that it was smeared with blood.

'Ready?' Barbatus asked. Without waiting for a response he lifted the shoulders and twisted the body.

Magnus did the same with the legs and over the corpse went, its partially severed head lolling.

'What's that?' Barbatus said, his eyes widening.

Magnus did his best shocked and amazed face. 'A knife, aedile!'

'Let me see.' Barbatus reached forward and picked it up by the sticky handle. He examined the blade and then wiped the blood off on Tuscus' tunic. 'That is unquestionably the murder weapon. It looks Eastern to me. What do you think, Magnus?'

'I think you're right, sir. That has to be the murder weapon. There're no signs of any other wounds on his back so this must have killed him with a single slash to the throat and then one of the murderers must have dropped the knife in his eagerness to get what they had really come for, there in that cupboard.'

Barbatus looked at the empty cupboard with the forced lock and stroked his chin. 'Yes, I think you're right. Which means that the murderers definitely took the scrolls, which puts Tacita in the clear: she couldn't have done the murder, and whoever did dropped the knife getting the cupboard open, so the horoscopes would have been gone by the time she found the body.'

Magnus looked solemn and shook his head slowly. 'So she's telling the truth.'

'It would seem so. Keep watching her; the murderers are bound to try and silence her at some point. Tell me as soon as they do.'

Magnus stood. 'Of course, sir.' He walked to the door, giving Cordus a cheery smile, and stepped out into the street. Looking about, he could see no sign of Cassandros. He walked towards the junction with the Alta Semita.

'Magnus! Magnus!' a high-pitched voice called.

Magnus looked up to see a small boy running towards him.

'What is it?'

The boy, nothing more than an urchin, paused to draw a few quick breaths. 'Cassandros sent me. He said to say: she's moving.'

'Which way did she go?'

The urchin pointed south, along Red Horse Street. 'That way, Magnus, towards the Viminal.'

'Did she now? Well, that is very interesting.' Magnus took a sestertius from his purse and put it on the boy's hand. 'Try to catch up with Cassandros and then run back to me at the tavern when we know where she ends up. Although something tells me I already know the answer.'

'So you'll delegate the organisation of the Brotherhood's participation in tomorrow's festival, Tigran,' Magnus said as his new counsellor finished studying the list of contributions from all the local traders and residents.

Tigran looked up at Magnus, seated across the desk in the back room. 'What?'

'You heard.'

'But that's far below me.'

'That's why you're delegating it, not doing it yourself.'

'But—'

'Tigran, the Brotherhood is not just about collecting money in return for protection, as you should well know having been with us for twenty-five years. We're also a religious organisation. First and foremost we tend the altar to the Crossroads' lares in order to ensure their blessing upon the whole neighbourhood. And then we have to represent the area in all the other festivals, religious or otherwise. Tomorrow is the festival punishing the dogs for failing to warn the defenders of the Capitoline Hill that the Gauls were climbing it. If it hadn't been for the geese, well … Anyway, that isn't important. What is important, though, is that you delegate someone, and I don't give a fuck who, to organise a group of the brothers to be a part of the procession up the Capitoline tomorrow with a half a dozen live dogs tied to forked poles.'

Tigran went to say something but Magnus raised his palm. 'Just do it. Servius used to. You need to know everything about the Brotherhood if you're to make a good patronus. What's more, the brethren expect it of you; they want to know that someone is thinking of everything. You know how superstitious they are; we all are. Just imagine what they would think if we fucked up a festival or forgot one? That's the sort of thing that leads to discontent, and discontent leads to weakness, and weakness is what Sempronius and the West Viminal bastards want to see in us so that they can push their influence into our territory.'

Tigran relaxed, slowly nodding, his eyes, hard, holding Magnus' remaining one. 'All right, Magnus, have it your way; I'll do your running around but I won't do it for long, is that clear?'

'It's not running around, it's managing the Brotherhood, and you'll do it for as long as I say.'

'Make me.'

'Do you really want me to?'

Tigran stood, still holding Magnus' eye, and then turned and walked out of the room, slamming the door.

Magnus watched him go with the exasperated look of a parent dealing with a troublesome but promising child. 'You leave me no choice, Brother.'

'I've left Lupus and the boy watching her,' Cassandros said as he sat down opposite Magnus at his table in the tavern, facing the door.

Magnus wiped a piece of bread around his bowl, soaking up the gravy from the remains of his pork, chickpea and lovage stew, and popped it into his mouth, chewing it at leisure.

'Well, don't you want to know where she went?' Cassandros asked, pouring himself a cup of wine. 'You don't seem very interested.'

'That's because I can guess.'

'Go on, then.'

'She's at the West Viminal headquarters.'

Cassandros looked in amazement across the table at Magnus as he concentrated on wiping his bowl clean. 'How the fuck—'

'Did I know? Easy: Sempronius is an unscrupulous piece of shit who's willing to involve himself in the domestic disputes of people not of his area if he can see the slightest bit of gain in doing so. So, as soon as Tacita comes back to our territory, let me know; she'll be able to go home now that the aedile has seen the body. I think we'll pop round for a nice chat and ask her how our mate Sempronius is, if you take my meaning? I'll be at Senator Pollo's house – send a message there.'

Senator Pollo swallowed his honeyed cake in evident confusion. 'But why would you want to organise the Vigiles raiding your own establishment, my dear Magnus?' Crumbs sprayed from his mouth, scattering across the desk in his tablinum. 'It's rather like a hound volunteering for the Punishment of the Dogs parade.'

'Yeah, well, let's just say that it will be of benefit to all of us: you, me, Caenis and the aedile.'

Pollo helped himself to another cake as a flaxen-haired youth, wearing a tunic a thumb's breadth too short for complete modesty, brought in a jug of wine and two cups.

Pollo paused, admiring the lad's half-concealed buttocks as he poured the wine, striking a pose that was not altogether natural but evidently insisted upon by his master so as to facilitate the view. 'Hmmm,' Pollo rumbled as the slave left, the glasses filled. 'Where were we? Ah, yes: of benefit to us all. If you say so, Magnus. When do you want it done?'

Magnus took a healthy slug of wine before answering. 'Firstly, it must never be known that I ordered it, so you'll have to get the tip-off to the aedile by a third party.'

'Someone not connected to either you or me? Do you have any suggestions?'

'You might like to ask your steward to have a quiet chat, incognito of course, with a Vigiles optio by the name of Cordus. He's not that bright, but bright enough to appreciate the value of a few denarii.'

'I shall send him down to the Quirinal depot forthwith.'

'Not just yet, Senator; there're a couple of things that I need to put in place first. I'll send one of the lads round when I'm ready.'

'Master?' the flaxen-haired slave said, standing in the entrance.

'What is it, my dear?' Senator Pollo smiled at the lad with obvious affection.

'A message for me?' Magnus asked.

The lad nodded, his long locks swaying to and fro.

Magnus stood and downed the rest of his wine. 'I'd better be going, Senator. You'll hear from me soon.'

'I didn't, Magnus, I swear I didn't.' Tacita knelt, grasping Magnus' knees in supplication. Cassandros and Sextus stood over her.

The blood remained congealed on the floor but the body of her husband had been removed; the infestation of flies, however, persisted.

Magnus gestured with his head to Cassandros; he pulled Tacita up to her feet. She howled and lashed out at Magnus. With a blurred-motion hand movement, he caught her wrist just before the nails made contact with his good eye. 'Stop lying to me, Tacita. I had you followed to the West Viminal and back again. Now sit down and tell me the truth and you might just get out of this in one piece. Did you get Sempronius to order the death of your husband?'

Cassandros and Sextus manhandled Tacita down on to a chair. Sextus kept his ham-like fists clamped onto her shoulders, keeping her there.

'Well?'

Tacita looked up at Magnus, tears welling. 'You wouldn't help me.'

'It was domestic; we can't have men living in fear of their wives ordering their deaths just because they might get a bit cross with them now and again. What did you offer Sempronius?'

Tacita cast her eyes down to stare at her hands folded in her lap. Tears were now flowing. 'I offered him money.'

Magnus was surprised. 'Money? How much?'

'Not much; all I could afford. It doesn't matter anyway because he wasn't interested in money; he was interested in something else.'

'So he asked for your husband's secret copies of his charts; you didn't offer them.'

Tacita looked up. It was her turn to be surprised. 'How do you know about them?'

'I'm the patronus of the local brotherhood and I talk with the aedile. So?'

'Yes, he said he would do it for the horoscopes.'

'Did he say how he knew about them? He must have been the only person other than you and Tuscus who did before they were taken.'

Tacita shook her head. 'No. I was shocked when he asked for them.'

Magnus thought for a few moments. 'All right, I believe you. So how did it happen?'

'I didn't want to hand them over before Tuscus was dead, for obvious reasons, so I made a deal that I would bring them once I had seen the body. I took them from their hiding place, hid them in my room and then went out and waited for the killers to strike. It was two men; they knocked on the door, Tuscus opened it, they went in and then, not long after, came out again and disappeared into the night. I waited until morning and then made the cupboard door seem as if it had been forced before taking the horoscopes to Sempronius' house.'

'Sempronius' house? Not the West Viminal headquarters?'

'No, his house, near the Viminal Gate; he made sure that I clearly understood that point. Only I didn't take them to his house after all; they seemed too valuable to give away just like that. I thought that I would be able to make a lot of money from them and then live in luxury somewhere outside Rome.'

Magnus was unsurprised by her greed. 'You double-crossed Sempronius? That was a foolish move.'

Tacita looked down, her eyes full of tears. 'I thought that I could get away with it if I got the Vigiles to keep me in their depot. So I decided to tell them that Tuscus and I had interrupted a robbery, the thieves killed Tuscus but I managed to get out of the house, having clearly seen the two men and that they had the charts, thus taking suspicion away from me. You see, I thought that, as a lot of influential people consulted my husband in secret, no one would want to look too deeply into how and why he was murdered because all the attention would be on finding the charts. I figured that I'd be quietly forgotten and could slip out of Rome.'

'And did you think that Sempronius would let you get away with that?'

Tacita shrugged. 'Sempronius couldn't go to the Vigiles and say that he had organised Tuscus' death at my request but I had refused to pay him afterwards; nor could I betray him because then he would implicate me in the murder. Either way we would be appearing in the arena together. I judged that his best policy was to remain quiet about the whole affair and let it go, as there was nothing to connect the two of us so no one would think to investigate him.'

'Nothing to connect you except for a misguided word yesterday afternoon. You should not have mentioned Sempronius' name to me, but I'm very glad that you did. Go on.'

'So I hid the charts again.'

'Where?'

Tacita hesitated and then thought better of it as the grip on her shoulders tightened. 'Back under the floorboards in the bedroom.'

'Whereabouts in the room?'

'Under the foot of the bed.'

Magnus gestured to Cassandros. 'Go and have a look, Brother.' He looked back down at Tacita. 'And then?'

'And then I went and reported the body to the Vigiles, saying that it was a robbery and that all my husband's duplicate horoscopes had been stolen by men whom I could identify.'

'Hoping that the Vigiles would keep you safe to prevent the murderers from killing you so that you wouldn't be able to identify them?'

'Something like that, Magnus.'

'But that didn't work because the aedile decided to use you as bait. And he still believes that there are mysterious killers out there looking for you. But we know different, don't we? Now that you're out, it's Sempronius who you fear.'

Tacita gave a sullen nod.

'And so you found yourself unprotected and decided that the only safe course of action was to give up the charts to Sempronius but the aedile had sealed off your house and you couldn't get them. So you panicked and decided to tell Sempronius that you would bring them as soon as you could get back into your house?'

Tacita hung her head. 'Yes.'

Magnus slapped his hand onto his forehead and groaned. 'Thereby telling Sempronius where the charts were.'

Tacita put her hand to her mouth in shocked realisation. 'But I'd been so careful.' She blinked back the tears as Cassandros came back in.

'Well?' Magnus asked.

'They weren't there, Brother.'

'What a surprise.' Magnus' tone implied the exact opposite.

'I found the loose floorboard and could see where they would have been but they weren't.'

'You stupid woman!' Magnus turned on Tacita, his fist raised; and then he paused, controlling himself. 'How long did you stay at the West Viminal headquarters after you'd told Sempronius that you couldn't retrieve the charts just yet?'

'I don't know. He sent a runner up here to check whether I was telling the truth and the Vigiles really had got the place sealed off. He told me that if the Vigiles found the charts and I couldn't complete my part of the bargain then I could buy my life with my husband's business and savings.'

'And the runner came back saying that you had told the truth and the house was still sealed off and so Sempronius said you could go, rather than just killing you there and then, because he was now going to fleece you of everything you owned, having already stolen the charts.' Magnus shook his head in disbelief as he turned his attention to Cassandros and Sextus. 'Stay here with her and bring her back to the tavern as soon as it's dark and then lock her up where we like to keep our guests. And if she makes a sound or struggles in any way, kill her.' He looked down at Tacita to make sure she had understood; her eyes left little doubt that she had.

'It will be tomorrow,' Magnus said in response to Tigran's question, 'during the procession punishing the dogs; Sempronius won't be at home.'

Tigran glanced across the street at a two-storey house as dusk descended upon the city. 'How do you plan to get in there? And if you do, where will you look for whatever it is you're looking for?'

Magnus pulled his straw hat further down to obscure as much of his face as he could, while Tigran was dressed in a plain tunic, Roman style to blend in. They walked at a slow pace past Sempronius' house, on a quiet side street off the Vicus Patricius, just before the Viminal Gate.

'How to get in is what we're here to think about. It's the tablinum that I want to get into so as to have a look in Sempronius' desk.' From beneath the wide brim of his hat, Magnus studied the front of the house: it had no windows onto the street in its ochre-painted facade other than the open-fronted shop to the right of the heavily constructed wooden door reinforced by iron strips. The shop, selling statuettes of gods and heroes as well as other decorative knick-knacks, Magnus knew to be nothing more than a subtle way to have guards outside the house without seeming to do so; indeed, the two burly shopkeepers lighting their lamps looked about as likely to be interested in decorative knick-knacks as Magnus was in fruit juice.

They carried on walking past. 'No alleys to either side,' Magnus observed. 'It's attached to both its neighbours. Let's have a look around the back.'

They turned left into a narrow lane, three doors up from Sempronius' house, expecting to find an alley dividing the houses from those on to which they backed.

'Mars' arse! He's chosen this place well. The only ways in are through the front door or over the roof.'

'Or through the walls,' Tigran reminded him.

Magnus shook his head. 'Too noisy and we haven't got the time.'

'Then we either fight our way in or trick our way in.'

Magnus slapped Tigran on the shoulder. 'I like that thinking, Brother. You see, Tigran, there is a fun side to being the second. Have you got any suggestions?'

'It would help if I knew why you want to get in there and have a look in Sempronius' desk, Magnus.'

'Ahh, I'm afraid that I can't tell you that as there are quite a few important gentlemen who would rather that the fewer people who knew about it, the better.'

'Careful gentlemen, are they?'

'You can never be too careful; one slip and—' Magnus stopped as if he had hit an invisible brick wall.

'What is it, Brother?' Tigran asked.

'Nothing; just something someone said. Or, rather, implied.' Magnus drew himself back to the present. 'What I can say is that there will be quite a reward for what I'm planning and you will share in it if you can get me into Sempronius' house.'

Tigran pondered the issue as they walked back to the Vicus Patricius and mingled with the crowds frequenting the brothels, catering for all tastes, that the street was renowned for. 'Well,' Tigran mused eventually, 'the only people likely to get past the guards and be allowed in by the doorkeeper would be known West Viminal brothers.'

'Yeah, I thought of that but dismissed it as I couldn't see how we would induce one to cooperate.'

Tigran grinned. 'He wouldn't need any inducement if he were dead.'

Magnus again stopped still and slapped his forehead. 'Now that is thinking worthy of a patronus. I'll get a few lads together and go to find one.'

'That's the closest one to our territory that's frequented by the West Viminal bastards,' Magnus said as he, Cassandros, Sextus and Lupus surveyed a crowded tavern nearly halfway down the Vicus Longus in the disputed area between the West Viminal and the South Quirinal brotherhoods.

The open-fronted establishment was much the same as any tavern in Rome: big pots of food embedded in the bars, amphorae upright in racks or in boxes of sand, a cooking fire beneath a grill filled with strips of chicken or pork, a lot of rowdy, drunken men and a decent sprinkling of whores to lighten their purses and see to their needs.

Magnus handed Lupus a few bronze coins. 'They won't know you, Brother; get yourself in there and buy anyone who looks to have had a few a few more and then make your excuses and get out and come back to us.' Magnus pointed to a similar-looking tavern further up the hill. 'We'll be in there.' He gave the young brother an encouraging pat on the cheek. 'Take your time; we'll be fine.'

'Now I've got you both alone, this is what I need you to do,' Magnus said as he, Cassandros and Sextus hunched over a table in the corner of the tavern, each with a cup in his fist, an empty plate in front of them and a belly full of grilled pork. 'Tomorrow, our headquarters is going to be raided by the Vigiles.'

Cassandros looked shocked. 'How do you know that, Brother?'

'Never mind how I know it; I just do. And I also know what they'll be looking for.'

Sextus shook his head in wonder. 'I don't know how you do it, Magnus. When I'm looking for something I often forget what it was before I've found it. But you even know what other people are looking for.'

'Don't you worry your head about it, Brother; you concentrate on what I want you to do first thing tomorrow morning. You remember that trader we were at today in the Saepta Julia?'

Sextus cast his mind back a few hours; it took some time but Magnus did not rush the process. 'Yes, Magnus; where you bought that knife.'

'Well done, Brother.' Magnus passed four denarii over the table. 'Go back there and pick up the scroll waiting for me; give him this money and no more. Then give it to Cassandros. Got that?'

Sextus slowly digested his orders. 'Pick up the scroll; give the man four denarii; give the item to Cassandros. Right you are, Magnus.'

'What is it, Magnus?' Cassandros asked.

'Never you mind; you just take it and keep it for me.'

'Where are you going to be?'

'Busy.'

Any more questions were forestalled by the arrival of Lupus, looking as if he had thoroughly enjoyed his mission.

'Here he comes,' Lupus whispered to Magnus as they peered out of a dark alleyway near the first tavern.

'Who's that holding him up?'

'A mate of his who turned up just before I left; I was pleased as it gave me a good excuse to leave. Anyway, our man, Pansa is his name, is well in hock to Bacchus.'

'Pansa? Good lad; he's perfect. He's a particularly nasty piece of work who has an unpleasant way with pincers when he wants to encourage someone to talk. I hope he's enjoyed his last commune with the god.' He signalled across the street to where Cassandros and Sextus were concealed in a doorway that Pansa and his mate were approaching, albeit by a ponderous route. 'Come on, Lupus.' Looking left and right, Magnus stepped out onto the Vicus Longus.

Ahead of them the staggering Pansa was having a little difficulty negotiating a set of raised stones set across the street, spaced so that cartwheels and draught animals could pass between them, used as a crossing point. Eventually his mate guided him through, having paused halfway to urinate over his sandals.

It was a mighty blow from Sextus' right fist that was the last thing that Pansa's mate saw that night, if, indeed, he saw it at all. Arching back, his nose crushed and his arms flying up, he collapsed with a dull thud onto the street, his head bouncing up once to crack back down and then loll to one side, to become just another victim of the feral night, ignored by all who passed.

Pansa swayed as he looked down at his erstwhile support, his eyes blinking as he tried to focus. The effort proved too much for him and he fell to his hands and knees, and then deposited a copious amount of vomit on to his mate's tunic.

'Come on, Pansa, my old friend,' Magnus said, hauling him up once his stomach had been emptied. 'You're coming with us. I've finally found a purpose for your miserable life.'

The morning of the second day after the calends of August dawned golden over the city, and was soon blanketed in the baking heat that had become the norm over the past few days. But the people of Rome were not to be put off by soaring temperatures from punishing the beasts who had failed so grievously in their duty almost four hundred and fifty years previously. And it was with a carnival atmosphere that they tied stray dogs by their front paws to Y-shaped sticks, their heads lodged in the fork, and paraded the struggling, howling animals through the city to the Capitoline Hill and then on to the Aventine in order to teach them the meaning of their duty.

With relief Magnus watched the six brothers who had been delegated to represent the Brotherhood set off with their lashed-up hounds and a good part of the local community following. As the end of the parade disappeared down the Vicus Longus, Magnus, picking up a skin of water and a fresh tunic and slinging them over his shoulder, called to Cassandros and Lupus to join him in the back room.

'When Sextus returns, Cassandros,' Magnus said, putting down his water-skin and tunic and then pointing at the leather satchel on the desk, 'put what he gives you in this and then before midday slip into Tigran's room and hide it under the mattress.' He took a key from the drawer in his desk. 'This is a duplicate; it'll get you in.'

Cassandros looked at Magnus questioningly, his brow furrowed as he took the key and picked up the satchel.

'Just do it, Brother; it's how I plan to stay alive.'

Cassandros looked down at the satchel. 'Right you are, Magnus.'

'Good lad. Then, once you've done that, make yourself very scarce until at least the eighth hour.'

'Why?'

'Never you mind.' Magnus turned to the younger brother. 'Lupus, go and get the handcart and bring it round to the side door.'

Without questioning the unusual request, the younger brother went to do as asked.

Magnus took a ring with three more keys on it from the drawer in the desk, turned and walked towards the door at the far corner of the room. Unlocking it, he passed through into a corridor, with padlocked, double doors leading to the outside world at one end and a couple of smaller doors along its length. Opening the first of these with the second key he stepped into a small cell.

'Good morning, Pansa. How's your head feeling today?' A whimper from the other side of the cell caused Magnus to glance left. 'Good morning to you too, Tacita. I'd like you to watch this.'

Pansa opened his eyes and looked up from the heap of rags upon which he had been sleeping; his wrists and ankles were bound. 'Magnus! What the fuck am I doing here? When Sempronius finds out you'll be dead.'

'I wouldn't think so, Pansa; in fact, I doubt very much that Sempronius will ever find out that you were here.' With one fluid movement, Magnus pulled a blade from the sheath hanging from his belt in the small of his back.

Pansa had barely a moment to react as Magnus grabbed his head and plunged the knife into his chest. The wind was knocked from him and he looked down in horror as Magnus rolled his wrist left and then right, shredding the muscle of his heart.

Holding the dying man's hair in his fist, Magnus pulled on the handle; the blade emerged with a slop of blood, staining the front of Pansa's tunic. A final croak, low and rattling, issued from his throat as he made the transition from life to death. Tacita's whimpers increased in volume as she watched Magnus wiping the blade clean on Pansa's hair.

'Did you see just how easy that was?' Magnus asked in a conversational manner.

Tacita nodded, her eyes transfixed on the corpse.

'Now, you have a choice: either I can walk out of this room having done exactly the same to you, or you can tell me the real truth as to how Sempronius knew about the charts.'

'But I have, Magnus.'

'No, Tacita, you haven't. Yesterday when I pointed out that you had given away the location of the charts you said: "But I'd been so careful." That implies that you had been concealing the whereabouts of the charts from Sempronius for some time. The truth, Tacita, or by the gods I swear your life means nothing to me.'

Tacita swallowed and then looked up at Magnus, eyes pleading. 'I told Sempronius about them a few days ago; although I said that I didn't know where Tuscus kept them as the hiding place wasn't in the house but I would find out where it was, retrieve them and sell them to him.'

'And you went to him and not me because you knew perfectly well that I would never countenance a wife stealing from her husband.'

Tacita gave a sullen nod. 'I thought that I could get my revenge on Tuscus for his whoring by selling the charts and at the same time get enough money to be free of him and still have nice things to wear. But then when he beat me and you refused to help I worked out how to have him killed and keep the charts to sell.'

'So you had been careful to conceal their location.'

'Of course, otherwise I knew that Sempronius would just steal them and I'd get nothing.'

'Which is now what you've ended up with because of that little slip of the tongue.'

Tacita now wept freely. 'I'm sorry I lied to you, Magnus.'

'No you're not.'

'What are you going to do with me?'

'I'll think about it.' Magnus slipped back out into the corridor and unlocked the padlock on the doors at its end.

Lupus was outside waiting with the handcart.

'Good lad,' Magnus said. 'Get Pansa in that and cover him up.'

'How am I meant to do that, Magnus? He won't want to cooperate.'

'He will, trust me. Now hurry up; I've got a timetable.' He handed Lupus the keys. 'Lock up when you've finished and put the keys back in my drawer. Get the tunic and the skin of water by the desk and bring them with you. I'll meet you at Lampmakers' Street as soon as I've done one thing, which will not take long.'

'But that's on the Viminal.'

'You're getting to know your way around, I see. Good lad. From an alley off it we can see Sempronius' house; I want to know when he's gone.' With a pinch of Lupus' cheek, Magnus left him to his work.

'In an hour's time, Magnus? I don't know if that can be organised.' Senator Pollo looked apologetic. 'Especially not with the Punishment of the Dogs going on at the moment. What makes you so sure that this is the right place?'

Magnus sat down opposite his patron. 'Sempronius organised Tuscus' death; Tacita admits that and admits that she was to pay for it with the charts that she was originally going to sell to Sempronius – although she never handed over the payment. Now, Tacita told me that she watched the killers come to Tuscus' door; he answered it and then let them in immediately, so he must have known at least one of them not to feel threatened by them. Also, Barbatus reckons that he was killed from behind, which is another reason to think he knew them as he was comfortable enough in their presence to turn his back on them. Now you said something that got me thinking: you said that most of the prominent people on the Quirinal had consulted Tuscus and probably from the Viminal as well.

'So who would Tuscus have been familiar enough with from the West Viminal Brotherhood to let them in after dark? My guess is only Sempronius himself; he'd been consulting Tuscus along with the other prominent people on the Viminal and Quirinal. When he heard about the charts from Tacita he would have, like you, been very anxious to get his back. Now, Tuscus wouldn't have found it unusual that Sempronius came after dark because that would be the normal time he came to consult him, not wanting to be caught out in the open by my lads. He would have been relaxed enough in Sempronius' presence to turn his back on him. Killing Tuscus would have been a mixture of business and honour for Sempronius, seeing as the astrologer had made a copy of his chart with the probable intention of using it for blackmail.'

Senator Pollo contemplated all that for a few moments and then slowly nodded. 'Added to the fact that Tacita states that Sempronius had been very insistent she was to take the charts to his house, that makes it reasonably certain they are still in there; if it was him who stole them, of course.'

'Of course it was him; no one else knew about them at the time. It has to be Sempronius and I'll bet that he thinks he's going to have a lot of fun with them.'

'But Barbatus hasn't got any jurisdiction on the Viminal; how is he going to organise a raid there with Quirinal Vigiles?'

'I think this has just got bigger than the Quirinal aedile. I think that you should get him to approach the prefect of the city and get him to raid the place with Urban Cohort lads.'

'Lucius Volusius Saturninus? But he and Sempronius have an understanding, as you well know; it was the prefect whom Sempronius bribed after he'd been condemned to the beasts when you managed to get him caught taking delivery of that ballista a few years back. How will we persuade him to do anything about it?'

'He's as worried as the rest of you. He was a part of that group that Barbatus was talking to outside the Senate House yesterday; you saw him.'

'Yes, you're right; he was, wasn't he?'

'I'm willing to bet that he has been consulting our little underground astrologer as well and therefore has a vested interest in getting the charts back as soon as possible before the Emperor finds out about them and he loses his nice cosy position. He's not going to let Sempronius' financial considerations to him compromise that. I would get Barbatus to see him now and have him act before Sempronius moves them somewhere safer; like out of the city.'

'Hmm, yes, I see what you mean. I'll send a message to Barbatus now before I go to the Capitoline for the ceremony.' The senator pushed himself up on to his feet and then paused. 'What about that raid on your premises that you wanted me to order?'

Magnus got to his feet. 'Don't worry about that any more, Senator. I'm just about to do something that will ensure that, after Sempronius' place is turned over, mine will be next in line.'

Magnus smeared mud over his tunic and mixed it with the blood on his face in an alleyway just off Sempronius' side street, about a hundred paces from his house. 'How do I look?'

Lupus studied him for a few moments. 'I couldn't recognise you.'

'Good. Now take off your South Quirinal amulet in case some sharp-eyed bastard notices it.' Magnus pulled his over his head as Lupus did the same. 'Are you ready?'

'As I'll ever be.'

Magnus slapped his shoulder, checked the horoscope chart and amulet were securely tucked in his belt, then bent down and pulled on Pansa's lifeless wrist, heaving up the body from the handcart and getting its arm around his neck. Lupus did likewise so that the corpse was slung between them.

With two quick glances, Magnus checked both directions of the side street. 'Good, it's busy. Hang on!' Looking up the street Magnus saw a couple of the West Viminal brethren leaving Sempronius' house with dogs tied to poles. 'I thought you said that Sempronius left home half an hour ago.'

'He did; I saw him leave.'

Puzzled, Magnus watched the two men disappear up the road with their burdens, one struggling and howling while the other, a sizeable beast, seemed to have accepted its fate and remained still. 'Right, they're gone. Go!'

They tore out of the alley, the corpse lolling between them. 'Get out the way! Get out!' Magnus bellowed at the top of his voice. 'Wounded man! Wounded man!' Barrelling along the street, forcing pedestrians aside, knocking more than a few to the ground, creating a wave of panic in their wake, they approached Sempronius' house at full tilt. 'They've got Pansa! Pansa!' Magnus shouted at the burly shopkeepers, lifting the corpse's head so that they could identify him. 'One of you help us get him inside and the other run for the doctor; it might not be too late.'

Both men leapt over the counter; one sprinted up the street as the other banged on Sempronius' front door. The viewing slat opened. 'Let us in, Quintus; they've got Pansa. We might be able to save him.'

The slot slammed shut, locks and bolts clunked and the door swung open. The shopkeeper stepped aside and Magnus and Lupus crashed in, dragging the corpse, whose toes left a trail of gore, through the vestibule and along the mosaic floor of the atrium. 'We'll put him on the desk in the tablinum!' Magnus shouted at a shocked-looking steward.

Without waiting for a yea or nay, they thundered on through into Sempronius' study at the far end of the atrium and heaved the body onto his desk, scattering styli and wax tablets. Bending down, with one hand pressing on the wound,

Magnus opened the bottom drawer a fraction and, pulling the horoscope from his belt, slipped Britannicus' chart and his amulet into it. 'How is he?' he shouted at Lupus, louder than necessary.

'Not good.'

'Those East Viminal cunts. I'll have them; we'll both have them, right now.' Together they turned and ran out into the atrium, past the shocked steward and then again through the vestibule and back out into the street, heading in the direction whence they had come. With his chest burning and breath rasping, Magnus just managed to keep up with his younger colleague. They turned into the alley where they had started as a column of Urban Cohort legionaries jogged, quick-time, from the Vicus Patricius towards Sempronius' house.

Skidding to a halt next to the handcart, Magnus doubled over and then took a huge breath, standing back up and leaning against the brick wall, his chest pounding. He pointed with one hand to the water-skin in the cart as he undid his belt with the other. 'Quick.'

Lupus grabbed the skin and burst into hysterical laughter. 'That was seriously good fun!'

Magnus joined his laughter, coughing and spluttering as Lupus sprayed water from the skin to wash the blood and mud from his face. 'I may be sixty-one, Lupus, but there is still plenty of fight and fuck left in me. Watch and learn, lad, watch and learn.' He slipped the stained tunic over his head, wiping his face as he did so, and then threw it away.

'I do, Magnus.' Lupus handed Magnus the fresh tunic, still shaking with laughter and with a wild look in his eyes.

'A keen lad like you could go far. Bring the handcart.' Doing up his belt, Magnus walked out into the street, looking the part of a respectable citizen.

Lupus jogged to catch up with him, the laughter slowly being replaced by a look of disbelief. 'That really was seriously good. They didn't know what to do, the arseholes. In and out, just like that.' He shook his head a few times and then looked quizzically at Magnus. 'But tell me, Magnus: why did we do it?'

Magnus glanced over his shoulder to where two Urban Cohort legionaries had taken up position outside Sempronius' house as the aged Urban prefect, accompanied by Barbatus and the Viminal aedile, made his way up the steps to the front door. 'Never you mind, Brother. Suffice it to say that we did.'

Magnus stood at a street counter on the Alta Semita, halfway between the Porta Collina and the South Quirinal's tavern, which he studied with interest while gnawing on a chicken leg.

'What are you waiting for?' Lupus asked next to him, wiping grease from his mouth with the back of his hand.

'The inevitable, Brother.'

'What's the inevitable?'

Magnus tore off a goodly hunk of flesh and, chewing on it, began to count down from a hundred in his head. 'That is,' he said, pointing the chicken leg towards his brotherhood's head-quarters, having only reached thirty-seven.

From the direction of the Viminal came Barbatus and a contubernium of Urban Cohort men.

'They're going into the tavern!' Lupus exclaimed, outrage in his tone. 'When was the last time we were raided?'

Magnus swallowed a mouthful and washed it down with unwatered wine. 'Oh, it's been a while; at least ten years, I should say. It hardly ever happens; the authorities generally leave us alone.' Magnus turned to Lupus, putting on his best perplexed face. 'I just don't understand it because, just as we were leaving Sempronius' street, I could have sworn that I caught a glimpse of the Urban Cohort lads raiding his house. They seem to be very busy today.' He carried on enjoying his chicken leg, watching the tavern as the Urban Cohort sealed off the front. 'Here they come,' he observed as further down the Alta Semita a door opened and a dozen or so of the brethren streamed out, splitting up and blending into the crowds in ones and twos.

An Urban Cohort soldier appeared in the doorway, looked left and right, and then pulled the door closed.

As Magnus finished off his second leg, Barbatus came out of

the front of the tavern, his escort behind him with two familiar figures in custody: one male, the other female.

'They're taking Tigran away,' Lupus said, his voice incredulous. 'We can't let that happen, can we, Magnus? And that's Tacita.'

'It would seem so. Time to go. We'll follow them down to the Vigiles depot and sort it out.' Magnus tossed a couple of bronze coins onto the counter but the stall-holder held up his hand. 'Very good of you, Festus.' Magnus scooped up the coins and strolled off down the street.

The Forum Romanum was bustling with spectators watching the annual ritual taking retribution on the canine inhabitants of the city for their great-sires not bothering to warn their masters that the Capitoline was under attack. Hundreds of the animals of all sizes were being held aloft, tied to their poles in great pain, in preparation for the procession up the Gemonian Steps to the shrine to Juventas, the goddess of youth and rejuvenation, which was situated in the Temple of Minerva. After sacrificing to the goddess the procession would move on to the Temple of Summanus on the lower slopes of the Aventine in the shadow of the Circus Maximus. None of the dogs would survive the ordeal.

But it was not the welfare of the animals that concerned Magnus as he and Lupus made their way through the throng: it was the timing of his day, which had started to go horribly wrong as soon as Barbatus had dropped Tacita at the Quirinal Vigiles depot and carried on down the hill with Tigran. Magnus had realised at once what that implied.

With the people of Rome in a carnival mood, the progress through the crowd was easier than normal since there was no need to push forward in order to hear someone's words as they declaimed from the rostrum or the front of the Senate House. Today traffic was far more free-flowing as the individuals moved around the Forum looking up at different dogs and laughing at their distress and agony as their front paws began to break under the strain.

As Magnus reached the Senate House, its members were just coming outside, having adjourned the morning session. They congregated around a goose, seated in state upon a deep cushion and covered in a silver cloak, waiting to lead the unfortunate dogs in their punishment, as a reward for its forebears honking and alerting the Romans defending the Capitoline to the nocturnal, Gallic assault.

'There he is,' Magnus said, spotting the rotund figure of his patron amongst the elite of Rome, many of whom had not dissimilar physiques. 'Senator Pollo! Senator Pollo!' He shoved his way through to the front of the crowd, continually shouting until the senator heard his name and turned towards him.

'What is it, Magnus? We're just about to start the procession.'

'I need a favour.'

'Now?'

'Now is the perfect time, sir.'

The senator mopped the sweat from his brow with a handkerchief and looked up the length of the steep Gemonian Steps. 'Very well. I've never enjoyed climbing to the summit of the Capitoline. What is it you want?'

'For some reason Barbatus has taken my second, Tigran, into custody; but it's not to the Quirinal Vigiles depot that they've taken him – it's to the Tullianum.'

'The prison? Are you sure?'

'Yes, we followed them down here; he's in there all right.'

'What do you expect me to do about it?'

'Barbatus took him in and I don't think he's come out yet. You need to get me in, sir. Trust me, it'll be for your benefit as well as mine.'

The door of the Tullianum, just at the bottom of the Gemonian Steps, creaked open a fraction and an eye peered out. 'Yes?'

Senator Pollo puffed himself up with self-importance. 'My name is Senator Gaius Vespasius Pollo and I have reason to believe that the aedile for the Quirinal is within. I wish to speak to him.'

'He's busy.'

Senator Pollo's jowls wobbled in indignation. 'Busy? My man, I can assure you that he's not too busy to see me. Now let me pass.' He pushed at the door. There were a few moments of resistance before it was released and he walked in with Magnus following, leaving Lupus, the bright sun and the festival spirit of the outside world far behind.

Magnus closed his eyes to adjust them to the gloom of the low-ceilinged interior; a couple of oil lamps on a crude table and a sputtering torch in a holder, on one soot-stained wall, provided the only light. It was, however, enough to see Tigran stretched out on the rack, his limbs taut as the wheel was tightened by a hirsute youth, with a face so flat that it seemed to Magnus that he had been repeatedly smashed against a brick wall.

Barbatus stood over Tigran, brandishing a scroll. 'What is it, Senator?'

It was Magnus who answered, stepping out from the senator's shadow. 'What has he done, aedile?'

'Magnus! I've got men out searching for you. I'm pleased that you've come to me of your own accord.' Barbatus held out the scroll. 'This is a horoscope; we found this in Tigran's room along with that scabbard.' He gestured to the scabbard lying on the table next to the lamp. 'The metal-work of which exactly matches the knife we found under Tuscus. What's more, the knife is Eastern in its appearance, just like this piece of shit. He murdered Tuscus and now I want to know where the rest of the missing charts are.'

'I didn't, Magnus,' Tigran said through gritted teeth. 'The horoscope and the scabbard were planted; I don't know who by. But he's wasting his time with me. Tell him.'

Magnus looked suitably confused. 'But aedile, I thought you raided Sempronius' house for the charts.'

'We did and your information was wrong; they weren't there.'

This time Magnus' surprise was genuine and he now understood why Tigran had been brought to the prison for questioning. 'They weren't there? Did you look everywhere?'

'We're still looking and we're also now searching the West Viminal's headquarters. The Urban Prefect has given orders to tear both places apart and scour the city for Sempronius. What we have found, however, is something so secret that I can't even admit to having seen it myself, and with it was a South Quirinal Brotherhood amulet, which led me to your tavern, where I found all the evidence I need in this Eastern shit's room. It looks like you're being circumvented by a subordinate, Magnus. I'd say you've got a bit of a problem.' Barbatus looked back down at Tigran. 'I'll ask one more time: where are the charts?'

'I don't know!'

'Believe me, I'll squeeze the hiding place out of you or you'll be as dead as one of those dogs being paraded outside.' Barbatus nodded to the hirsute youth. 'Another couple of clicks, Beauty.'

Beauty nodded furiously in understanding, delight at the order written all over his flat, down-covered face. He heaved on the wheel, putting his whole strength into turning it. The leather straps about Tigran's wrists and legs cut into his skin even more and blood started to seep from beneath them. The rack clicked into its new extension as Tigran's face contorted in agony.

Magnus visualised the two dogs coming out of Sempronius' house earlier; one struggling, one not. It was a moment of clarity. 'Stop!' he shouted, stepping forward. Beauty ignored the order until Barbatus cuffed him about the ear. 'You're mistaken, aedile; they can't be in Tigran's possession. He's definitely been set up.'

Barbatus looked unimpressed. 'What makes you think that?'

'Because I've realised where they must be.'

'Where?'

'Take him off the rack and I'll fetch them, but I need Tigran to come too.'

'Why?'

'Because I'll need help and I've only got one other man with me.' He turned to Senator Pollo. 'Sir, you might suggest to the Urban Prefect that he would be wise to have a century of one of the Urban Cohorts standing by in the Forum Boarium, near the Circus Maximus gates. Have them use "dead dog" as a password. He might like to be on hand too; it'll be much to his benefit.'

'And to mine as well, I hope, Magnus.'

'Very much to yours as well, sir. Very much.'

'Lupus, run and get Cassandros, Sextus and a half dozen of the brothers to meet us, as soon as possible, at the Circus Maximus main gates. And hurry!' Magnus said as he, Tigran and Senator Pollo walked back out into the sun to where Lupus waited. Lupus nodded and immediately began to forge a way down the Gemonian Steps now filled with people processing up them with howling dogs.

Magnus turned to Tigran, who was rubbing the sores on his wrists. 'You owe me for getting you off that before any damage was done.'

Tigran spat, rolling his shoulders and limping on pulled ankles. 'And how do I know that it wasn't you who planted those things? Someone did, because I've never seen that scabbard before, nor that horoscope. As to the amulet leading them to our tavern ...' Tigran looked hard-eyed at Magnus. 'Was it you? Was that why you wanted to get into Sempronius' house?'

'I was looking for something.'

'Don't play games with me, Magnus. Did you know about this raid, Senator?'

Senator Pollo rumbled with indignation, as if the question had no business being dignified with a reply. 'I must be getting back to rejoin the senators and find the Urban Prefect.'

Magnus quickly covered for the lack of a denial as the senator disappeared into the festival crowds. 'Well, it wasn't me, Brother; and if you're sure it wasn't you then I've got a fair idea who it was.'

'Who?'

'Tacita.'

'Tacita? But she was locked up in our place last night having spent most of the day in the Vigiles' depot.'

'After she came out of the depot she went to her neighbour's house and then on to the West Viminal headquarters. Ask Cassandros – he followed her there. She must have had the charts hidden with the neighbour, retrieved one of them and then delivered it with the amulet, which at some point she'd filched, to Sempronius or one of his men. Anyway, it doesn't matter, Brother, because we're going to get them back and buy your dispensation for Tuscus' murder.'

'I didn't murder Tuscus!'

'Really? The evidence suggests the contrary.'

'It was planted!'

'If you say so; but the aedile is going to take some convincing. Getting the charts back will greatly help your case, if you take my meaning?'

Tigran stopped suddenly. 'You bastard! It's you, isn't it? Barbatus said that you and he found the knife together. You placed the knife under Tuscus and then put the scabbard in my room, along with the horoscope. Of course! You didn't want to look for something in Sempronius' desk; you wanted to put something in it: the amulet.' Tigran grabbed Magnus by the collar of his tunic. 'Don't give me all that shit about Tacita. She's nothing to do with it now; she's out of the game. It's you, just you, Magnus. I should gut you here and now, you treacherous cunt.'

Magnus put his palms up in a conciliatory gesture. 'Now, now, Tigran. Whatever you may think I did doesn't actually make a bit of difference to the fact that, as far as the aedile is concerned, you are guilty of murder. The evidence was found in your room on a raid and an amulet connecting you to the theft of the charts of some very influential people has also found its way into his hands, thus corroborating, in his mind, what he suspects.' Magnus grabbed Tigran's wrist and jerked it from its grip. His tone became low and threatening. 'Now, you listen to me, Brother: you now need me alive. I was asked to investigate the murder and theft, and so I have done; it's just that I've made the results suit my purposes rather than have any bearing on the truth. Only I can get you out of this. If you kill me, either you'll have to run as far from Rome as you can or you can stay here for a brief appearance at the next games. Either way, your ambition of gaining a position of influence and respect by succeeding me as the patronus of the South Quirinal Brotherhood will have disappeared. Do we understand each other?'

Tigran held Magnus' gaze as hatred smouldered in his eyes. 'I'll kill you when this is over, then.'

Magnus let go of Tigran's wrist. 'Again, that will be a matter for debate. Now, we've got work to do. You make your mind up right now: are you going to help me get the charts or are you going to kill me and run?'

Magnus stepped onto the Gemonian Steps and smiled to himself in grim satisfaction as Tigran cursed and followed him.

The summit of the Capitoline was crowded as the ceremony centred around the small shrine to Juventas, and therefore very few could get inside. But the dogs died on Juventas' altar within the temple as the crowds cheered outside and presented more pain-ravaged victims for ritual slaughter, before they moved on to their final destination for the culmination of the festival in the Temple of Summanus.

'We want to find the West Viminal representation,' Magnus said to Tigran as they moved through the crowd.

'And then what?' Tigran asked, looking around and wincing at the high-pitched bestial screaming that saturated the temple precinct.

'Then we follow them at a discreet distance and wait to see when Sempronius turns up and who he's with, and hope that Cassandros, Sextus and the lads come quickly to the Circus Maximus.'

Tigran frowned. 'What do you mean, when Sempronius turns up?'

Magnus smiled. 'What would you do, Tigran, if you had certain items in your house that were so dangerous that to be caught in possession of them would be a death sentence, no matter who you were?'

'I'd get rid of them as soon as possible.'

'Exactly. Who wouldn't? But if you had gone to the trouble of stealing them, would you just throw them away?'

'Of course not, that would be a waste of time and effort.'

'So what would you do?'

'Sell them for a good price.'

'A good price, yes. But that takes some negotiation, and while those negotiations drag on the items are still sitting in your house, implicating you when you know full well that someone like us, enemies, suspect that you have them and would do all they can to make sure that you're caught in possession of said items. So what do you do?'

It was Tigran's turn to smile and he did so with genuine admiration for his patronus. 'I move them around, but not in a way that they are obvious or unprotected, until the negotiations are complete and then I make the exchange in a public place so that ownership is completely deniable should the transaction be interrupted by the authorities.'

'Exactly, Brother. And that is what Sempronius is currently doing.' Magnus pointed as he saw what he was looking for. 'What's that?'

Tigran followed Magnus' direction and shrugged. 'It's a dog on a forked pole. So what? There are hundreds of them.'

'Ah, but what do you notice about that one?'

'Well, it's not moving so it's most probably dead.'

'Well spotted. But, you see, I saw that dog this morning come out of Sempronius' house and it wasn't moving then, either. I didn't think much of it at the time, but then, when Barbatus and the Urban Prefect didn't find the charts in Sempronius' house, I suddenly wondered why you would want to parade a dead dog right at the beginning of the ceremony.'

Understanding spread across Tigran's face. 'Unless it was nothing to do with the festival but, rather, a convenient and clever hiding place to move the charts around. Meantime Sempronius negotiates his price with the purchaser.'

'And furthermore, because the procession has a fixed route, once negotiations are complete, the merchandise is easy to find having been perfectly safe all day, as who would think of looking inside a dead dog on the third day after the calends of August?'

'I think we will.'

Magnus slapped Tigran on the shoulder. 'Brother, I think you might be right.'

*

The procession made its way down the Capitoline, hurling a few of the wretched beasts, howling, off the Tarpeian Rock for good measure, before coming back out into the Forum around the Portico of Harmonious Gods. All the while, Magnus kept the West Viminal's dead dog in sight as they cleared the Forum Romanum, passing the Temple of Castor and Pollux in the shadow of the Palatine, and proceeding along the Vicus Tuscus to the Forum Boarium, which was filled with lowing cattle in pens and the calls of buyers and sellers alike.

As they passed between the cattle market and the great gates of the Circus Maximus, Magnus nudged Tigran. 'There's Lupus with Cassandros, Sextus and the lads. You stay here watching that dog while I go and get them.' He stepped out of the column and jogged to where his brethren waited in the shade of the circus walls as a century of the Urban Cohorts crossed the Sublician Bridge on the far side of the Forum. 'Cassandros, you go and be nice to their centurion and say "dead dog" to him; he'll understand.'

'And then what do I do?'

'If I'm right, then as the ceremony finishes at the Temple of Summanus there will be quite a commotion. Suggest to the centurion, in the politest possible way, that he might like to have his men surround the temple at a distance to prevent any miscreants getting away, if you take my meaning?'

'I think I do, Brother.' Cassandros grinned as he headed off towards the approaching soldiers.

Magnus gestured to Sextus, Lupus and the other brethren. 'You lads follow me, and be ready for a bit of a toe to toe.'

The goose was raised high on a pedestal outside the Temple of Summanus, so that it sat in state on its deep cushion, swathed in its silver cloak, overseeing the demise of its guarding partners with an aloofness that seemed to many to be bordering on disinterest. Dog after dog was despatched upon the altar within to the chthonic god of nocturnal thunder who had once, in the distant past, been as exalted as Jupiter himself but now was confined to a small temple next to the circus at the foot of the Aventine. Just why this god had been chosen to receive the sacrifice of the dogs, Magnus did not know, nor did he care as he scanned the crowds for the face of his bitterest foe who, he hoped, would finally meet his ruin within the hour.

And it was with a mixture of relief and shock that Magnus spotted Sempronius pushing his way towards the West Viminal brother holding the dead dog aloft.

'There he is, but look who he left at the edge of the crowd, Tigran.'

Tigran shaded his eyes against the sun as he looked south. He whistled softly. 'Well, I suppose they can afford what Sempronius is trying to sell.'

Magnus could but agree. 'And I imagine that Britannicus' chart that Agrippina commissioned didn't show the boy's future in a very good light, so they're hoping that it's amongst the rest of them. Well, they are going to be sadly disappointed.' He looked back over to where Burrus and Seneca were standing, folds of their togas pulled over their heads as much in deference to the god of the temple as to partly obscure their faces. 'Mind you, they know that the charts will give them leverage when it comes to securing their charge the succession in power over his younger step-brother. Well, Brother, they aren't going to like this.'

As Sempronius approached the dead dog, Magnus moved forward, signalling to Tigran and the rest of the brothers to follow. 'No blades unless they pull them.'

The dead dog was lowered as, all around, the howling of the few still left alive and the continual bovine lowing and shouts of traders from the cattle market blanketed the proceeding with a bestial cacophony. Sempronius, tall and still retaining the sculpted good looks of his youth despite his full head of hair being silver, took hold of the dog as his men closed around him, shielding his actions.

'Now!' Magnus urged in a hoarse whisper. He ran forward, with his brethren following, barging through the crowd, sending men and dogs toppling to the ground as he neared his objective. Lowering his shoulder, he rammed it into the midriff of a surprised West Viminal brother, thumping the wind from his lungs and propelling him back, as Tigran, Sextus and the rest of the brethren crashed into their opponents, exposing Sempronius as he pulled the dead dog's chest open. A fist slammed into Magnus' jaw, a flash shot across his inner-vision, but he kept moving forward as Sempronius looked up in surprise. With no time to run, he hauled the dog carcass up by its hind legs and swung it at Magnus. The head smacked against his cheek, just above where the previous blow had landed, cracking bone and tilting his head sideways with neck-wrenching speed, but still he pressed on, vision blurred, face throbbing, to leap onto Sempronius, crashing him to the ground with a crunching jab of his right fist. Strong fingers gripped his throat as around him other couples or groups grappled, gouged and punched, rolling about on the ground or still upright, in a scuffle of flying limbs and butting heads that spread from the epicentre of Magnus and Sempronius out through the crowd, so that within a few dozen heartbeats it was no longer an exclusive South Quirinal versus West Viminal affair.

And over the chaos came the sound that Magnus was waiting to hear: the harsh, rhythmical clattering of many hobnailed boots double-timing over stone. With a boost of effort that came from he knew not where, Magnus prised the fingers from his throat, his face so strained his glass eye popped out, rolling away to come to a stop next to a leather scroll case protruding from the dog carcass. Lashing at Sempronius' face with the heel of his palm, crunching the cartilage of his nose, which instantly spurted with blood, Magnus leapt after his eye and grabbed the case as the stamp of hobnails broke its staccato rhythm and the century charged into the affray. With the flats of their swords and the bosses of their shields they broke up the various combats, cracking heads and fracturing forearms and ribs as their centurion and optio shouted at the combatants to desist or risk a pierced death as their men grew gradually more blood lustful and out of control.

Gradually the soldiers prevailed and they hauled the conscious to their feet and kicked the unconscious and the few dead to ensure that there was no play-acting.

'I'll take that, Magnus.' The voice was nasal and slurred.

Magnus turned to see Sempronius, one hand clutching a blood-streaming nose, the other held out towards him. 'And who's going to make me give it to you?'

'You'll be surprised just how powerful my friends are.'

Magnus looked as unconcerned as was possible for a man with an empty eye socket. 'Mine aren't without influence either.'

'But I doubt they'll want to tangle with me,' Burrus said, coming up behind Magnus. 'There're not many who feel up to testing their strength against the Praetorian Guard. I think it would be best if you gave that to me.'

Sempronius looked outraged. 'But you haven't—'

'Paid you yet?' Burrus crooned, finishing the sentence. He reached around Magnus and grasped the case. It was with total amusement at the look on Sempronius' battered face that Magnus released it.

'You promised me five thousand denarii!'

'I did, didn't I? But only if you delivered the charts into my hand.' Burrus opened the lid and tipped the case so that a third of the roll of scrolls slid into his palm. 'I don't really see why I should pay you now, Sempronius; after all, I found these on a ruffian in the street.' Burrus turned. 'Wouldn't you say that was a fair interpretation of events, Seneca?'

Seneca, balding and grey with an ample chin and rotund figure, took the question very seriously. 'I would say that was ... what's the best word for it? A precise, yes, precise is precisely the right word, Burrus. I would say it was a precise interpretation of events and one that would stand up in a court – not that it would ever come to that for the dead can't bring cases before the court.' He looked at Sempronius and smiled with ice in his eyes. 'I think that even someone of your station would know that, Sempronius.'

Sempronius, still clutching his nose, seethed with impotent rage, his hateful gaze flicking from Seneca to Burrus to Magnus and then back again.

'I knew you'd understand,' Seneca purred as an old man in a senatorial toga hobbled through the crowd, leaning on a staff and on Barbatus, with a very nervous-looking Senator Pollo in attendance.

'Of course you know that he was cheating you,' Lucius Volusius Saturninus, the Urban Prefect, said, his voice reedy and weak as of a man in his eighties. 'The one you prize the most isn't in there.'

Burrus spun around. 'What do you mean, Saturninus?'

'I mean that I had Sempronius' house searched this morning and this was found. Show him, Pollo.'

Sweating profusely, more from his exposed position in a battle of wills between the powerful than the weather, Senator Pollo pulled a scroll from the fold of his toga.

'I think you both know what we're talking about,' Saturninus wheezed. 'Best not to refer to it out loud.'

Burrus and Seneca exchanged a worried look.

'The price is straightforward,' Saturninus assured them.

Burrus looked at the scroll case in his hand. 'All of them?'

'All of them.'

'I feel we have no choice in the matter,' Seneca said. 'We're ... how should I put it? We're being coerced, yes, I think that does it admirably; coerced is what we are.'

Saturninus took the single scroll from Senator Pollo. 'I wouldn't put it so strongly, Seneca; after all, we're all getting something we want. Centurion!'

The Urban Cohort centurion stepped forward at his direct superior's bidding.

Saturninus gave him the scroll. 'Centurion, take that case from the Praetorian prefect and then pass it to me. If I'm satisfied with the contents, give him the scroll.'

'And what if I'm not satisfied with the scroll?' Burrus demanded.

Saturninus gave a weary smile. 'Oh, you will be, prefect, believe me; and you'll be very pleased that you had something to buy it with. With that little thing I could have brought you and all your faction down; all of it, do you understand? The end to all your ambitions concerning the succession.'

Burrus' and Seneca's faces registered the truth of those words as the centurion passed the case to Saturninus, who inspected the contents. Satisfied, he nodded to the centurion and handed the case and the charts to Senator Pollo.

Snatching the chart, Burrus quickly unrolled it and breathed a sigh of relief.

'Our business here is done, I believe, prefect,' Saturninus stated. 'Centurion, take your men back to their barracks; it's all over and there's no need to detain anyone. Just a little misunderstanding, nothing more than that.'

The centurion saluted and went about his duty with barked commands and swipes of his vine-stick, leaving the former combatants to get to their feet and dust themselves off.

'You haven't heard the last of this, prefect,' Burrus said, handing the scroll to Seneca.

'I think I have, prefect; after all, who would believe that such a thing existed and that I had seen it?'

Burrus went to contradict the statement and, realising that Saturninus had a valid point, turned on his heel and pushed his way through the cordon of Urban Cohort soldiery.

Seneca shrugged, gesturing helplessly. 'We're in one another's confidence, Saturninus. I think that is the best way to express the situation. Yes, that will do nicely.'

'It will indeed, Seneca. And we both know what happens if one side should break that confidence?' Saturninus did not bother waiting for a response and turned to go.

'Prefect?' Sempronius said, catching up with him as Senator Pollo helped him away. 'I have lost a great deal of money out of this deal.'

With a force that belied his age and surprised Magnus, Saturninus rounded on Sempronius. 'You're lucky that you're not being taken to a cell in the Circus Maximus to wait for the next batch of hungry lions. Do you know what trouble you've put me to? Do you?'

Sempronius mouthed a reply but it did not vocalise.

'If it wasn't for certain arrangements that we have had in the past and are still current, that's exactly where you would be going now; so get out of my sight before I change my mind.'

'I'd take his advice if I were you,' Magnus said in a helpful and friendly manner.

Sempronius looked at him with loathing. 'Fuck off, Magnus.'

'That's exactly what I plan on doing, Sempronius. By the way, you owe me for covering up your part in Tuscus' murder.'

Sempronius looked confused. 'Why would you want to do that?'

'Because it suited me to conclude that someone else had done it in order to secure my position. And besides, I thought I had already got you with the chart I planted in your desk when I brought Pansa in. Never mind, next time.'

Sempronius' jaw slacked in disbelief. 'It was you that brought Pansa in!'

'Yes, it was. And a very nice place you've got too.' Leaving Sempronius spitting invective, Magnus signalled to Tigran and the rest of his brothers to come with him and turned to follow the Urban Prefect and Senator Pollo across the Forum Boarium.

'I felt myself to be a little too conspicuous there, I don't mind telling you, Magnus,' Senator Pollo said as Magnus and Tigran fell into step next to him.

Magnus looked down at the case. 'Not as conspicuous as you would have been had those got into the wrong hands, as they very nearly did.'

The senator shuddered at the thought. 'I can rely on your discretion, of course, Magnus.'

'That goes without saying.'

'What about the cause of all this?' Saturninus asked. 'The woman?'

'Tacita?'

'Yes,' Senator Pollo said. 'Can we rely on her discretion?'

Magnus knew that he had a duty of honesty with his patron. 'She started this for revenge and money; those are her two driving forces.'

The senator nodded. 'I see. Where is she?'

'In the Quirinal Vigiles depot,' Barbatus informed him.

Saturninus winced. 'That's no good. Let her go, Barbatus. Then, Magnus, you know what to do.'

Magnus knew only too well what was required. 'Tigran will do it, won't you, Tigran?'

Tigran grinned; it was not a nice sight. 'It will be my pleasure; she insulted me deeply.'

'As to the outstanding issue with Tigran,' Magnus asked, innocence in his tone, 'I believe the aedile still thinks he's guilty of murder.'

Barbatus shot Magnus a glance. 'Of course he is.'

'But surely, if he's about to do you all such a service by removing someone who may try to go to the Emperor telling all sorts of tales for money, then some accommodation could be reached?'

Barbatus looked at the Urban Prefect, who nodded his agreement.

'Very well,' Barbatus conceded, 'I'm sure we can overlook it, this time.'

Magnus glanced at Tigran, who grunted and shrugged a shoulder, and then turned back to Barbatus. 'That's most kind, aedile. There's just one more thing: you promised me a favour should I get the charts back. Now, clearly, you have them and it was from my hand that the Urban Prefect took them.'

Barbatus was unable to deny the fact. 'What do you want, Magnus?'

'Oh, nothing much, sir. Just this: obviously you'll keep their evidence that incriminates Tigran in Tuscus' murder.'

The aedile agreed. 'Of course I will.'

'The favour I would like is that, should something untoward happen to me before I move aside for Tigran, I would very much like you to find it again.'

Barbatus gave a half-smile with cold eyes looking at the easterner. 'I'm sure I will, Magnus. And I'll hand the evidence on to my successor next year.'

'That's very reassuring, aedile.' Magnus hunched his shoulders, raising his hands, palms up, giving Tigran, whose feelings towards the deal were very apparent, his best 'there's nothing I can do about it' face. 'I'm sorry, Brother, but it seems that if you want to succeed me as patronus then first you need to succeed in keeping me alive, if you take my meaning?'

COMING SOON FROM **ROBERT FABBRI**...

THE DEATH OF A TITAN. THE RISE OF DYNASTIES.
THE BATTLE FOR AN EMPIRE.

JOIN **ROBERT FABBRI**, AUTHOR OF THE BESTSELLING
VESPASIAN SERIES, AS HE EMBARKS ON A NEW
JOURNEY INTO THE HEART OF THE HELLENISTIC AGE.
AFTER THE DEATH OF ALEXANDER THE GREAT, WHO
WILL INHERIT THE THRONE AND CONTROL THE
WORLD'S MOST FEARSOME EMPIRE?

ALEXANDER'S LEGACY
TO THE STRONGEST
COMING 2020 AD